SCREWED

By Eoin Colfer

Plugged
Screwed

Artemis Fowl
Artemis Fowl and the Arctic Incident
Artemis Fowl and the Eternity Code
Artemis Fowl and the Opal Deception
Artemis Fowl and the Lost Colony
Artemis Fowl and the Time Paradox
Artemis Fowl and the Atlantis Complex

Benny and Omar
Benny and Babe

The Legend of Spud Murphy
The Legend of Captain Crow's Teeth
The Legend of the Worst Boy in the World

Airman
Half Moon Investigations
The Supernaturalist
The Wish List

And Another Thing . . .

SCREWED
Eoin Colfer

headline

First published in Great Britain in 2013
by HEADLINE PUBLISHING GROUP

1

Cataloguing in Publication Data is available from the British Library

ISBN 978 0 7553 9186 8 (Hardback)
ISBN 978 0 7553 9187 5 (Trade paperback)

Typeset in Electra by Avon DataSet Ltd, Bidford-on-Avon, Warwickshire

Printed and bound by CPI Group (UK) Ltd, Croydon, CR0 4YY

Headline's policy is to use papers that are natural, renewable and
recyclable products and made from wood grown in sustainable forests.
The logging and manufacturing processes are expected to conform
to the environmental regulations of the country of origin.

HEADLINE PUBLISHING GROUP
An Hachette UK Company
338 Euston Road
London NW1 3BH

www.headline.co.uk
www.hachette.co.uk

SCREWED

CHAPTER 1

Cloisters, Essex County, New Jersey

The great Elmore Leonard once said that you should never start a story with weather. That's all well and good for Mister Leonard to say and for all his acolytes to scribble into their Moleskine notebooks, but sometimes a story starts off with weather and does not give a damn about what some legendary genre guy recommends, even if it is the big E.L.. So if there's weather at the start then that's where you better put it or the whole thing could unravel and you find yourself with the shavings of a tale swirling around your ankles and no idea how to glue them together again.

So expect some major meteorological conditions smack bang in the middle of Chapter 1, and if there were kids and animals around they'd be in here too, screw that old-timey movie star guy with the cigar and squint eye. The story is what it is.

And the story being what it is, let's get to it:

I am lying in bed with a beautiful woman watching the morning sun light up her blond hair like some kind of electric nimbus and thinking for the umpteenth time that this is the closest to happy that I am ever likely to get and several degrees closer than I deserve after all the blood I've been forced to spill.

The woman is asleep, which is frankly the best time to gaze upon her. Sofia Delano doesn't like being stared at when she's awake. A casual glance is okay, but after five seconds of eye contact her insecurities and phobias kick their way out of the sack and you find yourself dealing with a whole different animal, especially if she hasn't been taking her lithium.

Various psychoses were not part of Sofia's nature. They were nurtured. When she was still a teenage bride, Sofia was psychologically hothoused by Carmine Delano, her abusive husband, until she began to exhibit symptoms of bipolar disorder, schizophrenia and dementia, at which point Carmine, the prince, thought to himself: *Bitch be crazy*, and bought himself a ticket to far away, leaving his young damaged wife to sit at home and pine. The guy hasn't been seen since. Not a peep, not a dicky bird.

And nobody pines like Sofia Delano. If pining was an art form, then Sofia is the Picasso of the pine. Her only distraction was tormenting the downstairs tenant, which happened to be me. Then six months ago I did her a pretty measly household service, and boom, she's convinced I'm her long-lost husband who hasn't been in the picture for twenty years. The last time Sofia was truly happy was when she and Carmine first dated in the late eighties, so consequently that's the decade Sofia's needle got stuck in. Her Madonna rig-out is pretty hot, her Cyndi Lauper is stunning, but I will say her Chaka Khan needs work.

We've made out a couple of times, but I can't in all conscience take it any further than that. I know couples often pretend to be with somebody else, but there's probably something illegal going on if one of them actually believes it. But kissing's okay, right?

And man, she can kiss. It's like she sucks the beats right out of my heart. And those eyes? Big and blue, rimmed with way too much eyeliner. Men have climbed into hollow wooden horses for eyes like that.

My hand grazed her boob once, but it was an accident, honest.

I think she knows who I am sometimes. Maybe in the beginning I was Carmine, but now . . . maybe there's a glimmer.

So if I'm so goddamn noble, how come I'm in bed with this delusional woman? First of all, screw you and your dirty mind. And secondly, I'm lying on top of the covers and Sofia is tucked in nice and safe under the duvet. This is the only time I've stayed over in six months, because last night we split a bottle of liquor-store red that had enough tannins in it to poleaxe an elephant and watched *Amélie*, which is possibly the best non-violent movie I've ever seen.

We laughed a lot.

In French accents.

I remember thinking: *It could be like this all the time.*

I've found that Sofia's sweet spot is meds plus two glasses of wine. Then I swim into focus and we can enjoy a movie date like two middle-agers in love. And I do love her. I love her like a high school kid loves the prom queen.

Simon Moriarty, my off-and-on shrink since the Irish army years, tells me that I am obsessed with something unobtainable and therefore forever pure. But what the hell does he know? There ain't a guy on this planet who could lie where I'm lying and not feel his heart swell.

And believe me, Sofia ain't *unobtainable*. She's been doing her level best to get obtained ever since we became pals. But I can't do it, and all this lying on the bed together ain't helping.

Sofia opens her eyes and I'm thinking, *Please God recognise me.*

And she says in a voice so husky it would make a cat purr, 'Hey, Dan. How you doing?'

And there it is, the perfect moment, so I snap off a blink photo before answering.

'I'm doing real good,' I say, and it's the truth. Any day that I ain't Carmine is a good day for D. McEvoy.

'Why are you out there?' she asks, trailing a finger down my face, her nail catching in my stubble. 'Come in here where it's warm.'

I could. Why not? Consenting adults and so forth. But Sofia could flip in a heartbeat and then who would I be?

Carmine?

A stranger?

And this girl doesn't need any more trauma or mind games.

So I say: 'Hey, how about I bring you some coffee?'

Sofia sighs. 'I'm forty in a couple of months, Dan. The clock's ticking here.'

I try to smile but it comes off like a grimace and Sofia takes pity on me.

'Okay, Dan. Coffee.'

She closes her eyes and stretches, arching her back, one long leg sliding out from under the duvet.

I think maybe I'll have some coffee too.

I leave Sofia propped up on her pillows with one of those cappuccinos from a sachet and her copy of *Caribbean Cruising*, which she's read a hundred times even though she hasn't left the building on more than a handful of occasions in the past twenty years. We both made a promise before I went. I pledged to come over after I'm finished at my casino to watch *Manon des Sources*, which is not one of my DVD favourites, and Sofia swore that she would swallow the pills I left in a cup on her locker.

I am optimistic that tonight could be another little slice of heaven.

This could be the beginning of something good. Sofia is getting her head right and I'm picking up a few words of French. The casino is staying afloat and no one has tried to kill me for half a year. Best of all, outside of giving a coupla drunks the bums' rush from the club, I haven't been forced to hurt anyone in a while.

I could get very used to that.

People can be content. It's possible. I've seen them in parks or outside theatres. Christ, I've even met a few contented people personally. It could be my turn.

Don't get happy, I warn myself. *The universe cannot suffer happiness for long*, which is probably not gonna be the title of any self-help books on the shelves next Christmas.

I haven't walked five blocks keeping my eyes open for contented people to bolster my argument when my cell rings. I know without looking that the caller is Zebulon Kronski, one of my few friends. I know this because he has set the Miami Sound Machine's 'Dr Beat' as his personal ringtone.

This little detail tells you a lot about my friend Zeb. You listen to five seconds of Cuba/Florida polyphonics and without ever meeting the guy you have an epiphany. So, Zeb's a doctor, obviously. He considers himself a player, hence the retro-cool Miami tune, and also he's something of a douche for going into a guy's phone and screwing with the settings. Who likes that? A man's phone is personal, you don't mess around there. I never heard anybody say: *Hey, you dicked around with my wallpaper. Great.*

This is all true: Zebulon Kronski is a douche cosmetic surgeon who sees himself as a player. And if we met under normal circumstances I can imagine me leaving the room with clenched fists so I wouldn't punch his lights out, but we met when I was with the UN peacekeepers in the Lebanon during wartime and under sea-trench levels of pressure, so we're bonded by blood and shrapnel. Sometimes having a wartime friend is the only way to make it through peacetime. The fact that we were on opposite sides in the Middle East doesn't matter; we're both too old to have any faith in *sides*. I put my faith in people nowadays. And not too many of them either.

And technically, I wasn't on a side. I was in the middle.

I wait till Gloria Estefan has finished the bar then swish my iPhone.

'Hello,' I say, adhering to the Irish maxim of not volunteering information.

'Top of the morning to you, Sergeant,' says Dr Zebulon Kronski, ear-shagging me with his Hollywood Irish accent.

'Morning, Zeb,' I reply wearily and warily.

I have an army buddy who would not even admit that it *was* morning over the phone in case it would help triangulate his position.

'You been practising that accent?' I ask him. 'It's good.'

'Really?'

'No, not really, you dick. That accent is so bad it's racist.'

This is a bit of a cheap shot as Zebulon has just begun taking acting classes and fancies himself a character actor.

I got the quirk thing going on, he once confided after a bottle of something illegal from the Everglades that may or may not have contained alligator penis. *A little bit Jeff Goldblum and a slice of that guy Monk. Know what I mean? I once did a walk-on in* CSI *some fucking city or other. Director said I had an interesting face.*

Interesting face? Sing it, brother.

Like a normal face except squashed between two sheets of plate glass. Then again, my own face ain't nothing to write home about. I've had the hard-man scowl pasted on for so long that the wind changed and it stuck.

Zeb is not impressed by my *racist* crack and so comes back strong, breaking some heavy news without any sugar coating.

'Mrs Madden died, Dan. We are uber fucked.'

Zeb and I both appreciate the term *uber*, so in the era of casual *awesomes* and total generational confusion over the terms *sick, bad, wicked and radical* we reserve *uber* for verbs that really deserve it.

My heart stutters and the phone seems heavier than a brick. I shouldn't have even contemplated contentment; this is what happens.

Mrs Madden dead? Already?

This is not right. I don't have any wiggle room in my life for trouble right now. My issues are packed tighter than shells in a magazine.

She cannot be dead.

'Bullshit,' I say, but it's just a stall to give my heart a chance to settle back into a rhythm.

'No bullshit, Irish,' says Zeb. 'I said *uber*. You don't fuck with uber, that's our code.'

Generally I would not be broken up when a lady that I did not personally know totters off her coil, even one from Ireland, but my own welfare is very dependent on Mrs Madden being alive enough to call her son once a week.

Here's what it is: Mike Madden, the beloved son, is the big fish in our small pond, and by big fish I mean the most vicious sunovan-a-hole gangster in our quiet burg. Mike runs all the usuals from the Brass Ring club on Cloister's strip. He's got maybe a dozen hooligans with too many weapons and too few high-school diplomas between them, all desperate to laugh at Irish Mike's jokes and put the hurt on anyone throwing a monkey wrench in the Madden machine. It's laughable really, this faux-Celtic dick with his Oirish lilt straight outta *The Quiet Man*. I came across a lotta guys like him in the corps: local warlords with delusions of cocksure, confusing brawn with brain, but they never held on to the crown for long. The next hard man was always coming down the pipe with a chip on his shoulder and an AK under his jacket. But Mike fell into a sweet set-up here in Cloisters, because it's too minor league for any self-respecting darksider to throw any bodies at it. He ain't as cash rich as other bosses, but he ain't fighting a turf war every second week neither. Plus he can speechify from morning to night and no one so much as whispers *Oh for fuck sake*.

Nobody but me.

Me and Mike had a tête-à-tête last year over a little fatal friction I had with his lieutenant. Zeb was in the mix too, which rubbed all participants the wrong way. The upshot being that I was forced to ask one of my Irish army buddies to make like an armed-to-the-teeth gnome in Mrs Madden's garden back in Ballyvaloo just to ensure Zeb and I kept breathing Essex County air.

I felt a part of my soul wither when I threatened a guy's mother. It was about as low as I've ever crawled but I couldn't see any other way clear. Every day since I struck that deal I have honestly believed that part of the fallout from dealing with the devil is that you remake yourself in his image. There was a time when threatening a guy's mother was not on the table no matter what the circumstances, especially considering what my own mom went through.

I would never have made good on that threat, I tell myself daily. *I am not that bad.*

Maybe I can claw my way back to how I used to be. Maybe with Sofia lying beside me in bed, her hair backlit to a golden nimbus by the morning sun.

Listen to me. I sound like Celine Dion on a boat.

Anyhow . . .

Irish Mike Madden was only promising not to butcher Zebulon and me so long as his mom was alive, or rather he promised to kill us just as soon as his mom passed away. The nuts and bolts aren't important as such. Basically now that his mom is gone, this guy Mike has Zeb and me strapped over a barrel with our pants down and half a pint of KY jelly wobbling on his palm.

Metaphorical jelly.

I hope.

I am in two minds about this latest development. I feel the familiar brain fatigue that comes with being tossed once more into the cauldron of combat, but also I am the tiniest bit relieved that Mrs Madden died and I didn't have anything to do with it. At least I hope I didn't have any thing to do with it. I better call my gnome when I get a minute, because the ex-army guy I had watching Mrs Madden is known for being a little pre-emptive. Maybe Corporal Tommy Fletcher got fed up keeping an eye out.

I hear Zeb in my ear.

'Yo, D-man? You passed out on the sidewalk?'

Yo? Zeb loves his adopted culture. He called me *bee-yatch* last week and I had to knuckle him quite seriously on the forehead.

'Yeah. I'm here. Just had the wind knocked out of my sails a bit with that news.'

'Ah, Jaysus. We're not pushin' up the daisies just yet.'

'So what happened to the mother? Natural causes, was it?'

I hope to Christ it was natural causes.

'Some of it was natural,' says Zeb, with titillating vagueness.

I gotta admit, for a long time I thought *titillating* meant something else.

'What do you mean, some of it?'

'Well, the snow and the lightning.'

'Go on. Tell me, I know you're dying to.'

'I wish you had FaceTime. This is a hard one to do justice without video.'

Zeb is really testing me now. I shouldn't have disrespected his acting skills.

'Zeb. Lay it out.'

'Lay it out? Who the fuck are you? Shaft?'

I shout into the phone's speaker. 'What happened to the bloody mother?'

I have lost it and so Zeb wins.

'Calm down already, Irish. What the hell?'

Zeb is all about the games. His favourite one is pushing my buttons, but I have some games myself. The army psychiatrist taught me a little about manipulation, which wasn't really on the lesson plan but he thought it might come in handy seeing as I was moving to NYC.

'Okay. I'm calm. But I gotta bolt now, meeting at the casino. Call me later with the blow-by-blow.'

I can hear the scrabble as Zeb sits up in his seat.

'Come on, Danny boy. You got time for this. Might be the last story you'll ever hear.'

'Tell you what, leave it on the machine and I'll play it back later.'

I've oversold it.

'Screw you, Danny. Goddamn meeting, my ass. You had me going for a second, but I'll take pity on you. Old Lady Madden went skiing, can you fucking believe that?'

I presume this is a rhetorical question, but Zeb waits for an answer.

'No, I cannot believe that,' I say deliberately.

'Well, believe it, Irish. This old lady strapped on her skis and struck out across the veld.'

'Veld. Field. That's not Hebrew, is it?'

'If you know what it ain't, then why interrupt? It's like you hate me.'

If there is something more exhausting than a conversation with Dr Zebulon Kronski then I will shoot myself in the face before attempting it.

'Now it's not downhill skiing, I'm not saying that, the woman was eighty-five for Christ's sake, but she takes herself and her dog across the *field* to see her older sister.' Zeb giggles gleefully. '*Older sister*. You Irish people are made of volcanic material or some shit.'

'Get on with it.'

'There's a storm brewing. Big smokestack clouds sitting on the hills, so Ma Madden decides to take a short cut. A fateful decision as it turns out.'

I gotta sit through this performance. No choice.

Fateful and smokestacks, fuck me.

'She clambers over a stile, and it took me a while to find out what the hell a stile was, let me tell you. So the old gal is Forrest Gumping over this ditch with her ski pole up in the air when an honest to God bolt of lightning hits the pole and blows Ma Madden clear into the afterlife. A bolt of motherfucking lightning.'

A bolt of motherfucking lightning. And there we have our weather reference, with apologies to Elmore.

'You gotta be kidding me?' I ask, totally non-rhetorical. I really want to know if Zeb is shining me on. He does this kind of shit all the time and nothing is off limits. Last year, in the middle of my own hair transplant procedure, he told me I had skull cancer. Kept it up for three solid hours.

'I kid thee not, Dan. Boiled her eyeballs right in the sockets. One in a million.'

This is bad news. The worst. Mike never struck me as a guy with shares in the forgive and forget business.

'Maybe Mike is a bigger man than we think,' I say, totally grasping. 'Maybe he realises that the club is a good earner and he's gonna let that thing we had slide.'

Zeb chuckles. 'Yeah? And *maybe* if my Uncle Mort had a pussy I'd snort cocaine off his ass and hump him. No way is Mike letting anything slide.'

Uncle Mort and I have clinked glasses a couple of times, so now Zeb is responsible for yet another grotesque mental image that I will have to repress.

I feel that sudden icy terror in my gut that you get when you've accidentally forwarded an e-mail about a grade A asshole to the grade A asshole.

'Zeb, tell me bereaved Mike is not sitting opposite you listening to you blather on about his poor recently deceased mother.'

'Course not,' says Zeb. 'I ain't a total moron.'

'So how do you know he ain't letting anything slide?'

'I know this,' says Zeb, calm as you like, 'because Mike sent one of his shamrock shmendriks over to pick me up. I'm in the back seat being chauffeured over to the Brass Ring right now.'

'I better get over there,' I say, picking up my pace.

'That's what the shmendrik said,' says Zeb and hangs up.

I am sincerely worried that my watchdog, Corporal Tommy Fletcher, has gone operational and wired this old lady up to a car battery. Violence never bothered him much, even though his Facebook profile describes him as a lovable teddy bear. I would go so far as to say that some of Tommy's more memorable wisecracks were inspired by moments of extreme violence. An example being one particular night in the Lebanon a few decades back when Tommy and I were Irish army peacekeepers trapped on a muddy rooftop with our colonel between a lookout tower and a bunker, listening to Hezbollah mortars shells whistling overhead. I was swearing to Christ I could hear the tune of 'Jealous Guy' in the whistles and thinking to myself: *Mud? There's not supposed to be mud in the Middle East.*

But the mud wasn't the major gripe. Worse than that slick paste or even the incoming fire was the fear of death coming off the three-man watch in waves, and how it manifested itself in our leader. The colonel who had been green enough to accompany his boys on watch rationalised that he wasn't even supposed to be here and therefore he couldn't possibly die.

Don't these stupid bastards understand? he repeated in a voice that grew increasingly shrill. *I only came out to show a little solidarity, for God's sake. They can't kill a man for that.*

The colonel was right; the Hezbollah didn't kill him, they just took one eye and one ear, which prompted one of Tommy's immortal quotes in the billet a couple of hours later: *Typical officer. Get on his bad side and he can't hear nothing, can't see nothing.*

Oscar Wilde had nothing on Corporal Thomas Fletcher when it came to sound bites.

I decide to jog across to the Brass Ring. Downtown Cloisters is only a few square blocks, and a cab would have to follow the mayor's new one-way system, which seems designed to transform honest citizens into raving psychopaths on their daily commute. Anyway, the run gives me a chance to clear my head, even though a shambling apeman in a leather jacket is bound to draw *what the hell was that?* looks from people who for a split second are convinced that they're about to be mugged.

Guys my size are not really supposed to move fast unless we're in a cage match, and usually I take it nice and non-threatening among the be-Starbucked civilians, but today is a quasi-emergency, so I pound the pavement over to the Brass Ring. I say *quasi* because I'm reasonably sure Mike is not gonna do anything violent in his own joint; plus if he wanted to kill me, Zeb would hardly be afforded the opportunity to give me the heads-up.

Mike knows all about my specialised skill set, as another tall Irishman might say, and he has a proposition for me. I just bet that fat faux-Mick has been planning his delivery.

You see, laddie. I'm a businessman. And what we got here is a business opportunity. Except he says *opera-toonity*. For some reason he can't pronounce the word right, and I wouldn't mind but he works it into every second sentence. Irish Mike Madden says *opera-toonity* more than the Pope says Jesus. And the Pope says Jesus a lot, especially when people sneak up on him.

Little things like that really get to me. I can take a straight sock to the jaw, but someone tapping his nails on a table or repeatedly mispronouncing a word drives me crazy. I once slapped a coffee out of a guy's hand on the subway because he was breathing into the cup before every sip. It was like sitting beside Darth Vader on his break. And I'll tell you something else: three people applauded.

It's about half a mile over flat terrain to the Brass Ring, so I'm nice and loosened up by the time I get there. I don't think I'm gonna have to crack any skulls, but it never hurts to have the kinks worked out. A person can't just spring into action any more once he gets past the forty mark. Once upon a time I could hump my sixty-pound backpack down twenty miles of Middle Eastern dust road; now I get short of breath putting out the garbage. Well, maybe that's an exaggeration. I can put out the garbage just fine but I was trying to make a point. Ain't none of us as young as we used to be, except for the dead. They ain't getting any older. And I might be joining their ranks if I don't focus the hell up and stop drifting off on these mind tangents.

Middle Eastern dust roads? Jesus Christ.

Mike bought the Brass Ring at a knockdown price after the previous owner found himself with a few extra holes in his person. The joint is about as classy as clubs get in Cloisters, Essex County. The facade has got a half-assed nautical theme going on which extends to the wooden cladding and porthole windows but not to the door, which is brushed aluminium with several chunky locks dotting the metal like watch bezels.

There's a guy out front, smoking. He's not that big, but he's mean and twitchy. Also, this goon isn't overly fond of me because I put a little hurt on him a while back. Actually I've kicked the living shit out of most of Mike's crew at one time or another, so while I am welcome in this club, it's the kind of welcome piranhas extend to raw meat.

'Yo, Manny,' I call, waving like we're tennis buddies. 'Mike is expecting me.'

Manny Booker jerks like he's been slapped, and I figure he's flashing back to our last meeting.

'Just fucking calm down, McEvoy,' he says, his hand strangling the air in front of his breast pocket. This is because he's aching to pull his cannon and shoot me, but he's under orders never to draw in public.

'I am calm, Manny, but you look a bit jumpy. You worried I'm not outnumbered enough?'

'We got your friend inside, with a gun pointed at his face.' Manny blurts this out, right on the street.

I can't look at Manny for too long because of his beard. He's got one of these Midlake folk singer bushes that are springing up on cool faces all over these days, which is okay, I don't have a problem with that, had a nice beard myself back in the nineties. What makes me squirm is the fact that his wiry nose hair is so long that it grows right into the beard, so in effect he has a beard growing out of his nose. I'm not surprised Mike keeps him on the door; who could get any work done with a nose beard hovering around the place? Fecker's beard hair is red, too, so from a distance it looks like Manny got himself punched in the face and is fine with blood all over himself.

Nosebleed beard? People are animals.

I give Booker a nice shoulder-check on my way in, just to remind him of past pains. You never know, if negotiations break down, he might choose to run away.

The Brass Ring has got nice carpet, chocolate brown with golden thread. Plush is the word. And the bar has a comforting walnut burnish that gives a drinker confidence in the barman before he ever sets eyes on him. Irish Mike and eight of his boys are seated in the lounge with their pieces right out on the table. And there, in the middle, sits Zebulon Kronski, spinning one of his war stories. I think it's the one about how we met in the souk outside UN headquarters in the Lebanon where Zeb had set up an underground cosmetic surgery, supplying fillers to religious fanatics.

'So, anyways. In marches Daniel palooka McEvoy just when I'm about to inject a syringe of fat into the militia guy's dick.'

Mike laughs, but his goons don't because they've seen me come in. They jump out of their seats, scrabbling for weapons. Two guys get their guns mixed up and argue like kids until one of them actually produces a photo of his gun that he keeps in his wallet.

It's embarrassing.

Mike's impulse is to stand up but he checks himself. He is the boss after all.

'Daniel, laddie,' he says. 'Sit yourself down.'

I walk around the tables a few times, mapping the layout, banking the positions of the chairs in case I have to toss a few.

Mike is antsy. 'Sit down, for fuck sake. You ain't a spaniel.'

In olden days, his boys would have guffawed at this, but now I'm a known quantity and it's like there's a gorilla loose in the room.

I sit between Mike and the bar, with the door in my eyeline and Zeb on my left in case I have to slap his stupid head for getting this ball of shit rolling downhill.

'Mike,' I say, giving him the sad face. 'Sorry to hear about your mother.'

Mike has a picture of his old ma in a lace frame pinned to his lapel. If this is an Irish custom, I never heard of it, and I lived there for twenty-odd years.

'Yeah, she was a great old dame.'

'How come you're not on a plane?'

Mike reddens like I'm making some kind of subtle accusation that he'd rather be here taking care of grudge business than in the auld sod burying his mother. Of course this is exactly what I'm doing. The thing about this situation is that Mike is holding nearly all the cards. The only thing he can't control is my attitude, so I don't intend handing over that last card until I have to.

'I am not exactly welcome in Ireland. They got a photo of me in the customs booth. I did a bit of Semtex business with *the boys.*' He drops me a wink on *the boys* so I know he's talking the Republican movement, though the mention of Semtex had pointed me in that direction.

'Yeah, that would be a problem. Why don't we cut directly to the part where you tell me why I'm here?'

Mike enjoys a bit of drama and so this request pains him. This pain shows in his expression, though with Mike's bar-fight potato head it's a bit like watching someone squeeze a fat old sponge.

'It ain't that simple, laddie,' he says, touching the picture of Ma Madden on his lapel. 'I'm grieving. I got the sweats, the shits and mood swings. I been drunk since yesterday.'

His guys mumble sympathetically. They sound like faraway monks.

Zeb pipes up. 'I got stuff for all that. Three pills twice a day. Pessaries though, so you gotta get them right up there.'

Tarantino is the man, but I never really bought those indoor triangular shootouts he's done a couple of times. Who's gonna get annoyed enough to start blasting with a barrel pointed at their own head? But now I'm starting to think that with Zebulon Kronski somewhere in that triangle, everyone's past caring about their own lives. Zeb could get the Dalai Lama to shoot dolphins. Here I am trying to jockey for some leverage and he just comes out with some shit about pessaries.

'Do me a favour, Mike,' I say hurriedly. 'Get this little prick outta here before someone can't take it any more.'

Mike clicks his fingers at Manny. 'You are so fucking right. I nearly strangled him three times already. The wife loves him, though. Her little miracle-worker Zeb.'

Something clicks with me.

Zeb ain't on the hook any more.

Just me.

Zeb has done more than make himself invaluable to Mike; he has made himself and his Botox needle indispensable to Mrs Madden. Maybe he's not as cavalier with his own life as I thought.

Manny hauls Zeb outta there and he's trying to make eye contact the whole way, but I blank him. Zeb's been running a game, and all the time playing it like we're down the same hole.

'Come on, Daniel. Danny boy. What is it?'

Zeb's got that guilty whine in his voice. He bloody knows. I want him to know I know, which kind of typifies the juvenile relationship we have, so I let him have a blast of my ire.

'You guys don't like Jesus, right? How about Judas? You got him in your book?'

I gotta hand it to Zeb, he's not a bad actor. He pulls off *shock* and *hurt* pretty well. First his entire head jerks with the force of my words, then the pain creeps into his eyes. Not too shabby.

'What are you saying, Dan? Talk to me.'

This is where Zeb's gig falls down. Anyone who is familiar with Dr Kronski knows all too well that his response to any false accusation is a bilingual litany of variations on the phrase *fuck you*.

I look him square in the eye. 'You're drifting out of character, Zeb. You've lost your motivation.'

His jaws are still flapping when Manny pushes him through the swing door and I cannot believe that I have risked my life several times for this ingrate. I don't want thanks but I would appreciate a little solidarity.

When Zeb leaves, a lot of the crazy leaves with him and it's just believable that Mike and I can do a little *mano-a-mano*, and then Mike says:

'Daniel. I know we're in a bit of a bind, but I think we should look for the opera-toonity here.'

Opera-toonity. I grind my teeth. I gotta make the best deal I can here, and blowing my top over a mispronunciation seems a little childish.

So I do not slap Mike in his greasy chops. What I do is say: 'Mike. You're grieving, man. You just lost your mom and that's major trauma for anyone, but for us Irish, it's earth-shattering.'

Pretty good, eh? I rehearsed that on the way over here.

'That's it exactly, Dan. Earth-shattering. You hit the nail on the head.' Mike fingers the lace on his lapel. 'But we have a duty to the dead, and that duty is to keep on living. We respect those who have passed on by grabbing life by the throat, as it were.'

Looks like I wasn't the only one rehearsing. I nod for a while, seemingly absorbing the wisdom of Mike's words, but actually trying to gauge if I could sink my fingers into his fat neck before his boys shoot me. It's doubtful. We got a table and ten feet of space between us.

'It's like this, Daniel,' says Mike. 'I got a proposition to make. This is a real opera-toonity for you to get out from under.'

He said it again and I feel my face spasm like I got slapped.

'Out from under? How far out?'

'Out from under in that I don't have to kill you no more.'

'Me and Zeb, you mean?'

Mike grimace-grins like it's out of his control. 'Well, not so much Zeb. He's like Mrs Madden's little pet doctor. She's got way more friends now. Everyone's a winner. But you, you're expendable.'

Fabulous. I'm expendable. When have I ever been anything else? They're gonna scrawl that on the body bag I get buried in. What's-his-name was expendable.

'Is that it? You don't have to kill me no more? What about protection on the club? Is that on the table?'

Mike laughs. 'No. That ain't anywhere near the table. That ain't even in the same zip code as the fuckin' table.'

This is good news, because if Mike wasn't expecting me to come back alive from whatever his proposition is, he would throw the monthly payment into the pot. Why not? Then again, I could be getting played.

Mike clears his throat for the big speech. 'You gotta ask yourself, Dan, why Mr Madden would give me an opera-toonity to get square.'

This is confusing: Mike is talking about himself in the third person but me in the first person.

'Should I take that opera-toonity?' continues Mike. 'Or should I throw that opera-toonity back in his face?'

You gotta be kidding me. I feel a vein pulse in my forehead.

'Because opera-toonities like this don't come along every day.'

Aaaargh. I gotta cut this off. 'Mike, let me ask you a question.'

In Mike's head he's already two

21

monologue, so this catches his breath in his throat. I plough ahead before he can find another excuse to say *opera-toonity*.

'What are you doing here?'

Mike squints his little beady eyes and for a moment they disappear entirely in his broken-vein face. 'What are any of us doing here, Daniel?'

'No. I mean, what are you doing *here*? In Cloisters. New Jersey is an Italian state. There are no Irish gangs in Jersey. You're like a boil on a supermodel's ass, Mike. You do not belong.'

Mike's chair squeaks when he leans back and I get to take in his entire corpulent frame, which five years ago might have been fearsome. All I see now is an ageing hard drinker squashed into an expensive suit which he is sweating the class out of. He's still got strength, but if he uses too much of it he could have a cardiac. In my uneducated opinion, Mike has got five years tops before the bacon grease pops his heart. Maybe I could have accelerated that process just by leaving Zeb in the room.

'The Italians don't want to fuck with me,' he says finally, actually answering my question, if not truthfully. 'We're a quiet little burg, laddie, and it wouldn't be worth the bloodshed.'

'Yeah, I guess,' I say offhand, implying that Mike would indeed inflict a lot of damage on an Italian crew.

Now this simple comment might seem at odds with all the argumentative junk I've been spouting, but I have a method. Back when I was in between tours in the Middle East with the Irish army, my appointed shrink, Dr Simon Moriarty, gave me a few tips to try to deal with the authority issues I'd been having. I can see him now, stretched out on the office couch that I should have been lying on, smoking a thick cigar and tapping the ash into a mug balanced on his Ramones T-shirt.

You see, Dan. Your average boss man bullied his way to the top, so deep down he doesn't think he deserves to be there. So, first you give him a few well-constructed insults, just to show you got the smarts. Then, when he's feeling good and intimidated, start drip-feeding compliments. A fortnight of flim-flam like that and he'll be eating out of your hand.

I don't have a couple of weeks, so I'll have to trust that Zeb laid the insult groundwork.

'Nah, the Italians ain't coming in here,' continued Mike, straightening his flat cap in a manner presumably meant to convey his hard-line attitude towards Italian gangsters. 'It's like that Spartan thing. They can't fit too many in here all at once and we can knock down spaghetti-Os all day.'

Spaghetti-Os. Nice.

'You certainly got the men,' I say, setting up another insult with a compliment. Mike's men flex their muscles, making their jackets squeak. 'Then again, I did beat the crap out of most of these guys on my lonesome, twice, while injured, a few months back. I could probably take four or five of them now, if I have to.'

Mike is ready for that. 'Oh no, laddie. We ain't getting suckered again. Calvin has a red dot painted on your skull right now.'

And not in the Buddhist sense, I'm guessing.

Calvin. I remember him. Young guy, all up on his police procedures. Says stuff like *trace evidence* and *DNA typing* with a straight face. Mike adores him. Moved the kid right up to number two last year. Suddenly I swear I can feel the laser dot on the back of my head.

'Okay, so let's cut to the chase. What am *I* doing here?'

'You mean metaphysically?' says Mike, proving that people can always surprise you.

'No. I mean, why am I sitting here in your new clubhouse when I should be in mine working on the refurb so you can up your rates?'

'You're here because I owe you a killing. You set my whole operation back months. Hell, laddie, you put my lieutenant in the ground. You saw the opera-toonity to hurt me and you took that op—'

I can't take it. Damn my impetuous nature. 'Hold on there a second, *laddie*. You think I wanted to put your guy down? You think that doesn't keep me awake? I gave him every chance to walk away, but no, your fuckwit of a lieutenant attacked me with a spike and I defended myself. I saw an *opera-toonity* to survive and I took it.'

Calvin sniggers and immediately apologises.

'Sorry, Mike. He said that word. You know, the one you say, the way you say it.'

Mike is upset that this entire conversation is not rolling out the way he expected.

'What word, Calvin? What fucking word would that be?'

I save Calvin's ass. 'You're a bully, Mike, you know that? Always trying to make excuses for your bullshit. You're gonna kill me and burn down my club unless I do something for you, right? So just tell me what that something is.'

I have obviously abandoned my psychological tactics at this point. I didn't last too long. Premature exasperation.

'Maybe I'm just gonna kill you,' says Mike, peeved at being predictable. 'You ever think of that?'

'No, Mike. Because if you wanted me dead, then four or five of your guys would be in the hospital and I'd have a flesh wound. Maybe.'

This comment sends us sailing past Mike's shit limit and he closes his eyes for a second. When he opens them again, we are in the presence of Dark Mike. Mike the Merciless. This guy has shed the veneer of civilisation like a snake sheds its dead skin. Irish Mike is carrying the race memories of bloody revolution, prison protest and back-alley shankings around inside him, and a few decades in New Jersey making the occasional pilgrimage to a Broadway show is not gonna wipe those away for long.

'Okay, you know what? Fuck you, Dan. Fuck you. I am getting a fucking migraine listening to your fucking shit.'

That's a lotta fucks all of a sudden. When I was a doorman full time, I developed a theory which stated that there was a definite correlation between the amount of *fucks* in a sentence and the imminence of the fuck-utterer taking a swing. Four fucks, and you took your hands out of your pockets.

The room seems to heat up. Mike's boys lean inwards like tall flowers attracted to the sun. They sense that the time to earn their salaries could be at hand.

'Here's the situation, okay?' says Mike, spit flecking his lips. 'I own this town and you fucking owe me, McEvoy. Whatever way you want to dress it up. So, there are two ways for you to get yourself out of the hole. Either Calvin plugs you in the head right now and I have to Clorox the floor, or I need a dummy to deliver a package to a guy called Shea in SoHo, who can be a little touchy. That's it. Two choices. A or B, no option C. Oh, actually, wait. There is an option C. Option C is Calvin shoots you in the balls first, then shoots you in the head.'

Option B sounds less immediately terminal than the others. Seems too easy though: deliver a package to a guy who can be a little touchy?

A *little touchy*. I bet that's the understatement of the century.

This is bullshit.

Mike is probably setting me up as the biggest fall guy in history. I could end up looking dumber than those Trojan guys who towed a hollow wooden horse into their until recently besieged city, gave the sentries a night off and had themselves a drunken orgy. On the plus side, I probably wouldn't stay dumb for long, as a swift death would surely be hot on the tail of the dawning dumbness.

'No, Mike. Screw that. I'll take my chances right now. Why don't we do a death-match scenario kind of thing? I'll take your boys two at a time.'

Mike reaches into his pocket and pulls out a baggie of cocaine, which he pours on to his palm and licks right off there like a donkey chowing on sugar.

'I gotta have something to take the edge off,' he says after a minute of zone-out. 'Otherwise, laddie, I would just kill you and fuck it. You think I don't know you're crapping bullets? You can give me lip until judgement day, but the truth is you're scared and that's a smart way to feel right now.'

Shit. Cocaine seems to have smartened Mike up.

'Yeah, I'm scared, but I ain't jumping outta this frying pan to put out your fire. I need more details. What's in the package? How do I know this Shea guy won't shoot me on the spot?'

'I could deliver the package, Mister Madden,' says Calvin, eager to claw his way back up the popularity ladder after the *opera-toonity* giggle.

Mike rubs his eyes with stubby thumbs. 'No, Calvin. You're my guy and I need you here. Shea is a livewire so I need a peacekeeper.' He looks at me. 'You're a peacekeeper, ain't you, McEvoy?'

Mike pulls an envelope from a drawer, takes out its contents and fans the sheaf on the table.

'Bearer bonds, McEvoy. Two hundred thousand dollars' worth. These are better than cash. I owe this guy Shea, and this is how he wants to be paid. These little bastards are fifty years old and have seen more blood than the Bay of Pigs, and yet they are squeaky clean and easier to transport than money. I want you to take these bonds and deliver them to Mister Shea at this SoHo hotel in the middle of the day. Simple as that. You do this one thing without any more of your wiseass bullshit and I will consider you twenty-five per cent outta the hole.'

'Twenty-five per cent, bullshit,' I say. 'Make it fifty.'

'Sure,' says Mike with a curling grin. 'Fuck it, fifty.'

Damn, I got played by Mike Madden.

'And what if I turn down your offer?'

'You know what.'

'Tell me. Spell it out, we ain't got no wires in here, do we?'

Mike licks the wrinkles in his palm and I see for the first time that the man is honestly grieving, in his own twisted way. When some guys are feeling blue they can't feel better until everyone else feels worse.

'If you don't do this for me I'm gonna do something to you, or that nutcase Sofia that you got under your wing, or maybe that partner of yours. I don't know. Something. I can't really think about it now, but it will be totally out of proportion, violence wise, to what you are owed. Nothing is more certain except those bearer bonds.' Mike's pupils focus to pinholes. 'So you guard those bonds like your life depends on it.'

Which of course it does.

He doesn't need to say it. I can infer.

27

CHAPTER 2

My day just got a whole lot more complicated and I can't help feeling that a large percentage of that is down to the poisoned chalice of friendship with Dr Zebulon Kronski. But my own mouth has gotta shoulder some responsibility too. Every time I have a face-to-face with Mike, I find myself back-talking and slinging zingers. When I get too anxious it's like my mouth runs independently of my mind, which is shrivelling like a cut of meat on a hot rock. Simon Moriarty, my sometime shrink, commented on this tendency during one of our sessions when I'd made a stab at humour to gloss over my shell shock.

'You have two problems, Sergeant McEvoy,' he told me as I stood by the window looking out over the quad.

'Only two,' I remember saying. 'We are getting somewhere.'

'You see that's one of your problems right there. All the chatter. The verbal diarrhoea.'

'Verbal diarrhoea gives me the shits,' my mouth said.

Simon clapped his hands. 'There it is again. The technical name for this tic is denial. You use it as a coping mechanism.'

'Denial. That word is too complicated for a lowly sergeant, Doctor.'

'Once upon a time you were vaguely amusing, but now you're wasting your own time.'

I relented. 'Okay, Simon. Tell me.'

'Denial is a classic defence mechanism. It protects the ego from things that the individual cannot cope with. So the patient will basically refuse to believe that he is experiencing stress, and I imagine you wisecrack in any stressful situation without even realising it. The more dangerous the situation, the more smartassed you get.'

I mulled this over. It was undeniably true that I often shot off my mouth and hit myself in the foot. I had thought this was bravado, something for other people to grudgingly admire.

Something occurred to me. 'Hey, Doc. You said I had a second problem?'

'That's right.'

'You planning on telling me?'

Simon scooted to the window on his office chair and lit a cheroot, blowing the smoke outside.

'Your second problem is that you're not very funny, and the only way people are going to tolerate a smartass is if he's amusing.'

This wounded me. I had always quietly thought myself reasonably witty.

Zeb is in the corridor begging Manny to hit him in the stomach.

'Come on, man, punch me,' he urges, yanking up his shirt tails to reveal a stomach with about as much definition as a bag of milk. 'Just do it. I've been working out with the Zoom Overmaster trainer to the stars DVDs. You couldn't hurt me if you tried. These abs are like rocks.'

I can see Manny Booker's brain going into meltdown. People do not usually ask to be assaulted, and yet hurting people is what he is employed to do. I put them both out of their misery by jabbing Zeb in the solar plexus on my way past. He collapses in a breathless ball and I can't say that I don't grin a little.

'You should ask for a refund on those DVDs, Zeb,' I say, still walking, which must look pretty cool if anyone's filming.

I'm tempted to stop and watch Zeb writhe on the carpet, but it's enough that I can hear him retch.

I am two blocks away before he draws level with me in his Prius. Someone told Zeb that Leonardo drives a Prius and that was it.

'What the fuck, Irish? You are testing our friendship.'

I keep walking. You can't enter into a debate with Zeb Kronski or it will drive you demented. All the same, I can't help thinking what I *would* reply.

I'm testing our friendship? Me? Because of you, I'm delivering a mystery envelope to a touchy guy in SoHo. Because of you, I am involved, yet again, in a life-or-death situation. The life being mine and also probably the death.

'I thought we were a team, Dan. Semper fi, bro.'

Semper fi, my Irish arse. He was a medic with the Israeli army, I was a peacekeeper for the UN. Not a marine between us.

I stride down the block and he cruises alongside like a john.

'Is this about Mike's old lady? Okay, I was getting in good there, man, but at a later date I was gonna bring you in to lay some emerald pipe. I was doing it for both of us.'

I grit my teeth. *Really? Both of us? So how come I've got this envelope in my pocket and you're off to inject Jersey housewives' faces with cheap Chinese filler? Doesn't seem fair.*

Zeb lights a fat cigar and fills the Toyota's interior with blue smoke. 'I was thinking long term. I shoot Mike's bitches up for a couple of years and then we're golden. How was I to know Mrs Madden would get herself electro-fuckin'-cuted?'

A couple more blocks then I'm at the casino and Zeb will find himself barred from Slotz.

'I can't believe you hit me,' says Zeb, who never could stay penitent for long. 'I thought you were my *bobeshi*.'

I am starting to believe that Zeb comes out with these incredibly dense statements just to trick me into engaging. If it is a ploy, it works every time.

I take two rapid steps to the Prius's window. 'You can't believe I hit you?' I shout, drawing looks from the clusters of mid-morning cigarette-break employees on the sidewalk. 'You were begging to be hit. You lifted up your shirt, for Christ's sake.'

'I wasn't begging to be hit by *you*,' argues Zeb. 'That other guy was a jelly roll. My abs coulda taken a shot from him.'

I change tack. 'And *bobeshi*?' I say, slapping the Toyota with my palm. 'Really?'

'Hey,' says Zeb. 'Take it easy on the car. Have you got something against the environment?'

'I'm a feckin' Irish Catholic and even I know *bobeshi* means grandmother. I'm your grandmother now?'

Zeb is unrepentant. 'Patients like the Yiddish, so I throw it in every now and then. Makes me seem wise or some shit. I was just going for the family vibe, like we're brothers. I'm more of a Hebrew guy to be honest, Dan. Is that what this whole sulk is about? I don't know Yiddish?'

It's a goddamn maze arguing with this guy. Like trying to hold on to an eel, if you'll excuse me mangling my metaphors.

I rest on the car for a moment, feeling it thrumming gently through my forehead, then I straighten.

'Okay. Go home, Zeb.'

'Are we good?'

'Yeah. Golden. Whatever. Just forget it.'

Zeb flicks ash on to the asphalt. 'What about my accent?'

I'm beaten now, he knows it. 'Your accent?'

'You said my Irish accent was bad. I worked on that, man. I watched *Far and Away* twice.' He screws up his face for a Tom Cruise impersonation. 'You're a corker, Shannon,' he lilts. 'What a corker you are.'

I feel like heaving on the footpath. I could be dead by nightfall and this dick is nursing a bruised ego.

'That's good,' I say for the sake of peace. 'Uncanny.'

Zeb's eyes find the middle distance. 'I coulda played the shit out of that role.'

'Maybe they'll do a reboot,' I say.

I know this term because Zeb and I spend a lot of our free time, as two single middle-aged bucks, watching TV. How cool and edgy is that? Most of our references are pop culture and our favourites at the moment are old episodes of the egregiously cancelled shows *Terriers* and *Deadwood*.

Whores get fuckin'.

Classic.

Why the hell would anyone cancel *Deadwood*? If that guy ever comes into my club he better have the viewing figures in his pocket.

Zeb perks up. 'Reboot. Fuckin' A.'

'Fuckin' A,' I agree wearily.

Seeing it all ahead of him, Zeb guns the Prius and shoots off down the street at the speed of a four year old on roller skates, and

I wonder not for the first time whether my life would be less pathetic without him in it.

Fuckin' A.

At the raggedy arse end of Cloisters' nightclub alley sits Slotz. My kingdom. About two steps up from a bordello. Most nights.

I won the lease for this place in a poker game a few months back, so I reckoned I may as well occupy the apartment that sits on top of it seeing as I'm already paying for it. The previous leaseholder lived elsewhere but kept the apartment up as what he tenderly referred to as a fuck pad. You can bet your last nickel that I brought in a team of industrial cleaners to steam the shit out of that place before I moved in, but I held on to the waterbed and a Jacuzzi which is coin-operated if you can believe that. I bet if Mike knew about the Jacuzzi coin box he'd want a slice of that too. I realise protection is a necessary evil, but these guys don't seem to realise that there is a recession on.

Zeb is not sold on the whole Jacuzzi idea.

Fucking jizz pools, he informed me one night when he actually scored a classy lady in the club and I gallantly offered the two of them a handful of change for a whirl in my deluxe power bath. *What do you think goes on under those bubbles? And how often do you clean the pipes? That pearly gunk has probably made its way into the water system by now. We're all down here chugging down some guy's tadpoles, smacking our lips and saying yum yum.*

I guess you don't have to be smart to be a doctor.

I try to stay positive about Slotz, but it's hard because of the spectre of shitholery hanging over the joint. This place has been a dump for a decade and a craphole for twenty years before that, but we're trying to change things. Me and my business partner Jason Dyal.

Jason is doing most of the work, to give the guy credit. He has been a revelation and a godsend. And if that reads a little over the top, it's because Jason is gay and I tend to overdo the praise thing just to show how cool I am with that. I get embarrassed when he starts bandying around words like queer and homo, but he says he's been holding it in for so long that he feels entitled to queer it up a little now.

I'm a queen in a safe environment, Danny, he told me a couple of months back. *So you're getting an eyeful of the real me.*

Fag away, I said, trying to get into the swing, which stopped him dead in his tracks.

I've stayed out of the swing since then.

So anyways, Jason has been my partner for several years, since we started bouncing this place. I always knew he was a tough-as-nails kind of guy, but I did not know that he also had natural business acumen and could handle a toolkit, which is not a euphemism. I stood in a porch with the guy for the best part of a decade through the rain and snow, holding doors for addicts and perverts, and knew damn all about him. Then again, he knew the square root of damn all about me. But now that we're business partners, we got a stake in each other's future, so mutual trust has entered the equation. This feels good on a day-to-day basis, but in the long term it's bad, because now Mike has someone else to punish for my sins.

So that's Sofia my kinda girlfriend on her good days.

Dr Zeb, my peacetime buddy from the Lebanon war zone

And Jason my tool-swinging business partner.

Three friends now. I'm turning into Miss Popularity.

Jason spots me coming in the front door and he climbs down from a stepladder and hails me.

'Hey, boss man. You came home. I was worried sick.'

'Less of the sarcasm, J. And we're partners now, remember?'

Jason looks like a linebacker in dungarees and a hard hat, and I know that if Zeb was here he'd ask him if he was going to a club with the rest of the Village People and Jason would laugh his ass off. I aspire to that level of nonchalance.

'Yeah, partners. I do all the work and you grace us with your presence when the day is nearly done.'

'Sorry, J. Won't happen again.'

Jason tugs a Post-it from his helmet where Marco, his boyfriend and our head barman, probably stuck it.

'Here's the to-do list for today.'

I hang my leather coat on the stand. 'Gimme the summary, J. I gotta wash and go. Mike trouble.'

Jason snarls. I can see the diamond twinkling in his incisor and I don't think there is a soul on this earth who would use the term *queen* to describe him right now.

'That Mike guy is a thorn in our side, Dan. Come on. We got skills, I think we could call in a few people and take him.'

Jason knows plenty about accountancy and remodelling spaces, and maybe he can crack heads pretty good, but he doesn't know shit about going tactical, and I don't just mean pulling the trigger, I mean living with yourself afterwards.

'No one's *taking* anyone, J. I gotta run an errand for Mike. You keep banging away here.'

Jason pouts, which is new. 'It's a bit more than banging away, Danny. This dump is going to be a palace by the time we're through. This whole area will be open plan. I swear I could pull down these partitions with my teeth, and the sweet part is we don't need a permit because the walls are not even on the original drawings.'

Being made partner has given Jason a real shot in the arm. He goes at everything with the enthusiasm of a five year old wired on Skittles.

'That's great. So what have we got on today?'

It's crazy; I'm making small talk like it's an ordinary day when I've got two hundred large in prehistoric currency burning a hole in my pocket. It occurs to me that it would not be beyond Mike to send someone after me to steal his own bonds and put me in the frame with Shea. In one move he could extricate himself from this guy's debt and get someone else to take the risk of sneaking up behind me.

Jason walks with me like we're in the halls of power, and I try to focus on what he's saying. 'Today we're breaking through from the back room to the roulette wheel. Practically doubles our space. I got a few of the boys coming over to help out. Throw on some nice green and yellow paint.' He eyes me pointedly. 'You're good with those colours, right?'

Shades of emulsion are way down on my list of concerns right now.

'Sure. Why not? And we're still gonna be open by Friday?'

'Not completely finished, but we can open, sure.'

'Good. You the man.'

It's true. Jason is the man. Without him and his goodwill network we couldn't afford the new coat of paint for this job.

I am gonna allow myself to think positive for five seconds, so I fake-punch and Jason fake-blocks. 'I got high hopes, J. We could actually make a living. All of us.'

'Fuck living,' says Jason. 'We're gonna make bank.'

I wince. It's an Irish Catholic pre-emptive guilt reaction to any expression of optimism. Pride comes before a fall. The Jewish folks have it too; as Zeb puts it: *You get too cocky, you get that cock cut off.*

Like many of Zeb's sayings it doesn't bear scrutiny but gets the point across.

Plus even banks ain't making bank these days.

I have a plan of sorts re the Mike/bearer bonds situation. Nip upstairs to my apartment to clean up and put on my stomping boots. Swing by the bus station, select a gun from my locker stash and take the bus into the city. Maybe I'll stop off at Spring and pick up a slice at Ben's, but that's not a priority and only works if I'm alive and the queue of tourists doesn't stretch too far around the block.

This is a pretty slapdash plan but I figure I'll have plenty of time to fine-tune on the bus.

But the best-laid plans come undone, and the casual ones unravel even faster. My shower and change proceeds exactly as envisioned but the gun-bus-pizza portion of my strategy lasts precisely five steps from the club when I notice an unmarked cop sedan idling beside the hydrant opposite. I know the two cops inside by the shapes of their heads. Coupla knucklehead detectives called Krieger and Fortz who Lieutenant Ronelle Deacon (my fourth friend) once informed me couldn't find their dicks with mirrors and a dick-o-scope, which cracked me up at the time. Now that level of incompetence seems a little ominous. Fortz looks like he's wearing a helmet and, with his long neck and slender skull, Krieger could have a light bulb on his shoulders.

Maybe they're not looking for me, I think.

Yeah, and maybe if Zeb's Uncle Mort had a pussy, and so on and so forth.

Krieger spots me in the mirror and attempts to exit the squad nonchalantly, which is tough to do when your partner has parked level with a hydrant. Krieger dings the door panel real good before he realises he's shut in there.

This would be a great jumping-off point for me if I wanted to get into some back and forth with these guys, but I'm feeling a little worn out with all the morning's repartee, plus I got an envelope in my breast pocket with big denominations inside it that I am pretty certain were not attained legally. With this in mind I decide to play it straight with these blues, no matter how much klutzing they get up to.

Fortz slides out the driver side but keeps his distance. I guess the word is out that I can knock people over pretty good.

'Morning,' says Fortz, hiding his bulk behind the door. 'Or is it afternoon?'

'Brunchtime,' I say, all cultured.

'Good one,' says Fortz, flopping his wallet open to give me an eyeful of the ID inside. 'I'm Detective Fortz and that dummy trying to get out of the car is Detective Krieger,' he says, a thumb hooked into his belt, keeping one hand close to his holster. 'You're McEvoy, right?'

Not much point in denying it. 'That's me, Detective Fortz of the force. What can I do for you?'

Fortz is living proof that evolution goes both ways. He's got the aforementioned helmet head look going on, with a skull that shines like a buffed bowling ball. The man is completely hairless as far as I can see and his features seem to belong to a much smaller face. It's as if his head kept growing but his eyes, nose and mouth said screw it at about age fifteen. His tongue lolls a bit when he's not speaking and another one of my doorman theories states that tongue lollers are quick to violence. Someday I'm gonna write all these nuggets down for future generations of doormen. Maybe I'll attain guru status and get on *Dr Phil*. I would love that, sitting on the chair opposite Phil, just close enough to smack that smug fucker in the chops. I probably wouldn't take the shot, but little dreams keep a person going.

Fortz swaps his wallet for a phone and checks the screen to show me how in demand he is.

'Lieutenant Deacon wants to see you,' he says. 'It's important.'

'You're running errands for the Troopers now?'

Fortz grins. 'Just lending a hand. We're all on the same team.'

I tell myself not to panic. Ronnie is straighter than Robocop and I haven't done anything bad yet today. 'Tell her I'll be in the club later and to come on down.'

'Nah,' says Fortz. 'She sent us to collect you, get it?'

In my imagination the envelope is glowing through the fabric of my jacket.

'What kind of appointment is this?' I ask, like there's a good kind.

'I think it's a doughnut-tasting sorta deal,' says Fortz, his little features jiggling with mirth like the last jelly beans in a bowl. 'Now, are you gonna get in back or do I have to start wondering why?'

Krieger has given up trying to get out of the car and I can tell by the set of his shoulders that he's sulking.

'Okay, I'm getting in. Just tell your partner not to shoot me. I ain't the one who locked him in the car.'

Fortz's eye roll implies a fractious relationship with his partner, soured by years of grumpy stakeouts and botched coffee orders.

'I think maybe I'll shoot him and pin it on you. How does that grab you?'

He ushers me into the back seat, still chuckling.

Blues. Comedians every last one. I read somewhere that cops develop a macabre and inappropriate sense of humour just to survive the job, but I reckon that mostly this disposition has been lurking under the surface looking for a way to climb out. Like a troll down a dark well.

Krieger is not pretty to look at even from behind. He's got these weird little clumps of hair sticking out from the back of his head like greasy stalactites and his shirt collar is clumping up his neck fat, which is weird because the rest of him is skinny as a matchstick.

As Fortz drives, Krieger has his arms folded and is giving off icy vibes. Fortz puts up with this for about two minutes, then . . .

'Come on, man,' he says, leaning across to dead-arm his partner. 'That hydrant thing was funny shit. Took some driving, too. *Talladega Nights*, dude.'

Shake and bake, I think.

Krieger slaps away the punch. 'Funny shit? How many times are you gonna pull that? I am sick to death of bashing the car door. You know I'm claustrophobic, Fortz, you asshole?'

'Course I fucking know. That's why it's funny.'

Much as I would like to consider these guys total idiots, I'd have to be deep in denial not to hear the similarities between their bitching and what Zeb and I get into on a daily basis. It's a little depressing.

'Hey, fellas,' I say, trying to keep it jaunty. 'You really want a civilian listening in on your domestics?'

Krieger twists around, poking his hand between the headrest and seat. I can't help noticing there's a Taser in his fist and the charge light is flashing green.

'No,' he says. 'I guess we don't.'

And he shoots me in the chest, which turns my entire universe electric blue. Through the neon I hear Krieger's voice saying: 'Moron brought that on himself.'

I wonder who the moron is?

CHAPTER 3

So, I'm spasming without dignity in the back of a police cruiser and since yours truly is the guy spinning this yarn, the traditional thing to do would be to throw in a dream sequence at this point or maybe a flashback. Fill in a few paragraphs, beef up the back story. Perfect *opera-toonity*, right? Except I can't seem to fully pass out.

This is bloody typical. Back in the Lebanon we used to prank Tase each other occasionally for giggles. Hilarious, right? Sending fifty thousand bowel-loosening volts coursing through a guy halfway through the weekly phone call to his fiancée. How we laughed. This went on for months until a staff sergeant went into a cardiac and had to be shipped home with his honourable discharge but without the use of his right leg. The point being that I got lit up a dozen times but most of the time it didn't put me out. Just like now.

Here I am grinding my teeth hard enough to crack the enamel. My entire body is stiff as an ironing board and there's a halo of agony buzzing around my head.

I should be out. This is too much pain.

I concentrate really hard and spit three words at Krieger.

'Hit . . . me . . . again.'

Krieger is a stand-up guy, so he obliges.

I do dream a little when I'm under. Mostly about Sofia Delano, which is to be expected since we got enough sexual tension humming between us to power a beer cooler.

The incident I flash on reveals a lot about me and my varied insecurities. I'm in my old apartment, downstairs from Sofia, and I come out of the shower to find her standing there in workout gear holding my towel on a finger.

'Oh baby,' she says, her voice sensual from years of Jameson and Marlboro. 'You look good.'

I don't feel like I look good, never have. But there's a woman in my bathroom who resembles 'Let's Get Physical' Olivia Newton-John telling me I look good, and that's never a bad start to the day.

'Thanks, Sofia,' I say, trying to cover my privates without using my hands. Tricky. 'You look good too. Great.'

She laughs. 'Baby, you have no idea. I've sent bigger men than you home with a limp.'

This is not fair. This woman is the right age for me, i.e. she falls within my ten-years-up ten-years-down parameters, she has the correct amount of sass, and sex appeal that's going to last until the day she dies, but she thinks I am her long-gone asshole husband.

She backs up with the towel and I have no choice but to follow.

'Oh baby,' she says and just the sound of her plump lips smacking on the B's makes me feel a little excited, ignoble and also weak-willed.

I cannot take advantage of a delusional woman, says my angelic side.

My other shoulder demon comes back with: *Yeah, but is there even a victim here? You'd be doing the dame a favour.*

I am half expecting another compliment from Sofia, which would be my undoing, but instead she says: 'I thought it was bigger, Carmine. Didn't it used to be bigger? You should see Dan's.'

Even though I'm not sure who's been insulted, the excitement drains out of me like air from a punctured balloon animal and I mutter some lame crack about perspective. Sofia doesn't laugh; instead she goes all metaphorical with:

'Like the playgrounds of my youth, all seems smaller now.'

Deep. Too deep for a semi-horny man getting out of a shower.

Sofia has a moment of lucidity and says, 'I gotta scoot, Dan. Carmine might call and if I'm not by the phone there will be freakin' fireworks.'

I pluck the towel from her fingers and nod. I wanted her to leave, but now that she's going I feel cheated.

Sofia kisses me so hard my shamed region forgets it's been insulted.

'That's better, baby,' she says with a smile that might even be for me.

I step back in the shower when she's gone.

I feel myself surfacing but Sofia's eyes are still there. Not the same sky blue though, more of a dirty petrol.

They are not Sofia's eyes, says my subconscious. *Notice the thick brows, not to mention the rubber gimp mask.*

I have a pretty open relationship with my subconscious. A little unhealthy even. We *dialogue* a lot, which kind of defeats the purpose of calling it a subconscious in the first place.

Still, my inner voice is right. Sofia does not sport thick brows. I flop around a little, trying to earth myself in whatever situation I'm in.

I feel a chair underneath me. Remembering the word for *chair* is not necessarily an indicator of no brain damage, but I'm optimistic. More information seeps through the haze. For example, the office chair seems to have me cuffed to it, and the room which me and the chair are in has swathes of satin streaming down from the ceiling. Also I seem to be naked apart from a pink leather thong, which I definitely did not snap on earlier this morning. This can't be real? Maybe the Taser rattled my neurons a little. I blink the world into focus and immediately wish that I hadn't.

There are two guys, presumably Krieger and Fortz, dressed in gimp masks and rubber aprons, dancing happy little jigs either side of a stool-mounted laptop. The floor is lined with plastic.

What happened to human beings? Once upon a time Marilyn Monroe holding an apple was the raciest thing on the planet. Now we gotta have middle-aged cops in gimp masks?

I cough a few times, which feels like it's inflating my brain, then say:

'You know, guys. Whatever happens, at least we have our dignity.'

Denial. That's what it is.

'Hey,' says Fortz, and I know it's him not from the single syllable but from the inverted cauldron shape of his head and the fact that his narrow-set eyes don't quite line up with the eyeholes. 'Look who's awake.'

Krieger whistles. 'Thank Christ for that. I thought the second dart might have killed him.'

45

Fortz punches his partner's bare shoulder, which is matted with fuzz. 'So why did you give him the second dart, moron?'

'I was angry with you, Dirk,' says Krieger, whose body language screams *bitch*. 'You've been ragging me all week.'

Dirk Fortz does his eye-rolling thing. 'Shit, Krieg. We're partners. Ragging goes with the turf.' He turns to me. 'That's quite a ticker you got there. I never saw a guy still jabbering after getting sparked.'

I have crescents of pain behind my eyes and would really like a nap, but I figure keeping the conversation going will delay whatever shit storm is drifting my way.

'Depends on the weapon. I got hit with fifty thousand volts last year, knocked me out of my skin. What've you got there? Thirty?'

Fortz's lip juts out through the hole in his gimp mask. 'Nah, it's fifty. Well, that's what it says on the barrel. You never know with these fucking things, right? A bullet's a bullet. But Tasers could be shooting fairy dust for all I know.'

'Feckin' electricity,' I agree good-naturedly, going for reverse Stockholm syndrome. 'That's some sneaky invisible shit.'

Krieger interrupts our bonding session. 'Dirk, we're at fifteen grand already,' he says, tapping the laptop's screen. 'We should get oiled.'

It's a little difficult to understand what Krieger is saying because of the mask. I really hope he didn't say *oiled*.

'Fifteen grand,' says Fortz, clapping his hands. 'Twenty is our reserve, which you should feel very proud of. Five more and we're good to go.'

Good to go? Nothing about this situation is good as far as I'm concerned. I have an idea what's going on here, and half of me almost doesn't want my suspicions confirmed. The other half of me blurts: 'What the hell is happening. Fortz?'

The detective scratches his beer gut and ignores the question. 'You probably guessed they make porn in this building, McEvoy. Friend of mine lets me use a room on occasion. Did you know that they shot the entire *Twelve in a Bed* series in that bed behind you. Sunny Daze made her debut in this very room.'

'No way,' says Krieger. 'You never told me that. I love her flicks. Especially *Good Daze and Bad Daze.*'

'That was a classic,' says Fortz and is lost for a moment in fond reminiscence.

I try again. 'Come on, guys. What am I doing here?'

Fortz picks up a scalpel from the table. 'Deacon said you were smarter than you look, so figure it out, why don't you? Let's look at the clues: you're handcuffed to a chair in a porn studio. There are two guys in rubber watching pledges mount up on a laptop with a built-in webcam. Whaddya think's going on? Poker night?'

It's pretty conclusive stuff, but cops have been known to concoct elaborate scenarios to trick confessions out of suspects. My old army buddy Tommy Fletcher told me that two Guards from Athlone once dressed up as al-Qaeda to try to get him to sell them a wheelie bin full of Stingers that they were convinced he kept in his yard.

I would have sold 'em the bin too, he admitted. *But they had one whiskey too many in a hot bar and their beards melted off. Coupla red flags right there.*

Tommy. What a fecking nutcase.

'Maybe you're trying to set me up,' I venture. 'Trick me into confessing something.'

'You got something to confess?' asks Fortz.

'Nothing worth this much trouble.'

'Bang goes that theory,' says Krieger.

'So that's it? You're just gonna auction me on line?'

'Yup,' says Fortz. 'People gotta pay to log on and watch us torture you to death. You would be amazed at how many sickos are out there.'

Not today I wouldn't.

This is the worst thing that has ever happened to me. I can honestly say that if Sofia wasn't depending on me, I would prefer to be dead. They say that there are no noble ways to die, but a heart attack is looking pretty good right now. And the way my heart is thudding in my chest, a cardiac is definitely achievable if I let my fear run riot.

'Come on, guys. There must be something we can do here. I gotta be more valuable to you alive than dead. I got certain skills.'

Fortz laughs. 'Listen to Liam fucking Neeson. Certain skills.'

Krieger pitches in. 'He could tell us where the package is? That would be worth something.'

Package? How do they know about Mike's envelope?

I go to standard first base. 'What package?'

Fortz shrugs. 'If you don't know, then you don't know and we ain't got a use for you apart from the auction.'

I have no play here. All these morons have to do is search my clothes and they're going to find the envelope. I can't believe they didn't do that already, too busy wiggling into their rubber aprons.

Maybe they are stupid enough for me to pull some sort of con.

'Detectives. You're making twenty grand? That's chump change compared to what I can offer you.'

The blues don't even bother answering, returning their attention to the screen's growing total.

I let my chin droop to my chest and make animal snuffles that are somewhere between chuckles and sobs.

Keep it together, soldier. You are not dead yet.

Fortz pinches his partner's midriff. 'Nineteen grand. Still rising.'

Krieger giggles and skips away. 'Quit it, Dirk.'

'Okay,' I say, recovering a little. 'Let's do what we're really here to do.'

'Which is?' asks Fortz, stepping closer.

We're here because these two protect-and-serve motherfuckers are greedy, and maybe I can appeal to that side of their nature.

'Negotiate,' I say.

Fortz waves the scalpel at me. 'Negotiate? What are you gonna negotiate with, Irish? Who gets to slice off your balls?'

This casual questions hits me like a sock in the gut and I feel myself hyperventilating. I've been in tight spots before, but this situation is so dark that I am a hair's breadth from total panic.

Fortz taps me on the cheek with the scalpel. 'Hey, Dan. Danny. Come on now. Gimme some of that crackling banter you're famous for. Let's give the perverts their money's worth.'

I suck the panic back down. 'I got the package in my jacket pocket on the floor right over there.'

'You got the package in your jacket pocket?'

Fortz elbows Krieger. 'Is this guy serious?'

'The boss said it was a long shot.'

'So he doesn't have the package. Who cares? We're getting paid on both ends.'

I am insulted that they doubt my integrity. 'I do have that

package. I was delivering it for Mike Madden. Why don't you pull it out, see what we have?'

Krieger and Fortz go into a routine.

'Why don't we do that?'

'Yeah, why don't we do that?'

'Seems reasonable?'

'Totally reasonable.'

Fortz conducts with the scalpel as he speaks. 'We would have to be total retardos not to go ahead and act on your suggestion.'

Krieger laughs at the word *retardos*, which is probably a new wrinkle in their double act.

'Do we look like *retardos* to you, McEvoy?' Krieger demands.

This seems like a trick question.

'No. Look, it's in my pocket.'

I figure if I get away from Krieger and his partner, I can worry about Mike killing me later. Also, if I do get away, then I will come back almost immediately and kick the living shit out of these two clowns.

'My package is worth two hundred large, which is a hell of a lot more than whatever you're pulling down here. And there's more where that came from.'

Give a little truth to sell a lie.

'Save your breath, McEvoy,' says Krieger. 'You're gonna need it for screaming.'

Fortz pats Krieger's shoulder in silent approval for this segue.

'Do you think we just happened to pick you up at random, Danny?' he asks, and then answers. 'No, we were told to pick you up and see if you knew where the package was. And it's obvious to me that if you think the package can fit in your jacket pocket, then you don't even know what the package is. That being the case, we are to dispose of you however we see fit and make sure the body is never found.'

'They ain't ever gonna find you,' says Krieger with some certainty, like this might be worrying me.

'We've read your file,' continues Fortz. 'We know all about your special forces tricks. I go into the jacket for whatever your package is and it explodes and covers me with acid or some shit. No. Not happening. We do our thing, then we take our time extracting that envelope with tweezers. But hey, thanks for filling us in on its pedigree. That information could come in very useful when we're *negotiating*.'

Bastard. Turning a man's own five-syllable word against him.

'Hey,' says Krieger. 'Now we're getting paid three ways. The boss, the perverts and his package.'

Fortz tosses the scalpel in the air and catches it neatly. 'Who doesn't love a good three-way?'

I was stupid and Fortz burned me.

You're panicking, Dan. Getting sloppy.

In a previous life, when I was eager to serve my country by getting the hell out of it, my army shrink gave me a spiel on being a hostage. Apparently UN peacekeepers were snatched with the same regularity as Robin the Boy Wonder, which was about once per week. Unfortunately for us, we did not survive with the same consistency.

Always negotiate from a position of power, or at least a position of perceived power, Simon Moriarty had advised. *Failing that, it's amazing how many of these klutzes don't know how to tie a knot.*

None of which applied to me now, as I was cuffed hand and foot and not technically a hostage. I was a commodity whose life would be traded for cash, bit by bit, saving the balls for last.

'You can't just snatch a guy off the street and think nobody will notice,' I say, trying not to bleat. 'You guys are cops, for Christ's sake. Ever hear of surveillance footage?'

Fortz's response is snide. 'Yeah, we heard of it, we know every camera in town. Why do you think we parked where we parked?'

'There's gotta be witnesses?' Definitely bleating now. I sound like a baby goat.

'Maybe,' admits Krieger. 'But by the time anyone figures you're missing, we, as stand-up cops, won't even remember talking to you. You remember seeing that guy, partner?'

'What guy?'

'The Irish guy.'

'What Irish guy?'

'Exactly.'

And then they bump sweaty chests, and I notice some matted hair transferral.

Their celebration is interrupted by the laptop, which tweets stridently like a canary. This unexpected sonic squeak is greeted by the cops with sudden hushed reverence, as though it is the Angel Gabriel's horn.

'A fucking canary!' whispers Fortz, and Krieger shushes him.

'Wait, Dirk. Don't jinx it. Let me check.'

He rushes to the computer and checks the screen. 'Private session,' he says in hushed tones.

'Cha-ching!' exults Fortz, pointing the scalpel skywards like Excalibur. 'Tell me.'

Krieger enunciates so clearly you could slice apples on the consonants. 'One hundred thousand dollars from Citizen Pain.'

Citizen Pain? I bet he doesn't use that name on dating sites. If I do manage to extricate myself somehow from this evil little room,

I am gonna track down the good citizen and teach him something about pain.

'I knew Pain would lap up the preview video,' says Fortz. 'He loves the special forces types. That guy is a slave to his dick, man.'

'Will I confirm?'

'Seal the deal, partner.'

Krieger wiggles his fingers like Oliver Hardy playing with his necktie, then sends an index finger diving towards the return key.

Click.

'Sealed and delivered,' he says. 'We have accepted his offer, the money is in our account.'

Sealed and delivered, I think. *They're talking about me. My person.*

I literally shudder at the thought of what was on that preview video they must have shot while I was out.

'When are we going live?' I ask, might as well.

'Right fucking now,' says Fortz. 'As soon as I tape your fat Irish mouth.'

Of course. Tape. These guys don't want their names flying around the internet. Even with the volume muted, there's always some smartarsed lip-reader.

Fortz has gotta get close to use the tape. This is my last chance to make a play.

'Cover this motherfucker,' he says, snagging a roll of tape from his kitbag under the table.

Yeah, Krieger will cover me okay but he'll think before shooting now that I'm private show material.

I tighten my core, searching for focus.

One chance. What've you got, soldier?

My fingers crab under the rim of the office chair and all I find

53

is chewing gum and the height adjustment lever. If I tug on that lever, this chair should drop suddenly, if it's working right.

Krieger aims his gun my way, but half his attention is on the computer. Fortz is coming at me in ever decreasing circles. Wary, like a hyena closing in on a dying lion.

I smell a pungent blend of talc, nerves and Speed Stick as Fortz closes in from the rear. Drops of his sweat spatter my head.

A shadow falls over me and Fortz's elbows rest on my shoulders. His pale hands descend, a strip of duct tape held delicately between the fingertips, trying to avoid the sticky side. Even when taping a kidnap victim, a person's gotta pay attention to the sticky side.

When I see the tape in front of my face, I pull the lever. The chair drops down maybe a foot and I go down with it. Fortz, who had been leaning on my shoulders, is put off balance by the sudden drop and I feel his entire weight on my back. I have a little play in my legs now, not enough for anything more than a hobble but maybe enough to throw some chaos into this situation. I swivel the chair so that Fortz's bulk is between me and Krieger's gun, then focusing all my energy into my knees, I explode upwards to the limit of my chains, which is enough to catapult Fortz towards his partner.

Over my shoulder I see Fortz go down heavy and awkward and he loses a shelf of teeth to the laptop's keyboard, which is a bonus. Krieger is bowled backwards and drops his gun in the tangle of limbs.

I have maybe five seconds before I get shot. And being body-bagged in this thong has definitely shot into the top five of my *Don't Let It End This Way* list, just above accidentally drinking bleach and below diving into a freezing lake to rescue a puppy only to find out that it is actually an old rag and the girl you're trying to impress hates dogs anyway.

As you can see, I have put quite a bit of thought into this list. Dr Moriarty would say I was anal, and the rig-out I'm wearing at the moment would do little to disprove that theory.

With the seat at its lowest setting I have enough play in my bonds for a bent-over stagger. My hands and feet are cuffed around the central column and this cheap-ass chair doesn't even have casters so I gotta heck along like a . . . gimp. Is it ironic that I am gimping while those dressed as gimps don't have to? I don't think so. I think it's just unfortunate.

Fortz has pulled off his mask and stuffed it into his mouth in a ridiculous attempt to stop his gums bleeding, but more importantly, Krieger is scrabbling on the ground for his gun.

Time to find the exit.

This room has no windows and only one door, which is blocked by two buttery cops, so I'm gonna have to go through the wall.

Go through the wall?

Even thinking it sounds ridiculous. Nevertheless, it's either that or the aforementioned ball-slicing. I crab-roll on to the bed with just enough momentum to come to my feet.

'Hey,' burbles Fortz through the blood. 'Stop! Police!'

In the words of the sweatband-wearing fuzzy legend J. McEnroe: *You cannot be fucking serious.*

I bet McEnroe said *fucking* all the time off-camera. You can just imagine it coming out of his face.

I bounce on the bed to work up momentum and behind me I hear scuffling and clicking. I just bet that's Krieger finding his gun. He may be a shitty cop, but usually the shitty cops are the best shots.

A bullet clangs into the chair's column, knocking me forward a step, and I decide to make use of this blast of kinetic energy to hurl myself towards the wall, praying for a single board of sheetrock. The way my day is going, my head is gonna connect with a water pipe.

Also, my use of the verb *hurl* may have been a little optimistic. *Lurch* might be a bit more honest.

Saints be praised, luck o' the Irish, the wall is a flimsy partition and I bludgeon my way through directly into the middle of a threesome. At least I only count three. One second I'm in a room with two decidedly out-of-shape cops and the next I'm on a bed with a bunch of extremely well-endowed young people who seem to be loving their work.

A line from *Ghostbusters* pops into my head: *Do not cross the streams, that would be bad.*

I duck underneath what I hope is a forearm and tumble to the floor.

A film crew are by the foot of the bed and the director jumps to his feet, all ponytail and pout.

'A eunuch? I didn't order a eunuch?'

I will replay that later and be offended.

After a moment's grace, my sudden apparition causes pandemonium. Even in the kinkiest pornographic scene no one is expecting a semi-nude middle-aged man to come crashing through the wall. I ain't even waxed, for heaven's sake.

The guys lose their tempers among other things and the girl's squeals sound a lot more authentic than the ones she was making a few seconds ago.

'Sorry,' I say automatically. 'Just passing through.'

Waiting in the wings is an aged fluffer standing sentry at a dessert trolley loaded with various accessories. She is the only one unfreaked out by my arrival. Her jaded heavy-lidded eyes tell me she has seen a lot weirder things than me in her day.

'Can you uncuff me?' I ask from the floor, shaking my chains urgently at her.

The woman squints at my shackles while the director calls *cut* over and over again in increasingly panicked tones and an expensive-looking light on an aluminium stalk keels over, exploding in a shower of white sparks.

'What kinda cuffs you got there?'

I glance nervously at the hole in the wall. 'Police. Standard issue.'

She laughs. 'Cop cuffs. I could open those with my tongue.' This idea is made even more unsavoury by her mouthful of nicotine-stained choppers.

'A key will be just fine, darlin',' I say, laying on the leprechaun.

The woman locates a key and goes to work on my cuffs. Meanwhile there is more activity behind me on the bed as Krieger attempts to climb through the hole.

'A gimp!' exclaims the director. 'I am not doing a gimp scene. What is this, nineteen ninety-two?'

I twist around just in time to see one of the working studs, an obscenely muscled man, deliver a right hook that just about takes Krieger's head off.

'Motherfucker has a gun,' he explains, which is enough to send the starlet shrieking from the room.

Krieger droops in the hole. Seventy kilos of dead weight.

A few clicks later I am a free man.

'Who the hell are you?' the director screams. 'What the hell is going on?'

I read someplace that it's acceptable for men to scream like girls if they're movie directors or being electrocuted.

'It's okay, people,' I say, climbing to my feet, trying to muster some gravitas in spite of my appearance. 'I'm police. Undercover. Those two were planning an illegal shoot. Just put all your permits and birth certificates on the table and I can have you out of here in five minutes.'

The room goes quiet and I can hear Fortz gurgling next door like a baby looking for a boob.

'Anything else I can do for you, honey?' says my saviour, with that kind of frown on her brow that lets me know she ain't swallowing word one of my bullshit.

I tuck the cuff key into my thong, well you never know, then scan her trolley for something useful.

'Can I borrow a dildo?' I ask.

This is not really a specific enough request. 'Sure. Which one?'

'The big one,' I say.

I think about killing Krieger and Fortz, I really do. The bastards deserve it. No doubt this ain't their first rodeo, so God knows how many lives I'd be saving by putting them in the ground.

But it's not in me to murder them, no matter how easily I could justify it.

Maybe this whole episode comes off a little comical with the thong and porno scene and so forth, but the reality is that I have never been so scared or sickened. There were times in the Lebanon when I endured some pretty harrowing depravity, but in that room my psyche grew a whole new layer of scar tissue.

I push Krieger back into the room, leaving him flopped on the bed, and climb through after him. Fortz is still in a puddle of fat and blood on the floor, bitching about his ruined mouth, like the day has dealt him a bum hand. He finds it in him somewhere to go for Krieger's gun and I heft the dildo and give him a solid whack on the temple, which is enough to put him down.

'You are lucky,' I shout at the unconscious cop, 'that I used this tool as a club and not in the fashion for which it was realistically moulded.'

My heart rate is still at around two hundred, which is in the danger zone for a man my age, but I feel a little better. The immediate peril is past and now all I have to worry about is Mike's errand and these two gimps coming after me when they wake up.

I dress myself, leaving on the thong because the porn crew, who have probably figured out that I am not in fact a cop, are peeping through the hole in the wall. Then I wave Mike Madden's envelope under Fortz's nose.

'You see this?' I say, but I doubt he can hear the question. 'I did have the package. I told you, but you wouldn't listen.'

The cops' gear offers up a bounty of weapons which I am glad to accept. Four handguns: two official Glock 19s and a couple of baby Kel-Tecs in their Uncle Mike's ankle holsters.

Matching guns. I bet Fortz even decides what weapons they carry.

I distribute the cache of weapons to my pockets but the dildo I leave in Krieger's twitching fingers, for spite, and snap off a photo on my phone to post on the police website.

These guys are lucky, I tell myself as I leave this room of nightmares for the first and last time. *If I catch so much as a glimpse of these cops ever again I will kill them both.*

I decide to tape the thong to my bathroom mirror later, Rocky style, to look at every morning, just to remind myself how much hatred I am capable of mustering up in case I should ever need to channel it.

All this rigmarole to give perverts their jollies.

The older I get the less I like this world and the more I appreciate anything good.

Like Sofia.

CHAPTER 4

As soon as the door closes behind me I feel weak as a kitten in a sack. The righteous adrenalin drains down to my feet and I have to lean my forehead against the wall to stop myself throwing up. The Taser burns on my chest feel like they might be smouldering and my thoughts are suddenly swirling down the drainpipe of my confused cortex.

At least that's what it feels like.

Maybe I should go back in there and put those cops down, because the first thing they're going to do is come after me. They have no choice.

On a purely practical level this is a good argument. Just finish off Krieger and Fortz and be done with it, but killing cops would pretty much ensure that my case never made it to trial, even with a buddy in the department.

I spent a night on the town with Deacon, that's friend number four if you're losing track, and her captain a few months ago and we ended up in the back room at Slotz with a bottle of Jack Daniels and sloppy grins on our faces. The conversation got around to the dumb excuses cops actually committed to paper for firing their weapons.

This one guy claimed that he had to shoot the suspect because the suspect was wearing a T-shirt with writing on it, the captain said, hand on heart. *The writing was quote 'un-American' and this dumb rookie motherfucker thought he saw the word 'jihad' in there somewheres.* The cap had paused for a slug of whiskey and we knew the punchline was coming. *And the rook felt he couldn't let this guy live 'cause he wasn't more than five miles from an airport at the time. Turns out the writing was from* Lord of the *fucking* Rings. *Elvish or some shit.*

And Ronelle said: *Elvish has left the building.*

How we had split our sides in drunken laughter at the time. That war story doesn't seem that funny now. If Krieger and Fortz ever do catch up with me, they will have their excuses all figured out in advance.

Ronelle Deacon is a cops' cop. True blue back to her grandaddy, who was one of the rare African-American members of the Texas police force and one of the famous group who stormed the university tower in seventy-seven to bring in the Austin City Sniper. Ronnie picked up the baton from her father, who walked a beat in Rundberg, where it takes guts to put one foot in front of the other when you're a black man wearing the blue. Ronnie was raised tough but straight. By the age of twelve she was spotting her daddy while he bench-pressed in the garage. By fourteen she was bench-pressing a hundred pounds herself, and by twenty-two she was a rookie in the NYPD, working hard on her arrest rate and harder on her studies so that she could make detective by thirty. She managed it with two years to spare.

Krieger and Fortz used my friendship with Ronelle to get me into their cruiser in the first place. They gotta know she's the first person I'm calling once my hand stops shaking. Them being cops won't mean shit to Ronnie, she hates bent cops more than normal criminals. So now she's on the danger list too. Fortz does not strike me as the kind of guy to leave loose ends floating around. They gotta come after me and then make Ronelle's death look like an accident.

I need to handle this.

I call Ronelle but it goes straight to voicemail, so I leave a terse message, trying to inject the words with urgency but not desperation.

Ronnie. It's Dan. We need to meet. I am uberscrewed.

My tone implies, I hope, that this is really serious. It strikes me that Ronnie doesn't know about the *uber* thing, and if you don't know that then the message could come off a little jokey. Hopefully she will infer from my tone. But more than likely Ronnie won't infer shit. She will listen to the words and apply the usual meaning to them. I have this terrible habit of reading in layers that nobody else sees or that are simply not there. It's like in my mind everybody's speaking in metaphors or broadcasting their intentions through micro-movements and I'm trying to dig down to what they really mean. That's what happens when you grow up with an abusive parent: always trying to read the signs, predict the mood, keep yourself clear when it breaks bad.

What you eventually realise is that when people blink, they are mostly just blinking, not spelling out some kind of code, or when they shift away from you in bed, it ain't because they don't love you any more, it's because you have sharp elbows.

Sometimes a tiger tiger burning bright is just a tiger.

I know this, but still years of beatings have made this habit reflex to me.

Watch for signs. Everything means something.

In a way, it's handy having had an abusive parent. Pretty much every bad thing I've ever done can be traced back to Dad on a big thick blame arrow.

For some reason I had thought myself in a detached house, out in the country a little. Maybe with a garden. Someplace the neighbours would be horrified when they found out it was a porn studio.

I cannot believe it. That house was always so quiet. Kept itself to itself and never threw parties.

But as I settle enough to take stock, I realise that my spatial sense has probably been bamboozled by the porn room's soundproofing. I am in a New York high-rise hallway, no doubt about it. I can tell by the street noises jostling each other in the stairwell. Traffic and fat throngs of pedestrians. New Yorkers shouting terse messages into their cells, the delighted cooing of tourists getting their first glimpse of Donald's golden tower or the Apple store, and a blend of Middle Eastern dialects that you wouldn't find in Guantanamo. The smells are familiar too: street food, hot asphalt and the rubber of a million tyres.

New York. Those clowns humped me to New York.

There is a tight elevator box to my left which would take me down to a back door, but I choose not to trap myself inside. Contrary to what the movies would have us believe, there is often not a handy escape hatch in the roof which is left unbolted in case of action hero distress. If you get caught in a lift, then you are, as the gamers say, totally pawned.

It's hard to keep up with the kidlingo. I said FUBAR to a college jock in the club recently and he looked at me like I was in black and white.

Tango & Cash, junior. Buy a DVD, why don't you?

So I don't get in the lift for that reason. But also because I have a phantom memory of being manhandled into that shaft with Fortz's snide laughter wet in my ear and just looking at the steel door gives me the shivers.

Feck it. I'm just gonna kill them.

No. I've done a lot of desperate things in my life, but I never killed a person when there was another way. Any other way.

That arsehole Fortz better learn from his mistakes, because next time I can't promise this level of self-control, especially when I've had time to brood on the wrong done to me.

After a few breaths to steady myself, I take the stairs. Three storeys down past a nail spa and a meat refrigerator and I'm out on the street. I turn right and walk head down just in case there is some sort of surveillance. Putting a little mileage between me and that building is my priority. When my heart stops pounding, then I can try to figure my whereabouts. It shouldn't be too difficult. All I have to do is ask my phone.

As it turns out, I'm way down Manhattan on 42nd and 8th, which is an area I know pretty well from my years bouncing the Big Apple clubs. I could jump a cab to SoHo and get this accursed envelope dropped off, but I need a little headspace to ride out the after-tremors of combat neurosis that I feel coming my way, and also food would be a very good idea. It's after two and I haven't eaten a crumb.

After two? How the hell did that happen?

Krieger must have given me a shot of something in the car, to make sure I stayed out. Another reason I should have finished those guys off. I decide to ask Zeb for a thorough once-over if I make it home, to make sure there are no alien chemicals floating around my system. A lot of sedatives cause side effects unless you get them flushed. Anything from amnesia to paranoia can crop up for days after taking a shot. The last thing I need is to be wandering around, convinced that people are trying to kill me but unable to remember who exactly.

I'd probably ask a cop for help and that cop would be Dirk Fortz.

I hike the dozen or so blocks to the Parker Meridien, glad of the density of human camouflage on the streets, and grab myself a small table in the famous Norma's breakfast restaurant.

Dirk Fortz. What kind of stupid name is that? It's like his parents couldn't decide if they were in Dynasty *or* Star Wars.

This guy has gotten under my skin in a way nobody else ever has. He didn't just want to kill me, he wanted to go beyond that.

My hands are shaking and I hide them under the table when the waitress comes over with the menu. Sorry, not waitress. Server. The *server* is maybe ten years younger than me, so just about eligible for the fantasy league, with an open face and eyes that are bright with good diet or speed.

'No need for a menu,' I say. 'I've been before. Bring me a pot of coffee and the French toast, with everything.'

The server's smile is so wide that she makes me believe in it. If there's one thing Americans know how to do, it's how to make people feel welcome.

Shit, I feel like a regular and I haven't been up the steps in years.

'French toast,' she says, writing the order on her pad. 'Some comfort food, huh?'

'Yep,' I say. 'I need a little comfort right now.'

I used to treat myself to breakfast here when I'd had a rough night on the doors. A lot of joints have the *Best Breakfast in New York City* sign in the window, but Norma's might actually deserve it.

I read the server's name tag. 'Nothing like French toast to make a guy feel comforted, Mary. You Irish, Mary?'

Mary is thrilled with the question. 'Oh my God. I am like, totally Irish. My great-grandad came over from County Wales.'

I am glad to have an excuse to smile. 'That's great. I got cousins in County Wales.'

Mary thrusts out her chest with some determination. 'Well, I hope you're hungry, cousin. 'Cause this toast will be big enough to feed an army.'

I like Mary already, and if I hadn't been recently electrocuted and abducted I might even put some effort in here. But I have bearer bonds in my pocket and the truth is Mary is probably working on her tip, and even if she wasn't, I feel a crazy loyalty to Sofia like a bipolar angel sitting on my shoulder.

Mary strides off to the kitchen and I lay my hands on the table, daring them to shake.

Deal with it, assholes, I beam at them. *You got stuff to do*.

Norma's is a lot swishier than my usual diner but sometimes you gotta tolerate a little class in the name of toast. Even at close to three in the afternoon, the high-ceilinged room is half full of businessmen loosening their ties and buttons, and out-of-towners here for the famous pancakes. I bet a girl like Mary could pull in a couple of hundred extra a day in tips.

Maybe I'll offer her a job.

While I'm contemplating my server's totally over-the-top reaction to my imagined job offer, in the real world Mary has plenty of time to grab a pot of coffee and swing back around to my table.

'Hey, cousin,' she begins, then freezes, staring at my hands. No, not my hands, something between my hands. I look down and see that I have put one of the Glocks on the table. I don't remember doing it. Why would I do that in a restaurant? I feel a cold sweat push through the pores of my neck.

Mary is not fazed for long. This gal works in NYC.

'Oh, I get it. Irish, right? So, you're a cop?'

It's nice when people invent your excuses for you. I wish it happened more often.

'This is a cop's gun,' I say truthfully, sweeping the Glock off the table. 'I was just making sure the safety was on. I wouldn't want to shoot any of your customers.'

Mary leans in close and pours me a cup of java that I know is top class just from the aroma.

'See those two guys in the corner with their eyes on stalks every time my ass swishes by?' she whispers.

'Yeah, I see 'em,' I reply.

Of course now that she has said the words *ass* and *swishes*, my eyes are going to be on stalks too.

'You can shoot those two if you like, Officer,' Mary says, and I feel her breathing in my ear, which almost cancels out the memory of Fortz doing the same thing.

The toast is everything I remember and twice as big, buried under fruit, cream and syrup, made all the sweeter by the discreet hip bump Mary throws me on the way past. It's like tossing a bone to a drowning dog. I appreciate the gesture, but it doesn't really improve my situation.

I go to work on the toast, which is so good that I grudgingly enjoy it even though any respite is temporary.

It's fuel, I tell myself. *There is a lot of business to get through before sundown. You still gotta make the trip to SoHo.*

I put down my cutlery and think about reneging on that deal.

After my brush with the wrong arm of the law, I can't help thinking that I could go fetch my weapons stash out of my locker at the bus station and deal with this Mike Madden situation myself. The Irish government spent a lot of money training me to do wet stuff and quiet stuff and it would be a pity to waste that investment.

Better the devil you know, right? This touchy guy in SoHo could be some goodfella arsehole who will not give shit one about my lousy day.

I go at the toast again and pour myself another cup of coffee, feeling the caffeine opening up my heart's throttle all the way.

Yeah. Just take Mike's whole gang out, why not? Wouldn't take more than an afternoon and a coupla clips.

Maybe in a war zone. But this is New Jersey we're talking about. Plenty of cameras and concerned citizens.

And if you screw up?

Then Mike will block the club's exits and torch the place. Jason, Marco and the girls would be gone.

Sofia. Don't forget Sofia.

Yeah. Sofia would be as good as dead.

So, hows about I just kill Mike? Cut off the snake's head?

Nope. Calvin is waiting in the wings. Maybe Manny too. There are plenty more snakes where Mike came from. And these guys love to make examples.

I decide to text Sofia for no more practical a reason than to make myself feel better.

So I send: *?*

That's all, just a question mark. It used to be: *Hey, what's up? How are you?* But we got a shorthand now and I guess that's progress.

A minute later I get back: *?*

Which means: I'm fine. How are you?

So I send: *L8?*

And get back a big smiley face.

Which is good. It means Sofia's taken her meds, or at least she's not in one of her near-suicidal troughs and she wants to see me later.

I feel a little guilty for making a date I might not show up to or be recognised at, but sometimes a man needs more than French toast to buoy him through the day's shenanigans.

While I have the phone in my hand I check for missed calls and see there are six from Mike and three from Zeb.

Screw those guys.

My malicious side half hopes that Mike takes Zeb hostage to hurry me along. A little light torture would not go astray on that guy. Nothing life-threatening, but as far as I know Zeb rarely uses all of his toes.

My Twitter icon is chirping, telling me that there is a tweet from my psychiatrist, who is doing online wisdom now, which he assures me was inevitable so he might as well be in the vanguard. I have never actually tweeted, but I do follow Dr Simon and Craig Ferguson, who is one funny Celtic fecker.

There is something compulsive about tweets, so I read Simon's latest:

Remember, my phobic posse: it's always darkest before the dawn unless there's an eclipse.

I wonder who that's supposed to comfort.

I swipe back to Sofia's brief final message and just the sight of that simple emotion makes me feel a couple of degrees warmer.

Sofia. Could there be a chance for us?

Shit. I'm gonna be writing poetry soon.

*　　*　　*

My proximity sense tingles and I know someone is standing before me. I know without looking that it's a woman. My subconscious throws up the clues: perfume, footsteps leading up to this moment, the sound of her breathing. A woman, but not Mary.

So I look up and there's a rich lady not three feet away, staring at me like she's seen her maid in Tiffany's. This gal is maybe forty but with ten years of that slate wiped clean by spas and exercise. She's got burnished blond hair framing her striking face, which is horsey in a good way, and a gym body being hugged very nicely by a red velour sweat suit which I just bet has something provocative writ large on the ass. I can tell this lady is rich by the glitter-ball diamond on her finger and the fact that a cluster of waiters are bobbing six feet away, worried that something might happen to her.

I have no idea what this is but I do not have time for it.

I go for pre-emptive dismissal.

'Lady,' I say. 'Whatever you think—'

She cuts me off. 'Mister McEvoy? Daniel McEvoy?'

This is a surprise. Rich folk do not generally recognise me, since I let my country club membership lapse when Enron went under.

'Who's asking?' I ask, seeing as we're in a noir movie.

Uninvited, the lady pulls up a chair.

'Daniel,' she says. 'I think that I may be your grandmother.'

We must be watching different movies.

Mary pours more coffee and reinforces her earlier hip-bump with a high-beam cleavage flash because, as a professional, she knows that statistically even the presence of another female will drop my tip by five per cent.

Get a grip, soldier. The girl is pouring coffee and you're forty-three years old.

I can't help it. I read layers of meaning into the actions of everyone around me. I guess it's because sometimes it seems as though *everyone* around me has bad intentions towards my person. And as my shrink Simon once told me: *Being paranoid never got anyone killed; not being paranoid on the other hand* . . .

The glam gran has slid on to the chair opposite me and is busy muting her phone so we don't get interrupted. She orders a grapefruit juice from Mary without even glancing at my lovely server, then eases herself into the story.

'I go to the gym here. It's really good. And I have a trainer who comes to my house. Pablo is fantastic. I'm more flexible now than I was at twenty.'

I don't comment; effective as Pablo's techniques may be, this is all preamble.

'You look good too, Daniel. Solid. Are you married? Do you have kids?'

I shake my head once to cover both questions.

'Me either,' she says. 'Not really. Any more.'

Three short sentences. All loaded.

'I'm really sorry . . . eh . . . Nana, but I'm under a bit of pressure today.'

She slaps her own cheek gently, dislodging a tiny puff of foundation, which I would have sworn she was not wearing.

'Oh my God. Where are my manners?' She offers her hand for a shake, at a weird sideways angle, like royalty. 'I'm Edit Vikander Costello.'

She pronounces Edit to rhyme with Michael Jackson's 'Beat It'.

I shake the hand. To be honest, it's less of a shake, more of an undulation, but I feel strength in the soft dry skin.

'Costello?' I say. 'So you married old Paddy?'

'Wife number four,' she says. 'The first to outlive him.'

This was something of a feat. Paddy Costello had always seemed to be carved from granite.

'So, you're not my blood grandmother?'

'No. I'm the later model. Version 4.0.'

'And how would you know about me, Edit? How could you possibly recognise me?'

'I've been looking for you, Daniel; for six months I've had Irish detectives on your trail. And you turn up here two blocks from my apartment on Central Park South.'

'Why are you looking for me? Did old Paddy leave me a whack?'

Edit was embarrassed and refolded her napkin. 'No. You were disinherited, along with your mother. I'm looking for you because Evelyn is missing and she's the only family I have left.'

Evelyn Costello. Just hearing the name shoots me back to nineteen seventies Dublin. My mother's baby sister, the girl who defied her own father to cross the Atlantic and visit with us. The girl who told my dad she would skewer his sausage with an ice pick if he ever accidentally wandered into the wrong room again.

That was so cool. We didn't even have an ice pick. No one I knew did.

Evelyn Costello. My first hero. I saved every penny for weeks just to make sure we did have an ice pick if she visited again.

My Aunt Evelyn who used to bring me to the swimming pool except for that time when she couldn't for some mysterious lady-reason that I didn't understand at the time and don't know a whole lot about now.

'Evelyn's missing?'

Edit began folding my napkin. 'Yes. She had addiction issues, like her mother. We put her in Betty Ford the last time she relapsed, but you know Evelyn, don't fence me in, right? She checked out and we haven't seen her in over two years. She missed her father's funeral.'

If Edit is expecting my *aw* face, she doesn't get it. I don't hold *fathers* in the same esteem as nineteen sixties sitcoms. One hundred per cent of my father figures were drunken, abusive devils who walked the earth.

Edit realises my heartstrings have not been plucked.

'Sure, they had their differences, but Ev loved her father, and Patrick loved her. It's a tragedy that she may not even know he's dead.'

She knows, unless she's been living under a rock, and even then most rocks these days have network. When Paddy Costello's heart finally shattered in his chest under the sledgehammer blow of a massive coronary, all the major studios had a video obituary ready to air. Big Paddy Costello; the last magnate. The man who built America, or some such shit.

My grandfather.

We know all about empire builders in Ireland. I saw a couple in the army too. I figure if a man is serious about putting together a major hunk of kingdom, then he's gotta keep a laser focus on that prize his whole life and burn anything that might distract him. His competitors, for example. His family, for example.

'I thought she might contact you, Daniel. You guys were close, right? She talked about you.'

It's true. We were close, even though she only stayed with us maybe a dozen times. Evelyn always had spirit. When I was fourteen and she was sixteen, she came home from a grabby date one night and gave me a stern lecture on the proper way to handle a girl's boobs. A boy never forgets something like that. Never ever.

'Yeah, we were close. Ev was like a big sister to me.'

Edit nods. 'Exactly. She said that. Danny's big sister, she looked out for you. So I thought that maybe you might have heard something . . .'

Edit Costello's face is downcast. She has had so many disappointments in life that she's shielding herself against another one. I hate to be the bearer of zero news but . . .

'No, sorry, Edit. I haven't spoken to Evelyn in twenty years. She sent me a few letters when I was in the army, but it was small-talk stuff. I heard she was in Betty Ford a few years back and sent a get-well-soon card. But I have no idea where she is.'

Edit holds herself steady so she will not slump. 'Of course. Why would you? At least I can call off those investigators, right?'

'Yeah. They didn't even narrow it down to a continent.'

We smile, but I'm stressed and she's disappointed so we don't exactly light up the room.

Edit runs her finger down the glass. 'Mr McEvoy. Daniel. Perhaps you could call me if Evelyn does make contact. She doesn't have to see me if she doesn't want to. I just want to know if she's okay. If she needs money, there's plenty there for her.' Edit closes her eyes halfway, like she's visualising mountains of gold. 'I mean plenty.'

Part of me hopes that there's an extra clause to that sentence, i.e. *there's plenty for you too*, but my step-gran has finished talking.

I take the card she pulls out from God knows where, then I see there's a zip pocket in her sweatband. I didn't know they made those. Handy.

'Sure. I'll call. But after all this time . . .'

Edit is so trim that she stands without pushing back the chair. 'I know. It's a long shot. But sometimes long shots pay off.'

I look in her eyes and she's got that desperate look. Like an addict at the race track.

'Look, Edit,' I say, not believing that I'm jumping into another hole. 'I got a few things on this week. Important stuff or I wouldn't put you on the long finger, but next week I can make some calls. Maybe Ev went over to Ireland. You ever think of that?'

'Yes, of course. She loved Dublin. I've had my investigators on the lookout for her too. No luck.'

I push my food aside, wishing I had a plate of hash browns and bacon instead of this kiddie food.

'These detectives of yours don't sound so hot. They couldn't even detect that I left the old country years ago. I know a few guys who have fingers in pies. I'll get back to you.'

'Thanks, Daniel,' says Edit, automatically sucking in her almost non-existent stomach, so I can see her ribcage through the velour. 'I'll make it worth your while.'

I gotta do something noble so as this meeting does not end with me looking like a pancake-eating hillbilly.

'That's not necessary,' I say, hoping my chin isn't smeared with breakfast. 'There's no charge for doing family a favour.'

Edit is affected by my grand gesture and she leans forward to kiss me on the cheek and comes away with syrup on her lips.

We both ignore it and she leaves, wet-wiping her face on the way to the door. I am such a douche.

My Twitter bird chirps. I swipe the phone screen and read:

Don't overanalyse everything. You know what the first two syllables of analyse are?

I can't help noticing that there's nothing written on the ass of my gran's sweat suit.

Classy.

*   *   *

I triple-tip Mary, and she rewards me with a smile that could almost make a man forget about the people trying to kill him. I decide in the afterglow of that smile that if Sofia ever boots me to the kerb, then I will definitely make the trip into Manhattan and see if I can tempt this lady to accompany me to another restaurant where she can actually sit down.

The thought makes me feel a little guilty, but at my age you gotta lay the tracks, right? There are not that many single fish in the sea any more.

I hit the john on the way out, and a good thing too, because I get an attack of the shakes and the whole pancake mess comes up again before most of it had the chance to go all the way down.

Goddamn Fortz and Krieger. Screw those guys.

What kind of sick individuals do roadside pick-ups for snuff streams? I regret letting those bozos live for a full minute as I lean over the bowl. It's amazing how one short sharp shock can completely change a person's views on murder.

Bozos? That's a bit mild. Arseholes at the very least.

On the plus side of this toilet break, it's a clean retch. I get it all up in one heave and feel instantly better.

French toast. Maybe that was ambitious.

I wash up as best I can and trot up the steps into the lobby all casual and energetic like no puking whatsoever has occurred in the fancy restroom. I am feeling a bit delicate though and susceptible to paranoia and I am convinced that every tourist gazing vacantly at their cell phone screen is actually snapping a picture of the big goon who just threw up in the stalls.

It is entirely possible that I am already a wanted man with my mugshot posted on the blues' website. Everyone with a badge in this great city could already have my photo and history on their smartphone.

I guess I'm banking on Fortz trying to take care of the McEvoy loose end himself before trusting it to his comrades.

At the very least there will be two bent cops on my tail.

Enough of this bullshit. I have a job to do.

But once these bonds are delivered, I gotta get right back on the Krieger/Fortz situation.

Only Ronnie can help me there.

I pick up a pack of Life Savers at the lobby concession then push through the revolving doors into the Manhattan afternoon. I feel like it should be midnight at the very least but the day's travails have managed to shoehorn themselves into the span of a baseball game, which, God forgive me for saying it, is the most boring thing to do on a sports pitch apart from sweep it. First time I went to a game half the crowd were gone before I realised it was over. Zeb brought me to a game and spent most of it pointing out the guys from the visiting team who had syphilis. Apparently half the dugout had the clap.

I am too frazzled for public transport, so I flag a cab on the corner of Broadway and tell the cabbie to head straight down to SoHo. You would imagine that the guy would be ecstatic with a plum fare like this, but he hammers on the steering wheel like I just admitted to boning his mom.

Usually I am sensitive to people's moods, even when they're assholes, but today is not usually so I knock on the Perspex.

'Two things, pal,' I say to him. 'First turn off this mini TV thing here. I could give a fuck about Lady Gaga's fashion sense.' This is kind of a lie, Gaga is fascinating and she can belt it out too. 'And second, if you don't stop beating on that wheel I am going to shoot you in the head with one of the four guns I got here.'

The guy shapes up a little after that, but if it ever comes to it, he will be thrilled to pick me out of a line-up.

Thanks to midtown traffic I got a little down time to call Tommy Fletcher in Ireland. I search through my phone's contacts and the cropped headshot beside his details flashes me back to our army days. I remember when that photograph was taken. It was on the day Corporal Tommy Fletcher lost his left leg during an early-bird mine-sweep. Tommy was bitching about the heat and flies that flew into your face like bullets. And there was sweat in my eyes and I could hear blood rushing in my helmet, and I could not believe that people were looking to me for leadership. Kids were watching us pass by like we were boring them at this point, and the old men lounged in Nike track bottoms and sandals drinking their tiny glasses of sweet tea, playing their version of backgammon, conversing in the haranguing tones that I used to think were arguments but now realised was just business as usual, paying us absolutely no mind.

I remember thinking: *This place should be a paradise. They got the weather, the ocean. Beautiful girls. Bloody hell, they got the best surfing in the Med.*

Then a Katyusha rocket streaked from the unfinished top floor of an apartment block, its vapour trail hissing like a snake. It missed Tommy and me but rolled the truck over Fletcher's leg. The shooting started then and we were suddenly in a vortex of bullets. To stop myself freaking the hell out, I decided I would save Tommy. One simple instruction for my brain that allowed me to slice through the confusion. I dumped my weapon and pack and slung Corporal Fletcher over one shoulder. After that I don't really remember much about the heroic rescue until we were back at the hospital. When the medic sliced off Tommy's trousers his leg fell off and on account of all the morphine in his system Tommy took it really well and said: 'Jesus Christ, kid. Be careful with the scissors.'

Later on, he made me sit on the bed beside him with the bagged severed leg across our knees for a photograph. And that's the one I use for his contacts.

I press call and Tommy answers on the first ring like he was hunkered over the phone.

'What do you want?' he says in a Belfast accent. Tommy is from Kerry, but that accent ain't scary unless you can see the psychopathic face it's coming out of. The Belfast accent on the other hand is what they should broadcast from satellites to scare off aliens.

'Tommy. It's me. Danny.'

'Jaysus, Sarge,' he says, reverting to his normal voice. 'This is freaky. I was punching the numbers to call you.'

The line is digital clear and it's like my old comrade is in the cab beside me.

'Yeah? Why's that, Tom? You got some news?'

'You are not going to believe what happened to that old cross-country lady you had me scoping.'

'I heard. Lightning. One in a million.'

Tommy draws a breath. 'Fucking act of God. I'd actually grown quite fond of that old bird, she had a grand arse on her.'

It's impossible to know whether or not Tommy is lying. Actually, that's not true. Tommy is always lying. It's his default setting. What's impossible is sorting the outright bullshit from the little white lies.

Why are these people always drawn to me?

'Okay, so you didn't get bored with the detail and take matters into your own hands?'

Tommy gasps. 'That is an outrageous suggestion, Sarge. Sure, I've done a few things in my time, but electrocute Marge?'

Alarm bells clang in my skull. 'Marge? Marge now?'

There's a little pause while Tommy figures how clean he's gotta come.

'Ah . . . The old dear spotted me, Sarge. Eyes like a bloody hawk after laser surgery. Started leaving sandwiches out in the garden. Lovely sandwiches. Lovely.'

It hits me then. Tommy was banging Irish Mike's mum.

'Jesus Christ, Tom.'

'What?'

'Jesus bloody hell Christ. Is there any situation where you can keep it zipped?'

Tommy was famous for literally screwing his assignments. There was a Ranger legend that Corporal Fletcher's thorough infiltrations of an Irish Republican cell meant that he was the real father of a current Sinn Fein Member of Parliament.

'Zipped? How can you say that?'

'Why?'

'I got a monster in these Y-fronts, Sarge. Everyone knows that. Zippers are an accident waiting to happen with a weapon like mine. Button fly only.'

Nice deflection. And I suppose me interrogating Tommy won't bring Mrs Madden back to life.

'She's definitely dead, Tommy? You saw the body?'

Tom sighs. 'The poor woman had a metal hip, she was fecking spit-roasted. I saw enough to know that this assignment is over. I shot some video on my phone that might be of some use to you.'

I close the phone. *Metal hip? Spit-roasted? I do not need video of that.*

No wonder Mike is pissed.

Five minutes later the video arrives. I can't look at it. The poor old dear was someone's mother, even if that someone was Irish Mike.

I spend the rest of the cab ride thinking. I try to focus on the lion's den that I gotta shortly and of my own volition stroll into, but the mind goes where it will and soon my thoughts drift to Ireland and my mother.

God love her, the poor unfortunate.

That's what people said to me afterwards.

Margaret Costello was a rebel. She rebelled herself right out of the frying pan into the fire. Mom hit puberty on the tail end of the free love generation, when it was all about sticking it to the man. And who was *the man* incarnate in New York City? Paddy Costello. Her empire-building, union-breaking, back-room-dealing, peerless son-of-a-bitch daddy. Paddy had bent so many good men to his will by threatening their children that his own kids seemed to him potential chinks in the Costello armour. He hardened his heart against them and put Margaret and Evelyn in convent schools with high walls, stern nuns and big knickers.

But Paddy needn't have worried. Nobody turned his kids; he managed to do that all on his lonesome. Evelyn took to the booze and pills like her mother, and Margaret married a guy that she thought she loved, because her daddy hated him.

I'm oversimplifying maybe. Perhaps my mother did love Arthur McEvoy for the first couple of years or so, until he started slapping her around every time she set foot outside the kitchen.

Mr and Mrs McEvoy moved back to Dublin, where Dad sat back and waited for the trust fund money to roll in. He believed himself to be, as they say in Ireland, *on the pig's back*.

Paddy, as they say in the US, did not play that shit. If his daughter wished to tie herself to exactly the kind of drunken throwback that gave the Irish a bad name in their new country, then she was on her own. Margaret was warned before the wedding: *Choose. The family or that man.*

Rebel Margaret squared her jaw and said: *I have found my family.*

So she was cut off.

Arthur McEvoy was not put out by this development. Grand-children will break any man's resolve, he thought and quickly sired a couple of sons to forever intertwine the McEvoys and the Costellos. Even insisted on naming the second boy Patrick.

How cravenly transparent is that?

Still Paddy did not come around, and the marriage descended into drunken violence, not bit by bit as is the usual pattern, but in a single day.

Margaret woke up with a charming rogue one morning and went to bed with a drunken devil. She felt like she had fallen off a cliff. The charming rogue never showed his face again. I find it difficult to believe that he ever existed. I certainly don't remember meeting him. Mom used to whisper stories to me and Pat when the three of us were squeezed into the same bed. How our daddy used to sing to her in bars, right out there in front of everyone. How he once climbed the tall oak in Carthy's field to pluck her wind-blown scarf from the highest branch. I loved my mom, but I never believed a word of those stories.

My mother made the choice to live for her children, and that along with visits from her baby sister kept her going, until a sozzled Arthur ran the family Morris Minor into a donkey outside Dalkey Village, killing everyone but me and the donkey. The donkey was knocked over the ditch, the car went into a wall and I was thrown clear into the army.

Because that's the sensible thing to do when your entire family has been killed in a traumatic accident caused by an alcoholic sociopath: join a bunch of homophobes in a small tent and learn how to murder people.

Still, I gotta admit. I was an empty vessel and the army filled me to overflowing with attitude, guns and knives.

A goddamn donkey.

This is exactly the kind of stuff, along with this latest skiing/electrocution malarkey, that makes the whole country seem like some kind of twee tragicomic fairyland. And don't even get me started on *Waking Ned Devine*. Thank Christ we have a few serious buckos like Jimmys Heany and Sheridan to give the country a bit of gravitas.

Fucking leprechaun, Riverdancing, thatched cottage, diddly diddly, *Quiet Man* bullshit.

So I got this envelope for this guy and believe me, I know what the obvious question is:

Why in the name of the holy virgin do I not take off to Mexico with the two hundred grand?

Because Mike made me a promise:

This is an important transaction, laddie, he told me back in the Brass Ring. *You get the opera-toonity to run, you better think again, because that's a deal-breaker and I go to work on your nearest and dearest. Mrs Delano gets the first visit.*

Nearest and dearest.

That used to be my little brother. We shared a room for all his life.

Even after all these years, thinking about little Pat brings on a cramp of pain. I can remember his smile of crooked teeth like an old sailor, but his eyes are lost to me.

I snuffle and think, *Edit. She has me maudlin when I need to be sharp.*

The cab driver speaks.

'Hey, bud. You crying back there?'

I pull myself together. 'That's Mister Four Guns to you, Mac. We there yet?'

The cabbie taps his window. 'We been there for ten minutes. You ain't having a flashback or something, are you? You ain't one of those flashback to 'Nam motherfuckers?'

Flashback to 'Nam? How old does this guy think I am?

''Nam sounds so quaint. It's all about the flashbacks to Desert Storm these days. Those Desert Storm vets are so smug and current, but the Iraq boys will soon wipe the smiles off their faces once their post-traumatics kick in.

'Don't worry. If I shoot you, it'll be on purpose.'

'Good to know,' says the cabbie, whose balls have descended. 'That's twenty-two fifty, buddy.'

I am tentatively liking this guy now, so I give him a fifty on account of I might not be coming out of this hotel and I would hate for the scumbags inside to fleece my wallet.

'Thanks, man,' says the guy. 'You want me to wait?'

I slide across the seat to the pavement side. 'You can, but I ain't giving you any more tips.'

The car is moving before my fingers leave the handle.

New York, New York, where it's okay to be an asshole so long as you're local.

Dan McEvoy, doorman theory number 3: New Yorkers believe absolutely that any place which is not New York is by geographical definition inferior to the great five-borough nation. The Bronx has got better seafood than the Cote d'Azur. The beaches of Staten Island are far superior to anything Rio de Janeiro has to offer, and it goes without saying that there isn't a commercial boulevard on the planet that can hold a candle to Manhattan's Fifth Avenue. Therefore most New Yorkers do not travel; why the hell would they? And the ones that do venture out into the vast mediocrity are businessmen or intellectuals and not likely to start trouble. Except for the East Village guys. Those artist types have been in buttoned-down uber PC mode for so long that they go batshit at the sight of décolletage. Jason and I always keep a close eye on anyone sporting a ponytail. Those bastards are likely to grab a server's boobs and claim they were only trying to liberate her.

I think it's pretty obvious that Jason and I had a lot of free time on our hands when we bounced Slotz and a person can only do so many sit-ups in a club lobby.

CHAPTER 5

Out on the street, I feel exposed. There's still plenty of foot traffic down here, but not so much that a marksman wouldn't be able to thread a bullet through it. I could certainly take someone's head off from a rooftop without a problem. The crowd is different here, more discerning, fewer trainers, and even the light is more oblique somehow, not so much in your face, in keeping with the subtle fashions of the SoHo natives.

I used to walk around this neighbourhood wasting a lot of mind-space feeling all superior and grounded, but right now I would hand over a couple of years of my life just to be a guy out shopping in tucked-away places for on-trend pieces.

The best thing to do, I decide, would be to get my big burly frame into the Masterpiece hotel.

Sounds like a pretty grandiose name for a boutique hotel: the Masterpiece, right? But on account of the fact that I've been here before, I happen to know that this is the nickname given to the building by the locals because of the ornate cast-iron facade that the area is known for.

The Masterpiece. I was here a few years ago with Zeb during

New York fashion week when Zeb was doing Botox outcalls and I was humping his wedge. This gorgeous, and frankly way out of my league, senorita zones in on me in the bar and within two lemon gingertinis is all over me like cling film on a frankfurter. I was sporting a goatee at the time, trying to draw attention from my expanding forehead, and this girl, who had a name like some herb or other, tells me that my moustache is overpowering my beard. She let slip later on that she was using me to piss off her boyfriend who was chatting up an ubermodel while she herself was merely a supermodel. How Zeb and I sneered at these sub-classifications, later when we were going home on our own. Also that's where I picked up the term *uber* which I already told you about.

Cilantro, that was her name.

The lobby is dark and moody with plenty of floating light orbs and wave machines. If I ever get a few beers in me and meet the interior designer, I'll probably let slip that this place reminds me of a strip club I once bounced in Jo'burg, except for the strippers wore longer skirts than the girls in here.

The concierge desk is a swathe of curved steel with a glass worktop that changes colour every few seconds, which causes the young lady behind it to wince with every fresh wash of colour. That's gotta be bad for the brain so I try to be extra nice.

'Hi. I have an envelope for Mister Shea.'

The girl is severe/pretty in her steel-grey smock but she's going to have frown lines before she hits twenty five if she can't get away from this desk.

'You can leave it with me. We don't allow delivery men in the private elevators.'

We don't allow. She's a shareholder now?

I persist good-naturedly. 'I'm also kind of a visitor. Can you call Mister Shea and tell him that the package from Mister Madden has arrived?'

Mister Shea. Another Irish name. They say there are twenty million Irish Americans and it looks like I'm gonna bump into most of them before this day winds down.

'You're Mister Madden?' she asks, picking up a phone the same colour as her smock.

'No, I'm Mister Madden's . . .' I search my brain for a term that will bestow upon me the importance I deserve. 'Gopher.'

I hope the girl will interpret my wry smile to mean that I am underplaying my own importance in this whole package-dropping enterprise. She does not.

'Mister Shea,' she says into the phone, frowning as the desk turns green. 'The gopher is here from Mister Madden.'

Five seconds later she hands me an electronic lift key which is ironically in the shape of an actual key.

'Penthouse apartment,' she says. 'The private elevators are at the back.'

Ironic hotels. Only in Manhattan.

I stop off in the restroom and deposit one of the Glocks in a stall just in case I have to shoot my way out, Wild West style. And by *Wild West* I mean Limerick not Texas. O'Connell Street can get a little jumpy after turfing-out time on the weekends. The other three guns I keep on my person hoping to hocus pocus at least one past the search that will undoubtedly be waiting for me at the top of the shaft.

I am walking blind into this situation with no idea what kind of scenario awaits me up there. I don't know the exits, I don't know

89

how many hostiles. Weapons, intentions, bargaining positions. Nothing.

The odds are good that things will not escalate in a chichi SoHo establishment. What kind of moron would kick off a gun fight in a place like the Masterpiece?

The elevator has mirrored doors and I study myself as the lights flicker upwards towards PH, trying to decide which version of Daniel McEvoy I'm gonna present to whoever is on the other side of them.

I'll give them a blast of ice-cold professional, I decide, but then reconsider. Let these guys underestimate me. Play it big and dumb, like a guy trying to *look* professional who is actually out of his depth. Keep the mouth under wraps. Speak when spoken to and no backchat. This was what Mike had advised:

Remember, act stupid, McEvoy. I want Mister Shea to feel this letter is being dropped off by a shaggy dog. So none of the usual back-answering bullshit. The more stupider you are, the faster they let you leave. If they ask you specifics about my operation, you ain't got any. Clear?

More stupider? This guy runs an organisation?

I do a little shadow boxing in the elevator to get my blood up, then practise my chosen look in the mirrored doors. I want Mister Shea to see a guy who's big and dumb but trying his darnedest to look bigger and less dumb. It's time to accept that I'm going through with this drop and use whatever skills I have to ensure I come out the other side.

In other words, I need to become a soldier again.

The elevator tells me in the sexiest voice I have ever heard that we have reached the penthouse. At this point most elevators would ding but this one actually sighs, which almost breaks my focus.

Soldier, I tell myself. *Stupid soldier time.*

The doors open on to a corridor with plush red carpet like you'd get spilling out of the Queen's plane, and there are three guys on sentry duty.

These guys ain't military; two of them are sitting down, for Christ's sake. One of the sitters is eating chicken. But the third sentry is in my face, waiting right there by the door, big smile all ready. One of those hearty smiles favoured by people in public office. It comes on like a light bulb but there isn't any warmth in it.

I size him up from behind my *dumb trying to look not dumb* eyes. He's big but a little soft, should've moved up a shirt size a while back but is holding on, strangling the buttons in their holes. He's got a flat face and a weird constellation of teardrop freckles that look like he shotgunned someone close quarters and got spattered. He's light on his feet and I can see muscle in his shoulders and arms. Also, I hate to say it, but there's plenty of smarts in those eyes, which is the best weapon of all, at close quarters. From far out, a good scope and steady hands will trump smarts every time.

'I got the package,' I say, trying to sound gruff. 'For Mister Shea.'

The guy speaks and I am surprised to hear actual first-generation Irish-Irish. Maybe he emigrated on account of the recession, but I doubt it. I bet he threw a few things in a holdall and skipped the country with the laser eyes of law enforcement searing the seat of his pants.

'We were expecting you, Daniel. We have been for the past couple of hours. Mister Shea is getting antsy.'

I don't even bother offering a platitude. I give him a shrug that could mean *traffic*, *fuck you* or both. That's what I like about shrugs: their ambivalence.

The guy beckons me out of the lift and my toe catches on the lip, which kind of puts a dent in my tough-guy routine, but also gives me an excuse to stumble forward and slip the lightweight Kel-Tec concealed in my paw into his jacket pocket.

'Easy there, big fella,' says the guy, like I'm a horse being led to the bolt room.

He pushes me away gently, then raises his arms high, wiggling his fingers.

'You trying to lev'tate me?' I ask, figuring my mispronunciation puts the comment in *dumb guy trying to be a smartass* territory.

'Just get 'em up,' he says, so I do. And he moves in for a thorough frisk. This guy knows how to frisk, I'll give him that. In some cultures we'd be married now. It takes him five seconds to locate the two remaining weapons and a couple of probing minutes to ensure that there aren't any more. No gentle hands here. This ain't JFK. Nobody's gonna be pressing molestation charges.

'You came prepared,' he says and passes my weapons off to one of the chair goons, who gets chicken grease all over the holster before tossing the hardware into a bucket under his chair. Greasy fingers on my stuff is one of my pet hates and the only reason I hold it together is because those guns haven't been in my possession long enough for me to consider them mine.

'Prepared is my middle name,' I say, which I figure sounds stupid enough to cancel out the levitation crack.

My frisker's laugh is about as warm as his smile. 'Really? That's nice, Daniel. Now, why don't you get your *prepared* arse into Mister Shea's office?'

Arse. Now there's a word you don't hear enough of.

'Couldn't I just give this envelope to you?' Might as well ask.

'Nope. This is one of those *in person* situations. Mister Shea is anxious to meet you.'

I am anxious to meet absolutely no more new people today.

'Okay, let's get this over with.'

I walk towards the door, each step laden with doom, which sounds melodramatic I know but that's how it feels. The tension churns my stomach and I am gripped by an almost irresistible urge to take on this group of sentinels and then knock on the door and introduce myself to this Shea person. The seated guys hop to attention like they can read menace in my aura and treat me to vicious squints. I may have rushed to judgement about these two with all their sitting/chicken scarfing. Vertical, they look pretty formidable. My urge to violence fizzles out and I decide to let this situation play out a little more.

'You guys stay out here and watch the elevator,' says Spatter to his boys. 'On your toes, please. No more bloody KFC.'

They're staying outside. This is good, unless something is about to happen in the room that Spatter does not want anyone to witness.

The thing about witnesses is they never start out that way. People see nothing and know nothing until law enforcement types help them remember. Most people can be pressured into turning, and a good boss knows that. So if mortal injuries are about to be inflicted, the fewer people who see it the better.

The door is cast iron and ornate and I realise that it is a scale reproduction of the hotel's facade, right down to the arched entrance.

'It's a little hotel,' I say, ladling on the stupid.

'That's right, Einstein,' says Blood Spatter, shouldering me out of the way, which gives me that one second of *up close* I need to reclaim the little nine-millimetre from his jacket pocket. He doesn't feel a thing and I feel a kinship with the tiny Kel-Tec now; this gun is truly mine as we've been through shenanigans together.

Now I have seven surprises for Mister Shea and his boys, I think, slotting the featherweight pistol into my own pocket. *Seven and one in the pipe*.

I don't want to kill anyone if I don't have to, but to be honest I'm less anti-homicide than I was yesterday. If I even smell rubber, then the gloves are coming off if you'll pardon the expression.

This day is turning into a long series of confrontational meetings with angry men. It seems that no matter how far up the food chain you go, the head honcho is always a bag of insecurities itching for some poor sap to underestimate his importance. This place, the Masterpiece, is pretty top end, but I just bet this Shea guy has a high-and-mighty routine he would switch on for all and sundry right down to the pizza boy. I never met a boss or an officer who was comfortable in his own skin.

As I go through the doorway, I'm visualising how it's gonna go. Even though Shea has been pacing all morning for me to show up with this valuable package, he'll probably make me wait while he finishes his salmon blinis or shouts sell sell sell into his iPhone.

I am dead wrong.

This guy is out of one of those weird backless stool-chairs running at me with a mouthful of hummus.

I do not believe this. That's my third thing: sucking coffee, greasy fingers, eating with your mouth open.

You know what? People are animals.

You're not a monkey, I want to tell this guy. *Shut your goddamn face*.

It's too much tension. So I giggle.

94

'It's about time, McEvoy . . .' he begins, then hears the giggle and his techno trainers squeak to a halt on the wooden floor. 'What? You're laughing at me?'

Shea has got bits of food in his limp goatee. How am I gonna take this person seriously?

I remind myself that I am pretending to be dumb. Or more accurately, dumber than I am. If I wasn't dumb, would I be here in the first place?

'No, sir, Mister Shea,' I blurt. 'I got this condition. It's a stress thing, Mom says. It's like A . . . D . . . something and another D. I got stuff, like medicine, but we're outta Cheerios so I didn't take it. You're like the real deal, Mister Shea, and I ain't never been in a penthouse. You know your door is like the hotel but shrunk down?'

I fear I maybe have played the shit-kicker card too strong but Shea is moved to laughter by my speech.

'Do you hear this bullshit, Freckles?' he asks Blood Spatter. 'Mike said he was a retard and for once the man was right.'

I have one new piece of information now and an inference: the head muscle's nom-de-goon is Freckles, which by the law of inverses means he must be meaner than a snake.

Shea zigzags himself back into the ergo-stool and I take a heavy-lidded look at the guy, trying to see past the hummus for the moment, though I'm not ruling out bringing it up later.

Shea isn't much more than a boy. Maybe twenty-two, dressed straight out of Abercrombie, probably stands in line with the other kids on the weekends. He's got acne traces on his forehead and really well-conditioned blond hair, artfully sticking up a hundred ways all at the same time. If this youngster is at the top of whatever organisation is being run out of this place, then he just got here.

Maybe the king is dead and this kid found himself on the throne.

Shea drums the desk a little with his forefingers and nods at me to sit.

'See, here's what happened, McEvoy.'

I do not want to hear what happened. Finding out what happened rarely leads to happy ever after.

'You can tell me if you want, Mister Shea,' I say, wondering how long they can possibly buy this dumb act for. 'But if I gotta repeat it back, Mister Madden says to record it on my phone.'

Shea smirks at Freckles and I know I'm screwed. 'No need to record anything, McEvoy. You won't be repeating shit.'

'Okay, then.'

Shea resumes his storytelling, shovelling food into his mouth from a deli carton as he speaks. 'Mike. Mister Madden. My dad let him have his own little operation out in the suburbs because he owed Mike a favour or two. Mike's deal is small time, who gives a shit? But now Dad is gone and we're in a recession, so all the small-times need to be amalgamated. You stack up a hundred cents and they make a dollar, right?'

'That is right,' I say, amazed.

'I sent a representative to speak to Mike. A friend of mine. Nice guy, grew excellent weed. Harvard graduate like me, you know.' Shea wiggles a finger and I see a Harvard ring all pimped out with diamonds. 'What a school. Wall-to-wall smart pussy.'

I nod along with the beat of his patter, waiting for the point.

'So there's a misunderstanding with one of Mike's people and now my boy is out of action for half a year at least and his nerves are shot to fuck, which really inconveniences me personally. My pot parties are legendary, man. You ever hear about my parties, McEvoy?'

'No. I never heard about 'em. Was I invited?'

This is outrageous bullshit, but they're hooked now. I hear snickering behind me.

'I wanna *do* Irish Mike,' continues Shea. 'But Freckles convinces me to settle 'cause he's tight with old Mikey.'

Shea's Harvard accent is slipping and I hear the nasal wah-wah of Brooklyn bashing through.

'So Mike agrees to partnering up and promises to reimburse me for my trouble and send me the name of the man who decked my boy in an envelope, as a peace offering. You got that envelope, Daniel?'

My confused look is now genuine, as I am not sure what Mike's play is if I'm supposed to be the guy who decked his Harvard buddy. He's gotta know I'm not going down easy.

Shea snaps his fingers and hummus plops on to the desk. 'Hey, rocket scientist. Do you have my envelope?'

I reach into my pocket slowly. 'I got it here somewheres. This jacket has so many pockets but my other jacket is at the cleaner's. It's at my mom's really but I don't like to say that in front of the guys so I say cleaner's.'

Shea nods at Freckles. 'Looks like we're talking to the dumbest guy on earth.'

Freckles taps his temple. 'He ain't all there, boss.'

'Don't call me boss,' snaps Shea. 'My father was boss. Like some plantation owner. Call me sir.'

'Yes, sir. Mister Shea. Just reflex. I'm an old dog, you know?'

Shea nods like *ain't that the truth*. 'Well, we know what happens to old dogs.'

Oh. Hello there. A little tension in the camp.

Shea drums the table again. 'Envelope, please.'

I slide it over and begin visualising my moves. Freckles has shifted slightly, out of my field of vision, so he's what my Ranger buddies would call the prime hostile. Shea is just a kid and I can tell by his posture that he's not a physical guy, but I still gotta factor him in. You never know who's a crack shot or can throw a knife. Maybe this prick grew up on *Duke Nukem* and can decapitate a rat at fifty paces.

I still can't figure the play. Why would Mike throw me into this mix? I'm chaos and unpredictability. If Mike wants to suck up to this varsity kid, surely he's gonna sacrifice one of those mooks he keeps around the Brass Ring. He should know that at some point I am going to see an opening and bludgeon my way through and then come home in the dark.

Shea counts out the bonds then slides one across to me. 'This word, dumbass,' he says, tapping the bond. 'What is it?'

'Bearer,' I say, sounding out the syllables.

'You know what that means?'

I can guess but I give him the answer he might expect.

'Something about being like naked?'

'It means that you're the bearer, the guy. I don't know if you're the actual guy but Mike has no use for you.' Shea slides the empty envelope back to me like it's Long John Silver's black spot. 'I think your boss is trying to kill two birds with one stone and, Mister Daniel McEvoy, you're one of those birds.'

I have a road-to-Damascus moment, the penny drops from a great height, and I see Mike's vision of the future stretched out before me. Irish Mike is as dumb as moss, but he has a condition that makes him very dangerous: he sincerely and in spite of all evidence to the contrary believes himself to be clever. A master strategist.

And I think he's bumped into some other dumb smart guy.

This is what I think: Freckles and Mike have partnered up.

Freckles asked Mike to send over a patsy so Freckles can shoot Shea and blame the patsy and step into the vacant top slot. This poor college grad is getting disinherited.

But Mike is also running his own game. Instead of sending some clumsy stumble bum he sends ex-military Daniel McEvoy in the hope that I will be forced to kill both of these guys just to stay alive.

I gotta admit it, he suckered me with that *fifty per cent outta the hole* bullshit.

'You got it wrong, kid,' I say, normal cadence, hoping he'll take notice. 'I'm not one of the birds. I'm the stone.'

This is a really good line and I can just imagine the movie trailer guy doing it in a promo, but it doesn't impress Shea much.

'You're speaking fast now? What, you're a smart guy all of a sudden?'

'Okay, everyone. The important thing now is that we all stay calm. I'm gonna lay out what I think is going on, and everybody just keep it in your pants till I'm finished.'

'You're gonna lay it out?' says Freckles. 'Who the fuck are you? Shaft?'

Second time today. One more and I gotta consider that I might be a little Shafty.

'What are you talking about?' says Shea. He ain't worried but at least he's listening.

'Shea. Focus on me now. Forget everybody else. This situation is about to escalate.'

'Yeah, escalate into you being dead.'

'I like the way you took my verb and used it again. That's good stuff, but listen now. I think you're being played here.'

Food jets outta Shea's throat as he guffaws. 'Played? Mister,

I invented the word. I come from the world of business. Great white sharks, man. I've worked the floor on Wall Street. The bear pit, man. These goons can't play me.'

This guy is in his own little bubble. I don't have the time it would take to get through to him.

I twist in my seat, keeping an eye on Freckles. 'I bet if you ask Freckles here to turn out his pockets, you're gonna find a silenced pistol in there somewhere.'

Shea is young and so still thinks he's immortal.

'Yeah? So what? The bullets are for you.'

'Really? You shoot guys in the penthouse now, Junior?'

Shea frowns. 'Shut the fuck up, dummy. Freckles doesn't have a silencer. Do you, Freckles?'

'Course not, Mister Shea. This prick is winding you up.'

'I thought he was stupid.'

'So did I. Mike said he was thick as pigshit.'

I lean back on the chair to give myself a bit of spring if I need it. 'Mike has played us all, gentlemen. He is one hundred per cent aware that I would be the most dangerous person in this room, and still he put me here with both of his prospective partners.' I see doubt flicker across Freckles' brow, so I press on. 'Oh yeah, it's win–win for old Mike. If you manage to plug me and your boss on the quiet and set me up as a patsy, then he's off the hook with the kid, in tight with the new king and settles a score with me. If I go operational on the two of you, then he's forgotten in the chaos and his little cottage industry in Cloisters stays independent.'

Shea is still eating but half listening too. 'But you ain't got a silencer, right, Freckles?'

Freckles is glaring death rays at me. 'No, I fucking ain't. But I got a gun. Can I please shoot this prick?'

I point a finger gun at the kid. 'He draws a weapon and you're history, Harvard.'

'Your gun, it don't have a silencer on it?' asks Shea.

His accent is pure Brooklyn now, university washed away.

Freckles frowns for a second and I see he's making a decision, and that decision is *fuck it*.

'No,' he says, pulling a gun from a holster behind his back, then a suppressor from his pocket and expertly screwing it to the barrel. 'But it does now.'

It takes him three twists to get the silencer on to his pistol, which gives me plenty of time to duck under his gun arm and come up underneath with the Kel-Tec already in my hand. I twist the small barrel into the soft flesh below his chin hard enough to tear the skin and say gently:

'Shhhhhh.'

Freckles freezes like he's perched on a landmine, and because he can't nod perceptibly, blinks twice to show he understands. He does not need to know how my pistol has come to be pointed at his brain, he just needs to know that it is.

'Good,' I say. 'Now drop your weapon.'

What the hell am I doing?

Drop your weapon?

This is not how battles are fought in the real world. A guy has a yearning to shoot you; you put that guy down. You do not purposely engineer the situation so that the guy gets to draw further breaths.

Freckles' gun makes a couple of clacks as it hits the floor, not enough to draw the boys in from outside.

'Come clean,' I say, and if he gives me so much as one syllable of bullshit, so help me God I will send him bullshitting into the afterlife.

'Power play,' he says. 'Me and Mike. I was moving him up.'

As I thought. Freckles and Mike; two Shakespearean wannabes spinning tangled webs.

I nod at Shea, who has stopped chewing and sits slack-jawed.

'From the horse's mouth,' I say.

And before Shea gets the words out, I know exactly what's coming:

'I could use a man like you.'

Then:

'Execute that motherfucker.'

Ah, Harvard. Thine veneer has faded like dew in the morning sun.

I should kill Freckles and Shea. I could do it easily with the silenced gun and probably take out KFC and his partner in the hall, but you're talking carnage. Mass murder.

And if I gotta do mass murder, I want to go the whole hog. Get Mike and his boys and Krieger/Fortz while I'm about it.

I'm drifting towards war criminal with those numbers.

And I like to tell myself, on the cold winter nights when I'm flashing on all the ghosts of violence past that haunt my sleep-deprived spirit, that I Am Not So Bad. Sounds juvenile, I know, but it's a good 3 a.m. mantra.

I Am Not So Bad. Sometimes I sing it to the tune of U2's 'In the Name of Love'. I try to remember not to do this if I have someone sleeping over.

'I can pay you, McEvoy,' says Freckles, making the inevitable counter-offer. 'I got some bricks of cash in my car. An escape fund. A hundred grand.'

I slap the back of his head, hard, knocking him over on to the desk into what doormen refer to as the Deliverance position.

'I bet you do, Freckles. Thanks for the tip.'

Shea glares at Freckles. 'You fucking shitbag. I trusted you.'

The older man's head is ringing and he is not interested in Shea's bullshit.

'Fuck you, Edward. You ain't even a man. I don't owe you shit.'

'Shoot him, McEvoy. Freckles is my employee, so I have more funds than he does. Stands to reason.'

I pick up Freckles' silenced gun and poke him in the arse cheek with it. 'That does stand to reason, Freckles. How are you, an immigrant from Donegal, gonna up that ante?'

'You can take the money and the car. Keys are in my pocket.' He wiggles his arse and the keys jangle. This is humiliating for him. No man should be forced to arse-wiggle after the age of fifty. There should be a waiver.

I follow the jangle and find a ring of keys, a valet ticket and a phone. No car key.

'These are house keys, Freckles.'

'It's the key ring, McEvoy. Remote starter.'

Now that is convenient.

'That is convenient,' I say, pocketing the keys, ticket and phone.

I can see the attraction of robbing folks now. You just go round with a gun and take what you want.

'So are you going to shoot this little prick?' presses Freckles. 'He's killing the business.'

Shea takes a handful of hummus and smears it across Freckles' cheeks. 'You go straight to fuckin' murder? We couldn't talk it over?'

The kid is still in cloud cuckoo land. I should shake him up a bit to make him think twice about coming after me should he survive. I take two rapid steps around the desk and force his head into his carton of food, mashing it in there.

'Like you were talking it out with me?' I say. 'Is that what you mean?'

'I was trying to scare you,' he protests.

'Bullshit. As far as you were concerned, you were talking to a dead man.'

'You were totally dead,' Freckles confirms. 'We had the plot all picked out, McEvoy. This prick wanted to shoot you himself, make his bones, like anyone even says that any more.'

I got one guy with his head on a table and another with his arse in the air. This is unsustainable. I need an exit strategy.

'Okay, over by the window, both of you.'

'But . . .' says Edward Shea, so I crack him on the crown with Freckles' silencer.

'Shut up, kid. Talking just gets you dead faster. By the window.'

They go, glaring and elbowing like two kids. Freckles is all mutter and bluster but he knows I could give him his gun back, put one hand in my pocket and still beat the bejaysus out of him, so he's gonna bide his time.

The effect by the window is what I'd hoped for. Sunlight blots out their features, makes it difficult to see who's who.

'Okay. Now drop your pants.'

Freckles has some balls, and he doesn't want to show them to me.

'Fuck yourself, McEvoy. I ain't going out with my pants down 'less I'm getting blowed by Jennifer Aniston.'

It's a nice ambition but Freckles has gotta accept that it's aspirational to say the least.

I cock the weapon. 'I'll call Jen. You get yourself ready.'

Freckles goes to work on a buckle in the shape of the classic Playboy bunny silhouette, which I'm sure would impress the hell out of Ms Aniston.

The one where the superstar blows the Paddy mobster.

'What about you, Shea? You got any conditions?'

'Sure. Why don't *you* blow me?'

All credit to the kid. Maybe he has some moxy too.

But he wiggles out of his little hipster jeans and holy shit, I cannot believe it. The two of them are wearing matching underpants. White Y-fronts with yellow piping.

I've been teetering on the brink of hysteria the whole day and this sends me tumbling over the edge. I cough through ten seconds of ragged laughter and wipe tears from my eyes, because blurry eyes when you're covering hostiles is for amateurs.

'You gotta be kidding me. I don't know why you guys are fighting. You have a lot in common.'

'I've been wearing these shorts for years,' says Freckles sullenly. 'Not this exact pair.'

'Yeah, that's right,' says Shea. 'I broke into your house and stole them.'

'I don't fucking know, do I?' says Freckles. 'Who can understand kids, these days. I saw a movie the other day where this Saw guy was peeling faces. What kind of shit is that?'

Freckles is showing initiative by trying to appeal to me as a fellow oldie, but it's having zero impact.

'Now, hold hands,' I order, stony faced. I know they'll object, which I have no patience for, so I shoot a hole in the headrest of Shea's stool, knocking it over backwards. The falling stool makes more noise than the bullet.

'Hold hands, girls. Squeeze fucking tight.'

What choice do they have? They hold hands. I wonder would they kiss, if I insisted?

The clatter brings a goon to the door. He raps gently.

'Eh, boss? Everything okay?'

'Don't call me boss!' screams Shea, impulsively I guess.

'Sorry, Mister Shea. You all squared away in there with the guy . . . situation?'

I wiggle the gun a little and Shea gets the message and calms down.

'Yeah, it's all cool. Come in here, both of you. There's a little heavy lifting to be done.'

I back up, keeping one gun on the window and the other on the door. This is the tightrope bit, keeping the balls in the air, to mix my circus metaphors. It's all smoke and mirrors and windows. And two douche clowns outside.

The clowns walk in with that tough guy, rolling shoulders nonchalance, and stop dead in their tracks when they catch sight of what is framed by the window.

'What . . .' says KFC.

'The fuck?' completes his partner with comic timing that would make Ferrell and Rudd crap themselves.

I feel myself waiting to see how these two would interpret the situation, so I decide to jump in.

'Okay, boys. Guns on the table.'

KFC moves a little faster than I'm expecting, jinking left and diving for cover, with the result that I shoot him in the calf rather than the foot and he face-plants into the desk, stunning himself. His partner is frozen by indecision and stands there shuddering until the opportunity has passed. His massive shoulders hitch as he begins to sob, disgusted with himself, and he takes his gun out and meekly lays it on the table. I frisk KFC and find a single pistol and a knife. I keep the knife hoping I don't have to go through a metal detector any time soon, as I am fast becoming a walking arsenal. The gun I place on the office table.

I grab KFC's collar and drag him to his feet.

'You better belt that,' I say, pointing to the bullet wound.

'You're dead, man,' he says, but it's just for show. His face is pale and he's already halfway into shock, but he has enough motor skills left to remove his belt and tie off the wound.

When I have everyone by the window, I give them my speech.

'Let me summarise the situation. You guys are some kind of hooligans. Drugs, money, whatever, I never heard of you.'

'Mostly drugs,' says KFC, a little addled by his situation. 'And we off folks and shit.'

'Great. Okay. We're all on the same page. So here's what happened; I got dragged into the middle of a gang dispute. Freckles here was gonna shoot the kid, and set me up as a patsy.'

KFC raises his hand. 'What's a patsy?'

I was not expecting interruptions. 'It's a stool pigeon.'

'No,' says KFC. 'You've lost me.'

I think maybe this guy is playing me with my own dumb act.

'Are you taking the piss?'

KFC is wounded. 'Nah, man. You shot me. My mind is a little fuzzy with the pain and whatnot.'

Whatnot? I like this guy.

'Okay. The deal is that Shea and Freckles want to kill each other. Is that clear enough?'

Everyone nods. Even Shea and Freckles.

'So you people have a schism in the ranks.'

KFC's hand goes up. I do not have time for this.

'A split,' I tell him. 'A split in the ranks. Okay?'

KFC leans on his bloody knuckles. 'Yeah. I got it. You couldn't shoot me in the arm? That's my career fucked.'

'I could shoot you in the arm now. Would that shut you the hell up?'

KFC realises that there is no right answer to this question and so wisely decides to keep quiet.

I get back to the point. 'The point is that this group is not working as a unit. I don't know who's loyal to who, but you guys need some private time to sort it out. You know, brainstorm or make a graph or whatever. This has nothing to do with me, so I'm gonna absent myself.'

Shea gets a little antsy. Probably wondering if Freckles has paid off his boys.

'Take the guns, McEvoy. You need to protect yourself.'

I shrug. 'I got plenty of guns. I'm gonna leave those two on the table there. I don't like to overstock in general. I only kill what I can eat, like the Apaches.'

Shea is sweating now. 'You can't leave me here. I'm not one of these guys.'

The kid is good as dead and he knows it. I wonder, will I feel guilty about this? Probably. But if an Irish Catholic made his decisions based on guilt avoidance then he wouldn't get out of bed in the morning, and he certainly wouldn't play with himself while he was in bed in the morning.

I back away from the group, mentally assigning survival odds to each one. My money would have been on Freckles, but he gets a handicap on account of the dropped pants. KFC is shot in the leg but his hand is already on the table. Shea is getting dead unless he jumps out the window or gets abducted by aliens in the next ten seconds, and the other guy is still blubbering. So overall, I gotta stick with Freckles.

I back out the door, holding my guns steady.

'Nobody moves until I'm in the elevator; after that you make your own decisions.'

It's a tense situation. Freckles is trying to hitch up his pants with knee flexes and KFC's hand is crabbing towards the weapons. I shoot a hole in the desktop to stop him jumping the gun.

'Nu-uh,' I say, like a kindergarten teacher to an impatient toddler. 'Wait for the elevator door.'

Shea is sobbing uncontrollably, squeezing Freckles' hand like the guy is his prom date. I try to feel sorry for him but the kid has got food on his face, which counts against him. I realise with a jolt that I am more pissed off with Shea over the hummus than the attempted murder.

Shit. That is messed up.

But there's a whole lot more to eating with your mouth open than just the chewing involved. It says: *I am arrogant. I don't give a shit. I care so little about you that I can't even be bothered to close my mouth.*

In my opinion if you see a person eating with their mouth open, then that person is probably psychopathic at the very least.

I need to do a little more research before I publish.

I knuckle the elevator button and I can hear the car cranking and the cables working in the shaft. Not far, I'm guessing. Maybe one floor down.

'You got options,' I tell the foursome. 'You can all just walk away.'

It's bullshit, I know, but I am trying to kid myself that I'm not passively murdering at least half of these people. I'm separating

109

myself from the bloodbath that is about to happen. It's like the Seven Degrees of Kevin Bacon game, except in reverse, with homicide and only one degree.

The elevator sighs and I skip smartly inside, jabbing the lobby button with my silencer. The gun battle commences before the mirrored doors slide across and give me a look at myself when I'm not expecting it. I flinch with every shot, like they're shooting at me. But also I flinch because in that unexpected reflection I catch myself looking like my father.

I try to deflate the swelling in my head with a zinger.

'You should have kept your mouth shut, kid,' I mutter at myself.

I Am Not So Bad. No no, I am not so bad. My arse.

The valet barely glances at me, I suppose one Mick tough guy looks much the same as another after thirty years of facial hardship. He just scans the ticket with his hand-held gizmo and five minutes later I'm buckled into a Cadillac which has more kit than the USS *Enterprise*.

Freckles' phone synchs with the on-board computer, which asks me if I would like to send a message, and this gives me an idea which could buy me a little time. I dictate a text from Freckles to Mike Madden that reads simply: *It's done, partner.*

Hopefully Mike will embark on the traditional celebratory shit-faced binge and will not know what hit him, when I hit him, as I now must. Maybe once upon a time I would have simply pointed the car westward-ho and kept my foot on the gas until the radiator split, but now I have taken responsibilities upon myself.

Sofia. Jason. Even Zeb. They have all wiggled through cracks in my armour.

If my armour was actual physical armour I would be bringing it back to the armour store and having stern words with the armour salesman.

It would be standard countersurveillance procedure for me to tool around SoHo for a while and shake off any tail that I might have picked up. For all I know the Feds are up on Shea's people and I could be popped driving a vehicle stuffed to the door panels with contraband, but I don't have time for spy games. People are in danger because I didn't lay down and die like I was supposed to, so I gotta deal with the threat.

I ask the car to call Sofia and it says:

'Call Sofia Dominatrix?'

Dominatrix? Freckles won't have my Sofia in his phone. But he has been busy in his down time.

'No. Negative. Cancel call,' I shout in my eagerness to not get into a row with a leather-clad hooker.

'Cancelling call,' says the car, in a voice that takes me a second to recognise as Clint Eastwood's.

Wow. Freckles is/was a tough guy. Even his software kicks ass.

I dictate the number as I swing the Caddy into Holland Tunnel and drum the steering wheel waiting for Sofia to pick up.

Three rings, then:

'Welcome to the House of Jesus. Can I interest you in our latest publication; *Living Rent Free in the House of Jesus?*'

This is a standard Sofia pick-up. She has a whole ream of responses calculated to make the caller instantly hang up. Another classic is: *This is an automated ordering service, please speak to be redirected to our credit card debit line.* My personal favourite is lifted from *Ghostbusters*. Sofia treats the unfortunate caller to ten seconds of harrowing screaming followed by the growled word: *Zuul.*

She calls this technique the Reverse Jehovah. I once asked her why she bothered keeping her line connected and she replied: 'You are such a sad sack. Don't you want to laugh whenever you can?'

I couldn't argue with that.

'I don't leave the house much any more,' she'd continued, poking my chest with a finger, backing me into a corner. 'And you have that stupid goddamn casino. So all I do is take junk calls and do my look. You like my look today, baby?'

I did like her look. She was done up in a leather coat belted at the waist, torn tights and earrings so big they could pick up stations from space. I think Paula Abdul might have been the inspiration.

'You look great. You sure do.'

Sofia stroked my cheek and I blushed like a virgin. 'If I look so great, then why don't you do something about it?'

I ask what I always ask when something like this comes up.

'What's my name? Who am I?'

Sofia's gaze muddied and she stamped her kitten heels. 'Why do you always ask me that question, Carmine? Ain't we been married long enough? I make all this effort and you quiz me up and down. You shouldn't be putting any questions to me unless the answer is *oh baby.*'

Sofia was up against me like a molten bar, her curves finding all my hollows.

I'm only human, for Christ sake.

I needed to cool her down and I knew just how to do it.

'Sofia, have you taken your lithium?'

She pushed me away in disgust. 'Lithium? You have all this jammed up on you, and you're asking me about meds? Christ, Daniel.'

And just like that the well was dry.

SCREWED

How come I'm always Daniel when she's not horny any more?

If Sofia is coming on really hot and heavy, I ask her what happened to Carmine. That cools her down real fast, and the only answer she's ever given me is: *The same thing that will happen to you if you don't stop asking about him.*

Which doesn't bode well for our fledgling relationship.

I speak into a little microphone on the visor, probably louder than I need to given the multidirectional specs of these things.

'Sofia? It's me, Daniel.'

'What's the code, Dan?'

I had forgotten Sofia Delano's paranoia. The weekly code was usually the title of an eighties dance-floor filler.

'Sofia, darlin'. I don't remember the code.'

'Well then you better stop calling me or I'll send some voodoo down this line that will shrivel your balls like raisins.'

That is a graphic threat and the superstitious Paddy in me swears that his goujons *are* tingling a little, which jogs my memory.

'The code is: *When the going gets tough, the tough get going.*'

'Dan, honey,' Sofia says, all treacle and promise now. 'Where are you?'

Girls putting on the baby voice usually makes me wince, but Sofia does it with such need and conviction that it would break the hardest heart. If old Paddy Costello had met someone like Sofia, he might have actually enjoyed his miserable life of untold wealth.

'I am on my way over,' I tell the microphone. 'I'll be with you in ninety minutes max.'

I'm coming up on the Newark Turnpike and traffic is slow but moving, which is about as good as it ever gets, so I might make it in an hour twenty.

'Are you feeling hot, baby?'

I think maybe Sofia Delano sincerely believes that sex is the only reason anyone would give her the time of day. This Carmine asshole screwed her up good. From what I can glean from her neighbours, Carmine was the jealous type who turned a vivacious young girl into a virtual recluse; think cat lady without the cats. People will go to extraordinary lengths for attention when they have been systematically starved of it for years. I remember having a physical as a kid and half hoping the pain in my head was a tumour because fathers always love their sick kids, don't they?

So I understand, sort of.

I tried to track down Carmine a couple of months ago to put Sofia out of her misery. I even put a computer genius friend of Jason's on the case, but the guy has disappeared off the face of the earth, like aliens took a shine to him. A guy like that is most likely dead or locked deep in the bowels of a Mexican prison. I can't help worrying about it, though. Bad pennies have a habit of showing up.

'No, Sofia. It's not like that. Some people might come to see you, before I get there. I want you to put the brace on the door and don't open up for anyone but me.'

'Are they bad people, Dan?'

She doesn't sound afraid, a little eager maybe, and I'm worried she won't lock the door because she'd appreciate the company. Mike could send over a couple of stone killers and my girl could mix them a shaker of martini. Then again, she might cut them open and tell the future in their entrails. I'm exaggerating at both ends, but the point is that Sofia can't tell good from bad when it comes to attention.

'Yes, these are bad people, Sofia. You have to trust me and lock the door. What weapons do you have?'

Sofia amps up the little-girl voice so I know she's lying. 'I don't have any weapons, Danny. No guns on this premises.'

'I know you have at least one gun, Sofia. I found a shell box in the trash.'

'So I like to scorch patterns on the carpet, that's not proof positive of a firearm.'

Shouting at ladies is bad so I stop myself from doing it.

'Please, Sofia. Protect yourself until I get there. Do whatever you have to do.'

'Whatever I have to do?'

'Whatever.'

There is a clunk as Sofia drops the phone. She is so excited that she has forgotten to hang up.

I don't fully understand the strange hold that Sofia has over me. There's an old Gaelic word *geasa* which is about as close as I can come to explaining it. My class learned all about *geasa* in school from this dick teacher we had one year: Mister Fitzgerald, liked all the kids to call him Fitz. Winked at the girls and gave the boys cigarettes. Creepy customer. So anyways, Fitz asks a question about *geasa*, what they were and so forth. This was a genuine hard question and holy shit if I didn't know the answer.

'Is that hand connected to your arm, Daniel?' said Fitz, when he saw who was volunteering. 'I should take a photograph.'

'*Geasa* are magical bonds,' I rattled off, before my brain lost it. 'Cast over a man to bind him to the woman who loves him.'

Fitz was stunned and I couldn't blame him. In the three months he'd been teaching me mythology, *I didn't do it* was only answer I'd ever offered. It wasn't that I was slow, I just didn't know the answers.

'Fuck me,' he said, big eyebrows arching like slugs.

115

It was a laugh. Fitz got suspended and I got to slit his tyres without anyone looking too deep into it.

I only knew this particular term because my mom, wise in the ways of Irish folklore to the extent that only the child of an immigrant can be, suspected that perhaps my father had reversed the trend and magically bound her to him. Maybe she was right. Margaret Costello McEvoy certainly never got free of her husband. He even bore her down into the dirt with him.

And when his elder daughter died, even then Paddy Costello had not broken and hurried to her graveside to comfort his grandson.

Guy's a rich asshole. Only difference between him and regular assholes is monogrammed shirts.

So, like I was saying, Sofia Delano has me under a spell. And I think the main reason I don't break free is that I don't really want to. Part of me hopes she's gonna snap out of it and we'll have end-of-days sex and then embark on a series of adventures in a Caddy convertible.

Even Zeb knows enough about mental illness to realise that I am being slightly optimistic, or as he put it: *You have your head shoved so far up your ass that you're working your own mouth from the inside.*

I could have misheard that metaphor, or it's possible that even Zeb didn't know what he was talking about; he does favour the graphic image. Among his more confusing references is the description of his morning boner: *Danny, I got a hard-on like a vengeful baboon who just won the jungle lottery.*

I have no idea what the hell that means, and I would emigrate before asking as Zeb would drone on circuitously for hours to justify his choice of words.

All I know for sure is that I cannot allow harm to come to Sofia because of my situation. I hope I can get to her before Mike hears the sound of his shit hitting my fan. Or as Zeb might say: *Before Mike realises his plan is more fucked than a waxed badger walking backwards through a flamingo patch with honey on its ass.*

See what I mean? Just thinking about what the guy would say is enough to bring on a migraine.

Sofia is squared away for now and there is no more I can do on that front until I get there, so I turn my mind to the other cold fronts that are closing in from the north and east. Jason I put on red alert with a quick text. He's gonna love that, tooling up his beefcake brigade. I pity the mobster who goes knocking on the Slotz door now. Jason's guys will kick the shit out of him, then do his colour palette.

If you have a fashion problem. If no one else can help you. Maybe you can hire the Gay Team.

Was that homophobic? Am I allowed to tease the other team at all?

Best to say nothing. Keep out of harm's way.

I make it to the city limits in just over an hour and then I gotta sit in off-ramp traffic for ten minutes while some fender bender gets sorted out. There are a couple of bike cops on buffer duty between the drivers so I don't lean on the horn and vent my frustrations. Mike's boys could be on their way to Sofia's apartment right now and I gotta sit here watching some Armani-wearing, winter-tanned hedge-fund asshole do kiddie hysterics over his E-Class bumper. The notion that I could toss him off the ramp and be on my way grabs hold of me and I have to squeeze the steering wheel until it cracks to stop myself acting on it.

By the time they get around to waving us through with traffic wands, I am so wound up that I take off like a bat out of hell, clipping a wand on my way past.

Way to stay below the radar in your stolen car, moron.

That's what Sofia does to me. All reason goes out the window.

I avoid Cloister's main street, such as it is, and go across Cypress to hang the technically illegal U-turn that everyone does which saves me a couple of blocks. Sofia's building is so commonplace that I often find it difficult to believe that she lives inside, that some of her mercury has not bled through to the walls, staining them with violent slashes of colour.

Now who's the psycho? Mood walls? I really should call Dr Moriarty and fill him in on some of my new theories.

I abandon the car on a yellow line and take the steps two at a time, catching a break when my ex-neighbour old Mr Hong shuffles out the front door dragging his shopping buggy on a cord trailing between his bowed legs, pulling tight against an area where I would not want a cord to be.

'Mister Hong,' I say, reflexively courteous.

'My balls are smarting,' he says to me crossly. 'Like they're tied in knots.'

The first hundred times he said this to me, I pointed out the cord dividing his nethers. Now I just make shit up.

'It's the New Jersey damp,' I say, not putting too much effort into it. 'Notoriously bad for balls.'

Hong grunts, produces a peach from somewhere, stuffs the entire fruit into his mouth and begins the daily race to gum the peach into a paste before it chokes him. I slip past into the brownstone lobby thinking: *We are all mad here.*

Sofia's place is on the third floor and I take great bounds up the stairway, shouldering the wall on each turn rather than slow down. I knock a dent in the sheetrock on the second floor and it occurs to me that I will have to pay for that at some point, which bothers me, because a person should get a pass when he is trying to save someone's life for Christ's sake.

The banister bears the brunt of my shoulder charge on the final turn and I make splinters of the railings, which crack loud enough to warn any intruder that I am on the way. Even a deaf intruder could feel the vibration of my thundering approach.

What happened to stealth? I was a specialist once upon a time.

No time for softly softly. My Celtic sixth sense that only predicts bad stuff is bubbling in my gut. It's like a spider sense that brings on the shits, which would be a very bad look for Peter Parker swinging over Manhattan.

Bad things have happened. I'm too late.

This notion is confirmed by Sofia's door, which yawns open, still creaking, so I'm seconds late. Seconds.

Oh Sofia, darlin', I think, fearing the worst. What other way is there to fear? *I did not protect you. I could not save you to be my own.*

If she is dead, I will hunt down that husband of hers and take my time with him, I promise myself. Maybe sell the video to Citizen Pain.

I barrel inside, my momentum carrying me across the room totally off balance.

Stupid amateur. Stupid.

First thing my senses pick up is the tacky resistance as my soles leave the floor. My life is a trail of bloody footprints so I know what's sticking to my boots. I look anyway to confirm it, and there is a lattice of blood following the grout patterns in the floor tiles, forming an irregular triangle. At the tip is a woman's head, cracked open by a blow, hair fanned like a dark halo. Sofia lies awkwardly, the quirky spirit bludgeoned out of her.

I forget everything I ever learned about violent situations. I do not compartmentalise. I do not defer my grief. Instead I behave like a civilian who has had the blindfold of civilisation whipped off to reveal a first look at the ugliness of the world.

I collapse from the inside out, tumbling forward as my brain cuts off motor commands. I fall to the floor cursing the men responsible for this brutality. I curse the banker at the off-ramp. Mike Madden, Zeb, Freckles. All those guys. A pox on their heads and a plague on their families.

All bullshit, of course. I'm the one who brought this on poor deluded Sofia. I kissed her on the lips and lit her up for the bogeymen.

So I curse myself and my bloodstained hands. I curse my tangent-driven mind that cannot seem to focus in even the most urgent circumstances. I cry for everything that has ever happened. The line of bodies that dog me from the past all the way back to the tangled pile of limbs inside a crushed car in Dublin.

I am a rotten fruit with barely a scrap of untainted meat left. One more bite and I am lost.

I am lying there on the floor, head half under the settee, watching the sunlight draw laser lines in the blood pattern, when Sofia's hand twitches and I notice the nails bitten to the quick.

Sofia doesn't bite her nails any more. She is proud of her painted talons. She likes to purr like a cat and scratch the air.

Not Sofia? Not dead?

This is too much for me. I feel dull and stupid, and left out of the joke.

I roll to my knees.

'Sofia?' I croak.

And she comes out of the kitchen, all in black, plenty of pockets, military style. Janet Jackson. Rhythm Nation.

'Hey, baby,' she says, a hammer dangling from her fingers, a ribbon of bloody scalp in its claw. 'You were right. Someone came a-looking for you, but I did what I had to do. No gun necessary.'

Who is on the floor? Who is nearly dead?

I need answers to fill this awful vacuum.

Crawling seems achievable. I crawl across the floor, dragging my knees through the darkening blood, and with infinite care turn the woman's head and gaze upon her face.

I have finally gone mad.

It was only a matter of time. I should pay attention now, because Simon is going to want details when we go over this in therapy.

The woman is my mother.

Dead these twenty-five years.

My sweet mom. Looking not a day older.

'Mom?'

I hear the word and I know it came from my mouth, but I am a little out of body right now. Shell-shocked on seashells by the seashore on Blackrock beach where we used to walk.

The woman's eyes flutter open and she coughs a lungful of booze fumes in my eyes, scalding them.

'Danny,' she says, like we talked yesterday. 'Something happened to my head. I forgot again.'

My long-term memory fizzles into life and I get it in a jumbled rush of memories: ice picks, chaste good-night kisses, boob lectures.

Not my mother. Her baby sister, with enough of a resemblance to fool my frazzled brain.

Clearly not your mother, idiot.

Evelyn Costello reaches up a hand. Her nail stubs are painted blood red. No, not painted. It's real blood, her own.

'Danny. I found you. You treating girls with respect, Danny?'

Her eyes flicker and she is gone again, borne off by head trauma.

Just as well. I need to think.

I feel Sofia behind me. 'Who is this, Carmine? You got some whore stashed away? Is that it?'

So I am Carmine again. Figures.

There's a lot of blood on the floor.

'No, Sofia. This is not some whore, this is my aunt.'

Sofia sniffs like this is such a crock. Who can blame her?

'Aunt? Really, baby?'

It's not her fault. Sofia was only doing what I told her to do, but suddenly I'm angry.

I jump to my feet and snatch the hammer. 'Yeah, really. You brained my aunt.'

Sofia knows crazy when she sees it and backs off.

'Sorry.' And she cocks a hip and salutes. 'Just following orders, Carmine.'

Dan-Carmine. Carmine-Dan.

Maybe I am Carmine. How hard could it be?

This is all too labyrinthine. There are too many strands for me to follow.

Soldiering was simple.

You have one enemy. His face will be darker than yours and he will be wearing desert shit. Not camo gear, genuine desert shit. Goatskin, rough scarves, vintage Levis.

122

Find your enemy.

Kill your enemy.

But here and now, my enemies are multitude and look all the bloody same. Mike, Freckles, Shea, KFC, Krieger and Fortz.

I need a friend. Someone who can out-sneaky the sneakers. A person with paranoia in his veins who owes me his life.

This apartment is too bright. Everything seems bleached. How does that happen with small windows?

Evelyn moans at my feet.

I need a doctor.

I pull out my phone to call Zeb.

He better not give me the runaround. I am not in the mood.

I punch Zeb's number, and while the phone chirps in my ear, I pray that my friend is not stoned already.

CHAPTER 6

So here's Evelyn Costello, the AWOL heiress who schooled me in the ways of mammipulation, which is not a word but should be, back in my life again after twenty years within four hours of me meeting her stepmother, who is ten years younger than her stepdaughter.

This is starting to sound like yee-haw heaven: *It gits so darn lonesome in the trailer park that there ain't nuthin' for it but to hump yore own sister.*

I know plenty of people that don't believe in coincidence, but I do. It happens all the time. It's usually petty stuff like meeting two guys called Ken inside an hour or buying a DVD on the very night a movie shows up on cable. Generally coincidences do not have immediate and obvious life-altering consequences. I suppose it's possible that Edit and Evelyn would plonk themselves in the middle of my stressful day by total coincidence, but it would be one hell of a twist of fate.

Now that I'm close to her, examining the head wound that Sofia inflicted, I notice that Evelyn smells just like I remember. Still using the same shampoo. Women do that: stay loyal to a product.

Men always think there might be something better out there. Men like Carmine.

I swab the wound with a little antiseptic, but that's all I do because anything more and Zeb will have one of his doctorial shit fits like I'm not a professional and did I think he spent six years in medical school just so some grunt could go around getting all surgical? It's not often Zeb gets to play real doctors and so he gets pissed if anyone steals so much as a peal of his thunder.

My Twitter icon chirps and spits out a nugget from Simon:

To Klingon22: Sure it's okay for you to be attracted to a Romulon. We are all the same under the latex.

I don't know who Klingon22 is but I would swap places with him in a heartbeat.

I lay Evelyn out on the sofa and am still watching over her when Zeb shows up. As usual, Sofia is less than happy to see his face, and as usual Zeb tries it on with her.

'Hey, Sofia baby,' he says, arms wide. 'It's me, your darling Carmine, back from the wars where I've been for the past coupla decades. They had me in a stockade, baby. Did stuff with bamboos and shit. All that kept me from spilling my guts was the thought of your sweet ass.'

Someone should write a book about Zeb and the series of shenanigans that his life so far is composed of. A book would be good, but not a movie because movies gotta have story arcs and through lines. And what kinda *through line* is: guy does dumb shit daily? Not much of one. Not a whole lot of character development there.

Sofia glares at me like I'm responsible for this douche. 'You got guns, Dan. Why don't you shoot this guy and do the world a favour?'

Zeb brushes past her. 'Nice. That's what I get for trying to be a gentleman.'

I wish Zeb wouldn't screw with Sofia, especially when she's in a hammer-swinging mood. One of these days he's gonna greet her with one of his casual misogynisms and she's gonna crack his skull like an egg. And when that happens, all the king's horses will not give a rat's ass.

Zeb squats beside me.

'Yo, movie star,' he says, dropping a Gladstone bag between his feet. 'What do we got here? Live flesh or dead meat?'

It worries me that the doctor doesn't notice his patient is breathing. I decide to defer the usual banter until Evelyn is patched up.

'Head wound,' I say tersely, not giving him much to work with. 'Couple of sutures, I'd say.'

Zeb leans in close and pokes Evelyn's injury with a grubby fingertip. 'I agree with your prognosis, Doctor Paddy. Of course the patient's skull could be fractured, in which case her brain fluid is leaking right now. She spasming at all? Or speaking in tongues? You know, *Exorcist* shit?'

'No. Just lying there. And could you take your finger out of my aunt's head?'

Zeb retracts the digit and examines the clotted blood on its tip. 'Aunt? So she's available?'

I am not sure what kind of low self-esteem issues Zeb has going on that make him want to screw anything that does not currently have a dick. Maybe he's just depraved. I vaguely remember that I once found his unrelenting horniness funny, but right now, with all the stress factors I have on my shoulders, I am a hair's breadth from punching him in the temple, even though he's the only one who can patch up Evelyn.

'Zeb. You are on my shit list at the moment because of the whole Mike thing, but if you do this for me, if you fix this lady, we're square, got it? You should take that deal, it's a good one.'

Zeb hums 'Tainted Love', which is one of his thinking songs, then pulls a huge hunting knife from the bag at his feet.

'Nice knife,' says Sofia, drawn in by the glint.

Zeb attempts to twirl the blade but only succeeds in fumbling the knife and almost cutting off his toes. 'Yeah, thanks, my little goyish princess. This beauty is a genuine reproduction of John Rambo's blade from *First Blood*. A collector's item.'

I am a little worried that Zeb is going too far with his movie star obsession but more worried that he's gonna excise half of Evelyn's scalp when all we need is a little stitching.

'Zeb, no cutting. She's been cut enough.'

Zeb sighs. 'Cutting? I thought you were a movies man, Dan. Don't you remember that scene? They're all doing it now, it's kind of a staple, but at the time Stallone was breaking new ground.'

I do remember it. The screwtop knife.

'Classic.' I have to admit it.

'*First Blood* was a movie?' asks Sofia. 'I could have sworn that was real.'

Zeb screws off the compass on the hilt of his knife and inside the handle is a needle and thread, sealed in a steripack.

'Sly didn't have a sealed packet,' says Zeb casually, like him and Stallone are bowling buddies. 'But then he didn't have to worry about his licence.'

Zeb is still at the honeymoon phase with his medical licence, having recently acquired it through some outrageous wheeler-dealing involving a fat envelope, two members of the state board and the mother of crazy weekends in Atlantic City. He hinted that at least three of Tiger Woods' mistresses were involved, but more specific information would no doubt be eked out over the coming years.

'You got any anaesthetic?'

Zeb snorts and raps on Evelyn's forehead. 'Are you kidding? I could amputate this chick's arm and she wouldn't flinch.'

He swabs the wound with a very un-Rambo-like baby wipe, then stitches Evelyn up. Two minutes and he's biting the thread. I gotta give it to him, the little bastard can be efficient when he feels like it.

'Good work, Zeb,' I say, enjoying the fleeting moment of sincere gratitude that Zeb will no doubt screw up by speaking.

'Yeah, well maybe when *Auntie* wakes up, I'll get a real thank you, know what I'm saying, Sarge?'

Reliable as a Swiss banker. Zeb adds fuel to the fire with: 'You think the nutjob has anything to drink? I'm parched, movie star.'

Sofia is apparently unperturbed by being referred to as *nutjob* and walks to the kitchen to fetch us a drink.

I am relieved to find Evelyn's breathing steady. I concentrate on that for a moment because I have so many urgencies to consider that I can't engage with any of them.

Something that Zeb said niggles at me, breaking through my funk.

'Hey, Zebulon, why are you calling me movie star? That's new.'

Zeb literally jumps to his feet, stumbling backwards a few steps, almost colliding with Sofia and her tray.

'Oh fuck! Oh shit, Dan! You don't know? You genuinely don't know?'

I groan. This sounds like big news, so Zeb won't give it up easy.

'No. So do me a favour and don't tell me. I got enough shit on my shovel at the moment, okay?'

I am not playing games here. My crisis dance card is pretty full.

Zeb walks up and down, agitated like he needs to Riverdance but is holding it in.

'Okay, screw it. I'm just gonna show you.' He pulls out his phone and opens a clip. 'This is up on YouTube. Fifty thousand hits and counting.'

My stomach lurches because my subconscious has figured it out. The rest of me needs to look at the screen.

Don't look.

I gotta look. How can I not look?

I'm warning you. This ain't gonna be a video of some kid wasted after the dentist.

So I look.

And it isn't a kid after the dentist. Or a cat punching a dog. Or some dreadlocked teen falling off his board.

It's me. Hitting a cop with an enormous dildo. The porn crew caught the entire episode. Maybe Zeb doesn't know my victim is a cop.

'You know that's a cop, don't you?' says Zeb. 'And that guy back there, weeping. Another cop. Detectives Krieger and Fortz. They been tagged about a hundred times, mostly by other cops lol'ing their cyber assholes off.'

'I thought that dildo was smaller,' I mumble, just to take the focus from the video.

Zeb's focus does not waver. 'It's perspective. Dildos always seem smaller when you're holding them.'

I am in no position to judge Zebulon right now.

Sofia plucks the phone from Zeb's hand and retreats to the corner with a bottle of whiskey. After a couple of replays she slugs from the neck and says:

'Nice thong, Dan.' And then, 'This is real but Rambo isn't? I'm confused.'

Me too. Most of the time.

My own phone brrrps and spits out a tweet. I check it even though screen checking hasn't been working out so well for me lately.

Life is not a rehearsal. Life is real. No do-overs. So put down that bottle of Grouse and go have safe sex with someone.

No do-overs. No take-backs. The genie is out of the bottle.

It's just a pity the genie is wearing a pink thong and wielding a dildo.

Somehow then I fall asleep, right there standing up. It comes out of nowhere. One second my neck is burning with embarrassment, and it seems like the next that I am blinking away the fog of a power nap.

'Huh?' I say, because it takes a second for the cylinders to fire in my brain.

A bit of advice for you: never answer the phone rising out of a deep sleep. First because your voice sounds like you spent twenty years sinking shots with Bob Dylan and Rod Stewart, and secondly you might say something not strictly relevant to the real world. I learned this the hard way when Tommy Fletcher called me on Irish time and I bolted upright in bed, blurting: *Terrorist pigeons, honest to Christ, they've trained the pigeons.*

Tommy reminds me of this often with great hilarity from his end. So my advice is when you hear that phone ringing, talk to yourself for a few seconds before answering. Gets everything moving.

Apparently I have been talking in my sleep, because Zeb is all caught up on the events of my hellish day.

'You putz,' he says, slapping my forehead with the heel of his hand. 'You were bored, was that it? You couldn't just take a meeting with Mike without it turning into Armageddon.'

I huff a little, but he's right. It's like I move people towards violence. Like they weren't really considering it until I showed up.

Bullshit. Mike's has violence on the brain like a poultice. And Shea picked out your burial plot before you even got there.

Those are violent people, but I can't deny that the common denominator in all their twisted scenarios is Dan McEvoy.

I lumber to the sofa and perch beside Evelyn's feet. Once you get past the shampoo smell, she stinks like a brewery, but she looks so peaceful. I could live with the booze sweats to be that peaceful.

'She gonna be okay?' I ask, figuring that prioritising is the way to get through this mess.

'She's gonna be fine,' says Zeb. 'You on the other hand are more screwed than my cousin Ada at a bat mitzvah. And she gets screwed a lot 'cause of her being the whore she is.'

Ada is the sweetest kid you ever met. Odds on she turned down Zeb's advances or wouldn't lend him money. But though we may disagree on Ada's whorey-ness, there is no arguing the fact that I am screwed.

I touch Evelyn's head and Sofia growls from her corner.

'Is there any way out of this?'

Usually I wouldn't turn to Zeb Kronski for tactical advice, but he's a slippery character and the tighter the hole the more he wriggles to get out of it.

Zeb paces a little. 'You got no power here, Irish. All you got here is liabilities.'

On the word *liabilities* Zeb does an unsubtle head tilt towards Sofia, who responds by rising out of her corner, whiskey bottle by the neck.

'Hey, I'm including myself in that package,' says Zeb hurriedly. 'We are all chinks in the McEvoy armour. Soon as Mike finds out his plan went to hell, he's coming here. Also you got the blues to worry about and whoever survived the Shea *massacre*.'

I wince. Zeb has been desensitised by *The Sopranos* and cocaine and thinks massacres are cool. He should know better; we've both been in war zones. Granted, he was self-medicating at the time.

'Why am I worrying about the blues?'

Zeb double-takes. 'What? Are you serious, man? You just dildoed out a beating to a couple of their guys in high definition.'

I suspect this might not be a correct use of the verb *dildoed*.

Sofia senses I might need a drink and so hands me the bottle. I have it halfway to my mouth before it occurs to me that I may want to stay sharp.

'No thanks, baby. One drunk family member is enough.'

Zeb stops pacing. 'Okay. Okay. Let me ask you, is this Edit person legit? Sounds pretty iffy to me. She asks about bag lady Evelyn, and suddenly your aunt shows up?'

That had occurred to me. 'Yeah, that occurred to me. I think Edit is cool. It makes no sense for her to bring Evelyn home, unless she's telling me the truth. If it was a money thing, then she would leave her stepdaughter rolling with the lowlifes.'

'Okay,' says Zen. 'That being the case, here's the plan: get the aunt home and beg for asylum.' He spreads his arms wide like he just presented me with a lost Shakespeare sonnet.

'That's it? You want me to drive back into New York where there are cops and gangsters looking for me?'

'Exactly,' says Zeb, swiping the bottle from my hand. 'Jason and his boys are all tooled up; anyway, Mike ain't going near that place in the daylight. I'll take Miss Fruitcake on my rounds and you deliver Evelyn to your hot grandma. Ain't nobody gonna break into a private apartment building in Manhattan. Rich folk have more security than the President. You'll be safer in there than in a safe. One of those safes with tungsten and shit in the door.'

I rub my chin against the grain of bristle. Tungsten and shit. Dr Kronski sure knows how to screw up a presentation. But if you ignored him being a dick, Zeb made a good point. Just one thing to clear up.

'Where will you take Miss Fruit . . . Sofia? She doesn't like leaving the building.'

Sofia steps up to Zeb, and if he had glasses they'd be steaming up.

'Miss Fruitcake doesn't leave the building,' she says firmly. 'Ever.'

'I can give you some pills,' says Zeb, who knows how to push people's buttons. 'And you get to inject people . . . in the face.'

Sofia's eyes glaze over and I know she is already gone.

Before we split up, Sofia plants one of those kisses on me that pulls my heart loose from its moorings. Initially I'm a little embarrassed to be kissing a lady right out in the open like that, but then Sofia grabs fistfuls of my hair and gives it an extra ten per cent, and I am lost in the moment. I want to appreciate this while it's happening, because every kiss could be the last one.

Eventually even Zeb is blushing and decides to puncture the romantic bubble.

'Dan, why don't you shoot off in your shorts already before you get us all killed?'

Sofia pulls away with a soft pop as she breaks the seal along with the spell.

'Dan,' she says, her eyes sparkling. 'I get to inject people in the face.'

'I'm happy for you, baby,' I say. This is not sarcasm. Anything that gets my Sofia outside in the sunshine is a good thing.

Evelyn is still out on the sofa. I heft her easily and she burps fumes into my face. I don't react well to whiskey belches usually, but she's family so you gotta make allowances.

'Come on, Aunt Evelyn,' I say, draping her arm across my shoulders. 'Let's get you to the car.'

Evelyn perks up for long enough to prove to me that her sense of humour is intact.

'I'll drive,' she says, then slumps heavily in my arms.

I sit Aunt Evelyn in the passenger seat of Freckles' Caddy, cinching the belt tightly to keep her secure. Being out on the road like this in a stolen car is not ideal, but *ideal* is a fond memory at this point. Compared to being strapped into a torture chair, driving a hot automobile ain't too much of a chore.

I go out of my way to drive past the club and am relieved to see Jason himself on the door, flanked by two of his construction crew, shooting menacing looks at the public in general and flexing their pectoral muscles in a synchronised manner that suggests they can hear music I can't.

Jason spots me driving past in the big Caddy and puts in a

call to my cell. I take the call through the car's system.

'Yo, boss. How's she cuttin'?'

This is an Irish rural expression that Jason picked up from me. He does my accent too, when he's feeling brave.

'Yeah, she's cuttin' fine but I got a lot of heat on me today, so I gotta keep out of the club. You cool to handle Mike if he shows?'

Jason growls into the phone. 'Yeah. I am so cool to handle that seersucker-wearing motherfucker.'

This is not good. J is at Defcon 2 already.

'Hey, partner. Take it easy. Mike has plenty of bodies to throw at this. We don't. It doesn't matter if you beat him down, he's just coming back with guns. So gently gently, comprende?'

'Got it, Dan. You gonna be all right, dawg?'

'Ten four, dog. I'm gonna be cool if I can steer clear of the five-o.'

Ten four. Dog. Five-o?

I have no shame.

Next thing you know I'll be putting my hands in the a-yuh.

The drive into Manhattan takes barely two hours but feels like it knocks about five years off my life. I'm seeing cops behind each windscreen and on every rooftop. If there's one thing the blues and the hoods have in common it's their desire to rain down vengeance on anyone who applies a little bodily harm to members of their fraternity. Adding dildoes and YouTube videos into the mix only serves to increase agitation on both sides.

The blues will have their vengeance and you can bet it will be entirely disproportionate.

My shrink, Simon Moriarty, once told me I was obsessed with

vengeance, to which I replied: *Obsessed with vengeance? Who told you that? I'll kill him.*

How we laughed. Happy times. I miss those days when all my issues were in my head. Nowadays it seems my problems are external and well armed.

I give Edit a terse call to let her know I'm en route with the package, and my chatter brings Evelyn around. She walks two fingers along her scalp, wincing as they make contact with the spongy ridge of sutures.

'Man,' she says. 'That was a bad one. You got anything to drink in this car, buddy? Something to help a girl straighten herself out.'

I'm starting to feel like the women in my life are actively trying to forget who I am.

'Evelyn. It's Daniel, remember? Margaret's boy.'

I sneak quick sideways glances at my aunt and watch her disintegrate. All that self-loathing is hard on the features. They say the eyes are the window to the soul but the face is a road map to the past, which would be a pretty good tattoo for those people who like whole paragraphs inked along their arms.

Evelyn's features collapse inwards as though she's been punched. Her mouth crinkles and purses, dragging her nose down and chin up. Her forehead is momentarily smooth then deeply lined once more as she draws breath. Her skin is dry and flaked across the nose, and sunspots dot her cheeks. She snuffles like a baby bear, then bawls aloud. I am embarrassed, and not because adults shouldn't cry. I've seen grown men cry on the battlefield. I did it myself a few times, hunched behind cover waiting for the ordnance with my name on it, but grown-ups don't *howl*. That's worse than letting the bowels go.

'Hey,' I say. 'Hey, come on.'

Genius, right? I should be a professional comforter. Surely I have a couple more platitudes in the barrel.

'It's okay, Evelyn. I'm here now.'

These pathetic uber clichés make her cry all the more. She is bleating now, like a goat, digging her nails into her own legs. I do not know what to do. I am seriously stumped. Should I pull over and give hugs or something?

So I do nothing. I ride it out, waiting for my aunt to run out of steam. Eventually she calms down, drawing the folds of her worn shirt tight as though hiding nakedness.

'Dan,' she says, voice thin from wailing. 'Daniel. Danny. I'm hurting, nephew. Could we stop at a liquor store? All I need is a hit. One belt.'

Hit, belt, slug.

All terms of violence. Why is that? Seems like something I should contemplate moodily at some maudlin moment in the future. Might be important, but I'd have to be loaded to get it.

Loaded. There it is again.

'No, Evelyn. We need to get where we're going. It's not safe to be with me right now. You picked a bad time to make contact.'

'Sorry,' says Evelyn, scratching her forearm. 'I was coming last week but something happened in Queens. I met this guy and he rolled me. Can you believe that? A guy rolled me. Once upon a time I was doing the rolling. You know, before the goods went south.'

'You're good. You look good. All you need is a weekend in one of those spas. Maybe a few shots of thiamine. You'll be fine.'

It's true, Evelyn does look good. She's a skinny drunk without a single strand of grey in her dark hair. I can see how she would work that face to roll guys. Zeb and me have this people-watching thing, where we try and figure out if a girl is actually beautiful or simply young. I figure it's okay for us to play this game seeing as we're so goddamn perfect our own selves. But the point is that some faces have a beauty that lasts. Others hit thirty and get plain overnight. Evelyn's beauty has longevity. She has fine features and the kind of clean neckline that people take photos of and show to their cosmetic surgeon. And it pains me to think of my mother's baby sister using her features to turn occasional tricks for beer money.

Evelyn flaps her lips. 'Vitamin shots? Spare me, Dan, okay. I been down that road a dozen times. All I need is a fifth. Maybe a coupla Percodan for this goddamn headache.'

I find myself losing patience faster than I normally would. Christ, I've been a bouncer half of my adult life. I deal with drunks on a daily basis. But this is Evelyn. Sweet, plucky Evelyn who's the image of my mother. So I slap the steering wheel with a palm and blurt: 'Pull yourself together, Aunt Evelyn. For Christ's sake, you're my mom's baby sister. You're the last of her.'

Evelyn laughs. No doubt she meets meaner characters than me in the gutter.

'Okay, nephew. Wow. I'm the last of her. That's deep or some shit. And here I was thinking I'm my own person.'

'That's not what I meant.'

'Relax, Danny. You could use a drink. What say we pull over and knock a couple back? Talk about the old days? You remember that thing with the ice pick?'

She has ruined that memory for me. Polluted it with her slovenly, alcoholic self.

Fecking alcoholics.

Selfish.

Disease, my arse.

'Please, Evelyn, just sit there, okay?' I am pleading now; funny how quickly it comes back. *Please, Dad. Just sit there. Let me make you a cup of tea.*

Evelyn tugs on her belt. 'I don't have much choice, do I, Dan? You kidnapping me?'

'Hey, you came to me, remember?'

'I thought we could hang out. Party a little, like we used to.'

Evelyn gave me my first sip of alcohol. Cooking sherry it was. Revolting stuff, but there was something glamorous about stealing it from the cupboard. The shine has worn off at this point. Nothing glamorous about a middle-aged woman with stains on her pants.

'You've partied enough. How did you find me?'

'Kept your postcards, Dan. Last one was from Cloisters.'

Ask a silly question. I bet my postcard pep-talks really helped Ev through withdrawal.

'So that's it? You're just working your way down the list?'

Evelyn finger-combs her matted hair in the visor mirror. 'Kid, you *are* the list.'

'So you don't need help?'

'Yeah, I need help, look at me. And I'll get it too, maybe in a couple of years. I still have some partying to do first.'

She rubs at some dry skin under one eye, then seems to notice that we're going somewhere. 'Dan, where are you taking me?'

'Home,' I say, hanging a right on to Central Park South.

I expect Evelyn to freak out, to scream and thrash in her seat, to curse her father's memory and swear that she'd rather be dead than set foot in that blasted apartment where her life was a cold hell on earth. But all she does is shiver like she just swallowed her first oyster, and say:

'Yeah, I guess.'

'You don't mind going back?'

'Nah, it's time. Edit is okay. And they have good booze up there. I heard stories, Dan. Stories about rich drunks who get their blood changed once a year. They can function, Danny. Run banks and all that stuff.'

I think maybe some of those functioning bankers were drinking meths these past few years.

'So why did you leave?'

Evelyn coughs for half a minute or so before answering. 'Leave? I was stupid, I guess. Poor little rich girl, right? I thought I knew about life, well I didn't know.'

I nod along to this. I have seen this sad story play out a dozen times; Rich kid thinks she has it tough, so lives on the credit card for a few years, then ends up with grazed limbs and blackouts. If she survives the cheap hooch, she runs back to the penthouse faster than you can say *delirium tremens*, which is also comically known as the Irish jig.

You know a country is in bad shape when they start naming alcohol-related illnesses after its inhabitants.

'To be honest, Dan,' says Evelyn, rubbing her nose with a sleeve, 'I don't remember why I left. Not specifically. I was always angry with Dad about something. Seemed important.'

We are stuck behind a horse and carriage loaded with tourists heading into the park. It always amazes me that people can do normal things when life-or-death stuff is happening not ten feet away. I remember seeing kids in the Lebanon playing mortar attack,

140

with shrapnel from actual mortar grenades, in a minefield, using blood from real corpses as fake blood.

Okay. Maybe not that last bit.

'Edit will look after you,' I promise Evelyn. 'It's time you got straight.'

'Tomorrow,' says Evelyn, and her eyes are flickering. 'I need a couple of shots of the good stuff first. Maybe a few hours' sleep. Tomorrow I'll go to the clinic.'

This is good enough for me. 'Okay. Tomorrow.'

Evelyn chuckles, and the decades of whiskey and smoke make her sound like an emphysemic octogenarian. 'Did you know Edit is ten years younger than me? My own stepmom. I wish she was a bitch, I really do, then you know, I'd have someone to blame besides myself. But she was cool. We never did too much group hugging in our family, but she was okay. Bailed me out a couple of times.'

The ultimate good deed in the eyes of a lush: bailout from the drunk tank.

Suddenly my eyes are watery and my laser focus is diffused by sentiment. This is happening to me more and more lately; a childhood memory bobs to the surface and gets me all mushy. I remember, back in Dublin, hiding out with Evelyn on the garage roof. She was teaching me how to roll a cigarette, which is a skill every kid should have in his arsenal, and I was thinking how she looked like my mom and I always wanted to marry my mom, but maybe I could marry Evelyn instead. So I said that to her, how we should get married, and she replied: *Sure, Danny. We can get married, but you gotta take it easy on my boobs, okay?*

Now look at the both of us: a drunk and a fugitive. Where did it all go wrong? Zeb has a saying for most occasions, and I think the most apropos one for this moment is: *Sometimes the ugly duckling don't turn into no swan, 'cause it's a fucking duck. And you know what happens to ducks? They get fucked.*

That's what we are, Ev and me, a couple of ugly ducklings. And I know what happens to ducks.

I like a nice four-star hotel, something minimal and modern where the plumbing hasn't had a chance to buckle under the onslaught. Five-star upscale joints usually bring on an attack of the unworthies. Especially ones like the Broadway Park House, an old-world Central Park South upscale joint with uniformed doormen shooting me the beadies the moment Evelyn and I are disgorged into the lobby by a revolving door. Smells like money in here; floor polish and whiskey fumes. Evelyn's nose goes up like a bloodhound's.

'Hey, Dan, you smell that?' she says. 'Why don't we—'

'No,' I say, cutting her off sharply. Whichever version of *just one drink* she is about to launch into, I've heard it before. I've heard them all.

Edit is pacing the lobby waiting, which is just as well because the doormen have formed a casual cordon around us and are getting set to tighten the noose. She catches sight of Evelyn and freezes like someone pulled her plug. It takes a few seconds to reboot, then she's across the shining floor and all over my aunt. Hugging her close, kissing her forehead. Evelyn grins and works her elbows like she's dislodging a puppy.

'I don't even really know this bitch,' she whispers to me between giggles.

If Edit hears this comment she doesn't let on, but after a few more seconds of flurried hugs and kisses, she backs off and straightens the skirt of her wraparound pattern dress which I happen to know, from watching the ruthless Joan Rivers eviscerate red-carpet celebrities on *Fashion Police*, is a Diane Von Furstenberg.

'Last season,' I say inanely. 'But an instant classic.'

'Thank you, Daniel,' says Edit, and I swear she is blushing a little, not because I noticed her dress but because she has let her emotions show in public. Getting emotional is anathema to the top one per cent. Nobody ever got rich by wearing a heart on their sleeve, unless it was someone else's heart. And this was especially true of Paddy Costello, who tried his darnedest to turn his kids into Vulcans and succeeded instead in pushing them somewhere to the left of Cheech & Chong.

Your mother is a whore, was my own father's comment on Mom's hippie politics. I remember him telling me in a bar, in front of all his drink buddies, *She screwed so many guys before you popped out, I ain't even sure you're mine*. Then he paraded the length of the bar collecting pound notes from all the soaks who bet him he couldn't make a tough little terrier like me cry. Pop was so thrilled with himself he even gave me one of the notes. I took it too, for my ice-pick fund. Screw him.

Terriers. *What a great show. What kind of moron cancels* Terriers?

Edit calms herself down with some yoga breathing and literally beams at me. Her teeth are white and even, like rows of Orbit spearmint, except for a slightly crooked fang. I read somewhere that orthodontists are leaving in a flaw these days for a more natural look.

'Daniel,' she says, shaking her head. 'I can't believe this is happening. You are my saviour.'

I am almost blushing myself. Edit is genuinely over the moon. There's no fakery here. I read people pretty good and my levels are all in the green with this woman. She may not be a straight shooter but she's shooting straight vis-à-vis Evelyn and myself.

'I didn't do anything,' I say, playing the *shucks ma'am* card. 'Just gave my aunt a ride home.'

Home. The words sets Edit off again. 'Yes, home. You are home, Evelyn. Please stay. Please. You are all I have. You too, Dan.'

I thought she'd never ask. 'Actually. I could use a hideout for a few days. My situation is complicated right now.'

'Of course. Of course. I have plenty of room. Stay as long as you need. In fact, longer than you need. Do you have any bags, Evelyn?'

Evelyn frowns. 'I had a trash bag full of stuff but the guy who rolled me in Queens took it, the bastard. What the hell does he need pantyhose for?'

Edit is confused. There are so many elements of her stepdaughter's statement that she can never relate to.

'Rolled you?' she says, almost afraid to ask.

Evelyn elaborates. 'Yeah. I had to do a little light hooking for beer money.' She winks. 'You know that story, right, Edit?'

One of the hovering bellboys snickers, and I decide this is the ideal moment to get my aunt squared away before both of us are tossed.

I take a good grip on Evelyn's belt and march her past the snickerer. 'Elevators back here, Edit?'

Edit's Louboutins (*Fashion Police*) tick tack the marble as she hurries to keep pace with my marching feet.

'Yes. Big golden doors. You can't miss them.'

That's not true. You could miss them. All the doors in this place are big and golden, even the restrooms. I take an educated guess and pick the set of golden doors with call buttons.

*　*　*

The Costello penthouse is more subtle now that Edit is pulling the curtain cords. I remember being here once before, the year before Dad introduced the family car to a concrete wall. I was fifteen and Mom brought me over for a reconciliation attempt. The logic being that I was the spitting image of Paddy himself as a young man and that gazing into the time-mirror might melt the ice packed around old man Costello's heart. Mom didn't really want to be there, but she didn't really want to be where she generally was either and so allowed Evelyn to talk her into coming over.

Father wants to see Dan, Evelyn had told us on her last visit. *Dan's a scrapper and you know Dad's a sucker for a spunky hardass.*

I remember sitting in the antechamber waiting for an audience feeling a little anxious about the phrase *spunky hardass*.

In those days, the Costello penthouse apartment was like something from the Acropolis, with honest-to-God Greek pillars and a couple of busts mounted on plinths. The decor was all from the testosterone school, including the mounted head of a twelve-point buck and a taxidermed mountain gorilla which was scaring the pants off me with its unblinking stare even though I knew its eyes were glass. I remember Mom hugging the gorilla and calling it Buttons, but that only made the thing creepier. If it had come alive at that moment and squashed her in its powerful black fingers I would not have been in the least surprised.

We were kept waiting for half an hour, then a light over the office door flashed green, which meant Mom was clear to enter.

She squeezed my hand and said, 'Okay, Dan, I'm going into the lion's den. Don't worry if you hear shouting. That's just how Paddy Costello communicates.'

Mom slipped inside, the double-height doors making her look elfin, and there was plenty of shouting, almost immediately. I

145

managed to contain myself until I heard the musical tinkle of breaking glass, then I thought *to hell with this* and barged into the sanctum.

I was feeling pretty good about myself in the role of protector. Only the previous week I had pushed my dad so hard that he cracked his spine on the tabletop, and I regularly messed up boys much older than me. Surely I could manage an old man.

Paddy Costello was not even the giant I had built him up to be, in fact I was half a foot taller than he was, but the guy had an energy coming off him in waves, an aura of harsh intimidation. He reminded me of a billygoat, with his spearhead Vandyke, wiry frame and wild darting eyes. Those eyes flitted from the trophy cabinet with its glass door, which had been shattered by the hurled book, to my mother, who huddled, scared, in a low wooden chair, then finally to me. The boy who had come to rescue his mother.

My grandfather spat on his own floor then pointed a stiff finger at me, as though I was to blame for the thrown book. I didn't know what to say to this old guy, I say old but I guess he was maybe fifty, but I needed something strong. My mouth went ahead of its own accord and said: 'Fuck you, old man.'

The *fuck you* didn't bother Paddy at all. It was the *old man* that riled him.

'Old? I could take your head off with a punch.'

I didn't bother responding to that challenge. I just arranged my feet the way my school boxing coach had taught me. Now either he would fight me or shut the hell up.

He did neither. Instead he chuckled, showing a mouth of craggy teeth, and crossed behind his desk to the trophy cabinet.

'Young Daniel. A chip off the Costello block, so they say. Seems like a day doesn't go by without someone filling my ears with stories of young Daniel.'

I did nothing but keep my eyes on him. Could be he was a tricky bastard.

'Daniel is bright and he's tough. Daniel could carry on the Costello business, if not the name.'

Paddy reached into the trophy cabinet, through the ring of jagged shards, ignoring the fresh cut on his index finger.

'Let me tell you something, Daniel,' he said, drawing out the book. 'I don't need someone to carry on my business or my name. I'm gonna live longer than a man has ever lived, and after that they'll put me into the ground. Then I could give a shit about the whole ball of wax. The whole world can go to nuclear hell and I won't know a thing about it. I regret nothing. There have been things I missed, but I ask no questions, because I have loved it, such as it has been.'

My mother once told me that her father only had two moods: bad and worse. I supposed that he was giving me a peek at worse.

Paddy thrust the book at me and I caught it on reflex.

'Here's a test for you, boy. That book is a signed first edition of *The Fountainhead*. You can sell it today for ten grand. There's a guy on Fifty-Ninth that would give you twelve. But if you hold on to it for a few years it could be worth ten times that. Choose wisely, boy, because this book is all you'll ever get from me.'

I looked down at the book with the spatter of his blood soaking into its leather cover, then at the man, my grandfather, who had given it to me. He wanted me to throw it back in his face, but I wouldn't, because when little Patrick was older, ten grand could get us to London. Far away from our father. I'd take Mom with me then, just as I would take her out of here now. So I said:

'You better take two steps back, old man, or you'll be going into the ground a lot sooner than you planned.'

He wasn't convinced I was serious, so I played the schoolyard trick of faking a punch. The old man wasn't used to that sort of behaviour. It had probably been a long time since someone faked out Paddy Costello, so he flinched and I laughed in his face. I saw in his eyes then that he would kill me if he could, right there in his office, and I knew I had sealed Mom's fate as an outcast, but there was no up side to being beholden to this man.

'Get out,' he spat. 'Take my . . . your mother with you. And do not ever come back.'

So I took my mother with me and I never came back. Until now.

And the book? I sold it the following day and hid the ten grand in the trunk of our car inside the first aid kit. It was incinerated when Dad rammed that wall.

I often remind myself that there are people worse off than me; in the Lebanon and so forth, or Calcutta. But on dark days, I can't help thinking that I've been cursed to live a certain kind of life. I try to take care of my friends and run a straight business, but instead I get people hurt or run foul of people who want to hurt me. Maybe I have some kind of dark destiny, or maybe that old maxim *the luck of the Irish* doesn't apply to me.

Years later, I spotted a second-hand copy of *The Fountainhead* at a stall on Mingi Street, the rambling souk adjacent to the UN HQ in Beirut. I tried to resist, but a person clings to anything with resonance in a war zone. So I paid my ten bucks and pocketed the paperback along with some editions of Will Eisner's *The Spirit*. I liked *The Fountainhead* fine, and I realised that Paddy Costello's whole *I regret nothing* speech was lifted from the book. I understood then that Gramps considered himself to be in the same principled genius bracket as Rand's architect Howard Roark.

When I hit on that notion, I laughed until tears rolled down my cheeks and the guy in the top bunk threated to smother me with his pillow. Of course I couldn't stop laughing then on principle, so there was a bit of argy bargy and I may have popped someone's shoulder out.

You might not believe it, but I like thinking about Grandad; it vindicates me for despising his ghost.

So anyways, Edit swipes us into the apartment, where every trace of Paddy Costello seems to have been replaced with stuff that Howard Roark might actually have approved of if he ever took a break from being noble. I don't know much about modern design but I bet most of the furnishings in here come from some Scandinavian store that ain't IKEA and the artwork looks so bovine and gloomy that it must be worth a fortune.

Evelyn is on her last legs; usually by this time in the evening she'd be keeping herself topped up with Everclear and getting set to commit to a major bender, but she hasn't had a drink in several hours and she's hurting. Edit leads us down a corridor longer than a subway car and into a guest bedroom that probably cost more to decorate than my entire club. Nice, though. Tasteful. Chocolate-brown rugs on golden wooden floors, and a king bed in the same colours set askew in the corner.

I lay Evelyn on the bed and she whimpers a little, begging me for a drink, and I can't help remembering how she used to be.

What's the word?

Vivacious.

Now she's a drunk, and drunks all have the same personality; a blend of cunning and pathetic. Evelyn looks pretty far gone in the face and it occurs to me that this beautiful room is going to look like a Portaloo exploded in here pretty soon. .

'She's bad,' I tell Edit. 'Running on fumes. It's gonna be a rough night.'

Edit sits on the bed and takes Evelyn's rough hand in her manicured fingers, and even that little snapshot tells a lot about how each woman spent the past decade.

'A doctor is coming, Evelyn. He'll make you feel better.'

'One drink,' Evelyn mumbles. 'I'm a goddamn heiress, aren't I?'

Aren't I? Ev's Manhattan/Hamptons accent is reasserting itself faster than that kid Shea jettisoned his.

'Of course you are,' says Edit soothingly and she gets in close to hug Evelyn tight, ignoring the grime compacted in the folds of her stepdaughter's clothing, ignoring the sour stale smell of alcoholism. 'Everything will be all right.'

When I said that, it sounded like Christmas cracker cliché, but when Edit says it, in her sing-song accent, it sounds true. I want to believe it myself.

Can everything be all right? Is that possible?

Edit offers Evelyn a couple of light sedatives and Evelyn gobbles them from her palm. You will never hear an addict ask *what's in that?* Whether it kills or cures doesn't really matter, as long as the edge is taken off. The mere fact that she has ingested a drug of some kind calms my aunt and she lies back on the bed, good-naturedly cursing us for arseholes until she nods off, snoring through a nose that looks like it may have been busted since I saw her last.

Only then does Edit allow her own shoulders to droop a fraction and the worry to show in her eyes.

'I've seen people come back from worse,' I say. 'She's got all her teeth, which is a good indicator. Once they lose their teeth there's not far to go.'

Edit shivers at the thought. In her ivory tower, people only lose teeth they don't like.

Then she laughs. 'You know what, Dan? I need a drink.'

I smile. 'You know what, Edit? Me too.'

I am surprised to find Buttons the gorilla still guarding the office door.

'I didn't figure you for a taxidermy girl,' I say, rubbing the big monkey's nose for luck.

Edit pushes through the doors. 'Buttons. Towards the end, he was all the company I had.'

I don't express my sympathies because I don't feel any. Edit is an okay lady, but she knew what she was getting into marrying a billionaire who could probably remember when Johnny Carson took over *The Tonight Show*. Sure, it cost her ten years of her life, but she came out of it pretty sweet.

Edit has left her mark on the office too. The trophy case has been replaced with a Japanese bamboo water fountain, and where Paddy's old desk used to squat now stands what looks like reclaimed railway sleepers on brushed steel legs.

I could never live here. Even the furniture has a philosophy attached to it. Trying to interpret the wallpaper would give me an aneurysm.

'Whiskey okay, Daniel? Irish, of course.'

'Of course.'

Edit pours a couple of generous shots from a bottle of Bushmills that looks nearly as old as I am.

'You better lock that cabinet when we're finished. Or better yet, have someone shift the entire cabinet out of here. Locking the door would only work for about ten seconds.'

Edit passes me a glass and we clink. 'You're right. Don't worry, Dan. I'm committed to this process. Evelyn will have the best treatment. No sending her away this time, I'll have her treated here.'

We sit on opposite ends of an L-shaped sofa with fake zebra cushions, our feet sinking into a patterned rug which is probably loaded with symbolism that I am too brutish to understand, and sip our velvety drinks in a civilised manner. I am so glad that Zeb is not here, as he would doubtless blanket-bomb this classy situation with crass comments in an attempt to get Edit to either sleep with him or lend him money.

Zeb told me once that society dames like to *fuck down*, as he called it. *Why else you think Rapunzel kept throwing her hair out the window? You honestly believe Prince Charming was the first swordsman up in that tower?*

When I was a kid I read 'Rapunzel' maybe a thousand times and that particular moral never occurred to me.

Something does occurs to me now. It took a while, but I am not accustomed to being around decent people.

'I admire you, Edit. What you're doing for Ev.'

My gran studies the pointed toes of her shoes. 'She's family, Dan. I'm all alone without her, and you too.'

'Maybe. But like she said, Evelyn's the heiress. She comes back and you're out of the driver's seat, right?'

Edit laughs. 'Oh God, no. I'm not that much of a do-gooder. Paddy was pretty hard on Evelyn. When she disappeared, he left everything to me, except a trust fund should his prodigal daughter ever come back. It's a big fund, don't get me wrong, but she's very much a guest in my home.'

This simple statement calms any niggling doubt I may have harboured about Edit. I think I've always been suspicious of saints. If I'd been Joseph the carpenter and the Virgin Mary had come home with the line that she'd been impregnated by the Holy Spirit, then Christianity would have gone a whole different way.

'I also should thank you for letting me stow away here for a few days. I'll be no trouble.'

'I know you won't, McEvoy.'

McEvoy?

What happened to Dan, Danny, Daniel, my hero?

Also a new tone, not hostile exactly, but definitely imperious. I suppose she's entitled.

'Don't worry, Edit,' I say, swirling what's left of my whiskey. 'I don't want to bring trouble to your door. Two days max and I'm out of here.'

'I'd say that's about forty-seven and a half hours too long for me, Mister McEvoy.'

I glance up from my sophisticated spirit-swirling to find Edit not even looking my way. She's got her BlackBerry out, searching for a number.

'What I said about Paddy leaving me the empire. That was true, but unfortunately thanks to this recession a lot of the businesses are pretty strapped at the moment. I can fix it, but I need a cash injection, which brings us to Evelyn's hefty trust fund.'

What's going on here? Edit is talking like a bitch now, but she can't be.

I read people.

'As for you. Evelyn phoned me a couple of weeks ago to ask for money. I tried to talk her in, but she wasn't ready. Said good old Daniel would sort her out.'

She finds the number and selects it. 'You know Paddy cut you off, right? But Ev was going to have the final laugh.'

Final laugh. It's grammatically correct, but not really in popular use. Edit slipped up there because she's Swedish. She would be so screwed for that in *The Great Escape*, if it was set in New York with American Nazis.

American Nazis? What is going on in my brain?

'Dear Aunt Evelyn put you in her will. If anything happens to her, you get the entire trust fund. Twenty-five million dollars.'

Twenty-five million dollars is always a nice thing to get in the post delivered by a stork, like babies.

'Luckily I've had two crooked policemen on my payroll since they worked in the city, so I sent them to pick you up and see if you knew where Evelyn was.'

The package. Evelyn was the package, not Mike's envelope. No wonder Fortz laughed when I claimed to have the package in my pocket.

'If not, they were supposed to kill you as a precaution,' continues Edit. 'And wait at your sleazy club for Evelyn to show.'

A precaution. Like a condom. We call those rubber johnnies in Ireland, which is pretty hard to take if your name is John, even harder if your name is Robert John.

'I am so glad you escaped from my pet policemen. I followed you from their torture room and it really has worked out perfectly. You brought Evelyn to my door. I cannot believe that. I should have hired you directly instead of Krieger and Fortz.'

Hey. Edit and I have people in common. She knows Fortz, I know Fortz.

'Whenever you're ready,' she says into the phone, and I know then that I'm screwed.

Or as Zeb would say: *more fucked than the chief fuckee of Fuckville during Fuckapalooza on the fuckteenth of Fuckuary.*

And worse, I've delivered Ev to the lion's den.

The lion's den with a gorilla in it. That's hilarious, so I laugh a little.

Edit laughs along with me.

'No,' she tells whoever's taking the call. 'I don't think he'll be any trouble now.'

There used to be a show on TV with that guy from *Oliver!* except he had a magic flute called Jimmy or Billy. Anyway it was a flute. There was big monster too but he was friendly. Genuinely friendly too, not like a grizzly bear who's gonna eat you as soon as his smaller food sources run out.

Balls. I've been drugged.

I'm on the main stage at Fuckapalooza.

Hello, Fuckville.

Focus, soldier. Rescue the civilian.

'I would prefer to just let you go,' said Edit. 'But Evelyn might refuse to change her will. Also, my little policemen don't want you and your big mouth on the loose. And they have been faithful and useful boys to me. So . . .'

I squint down at my feet and try to marshal them, but they seem so far away on long spindly legs that are definitely not mine. Some idiot has dropped a crystal tumbler and it tumbles down . . .

Of course it does. It's a tumbler.

. . . catching the light in its facets which is so beautiful that I want to cry.

What the hell did she give me?

I will have to rely on my trusty arms. I topple forward on to the rug, which I realise I can understand now.

Of course. It's so simple. The meaning of life is hidden in our fingerprints. All I have to do is take a photograph of my fingers and blow it up so I can read the whorls.

Edit lifts her feet daintily and swings them away from the broken glass, and over her shoulder I see the door open and Buttons the gorilla is standing in the doorway.

This sends me right back to my teen years, and I know Buttons heard me threaten his master and has been waiting for a chance to shut my mouth for good. I am suddenly more scared than I have even been. There is not a doubt in my addled head that Buttons intends to tear my head from its shoulders.

My life begins to flash before my eyes, which I do not want to happen because we all know what that means.

No. Not yet. I'm not ready yet.

The flashing continues regardless. I see my father stretching a Band-Aid across a cut on my knee, saying *good soldier, good soldier.* Did that happen? I don't remember him being human. There's Pat, my baby brother, with a pillowcase tied around his neck like a cape and the poker in his hand for a sword. He's going to catch a belt later for getting coal dust all over his clothes. I want to warn him, but my lips are sealed. I'm in the car now, on that last fateful journey, and I see for the first time that the only reason I'm alive is because the rear window was open to let out Dad's cigarette smoke. I hear the screech of the tyres and see the wall rush at our puny vehicle and Mom's hair fan out like it's underwater. I reach for Pat but he is ragdoll dead and I am flying.

Buttons shambles into the room and I see a smaller figure behind him that could be Tarzan or maybe Mowgli. I am afraid to look and I am frozen by chemicals but I see that Buttons has some kind of blackjack in his hand. He squats before me and I see the gorilla is wearing shoes.

'Don't do it here,' says Edit to the gorilla. 'I don't want any evidence if his cop friend comes looking.'

'Remember this, McEvoy?' asks the gorilla, dangling the club before my face. 'Every cop in the state knows what you did to me with this fucking thing.'

I have no clue what Buttons is talking about. I never touched him with a big dildo.

Buttons pulls his arm back, and I hear his laboured breath burr in my ear.

'Now it's your turn,' he says, and I close my eyes.

I read people pretty good, right?

CHAPTER 7

In every noir book I ever read there's a bit about the guy, the gumshoe, coming to after a beating. I never liked those passages because some of those scribes put their shit together pretty good, and it all gets a little close to the bone for a guy like me who's been clipped enough times to move down a bracket on the IQ scale. I'd swear I was a gifted kid; now I'm barely average thanks to Tasers, rubber bullets, spiked drinks, steel-toecapped boots and now a goddamn dildo. There was also a time with high heels and a spiral staircase but I don't know anyone well enough to tell them that story. And I will never go to a hypnotist's show just in case I might let it slip.

You come out of it different each time. Fast or slow. Easy or so damn hard you want to be dead. Sometimes the pain is so massive, so *everything*, that you feel it can no more come to an end than the universe itself. This is gonna be one of those times, I just know it. Drugs with a side of dildo? There is no way this is gonna be anything but a nightmare.

I feel myself surfacing and part of me is glad not to be dead, but most of me wants to stay down here in the cool dark and have no network for a while. My subconscious is running the show at the moment, though, and picks up on some red flags that need my immediate attention, and so sends me surging towards consciousness like an oxygen-starved swimmer pulling for the surface.

I hear a screeching noise that could be a large bird, something from the Amazon maybe, and my body is being vigorously shaken. Am I riding some huge Amazonian bird? Could that be it? How has my life arrived at this point? I stop worrying about the bird when I realise that I can't breathe. Imagine the panic our friend the oxygen-starved swimmer would feel if he broke the surface only to find no breathable air in the atmosphere. That is how I feel. Panic and pain are my motivators. How could I not have realised how happy I was back then, in the past, when I could breathe freely and there was no constant pain?

My eyelids open themselves, allowing my eyeballs to swell and bug out. No photos, please. I am in the back of a car which is skidding sideways towards a cowboy cushion on the freeway. The screeching is the protests of four melting tyres that were not designed for lateral hops. There are two familiar-looking heads in the front and they are howling in panic, slapping at each other like kindergarten girls in a yard fight, as if that can help. The side windows are filled with the elevated grille of the Hummer that has rammed us. I don't even know who's trying to kill me now. Probably everybody in both vehicles.

I do not give two shits about any of this. All I want to do is breathe. This is beyond a joke. Why can I not breathe?

I paw at my throat with handcuffed hands to find a seat belt cinched tight across my Adam's apple.

It's probably the belt across your windpipe that is stopping you breathing, genius.

And why am I handcuffed? Did Buttons handcuff me?

The belt is tight across my chest like a Band-Aid and I can't get a finger under it, so now I have a dilemma: leave the belt on and suffocate, or take it off and be killed on impact. Is this Murphy's Law or Hobson's Choice or Catch 22? I can never distinguish between those three. Murphy's Law has something to do with potatoes, I'm pretty sure about that. If this run of bad luck continues, they might have to coin a phrase in my honour, posthumously of course.

Daniel's Dilemma.

Catchy.

Got a ring to it.

Screw it. I have to breathe. My fingers crab down towards the safety buckle but the choice is taken from my hands when the car crashes into the impact barrel, smashing the barrel flatter than an unassembled coffee table, sending water seething through the cracks with enough force to fracture the side windows. The safety belt holds, but cuts through my clothing to the skin below. My shirt pocket bursts into flame and I cannot understand why until I remember the book of matches I keep in there to light the tipped cigars Zeb and I smoke to celebrate staying alive for another week. Is the matches' flaring symbolic somehow? I am showered with glass and water, which is painful, but at least the fire goes out. Every cloud, as they say.

I am held in place by the belt but I still cannot bloody breathe. For feck sake. Gimme a bloody break. God, Buddha, Gandhi, Aslan. Whoever. I remember that I have hands, and so when the body of the car settles on its buckled chassis and stops moving, I unsnap the buckle, slide across the seat and draw a greedy breath that feels like I'm swallowing glass, but I don't care. My brain was seconds away from starvation and I do not have spare brain cells to lose. I breathe again, deeper, and feel my panic subsiding. Confusion quickly fills the vacuum.

What is happening?

What part of my life is this?

Am I in Ireland or the Lebanon or Jersey?

I do not know exactly who the guys in the front are, but I imagine they were planning on doing me harm, so I am glad to see that they are not moving, their heads enveloped by the mushroom sprawl of airbags. Maybe they didn't survive. I think I am safe enough, conscience wise, to hope they didn't.

So this is a rescue? Could that be it? My friends have grouped together, pooled their resources and come to save me.

Doubtful. Do I have friends? No one springs to mind. Something about Madonna and the Bee Gees.

Two dead now. Tragic, what a band.

There is a horrendous creaking of twisting metal as the Hummer backs up a few feet, taking the side door with it.

I hope this is a rental, I think unkindly. *So those two bent cops will be hit with the bill.*

Cops? They're cops. I remember that now. Krieger and Fortz.

A shadow falls across me and I am relieved to see a human framed by a doorway which until recently had a door in it. I am relieved because the figure is human and not simian, though it is wearing an Obama mask.

Simian? Buttons. That couldn't be real.

The figure moves quickly, leaning in and grabbing fistfuls of my lapels.

My saviour, I try to say, but there is something hard in my mouth so I let it dribble on to my lap.

A tooth. One of my molars. All those years flossing, wasted. And I hate flossing too.

The guy is familiar.

'Thanks for rescuing me,' I say; well, you don't want to be rude.

'This ain't no fuckin' rescue, retard,' says a familiar voice.

Freckles. I remember.

Friend or foe?

Foe. Most definitely.

I spit out a lump of bloody gum. 'Freckles. I was rooting for you, dude.'

He drags me out of the car, gets up real close.

'Don't call me Freckles,' he says. 'My boss calls me Freckles and guess what? I *am* the boss now.'

It's a reasonable request. 'No problem. What do I call you?'

Freckles hustles me to the blacked-out Hummer. The freeway is quiet, so it must be very late or very early. Regardless, it won't take the blues more than a minute or two to get here, and a bashed-up Hummer won't be so hard to spot. I can see the Silvercup sign near the off ramp. There can be only one.

'You can call me Mister Toole.'

He has got to be joshing. 'Your name is Tool?'

Freckles hoists me so we're nose to nose. 'That's right. Ben Toole.'

Sometimes you gotta laugh, even though it could get you killed. 'Bent Tool? Get the feck out. What is wrong with parents?'

Ben blushes with rage and his freckles disappear. 'Ben . . . Toole. With an E.'

I am still not altogether together, if you know what I mean. My face feel like it's been flayed, my body is for shit, but I think it's important to keep the conversation going.

'Everyone knows there's an E in Ben, Freckles. I'm not a fecking tool . . . No offence.'

Freckles jabs me in the solar plexus, which is probably doing some damage but my pain levels are so off the scale that the blow doesn't even register.

'The E is in Toole. At the end.'

I get it. 'Oh, like O'Toole, without the O.'

This apparently is a vowel too far for Freckles, because he howls with that particular anguish brought on by decades of taunting and bundles me into the back of the Hummer. I get an upside-down glimpse of the driver and it's the kid, Shea.

I am confused.

Freckles climbs in behind me and slams the door.

'Did you see that, Ben?' asks the kid. 'I nailed those fucking cops. I fucking crushed them. Who's a college boy now? Who's got soft hands now?'

And then, I cannot believe this, they actually high-five each other. These guys are tight. It's like they watched *Sesame Street* and learned all about tolerance and seeing the other person's point of view.

Shea jerks a thumb towards me. 'Tell me we're going to torture this motherfucker, old school.'

Bent Tool pulls off his mask and knuckles me in the temple. 'You know it, kid. Old school.'

Old school? I remember when Run DMC were old school; now it's torturing the Irish guy.

Fecking old school, hummus-eating, Catch Murphy's 22 bullshit.

Shea follows Freckles' directions and pulls the Hummer into a chop shop two blocks back from Javits. I always wondered who had the brilliant notion to drop the city's biggest convention centre in this neighbourhood. Every year dozens of accountants and IT guys get themselves in hot water because they take the wrong cross street on the way back to their midtown Holiday Inn. The lucky ones get a couple of taps and their wallets lifted; the unlucky ones end up hooked on smack. I heard a rumour of a pimp who runs a speciality stable of ex-librarians that he picked off from the pack and turned out. Probably an urban myth.

I take advantage of the drive to pull myself together a little, and by the time Freckles hauls me out of the vehicle I am pretty certain that I was not handcuffed by a gorilla. On the negative side, whatever Edit gave me is wearing off and I realise that I am just about the most messed up I have ever been. My bruises have got bruises and those bruises have got welts, and don't even get me started on the lacerations. I reckon my left ear is cauliflowered for good and one of my eyes has a weird shelf above it that doesn't feel like any swelling I've ever had.

What I am is past caring.

If it was up to me, I would throw in the towel right now and spare myself the rest of this shitty day.

Freckles jostles me across the factory floor, which is occupied by luxury sedans mainly, but with a couple of cannibalised mopeds lying around like busted Terminators. There's a grease monkey in Texaco overalls poking around in the guts of a yellow cab, but he doesn't even take his head out from under the hood. I guess whatever goes down in here, he doesn't want to witness it.

With rough encouragement from the barrel of Freckles' pistol I stumble through an oil puddle to an office area which has been blocked off by a rank of filing cabinets on one side and a dirty partition on the other. Freckles sits me down in a plastic chair which squeaks with fright under the sudden trauma of bearing my weight. He never takes his gun off me for a second.

Shea follows and takes a moment to study a wall-mounted Miss July 1972 who is holding a wrench and biting her bottom lip like holding wrenches is pretty stressful.

'What the hell did you do to those cops, McEvoy?' asks Shea, when he is done with ogling. 'Whatever it was, they took it real personal.'

'I did a number on them with a dildo,' I say, which is about the strangest statement I'm ever likely to make. I don't elaborate because I can't. I only got enough energy for breathing. I try to speak any more and I could asphyxiate.

This suits Edward Shea just fine, because even though the whole dildo thing is an incredible conversation starter, he wants to get back to his favourite subject: himself.

'I bet you weren't expecting to see me again, huh, McEvoy?' he says, perching on the corner of the desk. And he's right, I would have bet big money on long odds that this particular fly was out of my ointment.

'Yeah, I bet you thought that the Shea kid was sleeping with the fishes.'

I nod, and it hurts my brain but it's easier than talking.

Did he really just say sleeping with the fishes?

'You wanna know what went down after you set us up to kill each other?'

I don't want to know. Why doesn't this kid just go play with himself or wait in line somewhere to buy *Call of Duty*?

Wait! I do want to know.

I can't nod any more, so I blink. Once for yes.

Shea starts talking without even registering my blink signal. Why would you ask a person if he wants to know something if you're just going to go ahead and tell them regardless? Between that and the hummus, I am running out of things to like about this kid.

'You did us a real favour, McEvoy,' says Shea. 'We've been bitching and sniping between ourselves since Dad died. Ain't that right, Benny T?'

Benny T? Who the hell is Benny T?

'That's right, Shea-ster,' says Freckles, flushed with pride at hearing his new Mafia-type handle.

I don't believe it, these dicks are celebrating their new partnership with buddy names.

Shea-ster and Benny T?

Just fecking kill me now.

'But now we been through shit together. That shit bonded us, McEvoy. You left us with two guns on the table, remember?'

I blink once.

'So the elevator closes and we all dive in scrabbling, but not Benny T because he's got a weapon on his ankle.'

Crap. I was so busy congratulating myself on setting up the big bloodbath that I forgot to check for concealed weapons.

'So Benny bends over and comes up loaded.'

'And I don't know who to shoot,' says Ben Toole, laughing a little rueful like he just discovered he was wearing odd socks.

'Yeah. He don't know who to shoot. Cracks me up.'

'And I sure underestimated this guy,' says Benny T, punching Shea's shoulder.

'The guy you leg-shot was hobbling to the door, so it was just the movement really. I saw him go and shot him.'

'Right in the heart,' says Shea. 'And from behind with a moving target, that's a hell of a shot.'

I want to point out that the hell of a shot was like three and a half feet, and a chimp with one eye could've made it, but I don't say any of this because it would cost too much and the comment ain't funny enough to warrant more suffering.

'So then the other guy, Frank? Yeah, Frank. He goes for the table and I wing him. I'm just fucking shooting at this point. Ain't got a strategy as such.'

Shea takes up the thread. 'So he goes down, screaming so fucking much he's gonna wake up the building. Freckles . . . I mean Benny T goes around the table to finish him off.'

'I'm not even factoring in the kid,' says Ben. 'Fuck the kid is what I'm thinking. I got time to spare now. But he showed me. You got some stones on you, Shea-ster.'

Maybe making these two hold hands was a mistake.

'I go for a gun,' says Shea. 'And when Benny gets around the far side of the desk, he finds to his surprise that I'm covering him and he's covering me.'

'This guy. This guy right here. Steady as a rock. He's facing down Benny T, who ain't got such a shabby rep, and not a fucking shake to be seen. You gotta respect that.'

Yeah, like I gotta respect musical theatre.

Actually that's not fair. I enjoyed the shit out of *Rock of Ages*.

'So we stay like that for a coupla minutes,' continues Shea. 'And it occurs to me that I haven't a fucking clue how to run the practical side of Dad's company.'

Benny laughs his fond laugh again. 'And it goes without saying that I ain't no books person.'

I think using the phrase *no books person* pretty much guarantees that you aren't one.

'So the kid walks around the desk and calm as you like puts two into the guy I clipped, finishes him off. Now we got stuff on each other, see?'

I figure Shea's dad must have been an ungodly arsehole and Ben never had any kids. It's like they have a second chance at life. I bet they got autumn-hued plans for kite-flying and shit.

'We got a bond now,' says Shea. 'A blood bond. We are two sides of the same coin.'

'This arsehole is probably wondering how we found him,' says Freckles.

To be honest, the arsehole is past caring. They found me, and knowing how they did it won't make me any less found. Actually, if they hadn't found me, I'd be dead by now.

'My car has GPS, moron,' says Freckles, knuckling my head like I'm stupid. 'I called the monitoring company and they told me where it was parked. We was staking out the hotel garage when the two cops came out and rolled you into the back of their cruiser. I oughta thank them really. Taking bodies out of hotels is a bitch.' He winks at Shea. 'As we know only too well, right, Shea-ster?'

'You got it. Benny T. I'm gonna feel it in my quads tomorrow.'

'These fucking kids,' says Bent Tool. 'Fucking quads and shit. I gotta whole new lingo to learn.'

'That's so wac,' I grunt, giving him his first lesson.

Shea pats himself down until he finds an energy bar and I think, *No, don't start eating.*

But he does, right up in my face. Making a gooey paste of the bar, smacking his beard-rimmed fleshy lips, which from this angle, God forgive me for even thinking it, look a bit like a pussy.

I think about head-butting Shea, but then I might get some of his crud on my face, so I hang my head low and wait for this to be over. He's still chewing, I can hear it.

'I went through your pockets, McEvoy,' says Freckles. 'Took back what was mine. Checked your calls. Seems the only text you sent to Mike was a confirmation that the kid was dead. Is that all Mikey knows?'

'Everyone knows,' I manage to splutter. 'I got a friend in the cops.'

'Nah,' says Freckles. 'Bullshit. You were trying to buy a little time. If I know Mike, he's out in what the fuck is it? Cloisters? Celebrating. Tying one on. For the next coupla days Irish Mike Madden, the double-crossing arsehole, is wide open. And let me tell you, I'm gonna drive a spike straight up that open arsehole.'

Normally I would not be too broken up at the idea of someone lethal paying Mike a visit, but then it occurs to me that I will be extremely dead before that happens, plus Zeb could be at Mike's too. Though if Zeb suffered a flesh wound or lost half a testicle I wouldn't be all that upset.

'I swear,' I say. 'I put the word out. You guys are fugitives.'

Shea buys it. 'We're fugitives, Benny.'

Freckles, the pro, ain't in the market for bullshit. 'My guy tells me there's nothing on the scanners or the website. Not a dicky. But just to be sure, we hang on to this guy for a few hours in case we need a hostage. I reckon if we ain't heard anything by morning, then we're in the clear.'

'So all we gotta do is wait until the cab is ready and have a few of the boys take you for a little drive.'

Freckles is an old hand at the body disposal racket. He won't shoot me here 'cause of me being a hefty sonuva bitch and it would take six of them to carry the dead weight. So they got a tricked-out death cab. I've seen these hearses in the Lebanon. I remember we seized a bog-standard-looking Renault one time to find the trunk all wired up with a freezer box for body parts. Freckles' boys will

169

transport me in the taxi, then make me climb down into a dug grave and shoot me on site. Makes sense. That's what I'd do too if I was a cold-blooded killer; maybe roll Krieger and Fortz in there for good measure and a couple of animal parts just to screw with the crime lab. And if I had a spare minute I'd scrawl a few verses of Klingon poetry on Shea's forehead with a Sharpie. I could tie up Homeland for months.

'Come on, Benny T,' says Shea then, and I swear his voice doesn't sound like it's broken yet. Maybe it's the excitement. 'Let's do it. Me and you.'

This is a step too far.

Oh, wait. Maybe I've misunderstood.

'Let's finish the job, T. We can kill this fucking mook. Me and you.'

Thank Christ. The kid just wants to kill me personally.

'I don't know,' says Freckles. 'This guy is a handful and I don't want you getting hurt.'

'Come on, Benny.' The kid is pleading now, like he wants to break Santa's rules and open a present on Christmas Eve. 'Tomorrow I'm back to the corporate life, but tonight I wanna be a gangster, like you.'

Shea makes a good argument. Presents it well. He totally sealed the deal with the *like you* there at the end. I bet he was on the debating team at Harvard.

'How can I turn down that face? Look at this guy, McEvoy. We're gonna run this town.'

I got the strength for nothing, but my body jerks spasmodically of its own accord and Bent Tool takes it as acknowledgement.

'You're gonna be Edward Shea's first execution, not counting the guy who was already winged. That's a great honour.'

Fab. Triffic. Can't hardly wait.

Thank you, Fuckapalooza. It's been a trip.

I must be in shock, or maybe whatever sedative Edit snuck into the whiskey is still in my bloodstream, because I'm taking all this impending death stuff very placidly. I'm vaguely aware that I don't want to die tonight, but I can't seem to muster much enthusiasm for the idea. I know this kind of torpor, this leaden lethargy, is a common symptom of PTSD, but I ain't PTS yet, I am smack bang in the middle of TS right bloody now. I reckon maybe the S from the last PTS is just kicking in. So what I'm feeling now is a result of the torture video. I really hope that Krieger and Fortz get shot making a break for Mexico. Ain't it funny that I feel stronger about them dying than me living?

Just in case there are a few folks who are unaware what the letters PTSD stand for, I can tell you that it ain't, as my buddy Zeb once suggested, Prison Twinks Suck Dick, though I gotta say I did laugh at that, which wasn't very enlightened of me. Zeb made the whole thing into a running joke. After I dragged him to Broadway with me to see that *Rock of Ages* show, he claimed to be suffering from post-dramatic stress disorder. I thought that was a bit forced.

They leave me alone for a few hours, popping in every now and then to make sure I am still tethered to the radiator with a chain they had handy that looks like it came north on the underground railroad a couple of centuries ago. I feel guilty for not attempting to escape but I simply ain't got the resources. I been knocked out twice, beaten with a frankly embarrassing blackjack and rammed with a Hummer. That's gotta be some kind of record.

So I sleep on the floor, and even the fact that I'll be taking a one-way trip when I wake up cannot keep me from passing out. I read an article in Simon Moriarty's waiting room once that said your subconscious already holds the key. Whatever the question is, you already have the answer inside you. So maybe my inner self is gonna pipe up with the key to this dilemma. I'll tell myself something I don't know. That would be really nice, 'cause generally all my subconscious does is give me phobias and behavioural tics. The trick is to wake up and shout the first word that comes to mind. It's called auto-manifestation or, to quote Zebulon, *a crock of psycho bobbemyseh*. I don't know what bobbemyseh means exactly, but I imagine it ain't complimentary. Good things rarely come in crocks.

I dream a little in those few fitful hours but that doesn't enlighten me any, unless good old Dad wrapping my head in duct tape saying *good soldier, good soldier* is the answer to the world's prayers.

Daddy dreams are a staple in my repertoire of nightmares, but this one is even creepier than usual and kicks my arse straight back to consciousness. I sleep-jerk myself awake to find the Shea-ster and Benny T gazing down at me, cracking up like I'm Louis C.K. on his best night ever.

'What did you say, McEvoy? Did you say what I think you said?'

Oh shit. What did I say?

'Motherfucker said *fluffer*,' says Freckles. 'Fucking *fluffer*.'

Shea draws breath. 'I gotta hand it to you, McEvoy. Ten minutes from grisly death and still thinking with your dick. Maybe you are as stupid as you pretended to be.'

Fluffer? I don't get it.

'Fluffer?' I say, relieved to be able to speak. 'Definitely fluffer? Not suffer, or even mother?'

Freckles shakes his big pumpkin head. 'Nah, it was fluffer, McEvoy. I heard that term often enough to know.'

Fluffer? Why does my subconscious have to be so vague?

Overalls guy is wiping down the taxi's trunk with a rag when I am escorted into the bay, flanked by Shea-ster and Benny T, or as I like to think of them Pussy Lips and Blood Spatter.

'We good?' asks Shea.

The guy nods and tosses him the keys. 'All good, Mister Shea. Just to remind you, we need her back later for the Albanians.'

Freckles closes his eyes, frowning. 'Fuck, I forgot about those assholes. Where are we putting them?'

'With the Russian guys, I think.'

'Oh, the Connecticut farm?'

'Nah, the recent Russians.'

Freckles types a reminder into his phone. 'Okay, the industrial park. I got it. You get backed up, you know?'

Shea is sympathetic and I think these two have a real chance of making their relationship work.

'Tough at the top, partner,' says the kid.

'Hey, at least we can share the burden.'

Freckles and Shea are being so sunny and optimistic that surely fate will drop the hammer on them soon.

Maybe I am the hammer. Why not, I was the stone earlier.

That's a nice thought.

Overalls skedaddles and Freckles pops the trunk. 'Okay, McEvoy. In you hop.'

I haven't decided whether I will meekly lay down or make them shoot me for spite. As it happens, the choice is taken away from me.

'Ain't no way I'm fitting in there,' I say. 'I think someone forgot to take care of business.'

The trunk has been converted to a large freezer and is packed to the rim with body parts wrapped in bags. I recognise KFC's face with its second skin of white plastic.

'Bloody hell fuckballs,' says Freckles. 'These were supposed to be taken care of.'

Fuckballs. Nice.

Shea pokes the ice, looking for space. 'No way this Chewbacca-looking motherfucker is going in there. It's so hard to find good help these days.'

I think it only fair to point out: 'You had good help, Shea-ster. And you shot them.'

Shea is embarrassed that his criminal empire is coming across a little half-arsed.

'Shut up, McEvoy. What's going on, Benny T? Who takes care of dumping the bodies?

Freckles points at KFC's head. 'This guy. Usually.'

'I think I see what happened here,' I say, half expecting a pop from Freckles, but he is busy placating Shea.

'Don't worry, partner. Maybe can do the whole lot in one run. It's a bit risky having McEvoy in back, but we could drive to the park, dump the frozen meat and we're back here in an hour. And after that, I am gonna treat you to the best breakfast in New York.'

'You talking about Norma's?' I ask.

'You know it,' says Freckles. 'You ever have the pancakes there?'

'I love those things.' I nod at Shea. 'Listen to this guy, forget the hummus for one day. Live a little.'

'Shit,' says Shea. 'Now I'm excited. Let's get this show on the road so I can order me a mountain of pancakes.'

And in this sneaky fashion, I have Pussy and Spatter visualising breakfast so clearly that they lower their guard a little and load me into the back seat when what they should have done was made two runs.

I got a chance now.

Freckles hooks the chain of my handcuffs over a custom karabiner set into the metal-framed back of the front seats and screws it tight.

It occurs to me that I should have kept my mouth shut. I had a much better chance of escaping if I was left here under guard while Freckles did the run with the first load of bodies, instead of being shackled in the back seat.

Balls.

Thanks for the help, subconscious.

Fluffer.

Fluffer.

I turn the word over in my head, hoping for the light-bulb moment.

What does a fluffer do? She fluffs before a shoot.

So they're gonna shoot me, should I fluff something?

Freckles is driving the cab along the river. The grey tsunami of the USS *Intrepid* looms over us and I can see Union City across the water, its night lights like one of Spielberg's mother ships. I never thought I would pine for Jersey, but right now those lights are like the promise of safety. At least over there I would have a decent chance of surviving the day, but we've passed the tunnel now, so I guess the day's gruesome business will be conducted on this side of the Hudson.

I call out to my captors. 'Hey, guys. Can you hear me?'

There's a sheet of reinforced glass between us with a tiny sealed hatch in the centre. I can see the guys talking but I can't hear a word, but obviously they can hear me 'cause Freckles presses a button on the dash and his voice crackles over the speaker system.

'What is it, McEvoy? You wanna go potty? Why don't you save it for when the kid plugs you. Your bowels are gonna empty anyhow.'

Shea is intrigued. 'He's gonna crap himself?'

'Sure. There's a good chance. Guys often let go. I've seen the strangest shit with corpses. Coupla guys got boners.'

'What? The guys doing the shooting?

'No. The guys who got shot. Dead as fucking doornails, sporting a bugle.'

'That is some gross shit, Benny T. Boners, oh my God.'

Seeing as they're already talking about boners, I decide to make my fluffer pitch.

'I just wanted you to know that I'm open to offers at this point. Sincerely. You saw what I can do back in the Masterpiece. I could be a real addition to your organisation.'

Shea claps his hands, delighted. 'This is unbelievable. I am genuinely incredulous.'

Of course you're incredulous, arsehole. That's because it's unbelievable.

I do not voice this aloud, as now is not a good time to further antagonise Shea.

When he finishes laughing, Freckles explains my motivation. He forgets to switch off the speaker so I hear the whole thing.

'Y'see, this is typical death's door behaviour. This guy is desperate now. He's even offering to work for the guys he humiliated yesterday. Anything to get him off that hook.'

'This happens all the time?'

'Oh sure. I had an Italian guy once offered me his daughter if I'd cut him loose.'

'Did you take the deal?'

'Nah. Cut his throat like a pig. Then I visited the daughter anyway.'

'Those Italians are badasses, right?'

Freckles shrugs. 'Once upon a time, maybe, but they spent too long at the top. Gone a little doughy, you know what I mean?'

'Sure. Doughy. Dad never told me none of this stuff. So which guys are the toughest?'

Listen to this kid. Like anyone's tougher than a bullet. Still, Freckles considers the question, doing this weird sucky squeaky thing between his lips that would be enough to get him punched in the face under different circumstances.

'As an individual, one person per se,' says Freckles when he's completed his squeaky thought process. 'I am the toughest individual in this city. You cross Benny T and I will hunt you down like a fucking dog. But as a group. Collectively per se. I'd have to say the Russians are the toughest bastards around. Those guys come outta some real hardship. Fuckin' Siberia. I seen pictures. They ain't scared of nuthin'. Micks and spics. They shit 'em. And I say that as a fifty–fifty Mick 'n' spic. I got Latin blood though it don't show.'

That's a lotta per se's for one statement.

'You a Latin scholar, Benny?' I can't help asking.

'I told you already: I got Latin blood. Here's another phrase for you regarding me humping your momma. *Vidi vici veni*. I saw, I conquered, I came. You can take that to the grave. Fuckin' fluffer, you sad sack of shit. Hey, maybe your mom was a fluffer.'

While they are cracking themselves up, I get it. It comes back to me.

Fluffer. Holy shit.

* * *

It's pretty quiet on 12th Avenue this early in the morning. It's that moral twilight between the hours of thievery and joggery. Freckles has got maybe thirty minutes to do his business before the ferries start chugging in, dumping their cargo of white-collar office civilians on to the island. There ain't a ray of sunlight yet, but the night is holding its breath, waiting for daytime to paint the high rises red. While Freckles is entertaining young Edward Shea with gruesome war stories, I have an exchange with my sub-conscious.

Where did you see a fluffer recently?

The porn house.

And what did she give you besides advice on penis enlargement pills?

A key for cop cuffs.

And what are you wearing now?

Cop cuffs.

What happened to that key?

I tucked it into the thong, because you never know, right?

So go fish in your thong for the key already, moron.

When are you going to stop being such a tool?

One second after you stop being such an idiot.

Gombeen.

Shitehawk.

I got a key in my thong, and as soon as I remember that, I feel the metal digging into my stomach. It's a step in the right direction having a key and so forth, but there's still a long way to go. Even if I slip these cuffs, I gotta get out of the cab and deal with Spatter and Pussy up front.

First things first. Get outta these shackles.

I knock on the glass with my forehead. 'Hey, kid. Do me a favour. Scratch my balls.'

Ain't a man alive who can ignore a request like this, rife as it is with such potential for hilarity.

The kid's jaw literally drops. 'Scratch your . . . Are you serious?'

'Come on, Shea. I'm trussed up here like the baby Jesus in his swaddling clothes.'

Freckles frowns, upset by my choice of words. 'Aw, come on, McEvoy. Why you gotta bring Jesus into it?'

'I'm tryin' to convey how itchy my balls are.'

'You should know better than to invoke Jesus, man. Our countrymen been killing each other for seven hundred years over shit like that.'

Now Freckles has developed some kind of political conscience. I guess it's all right to plug your fellow man so long as baby Jesus ain't invoked anywhere in the process.

'Also, maybe you got ball rot or something,' adds Shea. 'You think anyone is gonna touch your sack?'

Freckles nods wisely. 'I know what this is. When did your symptoms manifest, McEvoy?'

Never, I think, but I answer: 'I dunno. Last thirty minutes, maybe.'

'I thought so,' says Freckles, smacking the wheel. 'That itching is all in your head.'

I say the obvious: 'Actually, I'm pretty sure it's in my balls.'

'Nah, it's psychosomatic. A death's door ailment. I seen this shit before. A guy realises he's about to get his ticket punched and his body reacts by throwing up weird symptoms, takes his mind off it, see?'

Shea is nodding along, intrigued. If he had some paper, he'd be taking notes.

'Hey, Benny T. These are my balls and they feel like some malicious fecking goblin scuffed them lightly so they'd scab over, then dipped them in pepper. So, until we're talking about your balls, keep your shrinkifying to yourself.'

'Shrinkifying?' says Shea. 'Is that a word?'

'No. But it should be.'

'Bottom line,' says Freckles. 'We ain't scratching your balls. Maybe, if you ask real nice, the Shea-ster can shoot you in the crotch, which might alleviate it some.'

Shea slaps his knee, enjoying the hell out of his day. 'Consider it done,' he says.

'Please, guys,' I beg, tugging on my cuffs. 'I can't reach and I don't wanna go out with jock itch.'

Freckles laughs. 'That is indeed a pathetic way to go.'

And he shuts off the speaker.

Now I got licence to root around in my own underwear.

I played those fools. Played myself right into the back of a death cab on the way to my own hole in the ground. Ain't I the genius?

Actually, with KFC and that other guy in the trunk, I might not even merit my *own* hole.

And that is depressing.

I think my balls actually are itching.

I grind myself right up on the glass partition, trying to get a hand down my pants. Through the crook of my arm I notice we are off 12th and down by the river. I see that weird-looking melted pier, an altar to scores of busted planks and rotting tyres heaped at its base. I always used to wonder about that pier when I drove past, what its story was and so forth. Now I probably won't ever know.

Tragic, right? A man goes to his grave without comprehensive pier knowledge.

So anyways, I'm basically humping the partition trying to get at the key and Freckles turns the speaker back on so's I can hear them laughing. It's not like they need to worry, right? Freckles frisked me pretty good, even gave my privates a decent squeeze. So, they're cocksure I ain't armed. But I got a key and my hand is only a coupla inches away.

Ha. Wait. That pier collapsed from pier pressure.

Zing.

In your face, Zebulon. That is a genuine joke. I could send it in to Ferguson. Always the cautious optimist, I bank that joke for later, if there is a later.

My index finger brushes the key. So close.

'Oh,' I say, which sets Freckles off laughing again.

'Listen to this asshole,' he says in between chortles. 'We should take a drive to Connecticut for laughs. This guy is better than Howard Stern.'

So then they're off on a DJ debate. Apparently this Harvard girl that Shea once banged in a bathroom stall voiced the opinion that Howard Stern was a misogynist arsehole, and Shea happened to agree with that position. Freckles on the other hand was loudly opposed to this argument despite the fact that it quickly became obvious that he didn't understand the term misogynist.

I have to stop myself joining in, because I got stuff to do, staying alive and so forth.

I reach the key, pull it out between two fingers and slump gratefully on the seat. Usually when I sit down, I don't attach an emotion to it, but this time gratefully works okay.

Stage one complete.

I look down at my hands, the palms worn shiny like the hands of a fisherman, the fingers curved like a gorilla's, and they are shaking like I got a charge running through me, but I manage to hold on to the key, and after a minute of trying to thread that toy-sized key into a hole the size of a match head, I manage to free myself.

Correction, free my hands.

There's a long way to go before I can consider my entire self to be free. Ideally I could simply jump out of the car the next time Freckles slows to take a corner. But the central locking button is up front and there are no controls for the windows back here. I will have to trick Shea into giving me a shot at grabbing his gun, then I'll be in the driver's seat.

Metaphorically.

I butt the partition with my forehead, and because of my entertainment value so far on this trip, my captors are inclined to listen.

'Wassup, ballsack?' says Shea. 'You need some exfoliator for your asshole this time?'

That's not bad, but I don't have time. I need to provoke the kid with some outrageous remarks. It's not denial this time, or a coping mechanism, it's part of a general strategy that is too loosely thrown together to qualify as a plan.

'Listen, kid. I'm done screwing around. Do yourself a favour and turn me loose. Then you and Freckles can round up your big scary posse and get your gangster on with Mike.'

Shea is eating again, a big blueberry muffin that he had stuffed in some pocket and sat on, looks like. The muffin is flat as a cookie and he is picking off the edges like a fecking squirrel. I hate this kid.

'Turn you loose? You had more chance of me scratching your balls. I'm gonna shoot you, McEvoy. Deal with it. Visualise your next incarnation or some shit, I could give a fuck.'

'You ain't gonna shoot me, kid. Not you. The old man maybe, but you? Nah. I got a date with a bullet okay, but you ain't the one pulling the trigger.'

Shea twists in his seat to look back at me and I can see the first rays of sunrise behind his head, making him look like one of those pale Scandinavian Jesuses movie people were so fond of in the fifties.

'You ain't even my first, McEvoy. And I liked that other guy. He was my favourite.'

'Maybe, but he was wounded, immobile most like. Me you gotta get all the way from the car to the hole, and I ain't going easy. Also bigger guys than you shot me just before I killed them. I got more holes in me than Fifty Cent.'

I said Fifty Cent all wrong. Should be Fiddy or some such.

Respect for 'In da Club' though, classic. Jason and me used to play *celebrity beat down* on the door. Fifty Cent was the only guy who we put through to the next round without argument. Fucker's huge, plus he's got that smart/crazy glint in his eye.

Shea is getting a little angry, but tries to laugh it off. 'Listen to this dope,' he says to Freckles. 'Handcuffed on the way to his own execution, and he's still playing the big man.'

Freckles has his eyes on the road, lotta potholes down here. Homeless guys too. It's like Thunderdome by the river.

'He's just yanking your chain, kid. Pay no attention. You can shoot him right in his stupid mouth in about five minutes.'

'That gives you about five minutes to live,' I say.

Shea pulls out his gun and lays it on the partition. 'You want to shut the hell up? Maybe I'll shoot you right here.'

I laugh with a savage glee. Spraying the glass.

'Shoot me in a moving vehicle? You goddamn amateur. You wanna tell him, Benny T?'

'Tell me what?' Shea demands.

Freckles sighs. 'Shea-ster. It's your first day on this side of the fence. You ain't expected to know everything.'

'So why can't I shoot this prick now?'

I break the news. 'Because you're in a reinforced vehicle on uneven terrain. Firstly you'd most likely miss, then that bullet is gonna ricochet off all the metal round here and most likely kill the wrong person. And even if it don't, then the noise alone is gonna blow out a couple of eardrums and we'd all end up in the Hudson.'

Shea has a counterargument. 'Yeah? But you're in a sealed compartment, McEvoy, with bulletproof glass all around. All I gotta do is poke my pistol through this hatch and it's a million to one that a ricochet could come back. Plus the noise is gonna bounce off the glass.'

I try to look stumped by this line of reasoning. The place I go to for this expression is every single conversation I ever had with Sofia.

'Yeah . . . I guess.'

Shea is delighted that his youthful logic has trumped my veteran's wisdom.

'That's right, McEvoy. I can shoot you any time I feel like it. And guess what? I'm feeling like it right now.'

Come on, you little turd. Come on.

Shea slips the catch off the small door in the middle of the glass where real customers would pay their fare. The door opens with the soft hiss/pop of a seal being broken.

'Smile, motherfucker,' says Shea, poking the barrel of his gun through the hole. Freckles spots this out of the corner of his eye.

'No,' he blurts. 'Don't.'

Freckles may have been about to deliver more specific instructions along the lines of: *Don't give the ex-soldier access to your weapon as he doubtless knows a dozen ways to disarm you.*

But it's too late. As soon as the hatch opens, my hands are coming up. Shea ain't got much of a grip on the handle and so more or less delivers the gun into my waiting fingers.

I spin it around, flick off the safety, which the Shea-ster neglected to do, then stick my hand through the hatch.

Shea is stunned for a moment, then a petulance born of entitlement settles on his face like a crinkled mask.

'No,' he says. 'That's my gun. Give it back.'

Freckles needs a few seconds to come up with a plan, so he says: 'He's right, McEvoy. It is his gun.'

I cannot believe these two.

'Get out of the car,' I tell Shea. I need to separate them or they might try to out-bravado each other.

Shea's bottom lip juts. 'I am not going anywhere. Now you turn that gun over, right now, mister.'

I do something that anyone who has ever met Shea, except Freckles, has been praying for. I shoot him. Just in the arm, but the scar should draw admiring coos at his legendary pot parties. The noise is loud and flat like the snap of a dry branch, but most of it stays in the cab so I don't get disorientated, which is more than I can say for Freckles. Shea is disorientated too, but that's mainly from shock and pain. The blood drains from his face through the hole in his upper arm.

It was harsh, I admit it, shooting the kid and so forth, but some people never learn unless the lesson is public and humiliating.

'Get out,' I tell him again.

Shea's lip is wobbling and his body is racked with tension, and I don't blame him; getting shot is about the most painful thing that can happen to a body besides childbirth. The one thing a person learns once they've been shot is how little they want to get shot again. Shea nods. 'Okay. I'm getting out. Can you slow down a little, Benny?'

Freckles nods more times than are necessary. 'Yep,' he says. 'Yep, yep. Uhuh.'

I think he's answering questions in his own head.

'Slow down, Freckles,' I tell him. 'Just to thirty or so.'

Freckles does this, fingers drumming a fierce rhythm on the wheel. He probably doesn't intend it, but I swear he's tapping out the beat to George Michael's 'Faith'. Normally I would sing along, or at least whistle depending on the company, but at the moment I am trying to impress my determined professionalism on these two, so I ignore the rhythm, which is difficult and distracting.

The cab slows and I can see scrub and cracked asphalt in the high beams. The city is on our right and on the left a series of working piers stretch into the blackness of the Hudson. I bet there are more bodies buried down here than in the average cemetery. Hopefully I won't become one of them any time soon.

'Go,' I say to Shea. 'I'm gonna count to ten.'

Shea is crying and I don't blame him.

'Ten?' he says. 'Come on, man. Let me work up to it.'

'Three,' I say.

'You're skipping numbers,' he squeaks.

'Nine,' I say.

Shea hits the central locking button, pops the passenger door and is sucked out; he whips past like a tumbleweed and is lost in our wake, and the wind closes the door behind him.

He's probably dead, but technically I didn't kill him. Constructive suicide at worst.

No, no, no, I am not so bad.

Freckles steps on the accelerator as soon as the kid is gone and we both know why. He doesn't know about my aversion to killing people, so is convinced that I can't let him live. If Shea survives, he is done in this world of shadows, but Freckles would never stop coming. He's Irish, like me, and we know all about holding grudges. When it comes to vendettas, the Irish make the Sicilians look Canadian. Freckles would not be happy until both my knees were blown out and he's feeding me my eyeballs.

Eyeballs if I'm lucky.

Could be ball balls is what I'm trying to say.

I know, I should've left it.

So, the recently remonikered Benny T reckons his number's up and floors the accelerator, and the only thing preventing me from tumbling backwards is my arm hooked through the hatch.

'Freckles, slow down,' I shout. 'We can work something out.'

'Fuck you, McEvoy, you fucking prick,' he says. 'Fuck all you fucking Dublin bastards.'

According to the doorman rules of swearing, we are now officially in the red zone.

I push my arm further through the hole and screw the barrel into Freckles' temple.

'Maybe I'm gonna let you off with a warning. You ever think of that?'

Freckles doesn't even answer; instead his face comes over all grim and he swings the car ninety degrees anticlockwise.

'This is a bad idea,' I say, maybe aloud, maybe to myself.

'You like this one, McEvoy? You think you're the only one with balls?'

I smack Freckles on the side of the head with the gun, but there's no power in it and I'm at full stretch already. I see the speedometer needle jiggling around ninety.

I could jump, but at this speed I would snap like a dry twig. I should have bailed with the kid. Freckles knows I can't risk shooting him while his foot is on the gas.

The cab is headed for one of the less sturdy-looking piers, which is protected by a tin sign that says *No Access*. What kind of preventative is that? A fecking kid with roller skates could circumvent that security.

'I'm ready to go, McEvoy!' shrills Freckles, and I can see in his face that he ain't backing down.

I gotta shoot him. With him dead, things can't get worse.

I got no option but to plug this bug-eyed ginger shit for brains right this instant. Actually there should be a comma after *ginger*, otherwise it might read like Freckles has ginger shit, which would be a weird thing for me to be privy to.

'You ain't doing it, McEvoy,' shouts the ginger, shit for brains triumphantly. 'You ain't got the nerve.'

If we could freeze this for a moment, I would point out that Freckles is preparing to kill himself in order to avoid being killed by me, and surely there is a better way to resolve our issues.

But we can't freeze this moment, so I gotta pull the trigger or take a bath.

Shoot.

You've shot people before. Remember that time you were in the army? The hard bit comes afterwards.

188

Shoot.

'Freckles,' I shout over the rattle of tyres on gravel and the blood rushing in my ears. 'Don't make me do this. You're Irish, surely we can work this out.'

Sure, if we had seven hundred years.

Too late. We're on the pier now. A drum roll of planks underneath, my jaw rattles and then we are flying.

Freckles lets go of the wheel like he has time to roll out in mid air or some other frankly impossible move unless he's got bullet time on his cell phone, and last time I checked, the raciest thing Freckles had on there was Sofia the Dominatrix. He's got his legs out the door when we touch down and a giant fist of water slams the door on his torso, more or less cutting him in half.

We hit hard, the catastrophic deceleration jamming me against the partition, knocking the breath from my body. The windscreen bulges inwards and then pops out whole, allowing black water to surge forward, claiming the front area and Freckles' body. The only air pocket is the back seat area, so we go down fast.

I have serious hours logged in life-threatening situations but they are of zero use to me now. All I can do is ride out the crash and hope.

I try to breathe but my lungs won't oblige and I am seconds away from total panic. I don't wanna be not found. I don't want to be forever listed as missing, if anyone even bothers to add me to the list. There is something terrifying about the notion that you can be disappeared by circumstance, swallowed by the earth, and by the time the water gives up your corpse nothing will remain but algae-coated bones.

The car settles on the riverbed and the bump starts my lungs going again. And now that my brain has a little oxygen going to it, I start to take stock of my situation.

This whole thing is ridiculous.

Come on. In a death cab on the riverbed looking at a corpse floating in the *doors ajar* light. Silt floats through the window and a couple of fish that resemble nothing more than befinned turds swim inside to investigate.

My hand is cold. Why is my hand cold?

Because it's jammed in the fare hatch, dummy, otherwise you would have drowned by now. I am like that Dutch kid who stuck his arm in a dyke, except for it's a tricked-out cab not a dyke. I ain't Dutch and it's been a long time since anybody called me kid.

Freckles' crimped corpse floats up so we are face to face through the glass. He has held on to his expression of manic triumph, which makes me feel like a loser even though he is the dead one.

Something glows in Freckles' pocket and I am amazed to realise that my phone is still working and I have a call coming through. Luckily Freckles' pocket is within my grasp, so I drop the gun and wiggle my fingers in and snag my Hello Kitty handset. Now for the tricky part: I gotta whip my hand through, hoping the water shuts the hatch, and if it doesn't, I gotta get out the side door pretty sharp and pull for the surface.

I tug on my arm until it's ready to pop loose, then I take a couple of deep breaths, working up to a real lungful. My phone is still warbling in the flooded cab. Someone must really want to get a hold of me.

Okay. Stop wasting time.

I pull my hand through and the water forces the half-closed hatch the rest of the way, forming a reasonably tight seal. The water is still coming in, but at a drastically reduced rate.

Finally things are going my way.

Right. Stuck in a subaquatic coffin. My lucky day. I should rush out and do the lottery.

But I ain't rushing out anywhere. I won't even be able to open the door until the pressure equalises. And even if I could open the door, the rush of incoming Hudson would pin me to the back seat. So I gotta sit here and take deep breaths until the rear compartment is flooded, which means I will have to pop the little hatch myself, which goes against all my survival instincts.

I answer the phone. Might as well.

'Yep.'

'Where the hell are you?' asks Ronelle Deacon, my cop friend who used to work out of the four-roomed station in Cloisters (and two of the rooms were restrooms) but recently moved on and up as a lieutenant in the Special Investigations section of the New Jersey State Police.

'Where am I? You wouldn't believe it, Trooper.'

'You ain't by any chance wearing a pink thong and beating on some cops?'

'I wish,' I say sincerely. 'And it was a red thong, okay?'

'It's not looking good for you, Dan. My brethren are majorly pissed off.'

'Yeah, well I got the real story if you're interested.'

'I'm always interested in the truth, McEvoy. I am the last champion of the truth. Can we meet?'

'Maybe we can. I hope so.'

'Where the hell are you, Danny? The reception is crap.'

It is a testament to my phone plan that I still got bars underwater.

'I'm in a bit of a bind here, Ronnie. I'll met you in Pom Pom's, down in the Kitchen. You remember it?'

'Sure, we did that thing there with the guy from *Cheers*.'

'Yeah, but it wasn't *Cheers*. It was *Home Improvement*.'

'White guys, bad jokes. Who cares? When?'

'Soon as you can, I'll be there before you.'

'And if you're not?'

'If I'm not, dredge the river.'

'Dredge the river? What river? What's going on, Dan?'

'I can't explain now, Ronnie, but we're friends, right? You'd say we were friends, wouldn't you? You'd stand up and vouch for me at a service or something?'

'Yeah, we're friends,' says Ronnie, but her tone is wary, like she's talking a guy off a roof, so I hang up.

She said we were friends and that's enough for me.

The water is at my ankles now, feels more like sludge than water. No one ever jumped in the Hudson around here to get refreshed, but I can't go yet, I need to wait.

My phone reminds me that I have an unwatched video message. *Tommy's video.*

I'd rather watch that than Freckles' floating corpse, so I select it and press play, and what follows might be enough to tip the balance re the Mike Madden situation if I make it out of this underwater coffin alive. The video clip is almost riveting enough to make me forget my predicament, but then the small hatch pops its hinges, and bitter-smelling river water pours through. In seconds my knees are submerged in the icy water and there's a turd fish swimming Mobius strips round my feet.

I wait until I gotta tilt my head back to breathe, then I gulp down a lungful of oxygen and put my shoulder to the door. Luckily Freckles did not hit central locking after Shea bailed, so the door swings easily. I slide into the dark block of river and am swallowed like a speck, like nothing. If the Hudson takes me now, there will be little more than a ripple to show I was here.

When did I get so morbid? And why am I even thinking about mortality? I've been in training pools deeper than this wearing full gear.

I am in dark water, but above me shafts of red sunlight cut through the murk. I release the air slowly like I've been taught and kick for the surface, and it occurs to me that the sunrise is pretty special from this perspective.

Considering the twenty-four hours I've had, any fecking sunrise is most unexpected and appreciated.

I pull for the surface, feeling muscles that I haven't used for years protest and stretch. I ain't exactly dressed for subaquatic speed, but I am loath to part with my boots that have been with me since the army, and my leather jacket I bought from a guy called Anghel, who was a Romanian mercenary working for the Christian militia in Tibnin. Whenever I bought something from Anghel, he would promise not to shoot at me later that evening. So far as I know he kept that promise. Unfortunately I couldn't return the favour, and towards the end of my second tour I put a round in his leg when my patrol came across him and two of his buddies breaking into our compound. I didn't mean to kill him, but legs have a lotta veins and one thing led to another. Next thing you know I've cut down a guy I've known for two years over a couple crates of condensed milk.

Love the jacket though. Soft as butter.

The water runs shallow real quick and my feet touch bottom before I break the surface. I relax then and defer the moment just to kid myself I have a little control over my life.

But I can't control the shakes that envelop me from head to toe as I stagger ashore amid the harbour detritus. Styrofoam and foil wrappers, syringes and soda cans, planks warped and split by years in the water, dark strips of weed with fingertip touches, cereal boxes, bones that I hope are animal and most bizarrely a horse's head poking through its caul of plastic bin liner.

A horse's head sleeping with the fishes.

That's double points in Mafia Monopoly.

I rest my hands on my knees and hawk as much of the river as I can from my lungs. I don't see how any could have gotten in there, but a pint or so comes out all the same. My limbs seemed poisoned and weak, and my tongue feels chemically dry and scaled.

An old homeless guy is sitting on top of his shopping cart kingdom smoking an impossibly thin cigarette. He seems pretty jaunty, probably because for once he can compare his situation to someone else's and not feel too shit on by life.

'Morning, son,' he says. He's gotta voice that sounds like a bear went to elocution classes in Texas.

'Morning,' I return; after all, none of this crap is his fault.

He nods towards the river. 'New York cabbies, huh.'

That gets a smile outta me which I wouldn't have thought possible, so I give him twenty sopping bucks.

As I stumble up the embankment towards the brightening day, I glance behind me towards the spot that has become Freckles' tomb and I swear I see the glow of a *For Hire* sign shining piss-yellow from the depths.

I catch up with Shea pretty quickly, though in actual fact he was disorientated and stumbling towards me. We meet on the verge of the highway, two individuals who are not in full control of their emotions so maybe a reasonable conversation was never on the cards. He looks a fright, doused in his own blood from the bullet wound and a hundred grazes he must have incurred when he face-planted on the asphalt. Stupid dick doesn't even know how to tuck and roll. In fairness, I probably don't look much better: dildo-whipped and dipped in sludge.

When Shea catches sight of me, he squeaks like that square cartoon guy with the pants, and makes a run for the road. I am too goddamn weary to go after him so I let the kid run. Sadly for him, he slips on the verge and rolls practically to my feet.

I feel encouraged by this little favour from lady luck and feel my energy levels rising. I lean down, grab his lapels and hoist him to his tippy-toes. I have no idea what's gonna come out of my mouth but I start talking anyway.

'You see that pier down there?' I say.

Shea looks; there are several piers. 'Which pier?' he asks, terrified that he doesn't get to ask questions.

'Which fucking pier. The melted one. The collapsed one.'

'Yeah. I see it. All twisted and shit.'

'Yeah, twisted and shit. That's the one, Shea-ster. You know what made that pier collapse?'

'No. I don't.'

'Do you fucking know what made that pier collapse?'

Shea is crying now; he breaks down easily.

'No. I'm sorry, I don't know. I swear.'

I wait a beat, then: 'Pier pressure.'

He looks at me dumbly, as he has every right to.

'I . . . I don't get it.'

'Pier pressure,' I repeat then. 'Ha ha ha haaaa.'

I don't know if I am actually laughing maniacally or just saying ha ha ha haaaa. Either way it scares the bejaysus out of Shea, which is all he had left in him to scare, as I already scared the crap out of him back in the taxi.

I hoist the kid a little higher. 'Shit, sorry, that joke was for a friend of mine. What I meant to say was: if I ever see you again, I'll kill you. If anyone takes a shot at me, I'm gonna blame you and come looking. Understand?'

'I understand.'

'Good, 'cause Freckles was *my* favourite. You can't even eat with your mouth closed.'

'I'll sort that out,' promises Shea, and I know he won't cause me any more trouble for a few months at least. It's in his eyes. I toss him down the embankment where a cement bollard breaks his fall, and he curls himself around it like it's his wet nurse. I can hear him sobbing as I walk away. He should get that wound seen to or it might get infected.

I don't care. I'm gonna have to get this jacket dry-cleaned and it's his fault.

CHAPTER 8

Lieutenant Ronelle Deacon is the only cop I know who could play herself in a movie, especially if the movie was one of those 1970s blaxploitation flicks. She wears her Afro pulled back tight for the first section, then it blooms out behind her in an explosion of ringlets. Takes some confidence to wear a hairstyle like that, but Ronnie has more than confidence; she has anger hanging over her like a heat shimmer. Any time she walks into a room, every guy in there feels like he just got his boner rapped with a spoon. They don't know if they're horny or terrified. She's a one-woman flim-flam. A walking conundrum.

Ronnie and me got tossed together last year by one of her cases which was also one of my problems, and I saved her life a couple of times and she saved my bacon. It all turned out pretty good. She got herself a promotion and I got to keep breathing free air. Oh, and she tumbled me into the hay one night for a tension screw, as she called it. Sometimes that can be awkward between friends, but it ain't awkward between us because Ronnie doesn't really do friends the way normal people do, just people that aren't suspects at the moment.

Lieutenant Deacon keeps me waiting in the diner, but that's okay because I burn out a washroom drier getting the river outta my shirt. I am not even gonna attempt the pants. It's gonna take more than a wall-mounted Dyson to blast the Hudson from a pair of black jeans. So I'm in a booth working on some eggs and bacon, with a puddle of slime congealing around my nethers, when Ronnie finally breezes in the door like she's fashionably late for an awards gig and slides into the booth opposite me.

'McEvoy,' she says, working a toothpick between her strong white teeth.

'It looks like you're trying to be a cop,' I say. 'The toothpick is too much.'

Ronelle spits the pick on to the tabletop. 'Yeah? A pity I couldn't say the same about your toothpick.'

'Straight to that level, huh? No five-minute truce or nothing?'

Ronelle leans back, shucking the lapels of her long leather coat aside, giving me a good look at the gun and the badge.

'I only got one level, McEvoy. The Deacon level. That's where shit gets done.'

'You have your movie and tagline right there: *The Deacon Level.* Where shit gets done.'

'Is that why I'm here, Dan? So you can take a pop?'

These conversations are always tense because Ronnie lives on a hair trigger. She puts out more or less the same vibe whether she wants to kiss me or kill me. And that one night we did have a little tryst, you can bet your favourite organ that I kept her pistola out of reach.

'No, I got a few good tips for you.'

'I'm listening.'

'Remember that Arabian horse was stolen?'

'Scimitar? Apparently that nag was worth twenty million bucks. Mares lining up to get inseminated.'

'Yeah, well you can call off those dogs. Old Scimitar is in a trash bag down by Pier Forty-nine.'

Ronelle takes a note on her phone. 'That is indeed a juicy tip. Outta my zone but I can trade it in for something. What else?'

'A mob button man. Twenty feet out in a taxi. Bodies in the trunk and I'm betting you get enough DNA from the inside of that trunk to close a dozen unsolveds.'

Ronelle goes girlie for a second and giggles. 'Ooh. I love it when you say button man. Makes a lady go all quivery inside.'

This conversation is getting a little flippant for my liking.

'I'm in deep trouble, Deacon,' I tell her. 'The deepest.'

Ronnie places her iPhone on the table and makes a show of watching a video. 'I see that, Dan. Is that a thong you got going there?'

'So you saw the clip. I was severely provoked.'

Ronnie taps her screen. 'Looks to me like you were doing a spot of provoking yourself. That's two brother officers you're beating on there. Fortz has been decorated twice.'

'Decorated? Like a Christmas tree?'

Ronnie smiles, reminds me of a wolf I saw once. 'Christmas tree. You crack me up, Dan,' she says, displaying none of the traditional signs associated with cracking up.

'I need help, Ronnie.'

'Yeah, with your wardrobe for a start.'

'This is serious, Ronelle. A woman's life is in danger. It may already be too late.'

'Speaking of taglines, there's yours. Daniel McEvoy is the Pink Thong. Pray he's not too late.'

I pound the table. 'Pink? That's red. Any idiot can see it's red. The sequins make it look a little pink in the light. That's all.'

Ronnie is delighted. 'Whoa there, Thongmaster. I'm here, aren't I? Alone as requested, against orders and protocol I might add. So whose life is in danger and how do you account for this video?'

I lay it out in brief strokes. The abduction, the porn studio, my Aunt Evelyn. It's a good story, so Ronnie listens attentively. She may be a little out there, but Ronnie is one hundred per cent police. She said to me once:

I'm a straight cop, Dan. If you cut me, guess what happens?

Don't tell me, you bleed blue.

No. I bleed red, you moron, but I will read you your Mirandas before I beat the crap outta you for assaulting an officer.

When I'm finished talking, Ronnie lets it percolate for a minute, getting her questions straight.

'You ain't bullshitting me?'

'Nope. Straight up.'

''Cause if you're bullshitting me . . .'

'I am not bullshitting you. Do I look like a bullshitter?'

'You smell like one.'

'It's that fecking Hudson. I probably got hepatitis.'

Ronelle lines up the condiments.

'Okay. This woman Costello hires Fortz and Krieger to take you out of the picture?'

'Yeah. I reckon the torture porn was their own little wrinkle in the plan.'

Ronnie knocks over the salt and pepper. 'Those guys have been making skin crawl ever since they left the City Precinct under a cloud. They're in the wind now, last seen hobbling away from the scene of an accident out by the Silvercup.'

I am disappointed by this, as I had been wishing on a star that Krieger and Fortz had been found dead in their unit, having crapped themselves, with their dicks out, wearing mankinis.

Ronnie stands the ketchup and the hot sauce up on the napkin holder. 'So your aunt is stuck in the penthouse with the evil stepmom?'

'Is my aunt the ketchup?'

Ronelle scowls. 'No. Your aunt is the fucking sauce. What are you, retarded?'

'Sorry. Mayo, right. Yep, that's about it. My aunt and Edit are up in the napkin holder's penthouse.'

'You making fun of my diorama?'

'What? God, no. It's very effective.'

'Because this is legitimate policing techniquing. And if it ain't swish enough for Mister Pink Thong, maybe you should find yourself another blue buddy.'

I know Ronelle is playing me, but she's holding all the condiments.

'No. I like the diorama. It crystallises everything.'

Ronnie is placated by the effort I have put into my verb. 'Crystallises, huh? You really are desperate.'

'Come on, Ronnie, all I need for you to do is badge me into that penthouse. Then Ev can walk out of there of her own free will.'

Ronelle peels the paper from a sugar lump.

'Is that me?' I ask her. 'The lump?'

'It's not all about you, Dan,' she says and pops the lump into her mouth. On most days, when Ronnie does some tiny unexpected thing like this, it reminds me how singular she is, how striking. This morning I just feel helpless and outplayed.

'The problem is that you're wanted for questioning,' she says. 'I should be escorting you downtown right now.'

I like how this statement is going. Plenty of scope for a but, so I prompt.

'But?'

'But, I know how you are about protecting women, in your big dog, alpha bullshit, dick-swinging way.'

'So?'

'So if this aunt of yours were to turn up dead, you might cross out one of the Fs in our matching BFF tattoos.'

'Maybe a B too,' I say, playing along.

'So, we're gonna drive down there 'cause I have probable cause from a reliable source. Kidnapping or some bullshit. Is that enough for you?'

'Plenty, Ronelle. You're saving a life.'

Ronelle plants her elbows on the desk, which in itself is enough to scare off the waitress who was coming over with refills.

'But if you're setting me up, Dan, then I'm gonna look a little deeper into all the criminal shit that happened in your vicinity last year.'

I am prepared to take any deal at this point. 'Okay, Ronnie. I'll sign whatever confession you want.'

'And you promise me now: no throwing punches, none of your black ops, wet work bullshit.'

I am squirming to be off. 'No bullshit of any kind.'

'You better believe it, Dan,' says Ronelle, tossing a twenty on the table, even though she didn't have anything. 'I just got the lieutenant's desk and I want to hang on to it for a while.'

My phone burbles rather than tweets after its time in the river. I can't help checking it.

Stop waiting for that white knight to come rescue you. You are your own white knight.

I cover the phone with my hand.

Ronelle squints suspiciously. 'Got something interesting there, cowboy?'

'Nope,' I say, sliding out of the booth. 'Not interesting and not helpful.'

Ronnie slides out her side and suddenly we're standing very close to each other and I don't know whether I'm supposed to back away or not. Ronnie steps even closer and puts the flat of her hand on my back. Her eyes are two chocolate drops and her lips when she smiles could belong to a nice person. She's smiling now.

'Ronnie,' I say, but that's as far as I get because I don't know what to say next and also her hand is sliding lower under the band of my jeans.

This is all very public and I don't really have the time, but I can't help thinking back to the night we had together, which was pretty wild.

Something must show on my face because Ronnie laughs.

'Don't flatter yourself, McEvoy, I'm just checking something.'

She slips two fingers under the thong strap and snaps it good.

'Still wearing it, huh?'

I nod, hoping that none of the diner's half-dozen early birds are watching this little show.

'It's been a busy day and I don't carry spares.'

'That could be a problem,' says Ronnie, wiping the river mud from her hand with a napkin. 'You're never gonna get into the Broadway Park looking like a decrepit old bum.'

There was absolutely no need for *old* in that sentence.

* * *

We swing by a twenty-four-hour K-Mart on Broadway to pick up some clothes for me that don't smell of river sewage. With a little persuasion from Ronelle's badge, the manager relinquishes the employee's bathroom key and I spend a few minutes scooping crud out of my cavities and staring at myself in a mirror that seems to have some kind of fungus growing between the glass and the aluminium. I look pretty shook up, like the zombie version of myself, and this impression is reinforced by the sound of Michael Jackson's 'Thriller' playing over the store speakers, or maybe that's what put the idea in my head in the first place. I stand still to listen to the Vincent Price section, which I have always liked, and realise that there is no song playing over the speakers; in fact there are no speakers.

I need to pull myself together pronto.

I stuff most of my wet clothes in the trash apart from the boots and jacket, which I bag.

Outside the restroom there's an old Asian guy holding a cup, so I toss in a five, figuring I'll take whatever karma can be bought, and the guy says:

'Screw you, cue ball. I'm waiting to use the facilities.'

Shite. I can't put a foot right these days.

'Sorry, man. I assumed you were looking for a buck.'

''Cause I'm Korean, right?'

I am too weary for this and I'm afraid to stand up for myself in case I spark off another conflict.

'I apologise, okay? Whatever. Just give me back the five, or keep it, whatever. No bad blood. *Annyeonghi gyeseyo.*'

The old dude is patriotically unimpressed by my mangling of his birdsong language.

'Stop talking, cue ball. Your words hurt my brain.'

For some reason, getting into it with this ancient Korean brings on something of a mini breakdown. I think it's partly the randomness of it, this guy doesn't have a beef with me, and partly the cue ball thing. Sure I have a forehead the size of JFK's proposed new runway, but thanks to Zeb's surgical skills my bald patch is gone so I thought my hair wouldn't be such a target. Yet this restroom-waiting, empty-cup-holding, angry old motherfucker has nailed me twice already. Would it pain Jesus so much to send a few more decent people my way every once in a while? I know they're out there. Jason is one. Evelyn is another, underneath the layer of pickling.

Yeah. And Edit was one too. Remember?

I want to bawl like a drunken aunt. I wanna grind my teeth to stumps and punch the wall, but I don't, and the effort of containing it starts me shaking all over. For a moment I think I might actually be having a heart attack, then the moment passes and I collapse on to a chair beside the Korean guy.

He drapes his spindly arm around my shoulder and says:

'My son.'

And I think: *Wow. Is this guy going to surprise me by playing into his stereotype and delivering a nugget of wisdom?*

'I never see a man shake after taking a dump before.' He pats me on the back. 'That must have been a hell of a dump. Hollowed you right out. I think maybe I'll wait here a few minutes, let the extractor fan do its work.'

Clever but not very wise. I pluck my five dollars from his cup and go back outside into my life.

Twilight lasts a little longer in Manhattan because of the urban topography, and what light does manage to find a through line is faded and whittled until it arrives grey and limpid on the sidewalks.

Yeah, I know. You're thinking that maybe I should concentrate on the problems I got instead of contemplating early morning light in Manhattan. Limpid? Fuck me.

The Broadway Park House is exactly where I left it last night, standing sentry over Central Park, built on money so old it started off as goats. Ronelle pulls her Lincoln in hard, bumping the front wheel up on the footpath, letting the doormen know who's in charge before she even steps out of the vehicle.

The experienced guys get the message and hang back, but one young buck bristles at how the Broadway Park bay has been defiled and is over like a shot.

'Can I park that for you, ma'am?' he asks, pronouncing ma'am like his pops owns a plantation somewhere.

Ronnie doesn't even look at him. 'You don't touch my car, kid. And if anyone does touch it, I'm holding you responsible. Got it?'

The kid may have blurted out some kind of reply, but at that stage we are already through the door.

Ronnie has a menace about her that is particularly effective in post offices or hotels. Wherever people are responsible for shit. They take one look at Ronelle Deacon with her game face on and they start thinking: *Not me, please God not me.*

Ronnie strides through the lobby making a beeline for the concierge desk, snapping her fingers at a lady trying to hide behind the monitor.

'Hey, hey, sweetie,' she says. 'Get me Edit Costello on the phone.'

The lady makes a perfunctory attempt to uphold the hotel's privacy policy.

'Miss Vikander Costello does not wish to be disturbed. She sent a memo.'

Ronnie flashes her badge. 'See this, sweetie? This trumps the shit out of your memo. This takes your memo out back and beats the crap out of it. This bends your memo over and—'

'Very well, Officer,' says the lady, rightly guessing that Ronnie would continue with her graphic memo-defiling imagery for as long as was necessary. 'I'm dialling right now. Look, I'm dialling.'

Edit picks up and the concierge speaks to her in that enthusiastic yet deferential manner that makes rich folk feel good about having people serve them, then hands the phone to Ronnie.

'Miss Vikander Costello has kindly agreed to speak with you.'

Ronnie takes the phone and winks at me. This is not a friendly wink like a person might get from Fonzy. This particular wink says: *See how smooth I am? Now keep on keeping quiet and let me do my thing.*

Okay. *Let me do my thing* might be a little bit of stereotyping on my part, but that Korean guy knocked my powers of interpretation for six.

Ronnie tucks the phone under her ear and puts on a sad face.

'Yes, Mrs Costello, thank you so much for agreeing to speak with me.'

Thank you so much?

That ain't the Ronelle I know. She's running some kinda game.

'My name is Lieutenant Deacon, with the Jersey State Police. The thing is, we found a relative of yours down by the docks. His wallet identifies him as one Daniel McEvoy and, believe it or not, you are this bum . . . eh, this guy's next of kin. I was wondering if my associate and I could come up and talk to you about him. It won't take more than a minute, then I'm outta your morning.'

207

Ronnie nods for a couple seconds then smiles her dangerous, beautiful smile. 'Thank you so much, Mrs Costello. I appreciate you taking the time.'

She hangs up and points a stiff finger at me. Maybe I'm supposed to suck it. I honestly don't know any more. Obviously I can't read signs for shit.

'Okay, Associate. We are in. I do all the talking up there and I don't want to hear a peep outta your face.'

I'm glad I didn't suck the finger now. I'm pretty sure it would have been the wrong move.

Someone who is not Edit opens the door, which is good news for me as I get a pass into the apartment. The door-opener is a fit-looking fecker in his thirties wearing hemp shorts, and the name Pablo pops into my memory. Perhaps Edit is getting a workout session in before the business day kicks off.

Ronnie brusquely emasculates the guy.

'This is confidential police business, sir,' she says. 'I want you to point me in Mrs Costello's direction and then stay out here in the hall. If I need you to massage my glutes or something, I'll whistle, got it?'

The guy is wearing a Buddha T-shirt and a couple of string bracelets so I'm guessing he's not used to his space being violated by such negativity. I see in his eyes that he's about to lay some kind of bioenergy, chi, ask the universe line on Ronnie and that could put him in the hospital, so I intervene.

'Pablo's fine, aren't you, Pablo? He's at peace, right?'

Pablo blinks. 'Yes. Of Course. Miss Edit is waiting in her office. Just down the corridor.'

'Past the gorilla,' I say. 'I've been here before.'

*　*　*

Edit has that same desperately hopeful look strapped to her face that she wore in the Parker Meridien. It's a good look and only hardens a fraction when she sees who's waltzing in her door very much not dead.

'Lieutenant Deacon,' she says. 'I somehow got the impression that Mister McEvoy had been found drowned down by some docks or other.'

Deacon doesn't bother hiding her grin. Ronnie once told me that screwing with rich folks' schedules is the runner-up in her top five list of on-the-job perks. Buying drug-dealer bling in police auctions was number one. Couple of months ago Ronelle picked up a jewel-encrusted samurai sword for a hundred bucks which she is just dying to baptise with blood. I haven't visited since then.

'I don't know how you inferred that. It's certainly not the impression I intended to convey.'

This is a pretty pat statement and I get the feeling Ronnie has trotted it out before.

Edit nods slowly, taking her time signing some contracts on her desk. She is dressed in her gym gear, which seems a little out of place in the office, but she looks healthy and calm, and if I had to take her word over mine, I'd need to think about it for a minute.

Finally she lays the pen in a groove carved into her desktop.

'So, Lieutenant Deacon, if Mister McEvoy is not actually dead, what are you doing here?'

Ronnie isn't cowed by the wealth on display around her; in fact she thrives on this level of confrontation, which is why she might not rise much further in any police department.

'You have no idea why I'm here?'

Edit's smile acknowledges that she recognises an adversary.

209

'No. Why don't you tell me?'

Ronnie brushes some papers aside and perches on a corner of the desk.

'Mister McEvoy here . . .'

'Your associate.'

'Yes, my associate, swears that you hired two police officers to kidnap and possibly murder him.'

Edit has had a moment to compose herself and so does not overreact.

'Do the police provide those services? Surely not.'

'I don't, you can bet on that, but some of my brother officers don't have my scruples.'

'What do the officers in question say for themselves?'

'Nothing yet, but they will, you can bet on that too.'

'More betting? You appear to be gambling quite a lot, Lieutenant.'

'So you deny knowing these officers?'

'You are the first police officer ever to grace this office, apart from Commissioner Salazar, but that was a social occasion.'

I want to dive in at this point. I want to grab this woman by the throat and shake the truth out of her. I want to wrap Evelyn in a sheet and carry her to a hospital.

Ronnie seems to sense my frustration and shoots me a warning look. I shoot her a look back that says: *Get on with it. You have five minutes.*

Or if Ronnie's interpretation of looks and gestures is as bad as mine, my look could say *potato, potato, whiskey, potato* to her.

Ronnie changes tack before I decide to involve myself.

'We have security camera footage of Mister McEvoy delivering Evelyn Costello into your hands last night. Do you deny this?'

'I very much doubt you have any footage of anything,' says Edit. 'But no, I don't deny it. Daniel brought Evelyn home last night. He demanded payment for his services, can you imagine that?'

Ronnie ignores this accusation, which bumps her up a couple of places on my friend ladder.

'And you're holding Evelyn prisoner?'

Edit is confident enough to laugh. 'Prisoner? This is Evelyn's home. She has returned to her family.'

'And if she wishes to leave?'

'The door is right down the hall, but Evelyn came here because she wants to be here.'

It's killing me to hold my silence. I've been arguing with Zeb Kronski for the past couple of years. These people are amateurs.

'So we can see her? Get her side of the story?'

At this, Edit's mask of civility slips a little. 'No. Out of the question. Evelyn is sick and she needs her rest.'

Ronnie plays her last card. 'I can come back with a warrant.'

Edit stands and comes around the desk. The ghost of Joan Rivers spots that her tracksuit is Hermès but I can't think of a way to turn that fact to my advantage.

'I very much doubt that, Lieutenant,' she says with Scandinavian ice in her voice. 'You tricked your way in here and you are several postcodes away from your jurisdiction.'

We're losing ground. I am just gonna have to pop Edit gently and search the place. Ronnie is gonna have a fit, but once I find Ev, then everything should straighten out just fine.

'Okay, I'm outta my patch,' Ronnie says, but she's down to bluster now. 'But I know plenty of local guys who will run a search for me. Let me see Evelyn and that's the end of it. Why won't you do that one simple thing? Makes me suspicious, lady.'

Edit gets right up in Ronelle's face and I don't know two other guys who would have the town halls to do that.

'I do not care one tiny tad about how you feel, Deacon. Why do you not take your blackmailing associate and go back to your Jersey neighbourhood where I am sure there are cats that need rescuing.'

Tiny tad? Who says that? Immigrants from Sweden.

Ronnie plants her hands on her hips and I see that maybe I won't be the one to pop Edit. 'Yeah, well maybe you gotta few cats of your own that need rescuing.'

That doesn't even make any sense. Ronnie is going down in flames.

The door opens and a lady walks in.

'What's all the noise about, Edit?'

It takes me a second to realise that the lady is Evelyn, but not the same Ev that I dropped off. She's different. Calmer. There are cosmetic changes too. Her hair is cut short in one of those fashionable bobs that looks like someone hacked it out of the back of her head with a tomahawk but actually costs a fortune. Her brows are shaped and her skin glows like Vaseline. She's wearing a plush white robe and cloth sandals but I can smell the fresh booze on her from six feet away. So, not a totally new model. They musta had stylists working on her while she slept. I can't stay out of this any more.

'Ev, you don't have to stay here.'

Evelyn looks surprised to see me, like it's been years and she can't believe how much I've changed.

'Danny. Dan. You look good.' Her voice is lighter, less grit and one hundred per cent Manhattan penthouse.

'Since last night, you mean?'

'Was it only last night? Seems like a lifetime ago, so much has happened.'

Edit places her body between Evelyn and me, shielding her, touching her elbow.

'Don't get anxious, Evelyn. Daniel is just leaving.'

Ronelle gets to the heart of the matter.

'Evelyn. Miss Costello, are you okay?'

My aunt doesn't try to act, just sticks to her lines. 'Of course I'm okay. I'm home now. I've made a few mistakes, but with Edit's help I can get through this challenging time.'

Ronelle looks Evelyn up and down. 'You know something, McEvoy? Appears to me like this lady has already been saved.'

I can see where this is going, but I have to try.

'Ev, all of this is nothing. This is bricks and mortar. Edit tried to have me killed.'

I see the old Evelyn for a moment, like a flash from a sniper's scope, but then the robot is back: 'Daniel. What a horrible thing to say. Edit is my salvation.'

What a nice set-up, all ready for the spike.

'And you are mine,' says Edit, squeezing Evelyn's hand, which was probably soaked in paraffin before the French polish was applied.

Boom. Case closed. We are done.

For the sake of my mother, I gotta give it one last try. 'Ev, you're being manipulated, don't you realise? Edit needs access to your fund so she's gonna keep you here, topped up with the best booze, until you're broke. Then it's back down into the gutter for you.'

Ev walks deliberately to the drinks cabinet and pours herself enough Scotch to marinade a pig.

'I've been in the gutter, Danny, and I've decided I don't want to go back. Edit and I have an arrangement. I am investing in a few beleaguered companies in return for a twenty per cent shareholding in the Costello corporation.'

Shit. Beleaguered? I bet she hasn't used that word in a while. Well, she might've lain down in her Motel 6 room one evening and said: *After all that Thunderbird, one's liver is a little beleaguered.*

'You don't care that she tried to kill me?'

'I do care, Daniel. Of course I care. But I'm afraid it simply can't be true. We all know how you've been since the army. You see things. You talk to yourself. Have you considered that you might be suffering from PTSD?'

That's it. The final nail. I am thoroughly disgusted with my last relative.

'Okay, whatever. You two deserve each other. Paddy would be so proud.'

Evelyn downs half of her drink in one go. She's gonna love living up here. A never-ending supply of top-quality booze and she doesn't even have to resort to light hooking.

'Come on, Ronnie,' I say. 'This lady is beyond helping.'

Ronnie is not ready to go yet. She pulls out her phone and snaps off a couple of shots of Edit and Evelyn.

'You guys are all smug and victorious right now, but I'm gonna find Fortz and Krieger and link them back to you. I'm betting you used these guys before, back when they worked outta the city. And if you can do me a favour and have Daniel killed, that would make my case a whole lot easier to build.'

Edit and Ronnie lock eyes. Message sent; message received. I think Ronelle Deacon may have just saved my life.

I get a little maudlin in the elevator.

What is wrong with people? Why would Evelyn choose the dark side? Didn't the boob lectures and the ice-pick plot mean anything to her? I guess maybe they did at the time, but that was then and this ain't then.

Young Evelyn, the sherry thief, hadn't yet spent a few years rolling downhill, crashing through class fences, coming to rest in the shelters and hovels of America's great unsober.

I feel myself getting sucked into a mood. After what Ronnie just did for me, she doesn't deserve the silent treatment.

'Sorry to clam up on you, Ronnie. You did a good thing up there. Thanks.'

'Huh?' says Ronnie, looking up from her phone. 'I was checking my mail. You say anything worth listening to?'

I guess I didn't. 'No. Just, you know, talking.'

Ronnie pockets the phone. 'Well, the good news for you is that they found the site you were to be torture-porned on, complete with teaser video. That puts you in the clear. Ain't a jury on earth would convict a man for bitch-beatin' two sickbags who kidnapped him for a snuff shoot.'

'So, I'm free to go?'

'Yeah-ish. You still gotta come in for questioning but it ain't so urgent. Maybe you want to take a long shower first.'

For about ten years. 'I got a car here so I'll see you back in Cloisters?'

Ronnie gets out at the lobby, but holds the door.

'What I said up there, about you being dead helping me build a case.'

'I remember.'

'Well, it's true, but I'm thinking that maybe it wouldn't be worth it.'

The golden doors slide across and I see my own reflection looking dumb and defeated. I notice that the elevator panel has two close doors buttons but no keep doors open button, which is a little strange. Maybe rich folk are generally in a hurry. Faces don't glycolically peel themselves, I suppose.

Well, it's true, but I'm thinking that maybe it wouldn't be worth it.

I think that's the nicest thing Ronnie has ever said to me.

The elevator dings for the parking level and I wedge an old video store card into the runner to prevent the door from closing.

It's puerile I know, but I am desperate for the fleeting balm of light-hearted mischief.

Mom and Ev.

Dead.

To me.

On the bright side, I have a Cadillac packed with cash that Freckles ain't gonna have much use for where he's parked.

CHAPTER 9

The Caddy is in the parking garage where I left it, with the starter fob two inches inside the exhaust pipe. I don't know why I decided to hide the keys here; maybe my subconscious figured Edit out before I did. I fish the fob out of there and sit in the car for a while, just being cradled by the leather seats. Those plush leather seats are pretty darn comfortable and I want to take a minute just to appreciate, to enjoy something, even if it is the stolen car of a guy I just saw cut in half underwater. I got stuff to do, I know that, but some kind of news must be leaking through to Mike by now. He must know that the Masterpiece gambit pretty much played out exactly as he'd hoped. So why not let him enjoy his smugness a little longer while I sit here and stroke the soft kid leather.

The leather is so soft I want to cry. Why did they have to stitch it? Why would someone do that? All those pinholes of pain.

Balls. I think I'm having another breakdown.

Soldiers have this mindset that they gotta be tough as nails twenty-four seven. So we dampen down all the poison in our chests, forging a rancid cannonball to be fired at a later date, possibly at people who don't deserve it, in a crowded restaurant shortly before our divorce. Things got a little better with *The Sopranos*. Those therapy sessions really helped Tony, especially in season two. And if it's good enough for a Mafia don, then surely regular soldiers can't be accused of weakness for booking a few sessions.

Simon Moriarty was my saviour. If it hadn't been for that guy, I don't think I would have made it through six months of civilian life. I haven't called him in more than six months but I think now's the time.

I patch my phone through the Caddy's system and dial the Irish number. The international double brrrp is comforting and a little nostalgic, so I drift off for a while waiting for Simon to pick up.

I'm halfway into a dream where I'm calling a school friend of mine and hoping his mom will pick up when I realise someone is shouting at me.

'Huh?' I say, then, 'What?'

'Daniel,' says a familiar voice. 'Sergeant McEvoy.'

I'll be damned. That's Simon Moriarty's voice. 'Hey, Simon. What's up?'

'No,' he says. 'That's my line. You called me, remember?'

These shrinks are so perceptive.

'Yes. That is technically true. I did call you.'

Simon doesn't respond to this ridiculous time-waster. He just waits. He was always a bollocks for the waiting. I don't like a sound vacuum in a conversation, so I'll generally dive in with any old shite. Not this time, though. I ain't no punk newcomer to the couch game.

Screw you, I'm gonna wait you out, Simon.

Simon hangs up.

Feck. I been played.

I redial.

'Who is it?' says Simon, making me feel like a naughty kinder-garten student.

'Simon, please. I ain't got time for this.'

I hear the clunk/rasp of a Zippo being fired up, then a long crackle as Simon lights one of his tipped cigars. This is followed by a lengthy and horrible bout of coughing as he dislodges a pint of smoker's phlegm.

'Okay, Dan. I'm all yours, for ten minutes. The girls are with me this afternoon and I promised them no interruptions.'

Girls? 'I didn't know you had daughters.'

'I don't,' says Simon, straight-faced I imagine, and I hear two voices in the background singing Abba's 'Mamma Mia' and I wonder if the owners of those voices are wearing the outfits. I must listen for a few seconds too long because Simon speaking jolts me out of my reverie.

'Daniel. Come on, snap to it, soldier.'

'Oh, yessir. Sorry.'

Simon likes to throw in a bit of Pavlovian military jargon to get things moving, even though with his eighties rock star mullet, Cuban-heel boots and faded T-shirts he is about the least military person I know. In all the time he treated me, he never once arrived either on time or completely sober.

I'm not saying Simon Moriarty ain't good. In fact I doubt there is anybody better. Most shrinks I've done time with are all about the big revelation, but Simo is great for coping strategies that are of immediate use. And oh my God that's what I need today.

'I'm all tied up, Simon. Not really, like with ropes and stuff, but seeing as we're on the subject, I've been cuffed twice already today.'

'Big deal,' says Simon. 'I have one foot cuffed to the bedpost right now.' He barks a couple of times then, which I hope is not for my benefit.

I press on. 'There's a guy I work for who has me doing unsavoury stuff for him which I do to get out from underneath, but it never ends. Unsavoury stuff begets more unsavoury stuff and before I know it there are a bunch more guys all looking to take payment from me for something I did not start.'

Simon is silent for a long moment and I hear the girls are back around to the chorus.

'Could you be a little more vague?' he says eventually.

'I know I'm not giving you much to work with, but some of these things I'm being forced to do ain't exactly legal.'

'Okay. These unsavoury things. Is there any end in sight?'

I try to imagine Mike good-naturedly cancelling my debt and the picture won't take shape in my head.

'No. No, he's never gonna let me off the hook.'

'Okay. And do you have any roots in the community, anywhere you can turn for help?'

'My roots. There's this girl I know.'

'Ah yes, the delusional girlfriend. How is Sofia?'

I picture Sofia with a hammer in her delicate fingers, blood dripping from the claw. That picture takes shape no problem.

'Good days and bad days. She does recognise me occasionally, which has gotta mean something, right?'

'It's progress,' says Simon. 'But back to your problem. This man, who I'm guessing from our previous talks is Mike Madden, has you in a bind. All we ever talk about is this sadist Mike Madden. It seems to me that you are dealing with the symptoms rather than the root cause.'

I think Simon is trying to tell me something without telling me something.

'I don't follow.'

'Let me tell you a story. A parable, if you like. If they were good enough for Jesus, they're good enough for me.'

'Amen, brother.'

'This guy lived in a tent beside a bush.'

This is starting off real cryptic.

'Okay. Tent, bush. Got it.'

'Only the guy is allergic to the bush.'

'Is the bush flowering?'

Simon sighs. 'Stop dicking me around, Daniel. Just take it as read that I will include all relevant information. So if I don't say it, you don't need to know it.'

Is the bush flowering? What the hell is happening to me? Hanging with Zeb has turned me into a pain in the arse.

'Sorry, Simon. Continue.'

'Thank you. So the guy is allergic to the bush and wakes up every morning covered in hives. So he starts taking pills to get rid of the hives. Every night a fistful of pills. These are big horse pills, so it's a pain.'

'Okay. I'm seeing it.'

'After a while the pills aren't so effective any more, so he's gotta cover himself in lotion before bed. The stuff gets all over the sheets and stinks.'

'Am I the guy? Just tell me that much.'

Simon ignores the interruption. 'So it's pills and lotion and eventually an injection once a week. This bush is ruining the guy's life. So one day the guy calls his good-looking lady-killer friend who lives across the ocean.'

221

Aha, the mist is clearing.

'And he tells him all about the bush and the pills and the rest of his increasingly complicated regime.'

'What does the friend say?'

'First of all the friend calls him a tool, but then he tells the guy that he has two choices. Either he burns that bush right down to the roots, which is not really a practical option, is it?'

'Or?'

'Or he moves far away from that bloody bush where its pollen can never reach him again.'

I get it. I'm the guy and Mike is the bush.

Simon thinks I should move.

Or Simon has just advised me to burn the bush.

It's all about the interpretation, I suppose.

Well, if it's good enough for Jesus . . .

CHAPTER 10

Coupla hours later I'm all checked in to the Cloisters Holiday Inn across the road from the bus station. I took a twin room with a bed for me and a second for my stash of weapons, which lives in one of the station's lockers. I find it prudent not to store a bag of illegal arms at home.

My trove of weapons and bricks of cash is laid out on the duvet and I sit staring at it, like the dollars and guns are gonna tell me what to do with them.

Spend me on shit you don't need, says the money.

Shoot motherfuckers, says a Glock 9.

Not helpful, guys. Not helpful at all.

A custom sharpshooter rifle that I got in Chinatown from an Algerian, if you can believe that combo, clears its throat/barrel to speak.

Dan. All you gotta do is snap a Starlight to my back then wait in Mike's garden till he shows his face. Then we give that bastard a really bad case of heartburn.

'Did you hear that?' I ask the shamefaced Glock. 'That's what I call real advice. I'm so glad you're here, Sharpshooter, because if you weren't, I'd go out of my mind.'

Five minutes later I get a text from Simon.

Daniel. I hope you are not conversing with your guns. Remember we talked about this. It is not healthy to attribute blame to a rifle.

That's ridiculous. I would never blame Sharpie for anything. It's those fecking bullets.

I send my jacket down for an express clean, put my boots outside for a shine, work my way through a tray of carbs then lay down on my bed. I was considering squeezing on beside the weapons and cash, but that could seem weird if housekeeping called unexpectedly. It takes a while to swoon into that shadowy layer of pre-slumber, but when sleep is inevitable my entire being relaxes gratefully. This is my favourite time of any day, when I'm not quite alert and can't quite focus on my problems. To get to this place usually requires:

2.5 beers.

One sleeping tablet.

A transatlantic flight.

Or a marathon TV session. Me and Zeb once watched 24 season three in one sitting. I think I got bedsores.

Just before sleep descends, I realise that the strongest emotion in the McEvoy heart right now is loneliness.

Shit.

I thought fear would be number one. Or anger at all the people who are throwing a monkey wrench into my survival engine.

Loneliness.

Huh.

'Loneliness,' I say to Sharpie. 'Who'da thunk it?'

I have a few recurring dreams on my list, which account for about four out of seven nights. Three involve Dad and Dublin and I wake up scared because most of the crap in there actually happened. The fourth nightmare is my subconscious trying to be subtle.

It's just me, as an adult, seated at a school desk drawing up a family tree for everyone I ever harmed. By the time I'm done, the family tree has spread off the paper and is covering the walls, and my teacher, Brother Campion, is fondling my friend's Nash's buttocks and saying: *Daniel will go far, boys and girls. He will go far because he puts in the work. Dedication is the key.*

I wake up from this and I have somehow moved across into the other bed and the Glock is laying on my chest.

Which is why, ladies and gentlemen, I generally take sleeping pills.

Also, subtle? I don't think so. You don't really need a degree to interpret this vision.

I sit up and gulp down an entire bottle of ten-dollar Hawaiian water. It's expensive but at least I'll get a second use from the bottle.

I wipe the Sharpshooter and break it down so it fits in a Kevlar backpack. Sharpie doesn't mind being broken down, he's used to it. I pack the Glock too, and a couple of smoke grenades which I always bring just in case but hardly ever get the chance to actually use. I love the feel of those smooth cylinders, and just handling them helps me get into the soldier mindset, which is where I need to be.

Most of my clothes are black and the leather jacket is such a deep brown that it would be hard to tell the difference without a swatch card. Luckily, thanks to Johnny Cash, the all black look is cool for middle-aged men, so no one in the hotel bats an eye when I stroll out through the lobby wearing a backpack and dressed like I'm gonna jump out of a plane seven thousand feet over Kabul.

225

* * *

Mike's house is predictably showy, with honest-to-God Irish setter statues sitting atop the gate pillars, and a garden wall that he often claims to have shipped over from Ireland, where it used to be part of a Norman round tower. I believe this to be true because it is exactly the type of ridiculously over-the-top faux-Paddy bullshit that Mike mistakes for patriotism.

However, grand as it surely is, we are not talking about Skywalker Ranch here. Mike ain't pulling down that kind of moolah, so the Madden residence is the third house down on a swanky cul-de-sac. If you're ever looking for it, it's the one with the postbox in the shape of a leprechaun's head and the letters go in his mouth.

I bet the neighbours love Mikey.

Mike's Benz is in the drive, along with a Prius and a pink stretch limo. I hope the limo is something to do with one of the hooker-mobiles that Mike has roaming all over Jersey, otherwise there could be some kind of party going on in there, and I ain't trying to thread a bullet between the heaving bodies on a dance floor.

Mike could have unknowingly bought himself a reprieve from the reaper.

But seeing as I came out here, I might as well take a look.

I have parked down the leafy avenue that opens on to the dead end. It's dark now but there are enough street lights for me to be seen, so as soon as I get out of the car, the plan is to blend with the shadows of mature oak trees and work my way round the back of Mike's leprechaun lair.

Getting around back of Mike's house actually turns out to be a breeze. I was expecting the whole nine yards as regards security: external cameras with infrared, motion sensors or failing that maybe a big goddamn dog. But there's nothing. I imagine the house itself is alarmed up the wazoo, but the building and grounds are actually pretty helpful for an intruder. Plenty of shrubs and trees to lurk behind, and two big California-style floor-to-ceiling glass walls that run the entire length of the house.

I brought some AP rounds in case the glass turned out to be bulletproof, but it seems like I won't need them. Frankly, I'm a bit disappointed in Irish Mike. What kind of self-respecting gangster doesn't have a dog on the grounds?

I find myself a nice perch in the low crook of a horse chestnut tree and set up camp. I whisper nice things to Sharpie so he will not screw around while I'm assembling him, snap a Starlight to his back then take a look at the evening's entertainment.

The first room is an office or study with a large wooden desk and one of those gas fireplaces built to look like an old-fashioned range. Mike is sitting at the desk reading the cartoons from the day's paper.

Perfect. Just check the other room and away we go. I could be home in time for the late late showing of 80s copedy (WINAWBSB) *Sledge Hammer!*, which is hilarious. You will give yourself a pain laughing, trust me and seek it out.

As you can see, I am trying to appear nonchalant about this entire mission, but I ain't fooling anyone, not even myself. I am planning to gun down a guy in his own house, possibly a couple of rooms away from his wife and daughter. It doesn't matter who the guy is; my actions tonight are gonna weigh heavily for a long time and will possibly be the straw that busted the horse's arse vis-à-vis Daniel McEvoy getting into heaven.

Do it, says Sharpie. *Take the shot.*

I should. It's all set up. No witnesses in the room.

Pull the trigger.

My finger hovers and I try to make my brain send the command, but nothing happens.

Tell yourself again how there's no other way.

With Mike gone, my problems disappear.

Oh, yeah? What about Mike's number two, Calvin? You think he won't come looking?

At least I'll buy myself some time.

You are shooting a guy in the head in order to buy some time?

It will take Calvin a while to gets his ducks in a row.

I refer you to my last point re shooting a guy in the head.

Mike would do it to me.

You are not Mike. Do you wanna be Mike?

No. I don't.

I do not want to be Mike, but I have no choice.

I feel blood throb in my forehead and my eyes water. Why will my finger not do what it's told?

Mike is right there, seemingly close enough to touch. If I pull the trigger, a hundred things have to happen in the right order for the bullet in this gun to end up in Mike's brain. The odds against all these things occurring in the right order must be pretty good. My pulling the trigger is barely even the cause of that effect. The actual cause goes way back. Generations. To the forces that brought Mike and me here today.

But do you wanna be Mike?

That's the clincher. I was never going to shoot Mike, even if I thought I might.

'Balls,' I whisper.

You said it, brother, says Sharpie.

I say balls because there is no plan B.

I hear the muted tinkles of ladies' laughter and champagne flutes and swing the scope across to the second room.

There is a party going on.

Ladies are getting injected in the face.

The Prius.

Zeb, you prick. What the hell were you thinking?

When Zeb volunteered to take Sofia with him on his rounds, he neglected to mention that one of the stops was Irish Mike Madden's house. Mrs Madden must have a dozen of her lady friends in there, all sipping champagne and dancing around until it is their turn to sit in a reclined La-Z-Boy and have Zeb or his beautiful assistant inject a shot of Botox into their foreheads. Both Zeb and Sofia are swilling down booze too, which I am pretty sure is not best practice medically speaking.

One of the ladies slides into the chair, and Sofia straddles her, takes aim and, urged on by the whoops of the other ladies, sticks the syringe into a wrinkle between the lady's eyes.

This is insane. Lunacy. How are we supposed to survive when Zeb continues to fuck up faster than I can fix things?

My phone vibrates and I check to find a text from the man himself.

You will never guess where I am.

I text him back.

I know where you are. I'm looking at you. Get the hell out.

I watch him read the text and grin. He looks into the blackness of the garden and flips me the bird.

A minute later I get: *Chill. Mike will never think to look for Sofia here. As far as he knows she is my nurse.*

This is all about Zeb showing me what a tactical genius he is. In Zeb's mind it is more fun to parade Sofia into Mike's house for him to have the opportunity to not recognise than it is for him to put her somewhere Mike will never look in the first place.

I am so angry with him for putting Sofia at risk that I misspell *arsehole*. Luckily my phone recognises the word by now and helps me out:

Arsehole. Arsehole. Arsehole. Stuff is about to happen. Why do you think I am in the garden? Leave now!

I watch his face drop as he reads the text.

Yeah, that's right, shit for brains. As far as you know, this is serious.

I am gonna catch it later when Mike turns out to be unshot.

Flashes of movement from the office window catch my eye and I swivel the scope back to Mike's office. Mister Nose Beard, Manny Booker, is ushering a coupla guys into the office.

I find it hard to believe what I'm seeing.

Krieger and Fortz.

What is their connection to Mike?

It doesn't matter. I got all my rotten eggs in one basket here. I gotta improvise, replan on the hoof.

Various scenarios run through my head, but I know there is no way to take three guys with a rifle from out here even if I was cold-blooded enough to go through with my original plan, which apparently I am not. Shot one takes out the window and if you're lucky the prime target; maybe you get one more off in that second of frozen panic, but that's all she wrote. The other guys have dived for cover before you can refocus.

What I gotta do is leave Mike for the moment and follow Krieger and Fortz when they leave. Find out where they're crashing, phone it in to Ronnie then call Zeb to make sure he has stashed Sofia somewhere safe.

I break down the rifle and bag it, then train the scope on Fortz to try to figure out what's going on here.

Fortz talks for a while and Mike does his best Don Corleone wise nodding bit. At the end of the spiel, Fortz hands over a fat envelope with bills poking out the top, which Mike smoothly sweeps into his drawer, and I know what this meeting's about.

Fortz needs me found as a matter of urgency and Mike has the resources to do the finding, plus he wants me found himself. My life is being traded for dollars and not for the first time this week. I don't know why I even bother getting surprised any more.

Still, it is a fat envelope of cash, which is gratifying in a weird kind of way. If I have to be hunted down like a rabid dog, at least I'm a priority to someone.

I gotta stop playing Tarzan and get myself back to the car before Krieger and Fortz take off. Shouldn't be too difficult; I bet those two ain't so sprightly since that little whupping I laid on them. Just thinking about those golden moments is enough to make me smile.

Still, now is not the time for nostalgia. I have grievous bodily harm to plan.

I swing outta the tree and land on something that yields under my weight and whimpers. I hear a couple of rib-splintering snaps, and my boots come away sticky.

Balls.

I knew Mike had a dog.

I stoop low and hug the line of shrubbery leading towards the party window. The only reason someone would cut a dog open is so they can go about their business in peace.

There's another shooter in the garden.

I gotta warn Sofia.

*　*　*

I gotta come out in the open for maybe six feet between the foliage and the side of the house. Six feet takes maybe half a second, but nevertheless the shooter fires a bullet into that slot. The bullet takes me between the shoulder blades, swatting me with its sheer velocity, and I overshoot the party window and thunk on to the office glass not six feet from the three men who want me dead. The impact sets off a light sensor and I get lit up like Times Square on New Year's Eve. I slide comically down the window, leaving contact streaks that are going to take the maid a ladder, three rags and several hours to polish out.

Hello, Fuckapalooza.

Mike lifts his head expecting to see a big dumb dog who's walked into the window again, but instead sees yours truly, the man who has become his nemesis.

Or as Zeb put it: *You are the fucking monkey that stuck his spanner into Mike's machine.*

Which as far as I can make out is an amalgam of three sayings: the one about the monkey, the spanner in the works thing and the ghost in the machine one.

Why am I thinking about this now? Prioritise, idiot.

There's no point. I've been shot high in the back. There's no walking away from this one.

And you want this to be your final mental exercise? Dissecting Zeb's turn of phrase?

What *was* the monkey one?

Mike stares quizzically at me, not sure what to make of this apparition, but I could give a shit about his puzzlement 'cause I'm dying.

Or am I?

Okay, I'm flattened on to this window like a Garfield toy. But I've felt worse and survived.

But how can I survive a bullet between the shoulder blades? My heart has no right to be still beating.

The backpack. It's got a Kevlar hide.

I got shot in the backpack.

Thank you, baby Jesus.

And to think I nearly didn't take the backpack from the Algerian guy 'cause he wanted twenty bucks for it. Eventually he threw the bag in gratis with the flash bangs. I should call that guy and give him one of those true customer stories for his website.

Mike is out of his seat and coming towards me, his brow knitted as he tries to figure it out. In his place, I would be very concerned for the health of the poor Irishman stuck to my window and help him inside for a cup of tea, but Mike predictably doesn't go down the humanitarian route; instead he pulls a nickel-plated revolver from his armpit and points it at my head.

I don't know who Mike thinks he is, but I wish he would pick one stereotype and stick to it. I was just getting used to his Plastic Paddy act, and now he thinks he's Jesse James.

Nickel-plated?

Apparently Mike has decided to shoot first and ask questions through a psychic, because he cocks the weapon and places the barrel level with my eye, dinking the glass.

This is ridiculous. He's gonna shoot through his own window now, rather than slide the door across?

I see Fortz grinning behind him. I think he's grinning; it might just be the gumshield where his teeth used to be. When he realises that he just paid Mike several grand to find a man who was in his back garden all the time, it might alleviate his happiness somewhat. Every cloud, as they say.

I wish Sofia wasn't here. I don't want her to see me like this. With any luck my face won't be recognisable and she won't think to check my pecker.

Mike never gets the chance to fire, because someone else does it before him.

The second shooter.

I feel a vibration jump from the window to my cheekbone, then glass is showering over me. Through the rainbow hail I see Fortz's head disappear. I don't hear the shot, or the second one that makes Krieger's heart explode.

This guy is good. Three shots; three tens.

The window collapses inwards and I keel over into the house with it. Mike has already turned tail, and seconds later I hear his Benz growl as he makes his getaway. I realise that I will never know if Sofia and Zeb made it out because of that bloody Prius. I strain my ears listening for the polite hum of an electric motor and I think I actually hear it until I notice a beer fridge in the corner of the office.

Balls.

So I lie here, in the Deliverance position, waiting for the shooter to finish me off. Krieger is in my eyeline and I see that he still has a black eye from the punch that porn star dealt him. Of course the gore-ringed cavity in his chest is a little more serious. I tell myself to look away, but it is too late; the image is already seared into the gallery of horrors in my mind.

Maybe this will be my hell; a slideshow of all the dreadful things I have seen or caused.

Still alive.

It's true. The guy hasn't killed me yet. He could if he wanted to, no doubt about that. He managed to squeeze off three kill shots before anyone reacted. That's competition-level shooting right there.

So, why am I alive? The only thing I can think of is that the guy don't need me dead.

He was after Krieger and Fortz and probably thought I was about to warn them. Maybe he will leave me alone here and Mike can shoot me when he comes back. Oh, wait.

The dog has abruptly ceased to whine. The main man is coming.

I wish I could put up a fight, at least go out like a professional, but all I can do is lie here. I could probably make a supreme effort and thrash about a bit, but I don't want to die thrashing. There's something silly about that and I'd hate to go out silly. I realise that I never left instructions for anyone to look after Sofia. Maybe Zeb will take care of her and keep his pants zipped.

Sure. Zeb is king of the humanitarians. It's all about the fellow man with Zebulon.

I feel a strong hand press down on my backpack. Then the hand moves to my shoulder and the guy flips me on to my back like he's turning over his last card in a poker game. I see his gloved hand dripping with blood and I realise that he's just doing clean-up now. Finishing me is no more significant to him than putting the dog out of its misery.

The guy is all kitted out like a ninja except for his boots, which are army issue almost identical to mine. There's a rifle over his shoulder with a super-long suppressor on the barrel, which explains why I didn't hear any shots. I don't recognise the rifle but it looks expensive, top of the range. Sometimes you can tell on sight how valuable something is. Not wine, though. You would have to be one hell of a sommelier to put a price on a bottle based on the colour alone.

Ninja sniper shrugs his shoulder in a move that see-saws the rifle under his arm so the trigger guard lands in his fist and the silencer points directly at my face.

Nice move. Practised.

I could beg now, I got the breath. But this guy is a pro. I might as well argue with Arnold the Terminator from the first movie where he was relentless, but not the second one where Arnie turned good robot.

Then something happens. Seems like the guy recognises me. His head jerks back maybe an inch and I see his eyes widen a fraction.

'You,' he says.

And it is me. No denying it. I hope against hope that for once in my life, being me turns out to be a good thing.

'Yeah,' I cough, and it is no mean feat to cough and speak at the same time. I wasn't intending to cough, it just came out.

'Motherfucker,' says Ninja, and shakes his head. He makes a sound like three quick shots through a silencer; maybe he's laughing.

Ninja places the silencer's tip between my eyes, then wags a gloved finger at me, spattering my face with blood. The meaning is clear.

Do not come after me.

He needn't worry. I ain't ever coming after this guy. Shoot me once, shame on you; shoot me twice, shame on me, and I got enough shame in my life already, believe me.

As he wags his finger a fourth unnecessary time, Ninja's sleeve rides up a little and I see an inch of skin between glove and cuff. Sallow skin with two coloured string bracelets looped around the wrist.

I force myself to not think about this now. Do not show any recognition, because that could change Ninja's mind about sparing me. I close my eyes tight and act like I'm totally and utterly banjaxed. It ain't really an act.

I count to thirty, trying to concentrate on the numbers. Nothing else. No conclusions drawn, then I open my eyes, see the Ninja has gone and I think:

Pablo.

Feck me, it was Pablo. Edit's personal trainer obviously has a couple of non-gymnasium-based talents.

Krieger and Fortz were loose ends so they had to be clipped.

Why was I spared?

Stupid question. I was spared because Ronnie warned Edit that if anything happened to me, she would come looking.

Pablo got lucky that he shot my backpack.

It's genius really. Edit sends Krieger and Fortz to the local gangster's house to ask for help locating me. Then Pablo takes them out. Mike don't wanna be caught with two bent cops in his manor so he'll probably dispose of the bodies.

Sweet and neat. Except I threw my monkey dick in the machine.

Luckily my monkey dick was wearing a Kevlar backpack.

It takes me about five minutes to get to my feet and check the party room. Plenty of abandoned champagne glass littering the floor but no people. Zeb did what he was told for once and got Sofia the hell out of there. Another five minutes pass and I feel ready to tackle climbing the wall. But before quitting this rural abattoir I make myself pee in the water bottle from the hotel. I don't really need to go at the moment, but I carried the bottle all the way out here, so damned if I ain't gonna use it.

CHAPTER 11

I wake up in my hotel room to a tweet from Simon.

If you aren't sure how to interpret my words of wisdom, please ask. The last thing I need is patients doing stuff in my name.

I think Simon is granting himself absolution from whatever his flock of patients might get up to.

Messiah complex anyone? Paging Dr Jesus.

That phrase is a little redundant. I mean, who believes in Jesus any more? And if you want to see teenagers crap themselves laughing, try explaining what a pager used to be. You tell 'em about cassette tapes and they think you're one lying old Depends-wearing motherfucker.

The following is a transcript of a conversation I had with Jason's nephew:

Me: The songs were pressed on to a long tape. Six songs per side then you turned it over.

Nephew: Turned what over?

Me: The tape in the machine, but you had to be careful or the machine would eat the tape and you'd have to straighten it out with a pencil.

Nephew: Fuck off, Gandalf. You're making this shit up.

Five minutes later I get another message, this time from Mike.

Get over to the club now, laddie. We need to wrap this up. Be here by noon, or else?

Balls.

I was hoping Mike might be traumatised by last night. Also there was no need for a question mark at the end of his text. It's not as if we don't know what happens if I don't do as I'm told.

I'm gonna have to whip out Tommy's video. How much of it he watches is up to Mike.

So I'm on my merry way to get shot in the head. If I had to compile a list of possible traumatic moments in the life of an Irish male, the classic head shot would be right up there with the driving test and turning Pops on his side so the puke doesn't choke him, especially when the temptation is there to let the vomit do its work. It's nature, right? Who's gonna blame a ten-year-old kid?

Maybe I told you before that I'm not big on the whole flashback thing? I probably told you right before launching into a flashback thing.

But I don't have flashbacks per se; what I do have is a good memory for the bad times. I think of my mom and I see her weeping in a corner, dishcloth clutched to her breast masking the ripped blouse. I think on little Patrick and I see his moon face and those wonky teeth that would surely have needed braces, inkblot bruises covering his cheek, and him thinking he's a bad kid, that everything's his fault.

I got a head-shot memory too. From guess where? The Lebanon, big surprise, right.

Zeb says to me: *What's all this THE Lebanon shit? It's Lebanon, okay? You don't say THE Ireland or THE Israel.*

239

So I come back with: *You say THE United States.*

It went on like that for a coupla hours, until Zeb got one of his periodic boners and had to excuse himself for twenty minutes. That guy is like Old Faithful; when is he gonna slacken off? He's in his forties now, for feck sake.

Anyway, my head-shot memory. The UN trucked us over to Damour to throw stern looks at the locals who were hell bent on revenge on PFLP and DFLP militiamen who had just defiled a cemetery, dragging coffins out of their neat rows, executed a stack of Christians and painted a mural of Fatah guerrillas holding AK-47 rifles on the church wall.

A quick aside: revolutionary groups all got their go-to mural guys. A good inspiring mural can swing ten per cent of the don't-knows, not to mention make the revolutionaries feel validated. These guys are not just slopping paint on to walls; it's at least as legitimate an art form as graffiti. Banksy was never darkly satirical with automatic fire knocking chunks out of his canvas. It's the worst-kept secret in Irish republican circles that the artist who did a lot of the good stuff on the Falls Road was actually an Ulster Unionist who strapped on his orange sash on march day. I guess you get a pass if you provide a valuable service.

Anyway, back to the Lebanon. There we were in the rear of a truck driving straight into the aftermath of a massacre. I know for a fact, because we took a poll in the truck, that twelve point five men out of sixteen had no clue what PFLP or DFLP stood for, never mind the difference between the groups. I don't know how we arrived at point five of a guy in those calculations.

In the course of our sweep we happen on a Phalangist militiaman inside the gutted church with half a dozen Japanese Red Army terrorists trussed up in the aisle. There had been talk of Red Army guys helping out with the Popular Front but I always thought that was barracks bullshit. But here these guys were, Japanese no doubt about it, down on their knees being all stoic for the most part, about to pay the ultimate price for their role in the recent massacre. I don't know how a lone Phalangist managed the logistics of wrapping six enemy soldiers in restraints, but it was pretty clear that he was about to take advantage of their immobility to speed the Red Army boyos directly to whichever pearly gates they believed in, fervently hoping there would be a distinct absence of virgin hosts there to greet them.

We just kinda looked on for a second, a little perplexed to be honest. Intrigued too, like we were watching the whole show on TV. Peacekeepers aren't on anyone's side as such, so plugging this super-soldier would lead to one clusterballs of a debriefing. Tommy Fletcher let his trademark cow-scaring roar at the guy, followed by:

'Hey, gobshite. Step away from the prisoners.'

The Phalangist responded by shrieking in shock, then shooting the first Red Army guy in the head. The guy looked minorly disappointed for a second, like his car wouldn't start, then keeled over.

'Balls!' exclaimed Tommy and rushed the gunman. We all followed suit and there ensued a macabre version of duck, duck, goose, with us jabbering while the Phalangist dodged between the Red Army lads plugging as many as he could before we subdued him.

By the time we piled on, the guy had a score of five and he would have completed the set had his frankly ancient Luger not blown up in his hand and shredded his fingers.

Is that a funny story in retrospect? Is there a touch of humour to be gleaned from a domino line of Japanese terrorists?

Not for me.

I think on it too long and the strength of the images really drags me under. The guy with the gun staring in shock at his own mangled hand. The last Japanese soldier singing a simple melody high and clear. I've been trying to find that song ever since. Don't know why. It sounded like he was repeating the phrase *abandon we* but that can't have been it. Wrong language. The air in the church was baked orange and heavy with moisture, a miasma that clung to our uniforms. And Tommy squatting on the Phalangist, who was maybe eighteen, taking a poll as to whether we should report all of this or just go on our merry way and pretend nothing had ever happened.

So we took the path of no resistance. We cut the surviving prisoner loose, used the bonds to tie up the Phalangist, which must have earned us a grudging nod from the gods of irony, and got ourselves the hell away from that bloodbath, because there is no way to come out of a three-way balls-up like that smelling of anything but fear and death.

By the way, one night in the barracks we worked out what fear smells like and I still stick by the formula: fifty per cent stale sweat, thirty per cent gas and twenty per cent stink of your own private hellhole. Wherever the bad thing that happened to you happened.

When fear creeps up on me, my first sensory clue is the stink of that church with trussed corpses clogging up the aisle trumping the ghosts of brides being escorted by their proud fathers.

I voted the same as everybody else. Get the hell out.

Abandon we.

I know. Sounds a lot like a flashback, but I don't get flashbacks.

* * *

There's only one iron left in the fire now. It ain't my iron and I didn't light the fire, but I gotta put it out before this metaphor gets away from me and no one has a clue what the hell I'm talking about.

Writ simple: Irish Mike Madden reckons I still owe him. After all the shit that happened, Mike still reckons I got a tab to settle. I am starting to think it's never gonna be enough with this guy.

Also I know damning stuff like how he rolled me into the whole Shea/Freckles thing like some kind of Trojan Horse: shiny on the outside, deadly on the inside. And when you open a door to the inside, then the deadly comes out through the hole, like Achilles. I guess if you have to explain the imagery then the imagery is kind of redundant. Still, I think the Trojan Horse thing would have worked if I'd left it alone.

Anyways, now I gotta swing by his place and hope he's feeling magnanimous on account of how things turned out with the Shea situation. Not only is Mike out from under New York's shadow, but there's talk of him picking up the Shea slack, making him a genuine player, which could come in handy if any of the Jersey boys get fed up listening to stories about a Mick operating locally.

So, it is possible that Mike will call it evens and we can all get back to business.

Possible, but about as likely as a hyena spitting out a hunk of red meat which is then eaten by a supermodel, which is not probable firstly because hyenas don't ever not eat meat and supermodels hardly ever do, then there's the obvious hygiene issue and thirdly there's the geographical factor, as in there are not many supermodels hanging around sub-Saharan Africa.

Apart from Iman.

And Waris Dirie.

*Un*likely is what I'm trying to say.

I think my shrink was right. Maybe I am too much of a deconstructionist, but I would argue that it's undeniable at this point that watching *Fashion Police* can be educational.

In this spirit of optimism for the future, I do not bring any guns along. Also I know whoever's on the door will be giving me the cavity search.

From experience I know never to talk to Mike until he's had his first blow job of the day, which is usually about eleven. Even though Mike's blood is green, he's big on the whole English feudal lords conjugal rights law that got Mel Gibson so riled in *Braveheart*. So I stroll over just after the midday deadline to give Mike a chance to let off steam. To be honest, I feel a little weird being out on the street without anyone pointing a gun at me. Every now and then I do a little jinky sidestep just in case there's a guy on a rooftop watching me through a Zeiss, and I make it to Mike's block without anyone taking a potshot, so either I'm just paranoid or my zigzagging actually works.

I guess I should enjoy not being a target while it lasts.

Mister Nose Beard, Manny Booker, is outside on the door giving the world his best tough guy face, but I'm guessing he's sweating bullets inside the navy suit Mike forces his guys to wear. You put the facial hair and the suit together and you got a lot of heat bearing down on a little brain. That's a recipe for violent disaster.

I approach Manny slow and obvious, because I reckon this guy is close to the edge with me and it's my own damn fault. I can't help screwing with Booker because he's so earnest about the whole *gangsta* thing. He spends his days fretting over saving face or someone disrespecting him. Every little thing is end-of-days important to Manny. Just walking down the block he has to be bristling with menace. Someone should tell him that he just comes off as constipated. When God sends a guy that intense your way, it is your duty to take the piss; as my quotable buddy Zebulon Kronski said: *When you find a prick this big, you gotta play with it a little.*

Never a truer word.

So I make sure Booker gets a good look at me as I come up the steps.

'Hey, Manny,' I say. 'How you doing today? Beard looks good. Verdant.'

I realise that I have screwed with this boy too much and now he doesn't recognise sincerity when he sees it.

'Ver-fucking-what? Fuck you, McEvoy. I'll be doing good when I cut off your prick and ram it down your throat.'

I'd swear this is a line from some *Godfather*-lite movie.

'We all live for that day, Manny,' I say amiably, then I get down to business.

'How's Mike? Has he had his morning . . . ?'

Instead of finishing this question I wink twice, which is goodfella code for blow job.

'Nah,' says Manny. 'He's auditioning a new dancer. Calvin brought her in.'

Mike presides over a couple of lap dance joints on Cloisters' strip, which is precisely two blocks long. He considers it a good business practice to give every potential new hire a personal look-see. He runs a diner too, but the waitresses' interview ain't quite so stringent as they gotta carry stuff in their hands that Mike's gonna put in his mouth.

So Mike is still harbouring his morning tension. Not a great time to broker a truce.

'Okay. I'm gonna get a latte and come back in an hour.'

Manny glares at me. 'You fucking better come back in an hour.'

Here we go.

'I just said I was coming back.'

Manny tilts his head for maximum badness and his beard bristles. 'And I just said you fucking better come back.'

Manny is using the age-old tactic of intimidation through repetition with added fucketry (WINAWBSB).

I decide to throw him a curve ball. 'Yeah, you want something, Manny-o? Latte? No, you look like a skinny mochachino guy to me, right?'

Manny is predictably incensed by this exotic-sounding brew. I hear he once punched a lady in the throat because she asked him if he'd read *Twilight*.

'Mooha-fucking-what? Is that a fruity drink? Are you calling me a skinny fruit?'

I gotta lay off, or this goon is gonna knife me in an alley some night.

'Okay, Manny. Chill. I'll be back in an hour, honest. One gunman to another. Gangster's honour.'

Manny's phone rings. His ringtone is 'Eye of the Tiger' and we both bam bam-bam-bam along with it for a few seconds until he answers. That's the problem with having a good tune for your ringtone; sometimes you wanna hear the chorus.

'Fuck yeah,' he says. 'Fuckin' A.'

A man of many fucks. It's like Manny has a quota to fill.

'You ain't drinking no fag drinks, McEvoy. The boss seen you on the fucking security cam, so get up here and assume the position.'

I glower at the plastic beetle clamped to the door frame. It seems like I have a date with a horny Irish mobster.

* * *

Inside, the atmosphere is buzzing with anticipation. The lights are low and Mike and his guys are seated in a little semicircle in front of a makeshift stage with a screen rigged behind it. I can tell Mike is all amped up by the way he's slapping his thighs, and if the lights were any lower I swear he'd have his dick out. I need to get my spiel in now or I could be here all day.

'Mister Madden. Hey, Mike, we need to talk.'

Mike barely spares me a glance. 'Yeah, McEvoy. Gimme a minute, laddie. Maybe two. Sit your arse down.'

I seriously consider going operational right there. Technically I'm unarmed, but I can do a lot of damage without a gun. And these buckhawks virtually got their tongues hanging out, for Christ's sake. I could make a decent amount of bones go crack before Mike knew what was happening.

Attractive as this idea is, it would be suicide. They can take a dozen casualties, I can only take one. So I sit my arse down and run through the speech I gotta make to this bunch o' perverts.

Mike's number two, Calvin, hops up on the stage and pats the air for silence.

'Okay, guys. Mister Madden. I got something a little different here, but give it a chance. This gal is a money machine.'

'She better be,' says Mike, tugging the crotch of his trousers. 'The last gal you brought in danced like she was being electrocuted. I was paying that donkey money to keep her clothes on.'

Everyone laughs, but it is good-humoured stuff. Mike does not seem to be suffering any negative after-effects from the shootings at his home. Why would he? He's alive and several grand richer all for the price of two windows which probably needed replacing with bulletproof panes anyway. And today is another day in paradise for

247

Mike: ogle a dancer, take a few minutes in the back room, shoot me in the face.

It's all good.

A girl steps from behind a curtain and mounts the stage. She's something, no doubt about it: long gymnast's legs, shimmering belly-dancing rig-out and a face too pretty for these animals.

'Okay, Cal,' says Mike. 'She's a looker, I'll give you that, laddie. But I got plenty of lookers.'

'Wait, Mister Madden, you need the light show for the full effect.'

Calvin hops down from the stage and taps a few keys on his laptop. Psychedelic spirals swirl on the screen and one of Sade's better pop jazz classics fills the room.

Sade. There ain't a hetero alive who doesn't drift off into a soft-focus scenario when that lady sings.

The girl's movements match the mood perfectly. None of the usual bump and grind, this dancer is all about the slow seduction. Her arms do something a little Indian and her pelvis moves like there's a coupla extra joints in there.

It's very distracting.

Calvin knows he's brought in a winner.

'I told you she was a mover, Mister Madden,' he says.

Here we go. Three, two, one . . .

'I got something moving right here, laddie,' says Mike, bang on cue, then: 'Come on, darlin', enough of the tease, let's see the merchandise.'

The dancer undulates down from the stage like a human slinky. She knows who butters the bread around here and zeroes in on Mike like he's some kind of demigod. She's got eyes on her too, big brown numbers that could fool a guy into believing that this ain't a professional relationship. Just like every man Jack in the room, I forget all my troubles. I know in my heart of hearts that if this girl asked me to leave with her right now I would give it serious consideration. I never understood the Salome thing until this instant.

The dancer is up on Mike and he's trying to play it casual, like this kind of thing happens every day. I notice Calvin is a little jittery, like he's nervous about something, and then I notice something else. There ain't nobody without an Adam's apple in this room.

Holy shit. Brave move, Calvin.

I lean forward in my seat and wait for the explosion.

The dancer shucks off her sequinned top and there ain't any boobs underneath. The gal is a guy and I think Calvin may have overestimated his boss's tolerance levels.

It takes Irish Mike a moment to get it, but when he does, his reaction is comical. He executes a move that I can only describe as a reverse lunge, which I would not even have believed was possible for a portly geezer had I not seen it with my own eyes. He pulls out his gun and waggles it a little, giving genuine thought to killing everyone in the room.

'It's a male . . . guy,' he finally blurts.

I cannot stop myself and I know Zeb would be proud. 'A mail guy? Like a postman?'

Mike swings his gun towards Calvin, who may be the favourite but who's overstepped the mark this time.

'What kind of crying, Brokeback, queen of the birdcage bullshit is this, Calvin?'

'I thought you knew right off, Mister Madden,' says Calvin, and I swear he executes a craven little bow.

Mike breathes through his nose furiously, reining himself in. 'Yeah, I knew. Course I knew. Who wouldn't know? I screwed enough broads to know when someone ain't a broad.'

'Yeah. Of course. You're like a broad guru, Mister Madden.'

No one kisses arse less subtly than Calvin, but Mike's been getting his arse kissed for so long that he can't see the truth any more.

'That's right. A broad guru. You ask any woman in this town.' He sneaks a glance at the dancer, who is huddling behind Calvin.

'People pay for this?'

'Are you kidding? Big money. Mona was pulling in five grand in the Corral. Five grand per week.'

Money talks, as they say. 'Five grand? In one week.'

'Six days to be precise. She's off on Wednesdays.'

Mike snorts. 'She's a he is what she is. And she's on seven days from now on. Get her started in the Parlour tonight.'

'Sure thing, Mister Madden. She's grateful for the chance.'

Mike frowns, which he does when he's thinking. 'Yeah, but put up a sign or something. You know, some of the clientele ain't as perceptive as me. I don't want any of our counsellors getting a heart attack.'

Calvin is open to all suggestions. 'Yeah, a sign. Saying ladyboy or something like that.'

'How about mailman?' I say innocently.

Mike's brain is grinding through his options here; eventually he arrives at the conclusion that finding the whole episode hilarious is the best move for him.

'Mailman,' he says, slapping the thigh that was recently adjacent to a visible erection. 'That's a good one. You crack me up, laddie.' He drops Calvin a loaded wink that says it's time for serious business, and his number two hustles Mona out the side door.

'I like to make people laugh,' I say. 'When I get the opera-toonity.'

Mike squints. 'Hey, watch your mouth. Just 'cause we're laughing don't mean I've gone soft.'

Please Jesus, shut my stupid coping-mechanism mouth.

Mike sits up straight composing himself for the serious speech. Enough joking around with the strippers etc.

'You signed your death warrant last night, laddie,' he says, getting straight to it.

I reckon it was signed long before then; maybe I hurried on the execution a little, but I recently got beat on with a dildo so my judgement is a little out of whack. Also I got a card to play. The Tommy video.

'Okay, Mike. Why don't you give me a chance to make my case?'

'You nervous, Danny?' Mike asks, rolling an empty whiskey glass on the table. It click-clacks on each facet, which is really annoying, and I have to grind my teeth to stop myself slapping Mike's hand.

'I'm okay, Mike,' I say evenly. 'I been in deeper holes with worse people.'

Mike gathers himself, digging deep for some real anger.

'You came to my house,' he says finally. 'To my goddamn house.'

'I was in a hole, Mike. You put me there.'

'You crossed the line, McEvoy.'

This must be the code phrase because Mike's goons are up and drawing flashy weapons. It's difficult to believe that these Wild West types still exist in a first-world country.

I feel a familiar buzzing shroud settle on my brain, muffling the circuit breakers in there. Long-term-consequences evaluators are now unavailable.

'That's me, Mike. Always crossing your precious lines.'

'First I lose my mother, then I see you lurking in my garden putting my daughter's life in danger. We may be on the wrong side of the law, McEvoy, but there's a code.'

'Like your dear departed mother taught you,' I suggest.

Mike jumps on this, delighted that I have handed him a segue right into the next section of his speech. His fat potato face glows with the joy of a happy coincidence.

'Yes, exactly, laddie. Where I come from, a man looks after his family and does what his mammy tells him.'

'Whatever she tells him?'

Mike kisses a finger and smears the photograph pinned to his lapel.

'To the letter. My mam had a wisdom about her. I sometimes thought she had a touch of the fairy magic.'

Two of Mike's boys begin humming 'My Heart's Across the Sea in Ireland' so low that it's possible I'm imagining it.

'My mammy raised eight of us on three shillings a month. Eight!'

Feck me. JFK didn't get treated to this level of post-mortem rose-tinted spectacleness.

I lay on the Irish. 'Ah, sure, she was only a saint.'

'She was,' sniffles Mike. 'And I didn't even see her off.'

He switches tack in a heartbeat. Mercurial, that's our Mike.

'But I can see *you* off,' he grins with the tears still on his cheeks, following the wrinkles. His face reminds me of the irrigation channels in a rice paddy. 'You threatened my family.'

I can see where he's going. It's classic self-justification. Mike doesn't see himself as a monster, so he's gotta spell out his reasoning in case God is watching.

'Mike, before you wrap me in plastic, I got something to show you.'

'Really? You ain't gonna dick about, laddie? I am not in the mood. It's gone noon and I ain't busted a nut today.'

I pull out my phone, slowly. 'Mike, you need to see this. Your mam would want you to see it.'

Mike plucks the phone from my hand with pudgy fingers. 'A cell phone? Mam never even had a cell phone.'

'Not the phone,' I say. 'There's a video message on it, all keyed up. Just touch the screen.'

Mike's scowl intimates that someone of his importance should not have to be bothered with touching a screen, and in case the scowl might be misinterpreted, he vocalises too: 'Fucking little phones. I cannot be arsed, honest to Jaysus. A load of Bluetoothing wankocity.'

Wankocity? I am reluctantly impressed.

Calvin returns from shooing Mona into the dressing room just in time to offer his services as audiovisual guy.

'Mister Madden,' he says. 'I can cue that up on the big screen, no problemo.'

Mike tosses him the phone. 'Do it, laddie. I have a pain in my face with these gizmos. I stopped paying attention after VHS.'

While Calvin is e-mailing the video file to his MacBook I smile pleasantly at the man whose heart is about to be ripped out of his chest and dragged along the asphalt by the HD ghost of his own mother.

Is this cruellest thing I have ever done?

Possibly.

But in fairness I have suffered severe provocation. Occasionally I do stuff that doesn't make much of an impact at the time but loops around to haunt me for years. Until this moment the number one act of cruelty ever perpetrated by Daniel McEvoy on another human was the summer evening in the Curragh army training camp in County Kildare when I got peer-grouped into the hazing of a Donegal grunt for bringing down the squad's time on the assault course. Guy's jaw got busted and it was my kick that busted it. I felt the bone flex and crack under my boot. Never owned up to it. Let the blame get spread across the group. The Donegal guy washed out so maybe I saved his life, that's what I tell myself.

You're not a spineless bully. You saved his life.

Bullshit. I chose myself. I walked the soft road.

I am not so bad. No, no, no.

I think that guy's name was Mike too.

Is that an omen? Should I let Irish Mike off the hook?

I look into the wannabe godfather's deep-set eyes and it strikes me that he would probably drop the hammer on Sofia himself.

Screw mercy. I gotta get myself out from under this guy.

'Where the hell is that video, Calvin?' says Mike, pouting. 'I got stuff on, you know.'

Power makes children of grown men. My dad was the same. His trick was to build up a head of steam then invent a flimsy reason for it. He couldn't just throw a tantrum because he was an evil bastard. No, there had to be justification and God help whoever challenged his reasons. I remember him coming home from the track with a thundercloud on his shoulders having thrown a bundle at a nag that ran into the first fence and broke its own neck. He accused my mother of flirting with the milkman and gave her a ferocious slap, or a cross-court backhand as he often referred to the blow when he had a few whiskeys warming his gut.

The milkman on our street was eighty-seven, with an honest-to-

God wooden leg. For ten years I thought the guy was a retired pirate. You don't see wooden legs any more. Everything is carbon fibre these days.

Maybe it's thinking of my father that does it, but I am suddenly in a quiet rage.

'Hey, Mike,' I say. 'Before we look at this video, I want you to know that either way I am done with your shit.'

Mike isn't sure how to react. He wants to laugh it off but I think he hears the wire in my voice.

'Really, laddie? Done with my shit, are you? That's possible. That is entirely possible.'

I don't say anything but I get ready to come out of the chair, because there is an excellent chance that Mike will lose it once this movie starts rolling.

'Here we go, Mister Madden,' says Calvin, unaware that he could soon be the shot messenger of legend. 'See, what I did was add the video to a mail, then send it from the phone to my computer. Seeing as you have Wi-Fi in here, it was literally no problem. What took so long was the size of the video. I didn't want to compress it and sacrifice quality as we're putting it up on the screen.'

Mike looks so bored by this explanation that his head might roll off his shoulders.

'Kids,' I say, and Mike's eyes reply, *Tell me about it.*

It's nice that we're connecting. This will definitely be our last chance.

'Here we go, boss,' says Calvin, pressing the space bar with the same gravitas as the President launching a nuclear attack with the football.

Shit. I'm nervous. Giddy. I feel like giggling. Also I'm embarrassed for Mike, you know, 'cause he's a human being after all. And no son wants to look at what Mike's about to see. Except maybe that Greek guy Oedipus.

A video box appears on the screen.

'Ta-dah,' says Calvin, stepping back, trying to ramp up the importance of playing a video to compensate for his earlier faux pas. He is almost certainly going to regret that.

The film is excellent quality. Amazing what you can do with a phone these days.

As a techno-fool, Mike's default setting during any sort of computer activity is boredom. If someone were to ask Mike Madden whether he was a Mac or a PC he would probably say that he had some cousins in Waterford who were McDonalds. In spite of this I am not surprised when something on the screen slices through his ennui.

'Hang on,' he says, brightly. 'That's Mammy's room.'

On screen we see a bedroom that could have been lifted from an *Irish mammy's room* catalogue complete with patchwork quilt on the four-poster and enough throw pillows to choke a whale. There is an embroidered platitude hanging behind the wrought-iron headboard.

It *is* his mammy's room. I know because I have watched this clip and the big soft grin Mike's sporting is about to get wiped clean off his mug.

The camera swivels a little, bringing a elderly lady into the shot.

'Mammy had her hair done,' Mike breathes. 'And she has teeth.'

Mrs Madden coughs delicately then stares down the eye of the camera.

'This is a message for my son, Michael,' she says, and she is Irish mother incarnate, to be ignored at one's peril.

256

'Yes, Mammy,' says Mike automatically, and if any of his men want to get themselves gut-shot, now is the time to snigger.

'Michael, a dear friend of mine reliably informs me that you are up to all sorts of shenanigans in the United States of America. Now a man's business is his own and I am proud of what you've made of yourself, and I am fully aware that sometimes eggs need to be broken to make an omelette.'

'Yes, Mammy. Exactly, Mammy. Thanks, Mammy,' recites Mike, a beatitude of obedience.

'But Thump . . . my good friend has a good friend himself, and you are holding a gun to this man's head.' Mrs Madden's tone ratchets up an octave into the hysterical bracket. 'And he an Irish soldier.' The elderly lady sits forward. 'A soldier, Michael, like two of your own possible fathers.'

I've seen souls laid bare before but rarely with such brutal efficiency. For all intents and purposes, Mike is an eight-year-old boy weeing down his own leg.

'Mammy,' he says, pleading, as though this is live. 'All the boys are here.'

'Now you listen to me, Mikey boy,' says his mother, her eyes hard. 'You let this Daniel person off the hook. Throw him back, son, and kill yourself a couple of English boys if you have to get it out of your system.'

'I can't, Mammy,' whines Mike. 'I gave my word.'

Mrs Madden steamrolls over him. 'And I don't want to hear any old rubbish about debts or duty. I am your mother and I am *telling you* to call off the dogs. I never asked you for anything, Mikey, and I'm not asking now.' She leans towards the camera. 'Just do what your mammy tells you or I will haunt you for all eternity. Goodbye, Mike. Call me on Friday.' Mrs Madden smiles demurely at whoever is holding the camera. 'How was that, Thumper?'

'Thumper?' says Mike.

A male voice off-screen says: 'Perfect, Bunny.'

This voice has a Kerry accent, though sometimes it goes all Belfast if he needs that extra oomph of menace.

'Bunny?' Mike coughs the word. 'I . . .'

Words fail him. If I were him I would shoot the computer or Calvin before things get worse, but his wits are not about him at the moment.

And there's worse to come. Mucho worso.

'Turn off the camera,' says Mrs Madden.

'Oh sure I turned that off already,' lies Tommy Fletcher.

Tears spring into Mike's eyes and he stuffs his hand into his own mouth to stop a sob jumping out.

I feel guilty suddenly. Mike has seen enough. No son deserves to see what's coming up on this tape.

I think my point is made. I had intended to rub Mike's nose in it, but honestly I would prefer to shoot Mike than inflict this on him.

'Okay, Calvin,' I say. 'You can hit the pause.'

Calvin's eyes do not leave the screen. 'Shut the hell up, McEvoy. You ain't the boss of me.'

There isn't time to argue. Every second this video rolls is another nail in Mike's soul, so I rise and take two quick steps towards Calvin, and hit the space bar on his keyboard, freezing the video on Mrs Madden's face.

'You don't wanna see the rest of it,' I tell Mike. 'Trust me.'

'Mammy,' says Mike. 'Mammy.'

Manny and his nose beard choose this moment to pop in. 'Hey, Mike. Nice MILF. She dancing later?'

Mike reaches into his pocket and his hand emerges with the dull glint of brass adorning the knuckles.

'Get the hell out,' he says to me, and I swear to Christ I would not bet against this man right now even if he was going into the ring with Mike Tyson in his heyday.

I wink at Calvin and mouth, *I'll just get my phone.*

Five seconds later and I am outta there, not letting the door swat me on the arse and so on and so forth.

I hope Manny Booker doesn't get dead, because I like how his name rhymes with tranny hooker. The sound of breaking glass slides under the door and I know at the very least Manny's gonna be eating through a straw for a while.

Who cares? Let them prey on each other. Maybe Manny will come out on top.

I don't care, I tell myself. It was me or someone else who was not me.

The sharp crack of splintering wood spills out on to the street.

I check my phone for weirdly appropriate tweets. But there is nothing. Even my gadgets refuse to give me comfort.

Abandon Wii.

CHAPTER 12

The key to staying alive until you die is to not get yourself killed.

I saved this nugget till close to the end on account of how bleeding obvious it reads, which might bring on a little gnashing of teeth. But to most people *not getting yourself killed* involves nothing more than just doing what you're already doing and maybe cutting down on mayonnaise which is more or less liquid sugar.

Not so for Daniel McEvoy. Lately it seems that I gotta go far out of my way just to avoid the clusterfuck hotspots that are springing up all over this New Jersey picture-postcard town, which seems to be an oasis of calm and safety for almost everyone else.

I gotta admit to being a little aggrieved by all this attention from the grim reaper. Okay, you're on the front line wearing a flak jacket, you expect your daily dose of missiles and shrapnel, but I've been out of that game for nearly two decades now and still I'm dodging bullets on a daily basis.

At least I've earned some sort of reprieve from Irish Mike Madden, though I have no doubt it's temporary. Mike will figure a work-around soon enough and send me off on some other hare-brained suicide mission. I cannot keep this up indefinitely. I need to put a full stop on the Mike situation.

My Twitter bird chirps and I check Simon's latest characters of wisdom.

Normal is all about perspective. Unless you're killing people or exposing yourself to schoolgirls. That ain't normal.

When is it my turn to be normal?

I stand on the sidewalk outside Sofia's building and feel my heart pound just from proximity, and I think:

If you want to be normal, Dan, walk away now.

I don't walk away. I am not even tempted.

Sofia answers the door in a robe, hair wet and face scrubbed. I don't really know what to make of this. Usually when she isn't playing a part then she's lost to me in the shadowy folds of depression. These are the nights I bunk on the couch, just to make sure nothing bad happens. Sofia made it solo so far, but I feel responsible because I have allowed her to become dependent. My broad shoulders have taken some of her massive burden, and without me this beautiful lady would be utterly alone.

Or maybe it puffs up my ego to kid myself that Sofia Delano depends on craggy old war vet Daniel McEvoy.

'Hey, Dan,' she says and I can tell two things from this short greeting. One: Sofia knows who I am. And two: she's calm, which means she's taken her lithium.

It's easier for me when Sofia is on her meds, I'm not saying it isn't, but part of me wishes there was a place where her particular brand of electric crazy was acceptable right out on the street. When she turns on that personality I am drawn in like a moth to the neon.

Maybe we should move to Hollywood. Or Galway.

'Hi, Sofia darlin',' I say, laying my hands on her shoulders, like epaulettes. 'How are you feeling?'

She leans in to me, pressing her cheek to my chest, and if we could stay like this forever it would be fine with me, but sooner rather than later little Dan would start to get ideas. I savour the moment while it lasts, brushing her blond hair flat to her crown, thinking that cradling a woman's skull is about as intimate as it gets, and also thinking that I will not be voicing this theory to Zeb, who would laugh it out of court.

'I'm feeling better,' she says. 'Still cloudy in my stupid head, but better. I had a dream about a hammer.'

I pull her closer. 'That was a dream. No hammers around here.'

She shudders in my arms. 'Good. I've done stuff, Dan, but hammers? It's time to jump off the bridge when hammers come into it.'

'No hammers,' I say again. 'Just a nightmare. You need to keep taking your pills.'

Sofia backs off a few steps and I'm sorry I brought up the meds.

'You don't understand, Daniel,' she says, frowning. 'I'm not myself with the pills. They drain the life right out of me. Maybe I don't have the strength to hurt anyone but I can't really love anyone either. What I am is a cardboard cut-out. You can't understand how that feels, but it's not your fault.'

She holds out her hand, an olive branch, and I let her draw me inside.

'You're the only one, Dan. If it wasn't for you coming round, I don't know what would become of Sofia Delano. Nothing sunny, that's for sure.'

I shut the door with a swipe of my heel. 'I am coming around, darlin', for as long as you want me. Don't worry about that. Things will get better.'

She laughs because this is such a crappy line, but I don't mind, because laughing has gotta be good, right? Better than hammers.

'Better? Oh, Dan, you Irish asshole. How long you been around here? Things don't ever get better. All the nasty shit topples out of New York and whatever doesn't drown in the Hudson ends up in Jersey.'

This is a pretty grim metaphor and a little close to home for me, so I argue even though I know I'm wasting my time.

'It's not like that any more, darlin'. We're upmarket now. Cloisters is a fashionable satellite town. Property prices have barely dipped here at all.'

This argument is too boring to survive in a room with Sofia Delano.

'Oh my God, lighten up, Danny. Let's watch a couple episodes of that cowboy crap you like and have a beer.'

'It's *Deadwood*. And you shouldn't drink too much on lithium. It affects your levels.'

Sofia is already halfway to the fridge. 'Beer ain't drinking, Dan. I thought you were Irish.'

Beer and *Deadwood*, with Sofia snuggled into my chest. That sounds pretty idyllic, or as Zeb would say, *sweeter than a honey-coated hooker*, which may be offensive but makes a lot more sense than most of his chestnuts. I could sure do with an early night with the grand reopening of Slotz coming up tomorrow.

'All right, darlin'. One beer.'

'Maybe two,' she calls from the kitchen. 'And turn off your phone. I don't want your doctor boyfriend calling up.'

I put the phone on silent, telling myself to savour this interlude of sanity.

Sofia delivers my beer, clinks me with her own, then veers towards the bedroom.

'I'm gonna blast the worst of the wet out of my hair. Why don't you get working on that bottle and I'll come back with another?'

I sink into the sofa and I'm hunting between cushions for the remote control when the hairdryer whooshes into life.

I'm searching for a remote on a sofa. That's pretty normal. Sofia is drying her hair like a real person. Girlfriend material.

One night. Let me have one night.

I take a long pull on the beer, feeling its coldness spread calm down my chest. I must nod off for a minute because the next thing that happens is Sofia's hair tickles my nose as she lays her head on my chest.

'This is nice,' I say.

'Yeah,' she answers. 'I wish it could be like this all the time.'

It's like she plucks the wishes from the air over my head.

I can feel her heart beating through my shirt, like a bird's wings against the cage bars. Sofia is nervous.

'Something bothering you?'

'I should tell you about Carmine,' she says, and there is a tremor in her voice.

Generally I would be thrilled to finally engage in that conversation, but right now I am tired and selfish and all I want to do is appreciate this beautiful woman and keep her pressed against my chest for as long as possible.

'There's no need,' I say. 'Not right now.'

'I gotta tell you, Dan. If we're ever going to . . .'

Move on? Have a chance? One of those probably.

'Okay, but don't upset yourself. Just the bullet points.'

Sofia latches herself to my chest like a limpet. 'I was all alone, that's what it was. A silly teenager still listening to her Blondie records and wearing cheap make-up. My parents died and I was all alone in this house.'

I knew Sofia owns the building. She lives on the income from the four apartments. She would live a lot better if she had some guy doing a bit of janitoring instead of letting the residents DIY in lieu of rent.

'When I met Carmine, he seemed so exciting. He had a Mustang, you know, and he was like the opposite of my dad. We were engaged in six months. Married in a year. He was my first.'

I could cry, this story is so mundane. Seems like somebody like Sofia Delano would have a more dramatic downfall, not this everyday tale of woe.

'I don't know what went wrong. Maybe the sex, you know, I was pretty new to it. I did whatever Carmine wanted but he was never happy. Started drinking earlier in the day. He would take all the rent money and go out drinking for days.'

I pat her shoulder. It's a pretty pathetic gesture, but I'm a bit out of my depth.

'Carmine never let me out of the house and he wouldn't let anyone in. One day he kicked the postman down the street for saying hi. Poor guy said hi, that was it.'

I know all about that sort of insane, controlling jealousy. In my mind's eye Carmine is starting to look a little like my dear old dad.

That's why you love Sofia, dope. You're protecting your own mother.

This is hardly a revelation. Anyone who saw a couple episodes of *In Therapy* would pick up on that. Simon Moriarty threw that psycho-dart at me months ago. Still, I am struck by how true it is.

Maybe that's why you are reluctant to get under the duvet.

That's the down side of having a shrink: afterwards everything is distilled to burying Pops in the yard and copulating with Mom. Here's a little hint for you: you ever get sent to therapy, just admit to the Oedipus thing at the end of session two, and you'll shave six months off your sentence.

'He went away for longer and longer. Came back with tattoos and stinking of other women. Often he would call to make sure I was home and tell me to fix dinner and then show up three weeks later. If his food wasn't ready, he would hit the roof. It was terrible, Dan, awful. I was a wreck.'

You're still a wreck, I think, but there's no kind way to put this so I keep it to myself.

'Then one Christmas we had a big bust-up over the turkey. Too dry or not dry enough, I can't remember. He hit me with a spatula, Dan, a goddamn spatula. So I grabbed the meat thermometer and told him he was a dead man if he touched me again. I meant it, God help me; that man brought out the killer in me, but I still loved him.'

I know all about the killer inside. My mother never got the chance to kill my father. Perhaps I would have done it for her.

'So he left. Just went. For months he would call and tell me to get his food on the table. He never came back but for years he called. The bastard. Every time the phone rings I jump, and I always keep a plate of salad in the fridge, you know, in case.'

Bastard. Yep, that's one word for him.

'I burnt all the photos, Dan. Every one I could find, but I still see his face every damn place, every minute of every day.'

Sofia cries for a while and I feel like joining her, might be cathartic, but I think maybe she needs a rock to lean on right now, so I pat her shoulder and keep a stiff upper lip.

'Total bastard,' I say sympathetically. 'Arsehole.'

But a tiny craven part of me wonders what kind of salad and I hate myself for it and pray my stomach doesn't rumble now. Could be awkward.

Sofia cries for must be an hour, her small frame jerking against mine like a wounded animal, and I know we have reached a turning point.

'I'm going to stay on the medication,' she says finally, the words hitching out of her. 'I want a life, Dan. I want us to go out, to dinner or something. Maybe a movie.'

I'd like to stroke her hair but my arm is dead from the weight of Sofia's head.

'Baby, I would like that. Sincerely. I would love that.'

And I would. Sincerely. A movie theatre with those double seats, how great would that be? Jason tells me they tilt backwards. I've never seen an IMAX movie because experiencing awe alone seems indulgent; now there's a whole world of shared experiences that could open up to us.

Sofia sits up and sniffles. 'Oh my God. I must look like a panda. I'm gonna clean up a little, okay? And get you another beer. A cold one.'

'Okay,' I say, but I would have preferred to stay like this all night, dead arm or not.

I watch Sofia pad into the bedroom and it occurs to me that she is more miserable sane than insane.

I can change that. Just give me a month. Just let me have tonight, for heaven's sake.

I have just cued up an episode of *Deadwood*, the one where Al passes the kidney stone, when someone knocks at the door. Three sharp regulation police raps.

Balls.

* * *

Ronelle Deacon is outside, all cocked hip and coptitude, which is not a word but should be.

'Old guy buzzed me up,' she explains, because Hong must have made an impression. 'The balls guy, you know him?'

'Yep. Mister Hong. He's been cutting off the circulation for years.'

I must be squarely in the frame for something for Ronelle to track me down, and I'm hoping the preamble will give me a clue.

She throws me with: 'Remember when we went at it downstairs? That was some freaky stuff.'

I glance nervously over my shoulder. Sofia does not need to hear this. Maybe I should do a cowboy accent so she'll think the voices are coming from *Deadwood*.

Yeah, that's exactly what you should do. Let your psychotic girlfriend think the TV is talking about her.

So instead I step into the hallway.

'Ronnie, what's the deal? Did you get something on Edit? You didn't come looking for me to reminisce. Shit, you barely spoke to me on the freaky night in question when I saved your life a couple of times.'

I figure it's worth tossing the lifesaving factoid into the mix. You never know, Detective Deacon might have a tender spot that I haven't found yet.

Ronnie is leaning against the wall, navy raincoat hanging like a cape. She's so casual that I'm getting seriously worried.

'Yeah, I remember that night, Danny. You put in the effort, I gotta hand it to you. All the *GQ* foreplay and shit, but next morning your girlfriend clocked me with a frying pan.'

'It was a lasagne dish,' I correct her. 'That's Wile Coyote you're thinking of who got hit with a frying pan.'

Ronnie smiles, and her teeth are like predatory Tic Tacs in the gloom. 'You're missing the point, Dan. Bitch decked me, so payback was always coming down the pipe.'

She's here for Sofia.

I hate to trot out clichés, but I have a bad feeling about this. Ronelle wouldn't come down here personally unless there was some kind of prestige collar involved, and as far as I know, Sofia has only left the apartment a dozen times in the past decade, so what the hell could she have done? Did Zeb involve her in something when they were out together on his rounds?

'What's this about, Ronnie? If it's some petty ante bullshit, you owe me a pass.'

Ronnie straightens, hooking a thumb behind her hip holster, pushing out the gun.

'Murder one ain't no petty ante bullshit, McEvoy. You think I'm working late for parking tickets?'

Murder one? My first thought is that Evelyn has had some kind of delayed reaction to the hammer blow. It's possible.

'Murder? What are you talking about? Who is Sofia supposed to have killed?'

'You, Dan,' says Ronelle, grinning. 'Well, you know, not *you* you. Carmine you.'

Lotta yous in that answer so it takes me a second to unravel them.

'You're saying that Sofia killed her husband?'

'The real one, lucky for Danny boy McEvoy.'

I am stunned. Partly at the revelation but mainly because I don't doubt it enough.

A part of me always knew.

'Carmine is dead? Where did you find him?'

Ronnie blinks twice then sniffs like she's gonna spit, and I know there's a hole in her case.

'We ain't got the body per se.'

'No body, no case. What kind of bullshit is this? Is the crime rate so low you got time to be fucking around with hearsay?'

I wouldn't normally fire class A swearwords at the blues but Ronnie needs to know how against this I am.

'Hey, Dan. Mind your language. Just because I can kick your ass doesn't mean I ain't a fucking lady. Comprende?'

I am unrepentant. 'Well whaddya expect? Tooling in here on my night off and tossing out murder accusations without a body. I thought we were coming up on friendship, Ronnie.'

The back of my mind registers that I've got maybe half a minute to finish up here.

'This is business, Dan. I'm police first and foremost and I don't let capitals walk.'

I point a finger at Ronnie but stop short of poking. 'This is harassment, is what it is. Why are you even opening a book on this, after twenty years? Because you got whacked with a saucepan?'

'Lasagne dish.'

Being corrected is irritating, I see that now.

'You know what? You've got no paper to come in here, plus you are off my Christmas list. So why don't you clock the hell off or go pistol-whip some real criminals?'

Ronnie's smile never dims and I realise she must have something. The idea makes me sick to my stomach.

Sofia could never survive in prison. Hell, she wouldn't survive a trial.

'I need to know what you have.'

270

Ronelle walks forward and I either gotta step back or stand my ground.

Screw it. I stay where I am and order my spine to straighten up. This woman once threatened to shoot me in the privates, and the aftershock of that keen moment still passes through me whenever she violates my space.

'Tell me, Ronnie.'

'I don't need to tell you shit, civilian.'

'You can't walk in here.'

'You ain't the resident, *darlin'*. Step aside.'

'You need a reasonable suspicion at least, or else your case collapses in front of the judge.'

Ronnie's ebony face lights up and I know I've played into her hands.

'Reasonable suspicion? I think you could say I have one of those.' She pulls out her iPhone and opens a sound-file app.

'This is a 911 call. Came in last night; all the lines were busy so it went to overflow. We record them all. SOP. You know what that means, don't you, soldier boy?'

I have an urge to grab the phone and stomp it to smithereens. But those phones are tough little bastards so the likely outcome is that I would embarrass myself and probably break a foot to boot.

Foot to boot. I am hilarious.

I know that I am going to hear this message but I do not want to. Contrary to what Morpheus assured us with his red pill/blue pill speech, hearing the truth does not set a person free, and telling the truth usually earns the truth-sayer an overnight bench in the tombs waiting for his arraignment with some public defender kid still hung-over from an evening spent sucking jello shots from a stripper's navel. And if that image is suspiciously specific, it's only

271

because Zeb has used me a couple of times as his one phone call.

Ronnie taps the screen with a blood-red nail and the file begins to play. The voice is low and slurred but still fills the corridor and drifts into the room behind me.

'Amazing speakers on these little things, right?' says Detective Deacon. 'When I was a kid you'd have to lug around a goddamn boom box for this kind of sound.'

I don't join in the speaker quality discussion. Instead I listen to what my darling Sofia said to the cops when she dialled 911 in the grip of bleak depression.

'Someone needs to come take me in,' says Sofia's voice, then pauses and I can hear the whiskey clunk in the neck of a bottle as she swigs it down. 'I attacked a lady with a hammer. Can you believe that? I was a pageant queen. Now I'm getting hammered and hammering people.' A laughing jag then and more whiskey. 'It's not safe being me any more. I need to be locked away. You don't believe me? What about this? I killed my asshole husband. Oh yeah, I killed Carmine with his own pistol. Kept shooting till there was nothing left in the gun. I loved that man and he treated me worse than a dog. I shot my husband and I should go to prison. Can't be any worse than where I am now.'

Ronnie whistles. This is incriminating stuff and it's not over yet.

'No?' continues Sofia. 'Forget prison. You guys come down here, you better be ready to shoot me. I've got weapons. And anthrax, I have a bag of that. So shoot first and ask questions later. I am a danger to the public and I need to be dead. You guys listening? I'll be a-waiting.'

And that is the end.

Anthrax? Bollocks.

I decide to be brazen. 'Who's that supposed to be?'

All Ronelle Deacon can do is laugh, and I don't blame her. 'Yeah. Whatever, Dan. Just be on your way. I've got business here.'

'It isn't Sofia, if that's what you think.'

Ronelle shakes out her arms, which is a well-known precursor to police brutality.

'I knew who it was right away, Dan. So I checked into Carmine Delano. A nasty piece of work, small-time pusher and wannabe pimp. Turns out he beat the crap out of your lady friend for years before taking off. They found his car over in Wildwood by the pier. A little blood but nothing too suspicious. Everyone thought he had run off with one of his various lady friends. Now it's looking like your sweet Sofia filled him full of lead, washed down the car and dumped him in the ocean. So I gotta take her in, and run DNA on all the bloaters from around that time. I am presuming the anthrax comment was bullshit.'

My head is spinning. What the hell happened to *Deadwood*? That was only two minutes ago?

I want to protect Sofia but I don't know what to do. This problem cannot be coaxed out of existence with fists or snappy one-liners.

Unless we go on the run. I could truss up Ronnie and make a break for Canada.

Deacon reads the thought in my eyes.

'Oh no, you ain't thinking about running,' she says, incredulous. 'You think I came here alone after the anthrax thing? There are a couple of guys checking their safeties outside. The only reason Homeland ain't up in here is because I assured them that your woman is crazy.'

'Sofia is not crazy!' I mutter. 'She has issues and we're working through them.'

'Issues? Are you listening to yourself, Dan? You sound like a goddamn commercial for Valium or some shit. You gonna read me the side-effects now? No, let me tell you. The side-effects of dating Sofia Delano may include having to pretend you see shit that ain't there, watching her assault police officers and finding out that Looney Tune Mrs Delano busted half a dozen caps in her shitbag husband's ass.' Ronelle claps her hands, delighted with her little speech.

'You got a mean side,' I tell her like a spurned lover. 'I knew you were tough, Ronnie, and straight as an arrow. But you're wringing every drop of humiliation outta this arrest. Were you actually hoping I'd be here?'

She has the grace to blush a little. 'Just get out of my way, Dan. I only got one set of cuffs on me or I'd book you for obstruction.'

A man does stupid things for love, so I say: 'I ain't obstructing you. Not yet.'

Ronnie raises her eyebrows. 'Are you serious? You wanna get into it for a nutcase?'

My blood is up now, so the voice of reason in my head is barely a mosquito whine.

'Yeah, I wanna get into it. And Sofia is not a nutcase.'

As if on cue, I hear her small voice behind me. Every word saturated with despair.

'Yes, Daniel. I am. I'm a freaking nutcase.'

Sofia came up behind me in bed socks so I didn't hear a thing. Was a time a mouse couldn't surprise me, but now I'm getting old and my senses are as ragged as my emotions.

'No. No, darlin'. You say things you don't mean. You remember things that didn't happen, but it's nothing we can't fix.'

Looking at her standing there with every spark of the girl she used to be drained out of her by that monster Carmine, I realise that I believe maybe sixty per cent that she is innocent and the other forty per cent does not give a shit.

Whatever it takes. This woman will be happy.

'I'm here, Sofia,' I say, scooping her into my arms, and she seems smaller than she did minutes ago. There's a radical weight-loss plan: *Develop psychoses and homicidal tendencies and watch those pounds melt away.*

'We'll get through this,' I say. 'I ain't leaving.'

'That's touching,' says Ronnie, in the room now, thumb hooked through the cuffs on her belt.

I shoot her a poisonous glare. 'You enjoying this as much as you'd hoped, Detective?'

Ronelle scowls. 'No I ain't, Daniel. I'm closing a cold case here, which oughta be a feather in my cap, and you're making me feel like I shot this Carmine douche myself. Don't you know that gloating is one of the perks in this job?'

I hold Sofia tighter. 'Sorry to piss on your glory day, but this is a person we're talking about.'

Sofia pats my chest. 'Carmine is a person too. If I did something to him, something terrible, then I should answer for it.'

I don't see any way that Sofia is not going to Police Plaza for questioning. I hold up a finger to Ronnie.

'Just gimme a second, okay?'

'I'll give you ten, killjoy. Then I'm calling for assistance.'

Sofia pulls away from me. 'You gotta let me go, Dan.'

I grip her shoulders, making full eye contact. 'Okay, darlin'. They're going to put you in a cruiser and take you downtown for questioning. What they're really doing is fishing, because they got nothing but a phone call make by a drunken bipolar woman who doesn't remember a thing about it. Don't say a word until I get a lawyer down there, and even then your story is *you don't remember.* Got it?'

'I don't remember,' says Sofia, then gives herself away by attempting a brave smile.

My heart sinks. Sofia will say whatever I tell her until the interview room door clangs behind her, then she will say what the depression tells her. I feel my extremities tingle and a blackness eats at the edges of my vision, and for a second I understand Sofia's despair.

'It's okay, baby,' she says, reaching up to stroke my cheek. 'It's better this way.'

Ronnie taps her cuffs and I know my time is up. If I don't release Sofia right now, the back-up will come thundering up the stairwell.

'Just hold on for me, darlin',' I tell her, as close to tears as I've been for a while. 'Hold on until I get there.'

'I will, Dan,' she says, and I know it's all over.

She would sign a contract with Satan now if it meant earning herself the punishment her disorder thinks she deserves.

Ronnie has Sofia by the wrists and is gently pulling her from me when I register a figure at the door, and my Celtic sixth sense of doom informs me that things are about to get worse.

How the hell could things get worse?

The guy in the doorway looks like he had the crap beaten out of him by monkeys. His hair is all up on one side, and styled into a perfect quiff on the other. He's wearing a neon blue suit with honest-to-God shoulder pads that are either retro or way ahead of the fashion curve, and his fleshy upper lip is adorned by a Prince moustache that ripples like a worm in time to his heavy breathing. Physically, he doesn't appear to pose much of a threat, unless he clamps himself on to my face and smothers me with his beer gut, but for some reason the sight of this greasy character extinguishes the last spark of hope I was nurturing that this day might turn out okay.

'What the hell is going on here?' is the first thing out of his mouth. Plenty of attitude, like he's king of whatever hill he happens to be sitting on, and not a short guy with bad hair and a worse suit. Then he sees Ronnie and the twinklings on her belt and everything changes. The guy stands himself up straight and drops his eyes to the floor. Instant and total submission.

Ex-con, I realise. *And not all that ex.*

I glance down at Sofia. Her eyes are wide like she's witnessed the second coming of Elvis and she's taking those rapid little breaths that are music to any man's ears.

Then I get it.

Christ, no. This runt can't be him. I believe in coincidence, but this would be way beyond coincidence. This would be a goddamn miracle.

Detective Deacon takes the lead. 'What are you doing here, sir? There's an arrest in progress.'

The runt keeps his eyes down. 'I live here, Officer. This is my apartment.'

Ronelle laughs. 'You gotta be kidding me, right? You're Carmine Delano?'

'That's me, Officer,' he says, and with those three words Sofia is lost. All the work of the past year sloughs away as she steps out of my arms.

'Carmine,' she says, holding out her hands to this guy who abused her for years. 'Carmine, baby.'

The guy flicks his eyes upwards towards her and shakes his head.

Not yet, the motion says. *Wait until the cop leaves.*

The guy has been in prison all these years. Not dead, banged up.

Ronnie is having a hard time accepting such a mind-boggling coincidence.

'You're Carmine Delano?' she says again. 'Showing up here at this precise moment. Unbelievable.'

'Alls I did was come home, Officer,' says the man who purports to be Sofia's lost husband, come home at the very time his wife is about to be whisked downtown for his murder.

Ronnie knows prison discipline when she sees it. 'Show me your arm, convict,' she orders, and Carmine does not hesitate, dropping his duffel bag and rolling up one sleeve, revealing a forearm covered in ink.

'Prison tats,' says Ronnie. 'Aryan Brotherhood. My favourite. When did you get out?'

'Two weeks,' says Carmine sullenly. 'I did a twenty jolt without parole.'

'Where?'

'Eastham, Houston.'

Ronnie whistles. 'The pig farm? They do not fuck around down there. You got any ID?'

Carmine pulls an envelope from his jacket pocket and hands it over.

'Just my release papers.'

'Tell me what landed you in the farm, Mister Carmine Delano,' says Ronnie, studying the papers.

'Armed robbery, Officer. I was heading for Mexico and ran out of funds.'

'You kill someone, Carmine?'

278

Carmine shuffles like a guilty schoolboy outside the principal's office. 'A guy died in the bank. An old guy. Heart attack, they tell me.'

Ronnie stuffs the papers into the envelope. 'So, no parole. You were lucky not to end up with the needle and an audience.'

'Yes, ma'am,' says Carmine, but Ronnie is not impressed by his politeness.

'Ma'am? I don't think the Brotherhood call people like me *ma'am*. Ain't you noticed what colour I am, son?'

'I was just trying to survive, Officer.'

Detective Deacon palms the papers into Carmine's chest. Hard. 'Yeah? Well, that supremacist bullshit don't wash up here. I got your face in my lexicon now, Delano, so you better hope that nobody perpetrates any hate crimes, 'cause if they do, I'm coming directly to this address. Got it?'

'Absolutely, Officer. Those days are behind me. And I'm gonna get these tattoos lasered.'

'Good. Daniel here knows a cosmetic surgeon. He ain't the most reliable, but he's cheap.' She turns to Sofia. 'And you! Stop wasting police time with your boozy confessions. Next time I'll find something to charge you with.'

Ronnie might as well be in another dimension for all the attention Sofia pays to her. I know the feeling.

Deacon pulls the flap of her coat across the gun, badge and cuffs. 'Looks like you're out in the cold.'

I turn to Sofia, to see if this is true. I shouldn't have, because I'm invisible to her now. She will not even acknowledge me.

'Carmine, sweetheart,' she says, and I swear she is glowing. 'I knew you'd come back. I knew you loved me.'

'I dreamed of you every night, Sofia,' he says, and they are like dogs on leashes straining to get at each other. 'Even when I was being punked, I was thinking of you.'

Punked?

That should break the spell, but no.

'Poor baby,' she says. 'Did they hurt you?'

Ronnie punches me in the shoulder. 'You need a ride, soldier? Or you gonna get back to the club on that third wheel you got spinning?'

I swipe my *Deadwood* DVD box from the coffee table as if it's the last remaining shred of my pride. The disc is still in the machine, but it's gonna have to stay there.

'Can I sit up front?' I ask, hoping my bottom lip is not wobbling.

I walk towards the door with boots of lead, waiting with each footfall for a word from Sofia.

A farewell, a thank you.

Anything.

But not a single utterance is offered. She is ill, I know, and chained to this man by *geasa*, but that doesn't make my heart any less broken.

Just like that, I am out of the picture.

As the door closes behind us, I hear the thump of Sofia's feet racing across the wooden floor and into Carmine's embrace.

My phone tweets and I check it.

Cannibalism is not the only way to eat people alive. Love is just as effective.

I almost look around to see if Simon Moriarty is watching me.

CHAPTER 13

There's still a lot of activity at the club and I bet Jason could use a hand with the snag list, but my heart is heavy and my fingers are too thick for delicate work, so I sneak in the back way, like a teenager who has broken curfew to drink cider, and climb the boxy stairs to my apartment.

Dance music hammers the floorboards, but after years of living in the same building as Sofia Delano, I can sleep through any commotion that is not potentially lethal. I strip down to my shorts and lie on the bed, which can accommodate my entire body if I lie diagonally and don't move around too much.

In the end, it is not the decorating clamour itself which keeps me awake but the associated shenanigans. Jason and his boys are whooping it up while they work and I can hear the xylophone tinkle of shot glasses being raised every couple of minutes. The humanity gets to me and the sheer, boisterous happiness of those guys. I know that I would be more than welcome to trot downstairs and join the celebration, but I'd rather just lie here and be jealous. Anyway, grim moods are infectious and I would probably kill that party stone dead in twenty minutes. It would be like Jason's dad walking in wearing his *Gays Are the Spawn of Satan* T-shirt. A T-shirt which

Jason's dad actually owns. Jason came out by telling his father that if gays were the spawn of Satan, then that would make him the devil. Took the father a couple of days to figure it out.

So I lie here on the bed and indulge myself in a mopey funk, replaying the week's events over and over, but always coming back to the glassy adoration in Sofia's eyes when Carmine darkened her door. Shit, she would chug the Kool-Aid right out of the bottle for that guy.

I was fooling myself. I never meant anything to Sofia.

Nothing. Not a thing. She couldn't even remember my name.

For long hours my thoughts go round and round in ever-decreasing self-esteem circles until eventually I cry *fuck it* and trudge into the bathroom, where I find a bottle of triazolam that is almost in date and dry-swallow three pills.

I lie down again and watch the sun climb behind my linen blind like a cheap special effect in a silhouette puppet show.

Surely I will sleep now. Surely.

Even Sofia can't compete with three triazolam.

I sleep like a dead man and my dreams are vague, filled with dark shadows and glinting edges. The only splotch of colour is the crimson circle of a rising sun behind a blind, which turns into a pink thong, and any guilt I feel over the fates of Fortz and Krieger evaporates with the last wisps of the dream.

'Good riddance to those dicks,' I say to the ceiling, then roll out of bed for four score push-ups to prove to myself I ain't over that hill just yet. It is also a positive sign, physically and psychologically, that I am sporting a wake-up boner that any decent caveman could start a fire with, which means the push-ups aren't as deep as they would normally be.

There is life in the old dog yet, in spite of Sofia.

Yet even thinking her name deflates me more effectively than the memory of Fortz in an apron. I collapse in a heap of frustrated sweat and realise that I am not out of the emotional woods just yet.

Casino noise drifts up between the floorboards, which means that the crew are still renovating or I have slept right through the grand opening, which would be just dandy with me. Jason telling me to cheer the hell up is the last thing I need right now. But I gotta go down there; what kind of douche would I be if I didn't?

I throw on the Banana Republic grey suit that I bought in their January sale especially for this occasion, but it doesn't give me the boost I'd hoped for.

Now you are a cuckolded moron in a suit.

I check my phone for time and messages. I have missed plenty of both. It's eight thirty in the p.m. and I have a dozen missed calls and a psy-tweet.

To all my Twits: Be happy. Seize the day. Live in the now. What do you people want from me?

Looks like Dr Simon is tiring of his online practice. Maybe universal full-time access is not as much fun as he thought it would be.

I slip through the adjoining door from my apartment stairwell straight into a heaving throng of humanity. The club is seething with customers.

I am frankly amazed.

Jason has put in the effort with e-mail drops and so forth, but I never expected a turnout like this. There are guys crowded around the roulette wheel. A bunch of college boys are doing shots and tossing twenties at a blackjack dealer, and the booths are crowded with young bucks sharing pitchers.

Something about the crowd seems off, but I brush it away, glad to have a reason to celebrate something. Anything.

This is a good start. We can build on this.

I spot Jason working the room. Shaking hands and clapping shoulders like he's king of the hill.

He deserves it. If it wasn't for Jason, this place would just be another casualty of the recession.

I have to worm my way through the crowd to reach his side.

'Jason,' I call to him. 'Hey, J.'

Jason is wearing a powder-blue suit with a brooch at the neck of his shimmering silk shirt. He's had highlights put in, and replaced the diamond in his incisor with a ruby.

He looks good.

He sees me and I swear he seems nervous for a second.

'Dan. Where've you been? What do you think?'

I grab his shoulders like he's my brother. 'What do I think? This is amazing. Unbelievable. How the hell did you get all these people here?'

The big lug actually blushes. 'Social media, partner. I worked the keyboard. Lotta guys looking for a place like this.'

I grab a glass full of green stuff from a passing tray and salute him. 'To you, buddy. We might actually be able to pay the bills if we can hang on to some of these customers.'

Jason fake-punches and I fake-block, spilling half my drink. 'Fuck bills, man,' he shouts to the ceiling. 'We're gonna make bank.'

Looking around me tonight, that's not hard to believe, so I decide to ignore the Irish Catholic voice of sanctimony and pessimism that prevents me from ever getting too contented and for once in my life enjoy the moment.

I sink what's left in my glass. Tastes like lime jelly, but there's a kick to it.

'What the hell was that?' I ask when I finish coughing.

Jason blows a kiss towards the bar. 'Marco is a genius with cocktails. He calls that one a One-Eyed Serpent. You want another?'

I gotta stop now, or commit to the hangover.

Shouldn't I be taking charge here? Shouldn't I be making sure everyone's pulling their weight?

Then again, after the week I've had.

'What the hell,' I say. 'Keep 'em coming.'

Tonight, for once, I embrace the Irish stereotype.

Some time later, I am slouched in my office drunk-mumbling to myself.

Whenever I drink, there are three distinct stages: optimism, reproach, sing-song. I am bang in the middle of stage two at the moment, right on the guilt edge, berating myself that I am just like my father, and this sort of carry-on is what got my family killed before their time. One more drink and I'll be on the table crucifying the Pogues' 'Fairytale of New York', which is a song no one should be allowed to sing except Shane MacGowan and Kirsty MacColl.

'I am not my father,' I tell myself, then: 'You sure act like him. You sure look like him now. A drunken bum.'

And then, the saddest words a man can say aloud.

'Nobody loves me.'

I thump my heart as I say this, to make it more pathetic.

'Sofia doesn't even remember who I am. Oh yeah, she likes

looking at my thing when I come out of the shower. What am I? An object?'

Zeb arrives, as he was bound to with free booze floating around, and elbows his way into the office, and for a moment the thump of club sound waves enters with him and slaps me with a giant hand.

'Holy shit! Close that door,' I say.

Zeb obliges, swiping the door with his boot. His arms are full of cocktail glasses and there's a bottle of Jameson sticking out his jacket pocket.

He plonks his booty on my desk, squints at me and says: 'Fuck me, stage two. We better get some more booze into you, pal. I don't want to spend my night in here with a depressed Catholic. I'd rather take my chances out there with the ass bandits.'

I snort. 'Jason and Marco have both each other and standards, so I think your skinny arse is safe from banditry.'

I'm not sure if banditry is even a word, but for a man with the amount of alcohol in him that I have, that was not a bad sentence.

Zeb settles into the guest seat and downs three shots in quick succession.

'I gotta hand it to you,' he says. 'This took balls, literally, but you pulled it off. I should reacharound the desk and give you a shake.'

Zeb then collapses in a sneezy fit of giggles, like he's made several good jokes. I do not know what in the bejaysus is going on.

'Zeb, are you mocking me? Am I the butt of some joke?'

More giggles. Zeb actually sneezes into a shot, then drinks it anyway.

'Butt? Yeah, you're the butt all right.'

I am too emotionally delicate for this crap.

'Zebulon. I'm bloody drunk, okay? Your stupid labyrinths are too bendy for me.'

Zeb loves that one too. 'Bendy? Dude, we all gotta learn to bend.'

Okay. He's baiting me. Leading me towards that holy grail moment when I lose my cool and turn into a big lumbering bear. Well it ain't gonna happen.

Compose yourself, soldier. Be the bigger man.

With this in mind, I take a handgun from the drawer and place it on the desk.

'Zeb. I am feeling delicate and not in the mood for your cryptic shit. Spell it out.'

'What? You're gonna shoot me?'

I look him in the eye. 'Probably not, but this has been a tough week for me. I've been kidnapped for a snuff movie. Tortured by cops. Shot at by hoodlums, and I lost my girl. So tell me, what's with all the innuendo?'

I see a new expression on Zeb's face. I realise that the expression is pity. It doesn't suit him and won't last long.

'I can't just tell you, man. That's not how I roll.'

'But?' I prompt.

Zeb grins, and his teeth have a greenish tinge from the drink. 'I can give you hints.'

I sigh. 'Right. Hints. Make 'em obvious, though. My brain functions are compromised.'

Zeb pulls a sheet of paper from his Armani jacket.

'The new cocktail list.'

'Whatever.'

'Did you read it?'

'No. J gave me a One-Eyed Serpent.'

'Classic,' says Zeb, chuckling. 'Lemme list a couple more.'

'Knock yourself out. Before I do it for you.'

'There's the Manjoos.'

'Yeah, I think that one has mango in it.'

'Really? What d'you reckon the Twinkletown is made of?'

I know that one. 'That has a lit sparkler. Looks pretty cool.'

Zeb nods. 'Cool as all fuck, like the new colour scheme.'

I'm getting closer. 'Yellow and green.'

Zeb is vibrating with pleasure. The payoff must be huge. 'Yeah, yellow and green, or to put it another way, green and yellow. Which is what it says over the door now.'

This hangs in the air for a minute.

Green and yellow. Green and . . .

The penny drops with a deafening clang.

I get it. Holy reacharound.

'It's a—'

Zeb doesn't let me say it. 'It's a gay bar. You own a gay bar, dude.'

'All those guys out there?'

'Gay as game shows, brother. What are you? Blind?'

I feel blind. Blind and stupid.

'I know you're hoping for the big meltdown, Zebadora, but I ain't angry.'

Zeb's eyebrows shoot up. 'Angry? Are you kidding me? Jason's a fucking genius. These guys are not just gay, they're super-gay. Statistically the biggest spenders on the planet. Super-gay is a tough market to crack, but if you can tap into it, it's a frickin' gold mine.'

'A gold mine?'

'You betcha. These guys have got fat wallets and they ain't shy about opening them. Super-gays will pay twenty bucks for any cocktail with a dirty name. Tomorrow night, I'm parking a Botox-mobile outside.'

I am feeling a little stunned, so I revert to my bouncer habit of repeating what's been said to buy myself a little time.

'You're parking a Botox-mobile outside. You have a Botox-mobile?'

Zeb is delighted at how drunk and slow I am. Usually by the time I'm in this condition, he's having his stomach pumped in ER.

'Yeah, I got a Botox-mobile. It's on the roof beside my Transformer, you shmendrik.'

Aha! That's total crap.

'You don't have a Transformer,' I say. 'They're just in the movies.'

'No shit, McSherlock,' says Zeb, then downs a shot that appears to have an eyeball floating in it. He shudders as the alcohol hits his stomach.

'Was that supposed to represent an eyeball?' I ask.

Zeb chews and swallows. 'The drink is called a Ball Buster, so what do you think?'

The door opens and in walks Carmine, and before I know what's going on, there's a gun in my hand and it's pointed at his face.

'Hey,' says Carmine, raising his hands. 'What the hell, man?'

He sounds different; more California, less New York. Maybe it's the stress.

'This is the guy,' I tell Zeb. 'This is the prince who stole Sofia from me.'

Zeb folds his arms and leans back to watch the show. 'Well, I guess you better shoot him.'

Carmine kicks the leg of Zeb's chair. 'Screw you, Zeb. That ain't funny.'

It takes a second for these words to penetrate the jello coating my brain, then I say:

'You guys know each other? I guess I better shoot both of you then.'

Zeb is not in the least worried. I think I have been overplaying the *threatening to shoot him* card of late.

'Whatever, Dan. Just pay the man his money.'

'Yeah, pay me my money,' says Carmine. 'I was waiting outside that apartment for hours, man.'

Hold it a minute. What is going on here?

'Pay you? Pay him? For what?'

Zeb gets that mischievous look in his eyes that tells me he's gonna drag this out until I explode. Like I said, pushing my buttons is Zeb's thing.

'Come on, Danny boy,' he says. 'You're a smart Paddy. Use your brain.'

Zeb miscalculates my tolerance levels and reaches across the desk to tap my forehead. I might have tolerated this had I not once been tapped in much the same way by a guy who went on to do his utmost to make me dead. So maybe I associate one tapper with another, and perhaps I've had a few too many super-gay shots to drink, and so it's possible that I overreact a little.

I grab him by the wrist and yank him bodily across the desk. Zeb laughs, because he knows that deep down I am a big softy, so I smack him in the rice pudding cheek just enough to smart.

'Hey, fuck you, Danny. After all I've done for you.'

Sure. After all Zeb's done for me, I should snap his spine across my knee like the spear of a vanquished enemy. But Zeb has me pegged and knows that he's in no real danger, while all Carmine knows about me is what Sofia told him, which I would be willing to bet is sweet shag all.

So I twist Zeb's scrawny arm up around his back and frogmarch him out of my office. Too late my little pal realises what's going on and shouts over his shoulder.

'Don't say nothing. He's just a p—'

The rest of the P word is truncated by the slam and lock of the office door. I imagine the P word was not pal or prince.

Carmine stands in the corner all clenched fists and puffed chest.

'What the hell is going on here? I just want my money.'

I sit in my chair and begin casually removing bullets from my revolver. 'Here's the deal, Carmine. Zeb likes to string things out. Delay gratification as much as possible. Give me a goddamn migraine with all his bullshit. I ain't got time for that now.' I leave a single bullet in the cylinder, snap it shut with a flick of my wrist and spin it a few times. 'So what we're gonna do is play a little game I picked up in 'Nam.'

Carmine tries to sneer but his wobbling moustache gives him away. 'There ain't no such place as 'Nam.'

Surely he can't be for real. Then again, some people do think 'Nam was invented for the movies, that it isn't a real country and the war never happened. In fact, surveys have shown that more people between the ages of fifteen and twenty-five believe in Narnia than Vietnam.

'It's real all right. This is as real as it gets.' I point the gun at him. 'I am drunk and maudlin, so tell me what this is all about.'

It takes him about half a second to think *fuck Zeb* and then he spills his guts so fast the words are bumping into each other.

'I ain't no Carmine. I go to acting class with Zeb. When he found out about the 911 call, he asked me to impersonate the guy. Just wait outside the bitch's place until the lady cop showed, then do my thing.'

I feel such a tool. How could I ever have believed in Carmine's convenient materialisation? The odds against Sofia's actual husband turning up after twenty years, at the exact moment his abandoned wife is about to be dragged off to prison, must be immeasurable. Yet I swallowed the ball of lies without a murmur.

'What about the whole prison bit?'

'That's all true,' admits non-Carmine. 'The secret of acting is to stick as close to the truth as possible.'

'So you were locked up in Texas?'

'Yeah. Punked, too. My painful and humiliating honesty sold it to the cop. I exposed myself, metaphorically.'

I groan. This goddamn country. Everyone reads Stanislavsky.

'So Zeb offers you . . .'

'A grand.'

'A grand to impersonate Sofia's husband?'

'That's it, man. I doctored my release papers and impersonated the shit out of that husband.'

He did. I fell for it, so did Ronnie.

'What about Sofia?'

Non-Carmine smiles proudly, and feck me if there isn't a tear in his eye. 'She swallowed it totally. Imagine that. Al Pacino, fuck that guy. They should be giving me his Oscar.'

I shouldn't hate this fool so much, but I do. I guess he's become Carmine incarnate for me and it's difficult to see him as anything else.

'So? What did you do? You took advantage of Sofia? Is that it, method man?'

'I didn't take no advantages,' says the guy, but his rat's eyes flick up and down like he's looking for a bolt-hole and I know he ain't spilling the full beans.

'You ever see *The Deer Hunter*? I bet you did. A method man like you would eat that shit up.'

'Yeah, I seen it,' says non-Carmine, and there are lines of sweat lodged in his forehead.

I cock the revolver. 'Then you know what happens next.'

That did it. 'I tried to put the pipe to her. She's pretty fine for an old dame, but she kept calling me Dan.'

I figure a lowlife like this could live with being called Dan if it meant lying down with Sofia.

'And?'

'And she said my thing was smaller than she remembered. Got into my head. Undermined my confidence in the whole performance. Also I remembered how Zeb said you'd tear me limb from limb me if I interfered with the old lady, and that put me right off.'

Old lady? Sofia was not yet forty. I always have some crazy on tap and I let a little shine out through my eyes then.

'So you left her? Again.'

'Hey, hey, wait a minute, man. I ain't Carmine. I never left that lady before.'

I consider pulling the trigger a few times to teach this guy a lesson, but for what? All he did was keep Sofia out of prison. So I march him to the fire door and boot him into the alley.

'Hey, what the hell?' he objects.

I know I'm on shaky ground morally, seeing as this guy did me a solid, but he threw a few shapes at Sofia and I can't bring myself to actually give him the whole thousand, so I toss him three hundred and eighty, which is what I have in my wallet. Let him harass Zeb for the rest. I'd love to see him method-act six hundred and change out of Zeb's wallet.

It kills me to say it, but: 'I suppose I should thank you. Your performance was so real, so primal that I can't stop thinking how I hate you and wish you were dead.'

Non-Carmine looks like he might cry. 'Thanks, man. That's quite a compliment.'

But compliments only get you so far. 'So where's the rest of my fee?'

'Talk to Zeb,' I tell him. 'He'll sort you out.'

I don't know whether the guy is good with this suggestion or not, because I slam the door on him.

Now I gotta let Zeb back in and he's gonna be full to the eyeballs with smugness, asking for apologies and canonising himself for this good turn he's done me. I hate Zeb in self-satisfied mode. Come to think of it, I haven't been exactly falling over myself to consort with Zebulon Kronski in any of his humours lately.

I need to find a better class of amigo.

I open the office door and there the little bastard is, all folded arms and raised eyebrows, waiting for his apology.

'You got something to say to me, Dan?'

I might as well get it over with. 'Okay. I'm sorry, all right?'

'Really? What are you sorry for?'

He's like a Jewish Catholic priest, determined to prolong my act of contrition.

'I'm sorry for manhandling your divine person when all you did was look out for Sofia.'

Zeb reads my body language and rightly interprets the tremors in my shoulders as repressed violence.

'I accept your apology,' he says, and takes the seat nearest the booze. 'I assume you ejected Rafe?'

294

Rafe? Fuck me.

I nod and help myself to one of Zeb's cocktails.

'And you paid him, right?'

'Of course. A thousand in fifties. Money well spent.'

Zeb squints suspiciously at me but I distract him by stealing another one of his drinks.

'Hey, hands off, Daniel. Get your own. Just call Marco and have him send in a tray.'

I switch the subject again, moving Zeb two topics away from Rafe's pay packet.

'How did you know about the 911?'

'Are you kidding me? I shoot up both the switchboard girls and three of the patrolmen. I got ears all over that department.'

This is information I will not be passing on to Ronelle. It's always good to have an inside track in Police Plaza.

'And you couldn't just tell me?'

Zeb smiles sadly at how little I know him. 'Straightforward-like, that's not how the Zeb-man rolls.'

There are at least three things in that sentence that make me want to punch the Zeb-man in his smiling face.

The music from outside jumps a few notches and I realise I might have to rethink my living quarters. Eventually this beat beat beat crap would get to me. Whatever happened to melody? Or singers who don't name-check themselves every four bars?

Jason barges in, his face flushed, left hand pumping the air in time to the music.

Zeb shoots him with two finger guns.

'Who's a goddamn fairy genius?' he asks.

Jason points two index fingers at his own head. 'This guy, right here.'

I have to give it to him. 'You did it, J. This place is buzzing.'

'And you ain't angry?'

I go for blasé. 'Nah. Why would I be angry?'

'Lotta gays out there. Not just gays, super-gays.'

'That's a niche market,' I say, regurgitating Zeb's lecture. 'A gold mine if you can get in there.'

Jason rushes around the desk and hugs me. 'I knew you'd be cool, partner. Some people freak out, but not you, Danny boy. My man.'

'I am totally cool,' I say, feeling Jason's bicep flatten my right ear. 'But those guys know I'm straight, right?'

Jason releases my head and punches my shoulder, genuinely of the opinion that I'm kidding. 'Oh, I think they know you're straight, Mister Banana Republic. And anyways, it's a casino, not the prison showers. Though we might do that for theme night.'

'Theme night?'

'I got a million ideas, Dan. People are gonna cross the river for this place. We're gonna have a line round the block.'

It's good, I suppose. Being the boss of a thriving business. Making bank. But I can't help feeling a little nostalgic for the time when I was just a bouncer living underneath a crazy woman. I guess it is in my nature to never be satisfied. To seek out the flaws in every situation.

Maybe Sofia did put a full magazine into Carmine.

See what I mean.

The blood drains from my face and I feel like I have somehow phase-shifted into a dream state. I thought I was winding down and my girl's a murderess. Again.

'So, you gonna come out and listen to my speech, partner?' Jason asks, shifting on his feet, eager to get back out on the floor.

'Course I am. Wouldn't miss it for the world. I just need a little Dutch courage.'

I'm gonna have one more drink, then maybe sing a song. One song and then I'll call Sofia, if I can remember the code.

Zeb magnanimously sweeps a hand over his collection of cocktails, offering me my pick, which is very unlike him. I bet it has just occurred to the Zeb-man that he could do worse than be made a partner in my new super-gay club.

I choose a Ball Buster, complete with floating pickled onion testicle. Seems appropriate.

EPILOGUE

It's a week since Ronelle tried to arrest Sofia, and my life has gone back to quasi-normal, in that I am nominally seeing my alleged girlfriend for what approximates cosy evenings watching foreign fiction on TV.

I have arrived at the decision that even if Sofia did shoot Carmine, he probably deserved it, and I am in no position to judge after all the shenanigans I have been neck deep in for the past while.

Our relationship has shifted because now I realise that it's me who needs Sofia and not the other way around.

As Simon said: *Perhaps you like the fact that she doesn't know the real you, as your low self-esteem issues would have you believe that the real you isn't worthy of affection.*

Or as Zeb put it: *Sometimes the pit bull don't wanna screw the poodle. He just wants to make sure nobody else does.*

Both valid points, I think.

So, I'm kinda calming down a little. Enjoying the club doing so well, trying to sit with Sofia as much as possible but keeping alert for Mike, 'cause you know that potato-eating gangster won't stay outta my picture for ever. That video of his mom will be eating away at him like a ball of acid in his stomach. Not stomach acid obviously, a stronger kind.

Ronnie has called me a couple of times to make sure I'm behaving myself. I think her current attitude towards me is one of bemusement. It's like she knows I'm going down eventually and every day I spend above ground and outta the joint makes her smile and shake her head.

So I strapped my muzzle back on, good and tight. My hands feel empty without a gun in them, but tough shit, hands, you're gonna have to get by without Sharpie for a while.

But there are a coupla things.

Two loose ends I can't live with.

So I ask Jason if he can locate someone for me, and it turns out one of our new regulars more or less invented internet search engines. I can't say which regular because he's currently involved in over a hundred lawsuits, but it takes this guy about fifteen minutes on his new prototype phone to run down my cyber friend Citizen Pain. The guy who paid a hundred grand to see me tortured to death.

Turns out Citizen Pain is from Connecticut, and I was all set to take a bus over there and maybe bring a black dildo with me to administer some poetic justice. I think it was Benny Hill who said: *Revenge is a dish best served cold*, but mine was gonna be laid out piping hot, and I could relive it coolly later on.

It was a best of both worlds kinda plan.

I might be wrong about that quote, sounds a bit vicious for Benny Hill. But you never know, a lot of funny men have a dark side.

Anyway, like I say, I was all set to take a drive to Citizen Pain's place of employment and expose him for the arsehole he is, until Jason's guy texts me the rest of the particulars. Turns out Citizen Pain is not a crooked senator or a sex pest with a record as I had imagined in my mental scenarios. Turns out Citizen Pain is a lady in her fifties, and she is the director of the Connecticut office of a major third-world charity. This woman does the TV campaign, for Christ's sake; you know the one where the camera catches her weeping? You've seen that one, right?

So, if I go barging in there, this whole charity's going down the toilet, and I can't have that on my conscience. The last thing I need is nightmares featuring Sudanese kids pointing the fingers of blame in my direction. So I turn the evidence over to Ronelle and she agrees to handle it quietly, which is tough for her so I appreciate it.

The second loose end is Evelyn.

I am having a hard time believing that she would just dump me like that. We were real close once upon a time.

Tight.

She taught me about boobs.

My mom and her stood together against the grim might of Paddy Costello.

Could booze have changed her that much?

The straight answer to this is yes. Booze can mess people up. The first thing an addict loses is motor functions and the second to go is morals. I have seen guys renting their kids to strangers for the price of a carton of wine. So Evelyn could have flipped on me for a never-ending supply of penthouse-quality brandy, but she's had a few days now to acclimatise and perhaps regret selling her nephew out like that.

There is also the possibility that Edit blackmailed her with the threat of my death: sign the forms or Dan gets it, kinda thing. She's certainly devious enough.

It's not much of an incentive, I know, but maybe Ev loves me even more than I thought.

I gotta know. She looks like my mom, for Christ's sake, and there are not so many good people in my life that I can afford to summarily write one off.

So for the past few days, I've been calling the Costello penthouse and hanging up if Edit answered.

I know. Pretty childish plan, but I didn't know what else to do.

Yesterday I got lucky, and a maid or cleaner picked up who hadn't been briefed about me.

'Miss Evelyn?' she said. 'I give her the phone but she pretty hammered, so make allowances, okay?'

I reckon that lady was new. If she gets fired from Edit's, I'd hire her for Green & Yellow in a heartbeat. She tells it like it is.

I don't get long on the phone with Evelyn; almost as soon as she slurs *hello* down the line, I hear Edit's strident voice in the background.

'Who is it, Evelyn dear? Who is it that is calling on you?'

Who is it that is calling on you? Far too many words in that sentence.

I have maybe ten seconds, so I make them count.

'Remember the ice-cream sundae, Ev? I'll be there Monday at noon. And every Monday until you show up.'

I barely get that much out before the line goes dead.

It's been a long time since we had those sundaes. I hope Ev's alcohol-addled brain can locate the memory.

In any case, I'm gonna make the trip over and be waiting, every Monday at noon. Evelyn should be able to drag herself out of bed by then.

Cal Gerber's Tigon Hotel is down on the waterfront in Atlantic City, and is not what you'd call a classy joint. Okay, it's got a pool, but I bet they don't clean the filters too often, and there are slot machines in the lobby and vending machines in the hallways. Nevertheless, the location on the golden mile makes it one of the city's big earners, and the Gerber family are like Atlantic City's version of the Hiltons. Cal Junior, the son and heir, is regularly saying stupid smug shit to gossip mags, and Aeriel, the teenage daughter, is shunning the limelight and studying hotel management in university, but she has talked about her *secret tattoo*, which has caused no end of speculation in *US Weekly*.

But back before the hotel got celebrified, it was called simply the Royale, and its ice-cream parlour had a reputation for making the best sundaes on the strip. When Mom and I stayed there on our one trip to attempt to negotiate a peace with old Paddy Costello, Ev took me for a sundae every day. It was my favourite part of the trip and I've had a weakness for sundaes ever since.

Another reason I picked the Tigon for a rendezvous is that Jason and I once bounced the place during fight week couple of years back, when the hotel was paying double overtime for doormen. It is amazing how many rich white kids think they can take a professional 'cause they've watched a fight from the front row. One kid actually caught me with a soft right hook and broke a couple of his fingers. J laughed his arse off.

So I know all about the hotel layout, right down to the tables in the lobby Starbucks where the ice cream parlour used to be.

Tread softly because you tread on my dreams, as Bob Hope once said. The Tigon management hadn't so much trodden on my dreams as stomped them to death with hobnail boots.

I think it was Bob Hope, or maybe he was paraphrasing Benny Hill.

I park up a couple of blocks away in case they got cameras reading plates in the Tigon. I gotta admit I'm developing a fondness for the Caddy, and every time I think on old Bent Tool I get a little tear in my eye, from holding in the laughter. I have tried hard to feel guilty about how that ended up for Benny T and the Shea-ster, but whatever way I spin events in my head, I come out of it clean. Those guys wanted to kill me for something they knew I had no part in. That is blatant karma-fucking and the universe dealt with them for it. I cannot wait to see what the universe does to Pablo. That prick wears string bracelets, for crying out loud. You can't wipe his slate clean by lighting a coupla josticks.

The Tigon lobby is packed even at this time in the morning. Lotta desperate-looking people lugging buckets of Starbucks towards the slot machines. I nod at the doorman in solidarity for the bullshit he will undoubtedly endure before end of shift, then find myself a seat facing the doors.

If the parlour was still here, I'd probably order a couple of sundaes and try pushing a few nostalgia buttons, but I have to make do with a Frappuccino, which looks kinda summery at least.

I don't really expect Evelyn to show, not on the first day, and by twelve thirty I'm planning my next move when holy crap if she doesn't walk in the front door with Pablo holding her elbow and affecting a slight mince like he isn't a cold-blooded assassin.

I wonder does Evelyn know the kind of man Edit sends to keep an eye on her?

Ev looks good. Yet another hairdo; a pixie bob with autumn highlights (*FP*) and those oversized gilded shades that make her look like a very rich bug.

She has been off the street barely a week and already she's showing a wincing disdain for the three-star Tigon. She waves Pablo into a seat by the elevator, what Zeb would call the *hooker chair*, then totters towards me, wobbly on high heels and gin by the smell of her when she leans in for a kiss.

'What the hell are we doing here, Danny?' she asks, sitting opposite and taking a belt from the Frappuccino.

'The sundaes? Remember?'

Evelyn's wince grows more pronounced. 'Oh yeah. Dan the super-spy.'

I am getting a frosty vibe right off. This ain't gonna end in tears and hugs. Maybe just tears.

'I bet you're wondering why I brought you here today,' I say, sounding pathetic even to myself.

'Yeah, I kinda am,' says Evelyn. 'I had a seaweed wrap booked and I don't even know what the hell that is.'

Is this the real Evelyn? I remember her being funny and ballsy, but I haven't seen much of that aunt since the reunion in Cloisters. Maybe she hasn't been that person in a long while.

But I came here for a reason.

I blinker my face with a palm and talk behind it in case the ninja/Pablo can lip-read.

'Ev. Are you being blackmailed? Is that it?'

Ev is playing with her fingers.

Antsy.

She wants a drink.

I put my hands on hers and hold them still. 'Ev. Tell me now. Are you being forced to stay with Edit and sign her papers? Did they threaten to kill me?'

Ev shudders with the effort of holding herself together, but she doesn't answer.

I try another tack. 'Don't you remember your sister? My mother? How close we all were?'

She takes off her glasses with a shaky hand. 'Screw you, Danny. That's a cheap shot. Of course I remember how we were. Those days in Ireland, the three of us together. That was the happiest time of my life. I think about it all the time. In my mind there's a glow over the whole thing. Like it was magic.'

This is exactly what I wanted to hear, but I don't feel any better for hearing it.

'So what the hell is going on? I saved you.'

Ev's eyes are the only part of her face that seem honest. There's pain in there, and a lot of mileage at the corners.

'Saved me? You delivered me to Edit.'

'I thought I was doing the right thing.'

Evelyn covers half her face with the oversized glasses.

'Right thing? Danny, right and wrong are for people with choices. I'm beyond that now. I expected to be dead in a year, so I can ignore a little *overeagerness* on Edit's part if it means I get to sleep in a clean bed and have some chick do my hair.'

This sounds terrible. Awful. Like the last nail in hope's coffin.

'She tried to kill me, Ev. Those cops were gonna torture me.'

The corner of Ev's mouth twitches. Is she smug all of a sudden?

'Yeah? And where are those cops now, Danny?'

Suddenly I am cut adrift from the last blood member of

my family. Evelyn knows Krieger and Fortz are dead. It was a condition.

That's cold.

'Aunt Evelyn. Ev. I can look after you. Edit is dangerous.'

Evelyn applies some lipstick. It is almost impossible to see her as the pungent lush I poured into my car last week. This new image is stomping down on the old one.

'Listen, Danny. I left home, went on the road, turned my back on the family. I thought that was it. Daddy would cut me off the same way he did to Margaret. Until a few months ago, I thought I was destitute. You wouldn't believe what I did for a few bucks. I hurt people. I stole. I got with guys in bathroom stalls, Danny. For a shot of bourbon. So fuck all that, you know. Fuck it. I'm done with that life for ever. And if it means that I gotta watch my back, hell, I was doing that anyway.' She pats my hand. 'You're alive and I'm alive, and that's good. So you gotta stop calling me with your boy scout plans. I *am* saved, Danny. I saved myself.' She pauses to set up the next statement. 'And I saved you.'

It's probably true.

'The bad guys are dead and the good guys live to drink another day.'

Not all the bad guys are dead. 'I see you brought Pablo along.'

Ev laughs, and even her laugh is Manhattan and private schools now. 'Pablo is a nightmare. He makes me do these stretches. I can barely sit down. And the latest thing is I can only drink champagne, which is pretty low in calories apparently.'

'What an arsehole.'

'It's for my own good. I want to get into a bikini this summer. Also, he drives me. I don't have a licence, and even if I did, I'm pretty much permanently over the legal limit.'

I smile wanly. 'Everyone should have a Pablo.'

'Well, okay then,' says Ev, and I realise the meeting is over. 'If I can do anything for you, Dan. Any time. Please don't hesitate to call.' Her head tilts in concern. 'How are things with that local hoodlum, Irish Mike?'

Hoodlum? He's been called a lot worse by his own mother.

'Mike is fine. I handled it.'

'Great, good, fab,' says Evelyn Costello, rising to her expensively shod feet. 'So we see eye to eye, honey? We're both fine and let's just get on with things.'

She leans over and kisses my cheek, transferring a layer of lipstick.

'Edit and I are going to the Hamptons for a few weeks. We think it's a good idea to get me integrated with the brunch-lunch crowd.'

'Just smile and be yourself,' I advise, but it's all just empty words now. Just bullshit and passing time. We probably won't ever see each other again.

'You are my family, Danny. Never forget that.'

Yeah, family. Right-o.

All I can do is nod.

I feel so depressed, like I just woke up and found my leg amputated.

Evelyn walks out of my life, a little steadier than she re-entered it a week ago. You wouldn't peg her for a drunk unless you were raised by one. She pulls her hands close to her chest the way rich folk do when they're forced to wade among the plebs and waits for a sullen bellhop to get the door.

A fortnight ago she was rolling guys in motels for the contents of their wallets. Would I prefer that life for her? Who am I considering here? Evelyn's well-being or my bruised pride?

While I am considering this, Pablo comes over, helps himself to a seat and treats me to a suspicious eyeballing. He's wondering if I made him at Mike's. Did I figure it out that he was the ninja?

This guy is ice.

He's looking me over like I'm fish on a plate. I got stared at a lot as a soldier in someone else's country and also as a doorman on a casino, and usually I can give better than I get, but it's hard to glare convincingly at a guy who can do what this guy can do with a rifle. This goes on for about five minutes until finally I break.

'Fuck it, okay. I saw your bracelets when you flipped me over.'

Pablo slaps his knee. 'I knew it. I knew you recognised me. Shit, McEvoy, five more seconds and you would've been off the hook.'

Balls. Five seconds.

'So what happens now? Are you gonna come hunting?'

'Are you kidding? I never had a gig so sweet. Evelyn insists that you remain alive. She even said you had to be healthy, so I can't put you in a wheelchair or nothing.'

This is a major relief and I have to stop myself saying thank you.

'Good to know. But hey, I can kill you, right?'

Pablo laughs for a full minute, which is a little OTT, I think. 'I like you, Irish. You have a good imagination, but your aura is clouded and the way you walk is affecting your spine. I could help you with that. Total Dimensional Control. That's my system.' And then holy shit if he doesn't slide me a business card. 'Evelyn said whatever you want, so I could train you and she picks up the tab. Win–win.'

Being alive is win–win enough for me at the moment, but I take the card and study the details. I don't want to appear rude.

'Lemme have a look at the website and get back to you.'

'Sure, McEvoy. Whatever. No time limit on Evelyn's money.' He rises smoothly, and I see the power in his limbs, restrained but ready.

How did I not see before that this guy is a killer?

'Ciao,' says Pablo, all European, and then follows Evelyn into the parking lot without a backward glance.

This is about the least threatening sit-down I've had for months, and yet when Pablo disappears through the revolving doors, I stride quickly towards the restroom and lock myself in a cubicle until I stop shaking.

I call Zeb from the Caddy because I need to hear a friend's voice.

'Hey, Paddy McMickster,' he says. 'Did you catch up with that Citizen Pain guy?'

'That guy is a gal,' I tell him, then go for an obvious set-up. 'Ronelle went out there with the calvary to pick her up.'

Zeb sighs. 'Cavalry, man. Cavalry. Calvary is where Jesus was killed.'

'Yeah, well you'd know.'

One–nil.

'Ooh, the Mick is bringing it to the table. You in a party mood, Dan-o?

'You know what? Yeah, I am. It's been a tense couple of weeks.'

'What about karaoke tonight? We could do our "I Can't Go For That".'

'You know it. Hall and Oates kills every time.'

I remember something that could get me to two–nil for the first time this year.

'Hey, Zeb. Listen. You know that melted-looking pier down by the *Intrepid* we used to wonder about? Remember that one? I called the mayor's office and found out what caused the collapse.'

Zeb snorts. 'Yeah, don't tell me. Pier pressure, right?'

Dick.